The Complete Escapades of The Scarlet Pimpernel

Volume 1

The Complete Escapades of The Scarlet Pimpernel

Volume 1

The Scarlet Pimpernel

and

I Will Repay

Baroness Orczy

LEONAUR

The Complete Escapades of The Scarlet Pimpernel
Volume 1
The Scarlet Pimpernel
and
I Will Repay
by Baroness Orczy

FIRST EDITION

First published under the titles
The Scarlet Pimpernel
and
I Will Repay

Leonaur is an imprint of Oakpast Ltd

ISBN: 978-1-78282-730-6 (hardcover)
ISBN: 978-1-78282-731-3 (softcover)

http://www.leonaur.com

Publisher's Notes

Contents

The Scarlet Pimpernel

Contents

Chapter 1

Paris: September, 1792

A surging, seething, murmuring crowd of beings that are human only in name, for to the eye and ear they seem naught but savage creatures, animated by vile passions and by the lust of vengeance and of hate. The hour, some little time before sunset, and the place, the West Barricade, at the very spot where, a decade later, a proud tyrant raised an undying monument to the nation's glory and his own vanity.

During the greater part of the day the guillotine had been kept busy at its ghastly work: all that France had boasted of in the past centuries, of ancient names, and blue blood, had paid toll to her desire for liberty and for fraternity. The carnage had only ceased at this late hour of the day because there were other more interesting sights for the people to witness, a little while before the final closing of the barricades for the night.

And so, the crowd rushed away from the Place de la Greve and made for the various barricades in order to watch this interesting and amusing sight.

It was to be seen every day, for those aristos were such fools! They were traitors to the people of course, all of them, men, women, and children, who happened to be descendants of the great men who since the Crusades had made the glory of France: her old *noblesse*. Their ancestors had oppressed the people, had crushed them under the scarlet heels of their dainty buckled shoes, and now the people had become the rulers of France and crushed their former masters—not beneath their heel, for they went shoeless mostly in these days—but a more effectual weight, the knife of the guillotine.

And daily, hourly, the hideous instrument of torture claimed its many victims—old men, young women, tiny children until the day when it would finally demand the head of a king and of a beautiful young queen.

But this was as it should be: were not the people now the rulers of France? Every aristocrat was a traitor, as his ancestors had been before him: for two hundred years now the people had sweated, and toiled, and starved, to keep a lustful court in lavish extravagance; now the descendants of those who had helped to make those courts brilliant had to hide for their lives—to fly, if they wished to avoid the tardy vengeance of the people.

And they did try to hide and tried to fly: that was just the fun of the whole thing. Every afternoon before the gates closed and the market carts went out in procession by the various barricades, some fool of an aristo endeavoured to evade the clutches of the Committee of Public Safety. In various disguises, under various pretexts, they tried to slip through the barriers, which were so well guarded by citizen soldiers of the Republic. Men in women's clothes, women in male attire, children disguised in beggars' rags: there were some of all sorts: *Ci-devant* counts, marquises, even dukes, who wanted to fly from France, reach England or some other equally accursed country, and there try to rouse foreign feelings against the glorious Revolution, or to raise an army in order to liberate the wretched prisoners in the Temple, who had once called themselves sovereigns of France.

But they were nearly always caught at the barricades, Sergeant Bibot especially at the West Gate had a wonderful nose for scenting an aristo in the most perfect disguise. Then, of course, the fun began. Bibot would look at his prey as a cat looks upon the mouse, play with him, sometimes for quite a quarter of an hour, pretend to be hoodwinked by the disguise, by the wigs and other bits of theatrical make-up which hid the identity of a *ci-devant* noble marquise or count.

Oh! Bibot had a keen sense of humour, and it was well worth hanging round that West Barricade, in order to see him catch an aristo in the very act of trying to flee from the vengeance of the people.

Sometimes Bibot would let his prey actually out by the gates, allowing him to think for the space of two minutes at least that he really had escaped out of Paris, and might even manage to reach the coast of England in safety, but Bibot would let the unfortunate wretch walk about ten metres towards the open country, then he would send two men after him and bring him back, stripped of his disguise.

Oh! that was extremely funny, for as often as not the fugitive would prove to be a woman, some proud marchioness, who looked terribly comical when she found herself in Bibot's clutches after all and knew that a summary trial would await her the next day and after that, the fond embrace of Madame la Guillotine.

No wonder that on this fine afternoon in September the crowd round Bibot's gate was eager and excited. The lust of blood grows with its satisfaction, there is no satiety: the crowd had seen a hundred noble heads fall beneath the guillotine today, it wanted to make sure that it would see another hundred fall on the morrow.

Bibot was sitting on an overturned and empty cask close by the gate of the barricade; a small detachment of *citoyen* soldiers was under his command. The work had been very hot lately. Those cursed aristos were becoming terrified and tried their hardest to slip out of Paris: men, women and children, whose ancestors, even in remote ages, had served those traitorous Bourbons, were all traitors themselves and right food for the guillotine. Every day Bibot had had the satisfaction of unmasking some fugitive royalists and sending them back to be tried by the Committee of Public Safety, presided over by that good patriot, Citoyen Foucquier-Tinville.

Robespierre and Danton both had commended Bibot for his zeal and Bibot was proud of the fact that he on his own initiative had sent at least fifty aristos to the guillotine.

But today all the sergeants in command at the various barricades had had special orders. Recently a very great number of aristos had succeeded in escaping out of France and in reaching England safely. There were curious rumours about these escapes; they had become very frequent and singularly daring; the people's minds were becoming strangely excited about it all. Sergeant Grospierre had been sent to the guillotine for allowing a whole family of aristos to slip out of the North Gate under his very nose.

It was asserted that these escapes were organised by a band of Englishmen, whose daring seemed to be unparalleled, and who, from sheer desire to meddle in what did not concern them, spent their spare time in snatching away lawful victims destined for Madame la Guillotine. These rumours soon grew in extravagance; there was no doubt that this band of meddlesome Englishmen did exist; moreover, they seemed to be under the leadership of a man whose pluck and audacity were almost fabulous. Strange stories were afloat of how he and those aristos whom he rescued became suddenly invisible as they reached the barricades and escaped out of the gates by sheer supernatural agency.

No one had seen these mysterious Englishmen; as for their leader, he was never spoken of, save with a superstitious shudder. Citoyen Foucquier-Tinville would in the course of the day receive a scrap of paper from some mysterious source; sometimes he would find it in the pocket of his coat, at others it would be handed to him by someone in the crowd, whilst he was on his way to the sitting of the Committee of Public Safety. The paper always contained a brief notice that the band of meddlesome Englishmen were at work, and it was always signed with a device drawn in red—a little star-shaped flower, which we in England call the Scarlet Pimpernel. Within a few hours of the receipt of this impudent notice, the *citoyens* of the Committee of Public Safety would hear that so many royalists and aristocrats had succeeded in reaching the coast and were on their way to England and safety.

The guards at the gates had been doubled, the sergeants in command had been threatened with death, whilst liberal rewards were offered for the capture of these daring and impudent Englishmen. There was a sum of five thousand *francs* promised to the man who laid hands on the mysterious and elusive Scarlet Pimpernel.

Everyone felt that Bibot would be that man, and Bibot allowed that belief to take firm root in everybody's mind; and so, day after day, people came to watch him at the West Gate, so as to be present when he laid hands on any fugitive aristo who perhaps might be accompanied by that mysterious Englishman.

"Bah!" he said to his trusted corporal, "Citoyen Grospierre was a fool! Had it been me now, at that North Gate last week . . ."

Citoyen Bibot spat on the ground to express his contempt for his comrade's stupidity.

"How did it happen, *citoyen?*" asked the corporal.

"Grospierre was at the gate, keeping good watch," began Bibot, pompously, as the crowd closed in round him, listening eagerly to his narrative. "We've all heard of this meddlesome Englishman, this accursed Scarlet Pimpernel. He won't get through *my* gate, *morbleu!* unless he be the devil himself. But Grospierre was a fool. The market carts were going through the gates; there was one laden with casks, and driven by an old man, with a boy beside him. Grospierre was a bit drunk, but he thought himself very clever; he looked into the casks—most of them, at least—and saw they were empty, and let the cart go through."

A murmur of wrath and contempt went round the group of ill-clad wretches, who crowded round Citoyen Bibot.

"Half an hour later," continued the sergeant, "up comes a captain of the guard with a squad of some dozen soldiers with him. 'Has a cart gone through?' he asks of Grospierre, breathlessly. 'Yes,' says Grospierre, 'not half an hour ago.' 'And you have let them escape,' shouts the captain furiously. 'You'll go to the guillotine for this, citoyen sergeant! that cart held concealed the *ci-devant* Duc de Chalis and all his family!' 'What!' thunders Grospierre, aghast. 'Aye! and the driver was none other than that cursed Englishman, the Scarlet Pimpernel.'"

A howl of execration greeted this tale. Citoyen Grospierre had paid for his blunder on the guillotine, but what a fool! oh! what a fool!

Bibot was laughing so much at his own tale that it was some time before he could continue.

"'After them, my men,' shouts the captain," he said after a while, "'remember the reward; after them, they cannot have gone far!' And with that he rushes through the gate followed by his dozen soldiers."

"But it was too late!" shouted the crowd, excitedly.

"They never got them!"

"Curse that Grospierre for his folly!"

"He deserved his fate!"

"Fancy not examining those casks properly!"

But these sallies seemed to amuse Citoyen Bibot exceedingly; he laughed until his sides ached, and the tears streamed down his cheeks.

"Nay, nay!" he said at last, "those aristos weren't in the cart; the driver was not the Scarlet Pimpernel!"

"What?"

"No! The captain of the guard was that damned Englishman in disguise, and every one of his soldiers *aristos!*"

The crowd this time said nothing: the story certainly savoured of the supernatural, and though the Republic had abolished God, it had not quite succeeded in killing the fear of the supernatural in the hearts of the people. Truly that Englishman must be the devil himself.

The sun was sinking low down in the west. Bibot prepared himself to close the gates.

"*En avant* the carts," he said.

Some dozen covered carts were drawn up in a row, ready to leave town, in order to fetch the produce from the country close by, for market the next morning. They were mostly well known to Bibot, as they went through his gate twice every day on their way to and from the town. He spoke to one or two of their drivers—mostly women—and was at great pains to examine the inside of the carts.

"You never know," he would say, "and I'm not going to be caught like that fool Grospierre."

The women who drove the carts usually spent their day on the Place de la Greve, beneath the platform of the guillotine, knitting and gossiping, whilst they watched the rows of tumbrils arriving with the victims the Reign of Terror claimed every day. It was great fun to see the aristos arriving for the reception of Madame la Guillotine, and the places close by the platform were very much sought after. Bibot, during the day, had been on duty on the Place. He recognised most of the old hats, "*tricotteuses*," as they were called, who sat there and knitted, whilst head after head fell beneath the knife, and they themselves got quite bespattered with the blood of those cursed aristos.

"He! *la mère!*" said Bibot to one of these horrible hags, "what have you got there?"

He had seen her earlier in the day, with her knitting and the whip of her cart close beside her. Now she had fastened a row of curly locks to the whip handle, all colours, from gold to silver, fair to dark, and she stroked them with her huge, bony fingers as she laughed at Bibot.

"I made friends with Madame Guillotine's lover," she said with a coarse laugh, "he cut these off for me from the heads as they rolled down. He has promised me some more tomorrow, but I don't know if I shall be at my usual place."

"Ah! how is that, *la mère?*" asked Bibot, who, hardened soldier that he was, could not help shuddering at the awful loathsomeness of this semblance of a woman, with her ghastly trophy on the handle of her whip.

"My grandson has got the smallpox," she said with a jerk of her thumb towards the inside of her cart, "some say it's the plague! If it is, I sha'n't be allowed to come into Paris tomorrow." At the first mention of the word small-pox, Bibot had stepped hastily backwards, and when the old hag spoke of the plague, he retreated from her as fast as he could.

"Curse you!" he muttered, whilst the whole crowd hastily avoided the cart, leaving it standing all alone in the midst of the place.

The old hag laughed.

"Curse you, *citoyen*, for being a coward," she said. "Bah! what a man to be afraid of sickness."

"*Morbleu!* the plague!"

Everyone was awe-struck and silent, filled with horror for the loathsome malady, the one thing which still had the power to arouse terror and disgust in these savage, brutalised creatures.

"Get out with you and with your plague-stricken brood!" shouted Bibot, hoarsely.

And with another rough laugh and coarse jest, the old hag whipped up her lean nag and drove her cart out of the gate.

This incident had spoilt the afternoon. The people were terrified of these two horrible curses, the two maladies which nothing could cure, and which were the precursors of an awful and lonely death. They hung about the barricades, silent and sullen for a while, eyeing one another suspiciously, avoiding each other as if by instinct, lest the plague lurked already in their midst. Presently, as in the case of Grospierre, a captain of the guard appeared suddenly. But he was known to Bibot, and there was no fear of his turning out to be a sly Englishman in disguise.

"A cart—" he shouted breathlessly, even before he had reached the gates.

"What cart?" asked Bibot, roughly.

"Driven by an old hag—A covered cart—"

"There were a dozen—"

"An old hag who said her son had the plague?"

"Yes—"

"You have not let them go?"

"*Morbleu!*" said Bibot, whose purple cheeks had suddenly become white with fear.

"The cart contained the *ci-devant* Comtesse de Tourney and her two children, all of them traitors and condemned to death."

"And their driver?" muttered Bibot, as a superstitious shudder ran down his spine.

"*Sacre tonnerre*," said the captain, "but it is feared that it was that accursed Englishman himself—the Scarlet Pimpernel."

CHAPTER 2

Dover: "The Fisherman's Rest"

In the kitchen Sally was extremely busy—saucepans and frying-pans were standing in rows on the gigantic hearth, the huge stock-pot stood in a corner, and the jack turned with slow deliberation, and presented alternately to the glow every side of a noble sirloin of beef. The two little kitchen-maids bustled around, eager to help, hot and panting, with cotton sleeves well tucked up above the dimpled elbows, and giggling over some private jokes of their own, whenever Miss Sally's back was turned for a moment. And old Jemima, stolid in temper and solid in bulk, kept up a long and subdued grumble, while she stirred the stock-pot methodically over the fire.

"What ho! Sally!" came in cheerful if none too melodious accents from the coffee-room close by.

"Lud bless my soul!" exclaimed Sally, with a good-humoured laugh, "what be they all wanting now, I wonder!"

"Beer, of course," grumbled Jemima, "you don't 'xpect Jimmy Pitkin to 'ave done with one tankard, do ye?"

"Mr. 'Arry, 'e looked uncommon thirsty too," simpered Martha, one of the little kitchen-maids; and her beady black eyes twinkled as they met those of her companion, whereupon both started on a round of short and suppressed giggles.

Sally looked cross for a moment, and thoughtfully rubbed her hands against her shapely hips; her palms were itching, evidently, to come in contact with Martha's rosy cheeks—but inherent good-humour prevailed, and with a pout and a shrug of the shoulders, she turned her attention to the fried potatoes.

"What ho, Sally! hey, Sally!"

And a chorus of pewter mugs, tapped with impatient hands against the oak tables of the coffee-room, accompanied the shouts for mine host's buxom daughter.

"Sally!" shouted a more persistent voice, "are ye goin' to be all night with that there beer?"

"I do think father might get the beer for them," muttered Sally, as Jemima, stolidly and without further comment, took a couple of foam-crowned jugs from the shelf, and began filling a number of pewter tankards with some of that home-brewed ale for which "The Fisherman's Rest" had been famous since that days of King Charles. "'E knows 'ow busy we are in 'ere."

"Your father is too busy discussing politics with Mr. 'Empseed to worry 'isself about you and the kitchen," grumbled Jemima under her breath.

Sally had gone to the small mirror which hung in a corner of the kitchen and was hastily smoothing her hair and setting her frilled cap at its most becoming angle over her dark curls; then she took up the tankards by their handles, three in each strong, brown hand, and laughing, grumbling, blushing, carried them through into the coffee-room.

There, there was certainly no sign of that bustle and activity which kept four women busy and hot in the glowing kitchen beyond.

The coffee-room of "The Fisherman's Rest" is a show place now at the beginning of the twentieth century. At the end of the eighteenth, in the year of grace 1792, it had not yet gained the notoriety and importance which a hundred additional years and the craze of the age have since bestowed upon it. Yet it was an old place, even then, for the oak rafters and beams were already black with age—as were the panelled seats, with their tall backs, and the long, polished tables between, on which innumerable pewter tankards had left fantastic patterns of many-sized rings. In the leaded window, high up, a row of pots of scarlet geraniums and blue larkspur gave the bright note of colour against the dull background of the oak.

That Mr. Jellyband, landlord of "The Fisherman's Rest" at Dover, was a prosperous man, was of course clear to the most casual observer. The pewter on the fine old dressers, the brass above the gigantic hearth, shone like silver and gold—the red-tiled floor was as brilliant as the scarlet geranium on the window sill—this meant that his servants were good and plentiful, that the custom was constant, and of that order which necessitated the keeping up of the coffee-room to a high standard of elegance and order.

As Sally came in, laughing through her frowns, and displaying a row of dazzling white teeth, she was greeted with shouts and chorus of applause.

"Why, here's Sally! What ho, Sally! Hurrah for pretty Sally!"

"I thought you'd grown deaf in that kitchen of yours," muttered Jimmy Pitkin, as he passed the back of his hand across his very dry lips.

"All ri'! all ri'!" laughed Sally, as she deposited the freshly-filled tankards upon the tables, "why, what a 'urry to be sure! And is your gran'mother a-dyin' an' you wantin' to see the pore soul afore she'm gone! I never see'd such a mighty rushin'" A chorus of good-humoured laughter greeted this witticism, which gave the company there present food for many jokes, for some considerable time. Sally now seemed in less of a hurry to get back to her pots and pans. A young man with fair curly hair, and eager, bright blue eyes, was engaging most of her attention and the whole of her time, whilst broad witticisms anent Jimmy Pitkin's fictitious grandmother flew from mouth to mouth, mixed with heavy puffs of pungent tobacco smoke.

Facing the hearth, his legs wide apart, a long clay pipe in his mouth, stood mine host himself, worthy Mr. Jellyband, landlord of "The Fisherman's Rest," as his father had before him, aye, and his grandfather and great-grandfather too, for that matter. Portly in build, jovial in countenance and somewhat bald of pate, Mr. Jellyband was indeed a typical rural John Bull of those days—the days when our prejudiced insularity was at its height, when to an Englishman, be he lord, yeoman, or peasant, the whole of the continent of Europe was a den of immorality and the rest of the world an unexploited land of savages and cannibals.

There he stood, mine worthy host, firm and well set up on his limbs, smoking his long churchwarden and caring nothing for nobody at home, and despising everybody abroad. He wore the typical scarlet waistcoat, with shiny brass buttons, the corduroy breeches, and grey worsted stockings and smart buckled shoes, that characterised every self-respecting innkeeper in Great Britain in these days—and while pretty, motherless Sally had need of four pairs of brown hands to do all the work that fell on her shapely shoulders, worthy Jellyband discussed the affairs of nations with his most privileged guests.

The coffee-room indeed, lighted by two well-polished lamps, which hung from the raftered ceiling, looked cheerful and cosy in the extreme. Through the dense clouds of tobacco smoke that hung about in every corner, the faces of Mr. Jellyband's customers appeared red and pleasant to look at, and on good terms with themselves, their host and all the world; from every side of the room loud guffaws accompanied pleasant, if not highly intellectual, conversation—while Sally's repeated giggles testified to the good use Mr. Harry Waite was making of the short time she seemed inclined to spare him.

They were mostly fisher-folk who patronised Mr. Jellyband's coffee-room, but fishermen are known to be very thirsty people; the salt which they breathe in, when they are on the sea, accounts for their parched throats when on shore, but "The Fisherman's Rest" was something more than a rendezvous for these humble folk. The London and Dover coach started from the hostel daily, and passengers who had come across the Channel, and those who started for the "grand tour," all became acquainted with Mr. Jellyband, his French wines and his home-brewed ales.

It was towards the close of September, 1792, and the weather which had been brilliant and hot throughout the month had suddenly broken up; for two days torrents of rain had deluged the south of England, doing its level best to ruin what chances the apples and pears and late plums had of becoming really fine, self-respecting fruit. Even now it was beating against the leaded windows, and tumbling down the chimney, making the cheerful wood fire sizzle in the hearth.

"Lud! did you ever see such a wet September, Mr. Jellyband?" asked Mr. Hempseed.

He sat in one of the seats inside the hearth, did Mr. Hempseed, for he was an authority and important personage not only at "The Fisherman's Rest," where Mr. Jellyband always made a special selection of him as a foil for political arguments, but throughout the neighbourhood, where his learning and notably his knowledge of the Scriptures was held in the most profound awe and respect. With one hand buried in the capacious pockets of his corduroys underneath his elaborately-worked, well-worn smock, the other holding his long clay pipe, Mr. Hempseed sat there looking dejectedly across the room at the rivulets of moisture which trickled down the window panes.

"No," replied Mr. Jellyband, sententiously, "I dunno, Mr. 'Empseed, as I ever did. An' I've been in these parts nigh on sixty years."

"Aye! you wouldn't rec'llect the first three years of them sixty, Mr. Jellyband," quietly interposed Mr. Hempseed. "I dunno as I ever see'd an infant take much note of the weather, leastways not in these parts, an' *I*'ve lived 'ere nigh on seventy-five years, Mr. Jellyband."

The superiority of this wisdom was so incontestable that for the moment Mr. Jellyband was not ready with his usual flow of argument.

"It do seem more like April than September, don't it?" continued Mr. Hempseed, dolefully, as a shower of raindrops fell with a sizzle upon the fire.

"Aye! that it do," assented the worthy host, "but then what can you 'xpect, Mr. 'Empseed, I says, with sich a government as we've got?"

Mr. Hempseed shook his head with an infinity of wisdom, tempered by deeply-rooted mistrust of the British climate and the British Government.

"I don't 'xpect nothing, Mr. Jellyband," he said. "Pore folks like us is of no account up there in Lunnon, I knows that, and it's not often as I do complain. But when it comes to sich wet weather in September, and all me fruit a-rottin' and a-dying' like the 'Guptian mother's first born, and doin' no more good than they did, pore dears, save a lot more Jews, pedlars and sich, with their oranges and sich like foreign ungodly fruit, which nobody'd buy if English apples and pears was nicely swelled. As the Scriptures say—"

"That's quite right, Mr. 'Empseed," retorted Jellyband, "and as I says, what can you 'xpect? There's all them Frenchy devils over the Channel yonder a-murderin' their king and nobility, and Mr. Pitt and Mr. Fox and Mr. Burke a-fightin' and a-wranglin' between them, if we Englishmen should 'low them to go on in their ungodly way. 'Let 'em murder!' says Mr. Pitt. 'Stop 'em!' says Mr. Burke."

"And let 'em murder, says I, and be demmed to 'em." said Mr. Hempseed, emphatically, for he had but little liking for his friend Jellyband's political arguments, wherein he always got out of his depth, and had but little chance for displaying those pearls of wisdom which had earned for him so high a reputation in the neighbourhood and so many free tankards of ale at "The Fisherman's Rest."

"Let 'em murder," he repeated again, "but don't lets 'ave sich rain in September, for that is agin the law and the Scriptures which says—"

"Lud! Mr. 'Arry, 'ow you made me jump!"

It was unfortunate for Sally and her flirtation that this remark of hers should have occurred at the precise moment when Mr. Hempseed was collecting his breath, in order to deliver himself one of those Scriptural utterances which made him famous, for it brought down upon her pretty head the full flood of her father's wrath.

"Now then, Sally, me girl, now then!" he said, trying to force a frown upon his good-humoured face, "stop that fooling with them young jackanapes and get on with the work."

"The work's gettin' on all ri', father."

But Mr. Jellyband was peremptory. He had other views for his buxom daughter, his only child, who would in God's good time become the owner of "The Fisherman's Rest," than to see her married to one of these young fellows who earned but a precarious livelihood with their net.

"Did ye hear me speak, me girl?" he said in that quiet tone, which no one inside the inn dared to disobey. "Get on with my Lord Tony's supper, for, if it ain't the best we can do, and 'e not satisfied, see what you'll get, that's all."

Reluctantly Sally obeyed.

"Is you 'xpecting special guests then tonight, Mr. Jellyband?" asked Jimmy Pitkin, in a loyal attempt to divert his host's attention from the circumstances connected with Sally's exit from the room.

"Aye! that I be," replied Jellyband, "friends of my Lord Tony hisself. Dukes and duchesses from over the water yonder, whom the young lord and his friend, Sir Andrew Ffoulkes, and other young noblemen have helped out of the clutches of them murderin' devils."

But this was too much for Mr. Hempseed's querulous philosophy.

"Lud!" he said, "what do they do that for, I wonder? I don't 'old not with interferin' in other folks' ways. As the Scriptures say—"

"Maybe, Mr. 'Empseed," interrupted Jellyband, with biting sarcasm, "as you're a personal friend of Mr. Pitt, and as you says along with Mr. Fox: 'Let 'em murder!' says you."

"Pardon me, Mr. Jellyband," feebly protested Mr. Hempseed, "I dunno as I ever did."

But Mr. Jellyband had at last succeeded in getting upon his favourite hobby-horse and had no intention of dismounting in any hurry.

"Or maybe you've made friends with some of them French chaps 'oo they do say have come over here o' purpose to make us Englishmen agree with their murderin' ways."

"I dunno what you mean, Mr. Jellyband," suggested Mr. Hempseed, "all I know is—"

"All *I* know is," loudly asserted mine host, "that there was my friend Peppercorn, 'oo owns the 'Blue-Faced Boar,' an' as true and loyal an Englishman as you'd see in the land. And now look at 'im!—'E made friends with some o' them frog-eaters, 'obnobbed with them just as if they was Englishmen, and not just a lot of immoral, God-forsaking furrin' spies. Well! and what happened? Peppercorn 'e now ups and talks of revolutions, and liberty, and down with the aristocrats, just like Mr. 'Empseed over 'ere!"

"Pardon me, Mr. Jellyband," again interposed Mr. Hempseed feebly, "I dunno as I ever did—"

Mr. Jellyband had appealed to the company in general, who were listening awe-struck and open-mouthed at the recital of Mr. Peppercorn's defalcations. At one table two customers—gentlemen apparently by their clothes—had pushed aside their half-finished game of dominoes, and had been listening for some time, and evidently with much amusement at Mr. Jellyband's international opinions. One of them now, with a quiet, sarcastic smile still lurking round the corners of his mobile mouth, turned towards the centre of the room where Mr. Jellyband was standing.

"You seem to think, mine honest friend," he said quietly, "that these Frenchmen,—spies I think you called them—are mighty clever fellows to have made mincemeat so to speak of your friend Mr. Peppercorn's opinions. How did they accomplish that now, think you?"

"Lud! sir, I suppose they talked 'im over. Those Frenchies, I've 'eard it said, 'ave got the gift of gab—and Mr. 'Empseed 'ere will tell you 'ow it is that they just twist some people round their little finger like."

"Indeed, and is that so, Mr. Hempseed?" inquired the stranger politely.

"Nay, sir!" replied Mr. Hempseed, much irritated, "I dunno as I can give you the information you require."

"Faith, then," said the stranger, "let us hope, my worthy host, that these clever spies will not succeed in upsetting your extremely loyal opinions."

But this was too much for Mr. Jellyband's pleasant equanimity. He burst into an uproarious fit of laughter, which was soon echoed by those who happened to be in his debt.

"Hahaha! hohoho! hehehe!" He laughed in every key, did my worthy host, and laughed until his sides ached, and his eyes streamed. "At me! hark at that! Did ye 'ear 'im say that they'd be upsettin' my opinions?—Eh?—Lud love you, sir, but you do say some queer things."

"Well, Mr. Jellyband," said Mr. Hempseed, sententiously, "you know what the Scriptures say: 'Let 'im 'oo stands take 'eed lest 'e fall.'"

"But then hark'ee Mr. 'Empseed," retorted Jellyband, still holding his sides with laughter, "the Scriptures didn't know me. Why, I wouldn't so much as drink a glass of ale with one o' them murderin' Frenchmen, and nothin' 'd make me change my opinions. Why! I've 'eard it said that them frog-eaters can't even speak the King's English, so, of course, if any of 'em tried to speak their God-forsaken lingo to me, why, I should spot them directly, see!—and forewarned is forearmed, as the saying goes."

"Aye! my honest friend," assented the stranger cheerfully, "I see that you are much too sharp, and a match for any twenty Frenchmen, and here's to your very good health, my worthy host, if you'll do me the honour to finish this bottle of mine with me."

"I am sure you're very polite, sir," said Mr. Jellyband, wiping his eyes which were still streaming with the abundance of his laughter, "and I don't mind if I do."

The stranger poured out a couple of tankards full of wine, and having offered one to mine host, he took the other himself.

"Loyal Englishmen as we all are," he said, whilst the same humorous smile played round the corners of his thin lips—"loyal as we are, we must admit that this at least is one good thing which comes to us from France."

"Aye! we'll none of us deny that, sir," assented mine host.

"And here's to the best landlord in England, our worthy host, Mr. Jellyband," said the stranger in a loud tone of voice.

"Hi, hip, hurrah!" retorted the whole company present. Then there was a loud clapping of hands, and mugs and tankards made a rattling music upon the tables to the accompaniment of loud laughter at nothing in particular, and of Mr. Jellyband's muttered exclamations:

"Just fancy *me* bein' talked over by any God-forsaken furriner!—What?—Lud love you, sir, but you do say some queer things."

To which obvious fact the stranger heartily assented. It was certainly a preposterous suggestion that anyone could ever upset Mr. Jellyband's firmly-rooted opinions anent the utter worthlessness of the inhabitants of the whole continent of Europe.

CHAPTER 3

The Refugees

Feelings in every part of England certainly ran very high at this time against the French and their doings. Smugglers and legitimate traders between the French and the English coasts brought snatches of news from over the water, which made every honest Englishman's blood boil, and made him long to have "a good go" at those murderers, who had imprisoned their king and all his family, subjected the queen and the royal children to every species of indignity, and were even now loudly demanding the blood of the whole Bourbon family and of every one of its adherents.

The execution of the Princesse de Lamballe, Marie Antoinette's young and charming friend, had filled everyone in England with unspeakable horror, the daily execution of scores of royalists of good family, whose only sin was their aristocratic name, seemed to cry for vengeance to the whole of civilised Europe.

Yet, with all that, no one dared to interfere. Burke had exhausted all his eloquence in trying to induce the British Government to fight the revolutionary government of France, but Mr. Pitt, with characteristic prudence, did not feel that this country was fit yet to embark on another arduous and costly war. It was for Austria to take the initiative; Austria, whose fairest daughter was even now a dethroned queen, imprisoned and insulted by a howling mob; surely 'twas not—so argued Mr. Fox—for the whole of England to take up arms, because one set of Frenchmen chose to murder another.

As for Mr. Jellyband and his fellow John Bulls, though they looked upon all foreigners with withering contempt, they were royalist and anti-revolutionists to a man, and at this present moment were furious with Pitt for his caution and moderation, although they naturally understood nothing of the diplomatic reasons which guided that great man's policy.

By now Sally came running back, very excited and very eager. The joyous company in the coffee-room had heard nothing of the noise outside, but she had spied a dripping horse and rider who had stopped at the door of "The Fisherman's Rest," and while the stable boy ran forward to take charge of the horse, pretty Miss Sally went to the front door to greet the welcome visitor. "I think I see'd my Lord Antony's horse out in the yard, father," she said, as she ran across the coffee-room.

But already the door had been thrown open from outside, and the next moment an arm, covered in drab cloth and dripping with the heavy rain, was round pretty Sally's waist, while a hearty voice echoed along the polished rafters of the coffee-room.

"Aye, and bless your brown eyes for being so sharp, my pretty Sally," said the man who had just entered, whilst worthy Mr. Jellyband came bustling forward, eager, alert and fussy, as became the advent of one of the most favoured guests of his hostel.

"Lud, I protest, Sally," added Lord Antony, as he deposited a kiss on Miss Sally's blooming cheeks, "but you are growing prettier and prettier every time I see you—and my honest friend, Jellyband here, have hard work to keep the fellows off that slim waist of yours. What say you, Mr. Waite?"

Mr. Waite—torn between his respect for my lord and his dislike of that particular type of joke—only replied with a doubtful grunt.

Lord Antony Dewhurst, one of the sons of the Duke of Exeter, was in those days a very perfect type of a young English gentlemen—tall, well set-up, broad of shoulders and merry of face, his laughter rang loudly wherever he went. A good sportsman, a lively companion, a courteous, well-bred man of the world, with not too much brains to spoil his temper, he was a universal favourite in London drawing-rooms or in the coffee-rooms of village inns. At "The Fisherman's Rest" everyone knew him—for he was fond of a trip across to France, and always spent a night under worthy Mr. Jellyband's roof on his way there or back.

He nodded to Waite, Pitkin and the others as he at last released Sally's waist and crossed over to the hearth to warm and dry himself: as he did so, he cast a quick, somewhat suspicious glance at the two strangers, who had quietly resumed their game of dominoes, and for a moment a look of deep earnestness, even of anxiety, clouded his jovial young face.

But only for a moment; the next he turned to Mr. Hempseed, who was respectfully touching his forelock.

"Well, Mr. Hempseed, and how is the fruit?"

"Badly, my lord, badly," replied Mr. Hempseed, dolefully, "but what can you 'xpect with this 'ere government favourin' them rascals over in France, who would murder their king and all their nobility."

"Odd's life!" retorted Lord Antony; "so they would, honest Hempseed,—at least those they can get hold of, worse luck! But we have got some friends coming here tonight, who at any rate have evaded their clutches."

It almost seemed, when the young man said these words, as if he threw a defiant look towards the quiet strangers in the corner.

"Thanks to you, my lord, and to your friends, so I've heard it said," said Mr. Jellyband.

But in a moment Lord Antony's hand fell warningly on mine host's arm.

"Hush!" he said peremptorily, and instinctively once again looked towards the strangers.

"Oh! Lud love you, they are all right, my lord," retorted Jellyband; "don't you be afraid. I wouldn't have spoken, only I knew we were among friends. That gentleman over there is as true and loyal a subject of King George as you are yourself, my lord saving your presence. He is but lately arrived in Dover and is setting down in business in these parts."

"In business? Faith, then, it must be as an undertaker, for I vow I never beheld a more rueful countenance."

"Nay, my lord, I believe that the gentleman is a widower, which no doubt would account for the melancholy of his bearing—but he is a friend, nevertheless, I'll vouch for that—and you will own, my lord, that who should judge of a face better than the landlord of a popular inn—"

"Oh, that's all right, then, if we are among friends," said Lord Antony, who evidently did not care to discuss the subject with his host. "But, tell me, you have no one else staying here, have you?"

"No one, my lord, and no one coming, either, leastways—"

"Leastways?"

"No one your lordship would object to, I know."

"Who is it?"

"Well, my lord, Sir Percy Blakeney and his lady will be here presently, but they ain't a-goin' to stay—"

"Lady Blakeney?" queried Lord Antony, in some astonishment.

"Aye, my lord. Sir Percy's skipper was here just now. He says that my lady's brother is crossing over to France today in the *Daydream*, which is Sir Percy's yacht, and Sir Percy and my lady will come with him as far as here to see the last of him. It don't put you out, do it, my lord?"

"No, no, it doesn't put me out, friend; nothing will put me out, unless that supper is not the very best which Miss Sally can cook, and which has ever been served in 'The Fisherman's Rest.'"

"You need have no fear of that, my lord," said Sally, who all this while had been busy setting the table for supper. And very gay and inviting it looked, with a large bunch of brilliantly coloured dahlias in the centre, and the bright pewter goblets and blue china about.

"How many shall I lay for, my lord?"

"Five places, pretty Sally, but let the supper be enough for ten at least—our friends will be tired, and, I hope, hungry. As for me, I vow I could demolish a baron of beef tonight."

"Here they are, I do believe," said Sally excitedly, as a distant clatter of horses and wheels could now be distinctly heard, drawing rapidly nearer.

There was a general commotion in the coffee-room. Everyone was curious to see my Lord Antony's swell friends from over the water. Miss Sally cast one or two quick glances at the little bit of mirror which hung on the wall, and worthy Mr. Jellyband bustled out in order to give the first welcome himself to his distinguished guests. Only the two strangers in the corner did not participate in the general excitement. They were calmly finishing their game of dominoes and did not even look once towards the door.

"Straight ahead, *Comtesse*, the door on your right," said a pleasant voice outside.

"Aye! there they are, all right enough." said Lord Antony, joyfully; "off with you, my pretty Sally, and see how quick you can dish up the soup."

The door was thrown wide open, and, preceded by Mr. Jellyband, who was profuse in his bows and welcomes, a party of four—two ladies and two gentlemen—entered the coffee-room.

"Welcome! Welcome to old England!" said Lord Antony, effusively, as he came eagerly forward with both hands outstretched towards the newcomers.

"Ah, you are Lord Antony Dewhurst, I think," said one of the ladies, speaking with a strong foreign accent.

"At your service, *Madame*," he replied, as he ceremoniously kissed the hands of both the ladies, then turned to the men and shook them both warmly by the hand.

Sally was already helping the ladies to take off their travelling cloaks, and both turned, with a shiver, towards the brightly-blazing hearth.

There was a general movement among the company in the coffee-room. Sally had bustled off to her kitchen whilst Jellyband, still profuse with his respectful salutations, arranged one or two chairs around the fire. Mr. Hempseed, touching his forelock, was quietly vacating the seat in the hearth. Everyone was staring curiously, yet deferentially, at the foreigners.

"Ah, *Messieurs!* what can I say?" said the elder of the two ladies, as she stretched a pair of fine, aristocratic hands to the warmth of the blaze, and looked with unspeakable gratitude first at Lord Antony, then at one of the young men who had accompanied her party, and who was busy divesting himself of his heavy, caped coat.

"Only that you are glad to be in England, *Comtesse*," replied Lord Antony, "and that you have not suffered too much from your trying voyage."

"Indeed, indeed, we are glad to be in England," she said, while her eyes filled with tears, "and we have already forgotten all that we have suffered."

Her voice was musical and low, and there was a great deal of calm dignity and of many sufferings nobly endured marked in the handsome, aristocratic face, with its wealth of snowy-white hair dressed high above the forehead, after the fashion of the times.

"I hope my friend, Sir Andrew Ffoulkes, proved an entertaining travelling companion, *Madame?*"

"Ah, indeed, Sir Andrew was kindness itself. How could my children and I ever show enough gratitude to you all, *Messieurs?*"

Her companion, a dainty, girlish figure, childlike and pathetic in its look of fatigue and of sorrow, had said nothing as yet, but her eyes, large, brown, and full of tears, looked up from the fire and sought those of Sir Andrew Ffoulkes, who had drawn near to the hearth and to her; then, as they met his, which were fixed with unconcealed admiration upon the sweet face before him, a thought of warmer colour rushed up to her pale cheeks.

"So, this is England," she said, as she looked round with childlike curiosity at the great hearth, the oak rafters, and the yokels with their elaborate smocks and jovial, rubicund, British countenances.

"A bit of it, *Mademoiselle*," replied Sir Andrew, smiling, "but all of it, at your service."

The young girl blushed again, but this time a bright smile, fleet and sweet, illumined her dainty face. She said nothing, and Sir Andrew too was silent, yet those two young people understood one another, as young people have a way of doing all the world over, and have done since the world began.

"But, I say, supper!" here broke in Lord Antony's jovial voice, "supper, honest Jellyband. Where is that pretty wench of yours and the dish of soup? Zooks, man, while you stand there gaping at the ladies, they will faint with hunger."

"One moment! one moment, my lord," said Jellyband, as he threw open the door that led to the kitchen and shouted lustily: "Sally! Hey, Sally there, are ye ready, my girl?"

Sally was ready, and the next moment she appeared in the doorway carrying a gigantic tureen, from which rose a cloud of steam and an abundance of savoury odour.

"Odd's life, supper at last!" ejaculated Lord Antony, merrily, as he gallantly offered his arm to the *Comtesse*.

"May I have the honour?" he added ceremoniously, as he led her towards the supper table.

There was a general bustle in the coffee-room: Mr. Hempseed and most of the yokels and fisher-folk had gone to make way for "the quality," and to finish smoking their pipes elsewhere. Only the two strangers stayed on, quietly and unconcernedly playing their game of dominoes and sipping their wine; whilst at another table Harry Waite, who was fast losing his temper, watched pretty Sally bustling round the table.

She looked a very dainty picture of English rural life, and no wonder that the susceptible young Frenchman could scarce take his eyes off her pretty face. The Vicomte de Tournay was scarce nineteen, a beardless boy, on whom terrible tragedies which were being enacted in his own country had made but little impression. He was elegantly and even foppishly dressed, and once safely landed in England he was evidently ready to forget the horrors of the Revolution in the delights of English life.

"*Pardi*, if zis is England," he said as he continued to ogle Sally with marked satisfaction, "I am of it satisfied."

It would be impossible at this point to record the exact exclamation which escaped through Mr. Harry Waite's clenched teeth. Only respect for "the quality," and notably for my Lord Antony, kept his marked disapproval of the young foreigner in check.

"Nay, but this *is* England, you abandoned young reprobate," interposed Lord Antony with a laugh, "and do not, I pray, bring your loose foreign ways into this most moral country."

Lord Antony had already sat down at the head of the table with the *Comtesse* on his right. Jellyband was bustling round, filling glasses and putting chairs straight. Sally waited, ready to hand round the soup. Mr. Harry Waite's friends had at last succeeded in taking him out of the room, for his temper was growing more and more violent under the *Vicomte's* obvious admiration for Sally.

"Suzanne," came in stern, commanding accents from the rigid *Comtesse*.

Suzanne blushed again; she had lost count of time and of place whilst she had stood beside the fire, allowing the handsome young Englishman's eyes to dwell upon her sweet face, and his hand, as if unconsciously, to rest upon hers. Her mother's voice brought her back to reality once more, and with a submissive "Yes, Mama," she took her place at the supper table.

Chapter 4

The League of the Scarlet Pimpernel

They all looked a merry, even a happy party, as they sat round the table; Sir Andrew Ffoulkes and Lord Antony Dewhurst, two typical good-looking, well-born and well-bred Englishmen of that year of grace 1792, and the aristocratic French *comtesse* with her two children, who had just escaped from such dire perils, and found a safe retreat at last on the shores of protecting England.

In the corner the two strangers had apparently finished their game; one of them arose and standing with his back to the merry company at the table, he adjusted with much deliberation his large triple caped coat. As he did so, he gave one quick glance all around him. Everyone was busy laughing and chatting, and he murmured the words "All safe!": his companion then, with the alertness borne of long practice, slipped on to his knees in a moment, and the next had crept noiselessly under the oak bench. The stranger then, with a loud "Goodnight," quietly walked out of the coffee-room.

Not one of those at the supper table had noticed this curious and silent manoeuvre, but when the stranger finally closed the door of the coffee-room behind him, they all instinctively sighed a sigh of relief.

"Alone, at last!" said Lord Antony, jovially.

Then the young Vicomte de Tournay rose, glass in hand, and with the graceful affection peculiar to the times, he raised it aloft, and said in broken English,—

"To His Majesty George Three of England. God bless him for his hospitality to us all, poor exiles from France."

"His Majesty the King!" echoed Lord Antony and Sir Andrew as they drank loyally to the toast.

"To His Majesty King Louis of France," added Sir Andrew, with solemnity. "May God protect him and give him victory over his enemies."

Everyone rose and drank this toast in silence. The fate of the unfortunate King of France, then a prisoner of his own people, seemed to cast a gloom even over Mr. Jellyband's pleasant countenance.

"And to M. le Comte de Tournay de Basserive," said Lord Antony, merrily. "May we welcome him in England before many days are over."

"Ah, *Monsieur*," said the *Comtesse*, as with a slightly trembling hand she conveyed her glass to her lips, "I scarcely dare to hope."

But already Lord Antony had served out the soup, and for the next few moments all conversation ceased, while Jellyband and Sally handed round the plates and everyone began to eat.

"Faith, *Madame!*" said Lord Antony, after a while, "mine was no idle toast; seeing yourself, Mademoiselle Suzanne and my friend the *Vicomte* safely in England now, surely you must feel reassured as to the fate of *Monsieur le Comte*."

"Ah, *Monsieur*," replied the *Comtesse*, with a heavy sigh, "I trust in God—I can but pray—and hope—"

"Aye, *Madame!*" here interposed Sir Andrew Ffoulkes, "trust in God by all means, but believe also a little in your English friends, who have sworn to bring the Count safely across the Channel, even as they have brought you today."

"Indeed, indeed, *Monsieur*," she replied, "I have the fullest confidence in you and your friends. Your fame, I assure you, has spread throughout the whole of France. The way some of my own friends have escaped from the clutches of that awful revolutionary tribunal was nothing short of a miracle—and all done by you and your friends—"

"We were but the hands, *Madame la Comtesse*—"

"But my husband, *Monsieur*," said the *Comtesse*, whilst unshed tears seemed to veil her voice, "he is in such deadly peril—I would never have left him, only—there were my children—I was torn between my duty to him, and to them. They refused to go without me—and you and your friends assured me so solemnly that my husband would be safe. But, oh! now that I am here—amongst you all—in this beautiful, free England—I think of him, flying for his life, hunted like a poor beast—in such peril—Ah! I should not have left him—I should not have left him!—"

The poor woman had completely broken down; fatigue, sorrow and emotion had overmastered her rigid, aristocratic bearing. She was crying gently to herself, whilst Suzanne ran up to her and tried to kiss away her tears.

Lord Antony and Sir Andrew had said nothing to interrupt the *Comtesse* whilst she was speaking. There was no doubt that they felt deeply for her; their very silence testified to that—but in every century, and ever since England has been what it is, an Englishman has always felt somewhat ashamed of his own emotion and of his own sympathy. And so, the two young men said nothing, and busied themselves in trying to hide their feelings, only succeeding in looking immeasurably sheepish.

"As for me, *Monsieur*," said Suzanne, suddenly, as she looked through a wealth of brown curls across at Sir Andrew, "I trust you absolutely, and I *know* that you will bring my dear father safely to England, just as you brought us today."

This was said with so much confidence, such unuttered hope and belief, that it seemed as if by magic to dry the mother's eyes, and to bring a smile upon everybody's lips.

"Nay! You shame me, *Mademoiselle*," replied Sir Andrew; "though my life is at your service, I have been but a humble tool in the hands of our great leader, who organised and effected your escape."

He had spoken with so much warmth and vehemence that Suzanne's eyes fastened upon him in undisguised wonder.

"Your leader, *Monsieur?*" said the *Comtesse*, eagerly. "Ah! of course, you must have a leader. And I did not think of that before! But tell me where is he? I must go to him at once, and I and my children must throw ourselves at his feet and thank him for all that he has done for us."

"Alas, *Madame!*" said Lord Antony, "that is impossible."

"Impossible?—Why?"

"Because the Scarlet Pimpernel works in the dark, and his identity is only known under the solemn oath of secrecy to his immediate followers."

"The Scarlet Pimpernel?" said Suzanne, with a merry laugh. "Why!

what a droll name! What is the Scarlet Pimpernel, *Monsieur?*"

She looked at Sir Andrew with eager curiosity. The young man's face had become almost transfigured. His eyes shone with enthusiasm; hero-worship, love, admiration for his leader seemed literally to glow upon his face. "The Scarlet Pimpernel, *Mademoiselle*," he said at last "is the name of a humble English wayside flower; but it is also the name chosen to hide the identity of the best and bravest man in all the world, so that he may better succeed in accomplishing the noble task he has set himself to do."

"Ah, yes," here interposed the young *Vicomte*, "I have heard speak of this Scarlet Pimpernel. A little flower—red?—yes! They say in Paris that every time a royalist escapes to England that devil, Foucquier-Tinville, the Public Prosecutor, receives a paper with that little flower designated in red upon it. . . . Yes?"

"Yes, that is so," assented Lord Antony.

"Then he will have received one such paper today?"

"Undoubtedly."

"Oh! I wonder what he will say!" said Suzanne, merrily. "I have heard that the picture of that little red flower is the only thing that frightens him."

"Faith, then," said Sir Andrew, "he will have many more opportunities of studying the shape of that small scarlet flower."

"Ah, *monsieur*," sighed the *Comtesse*, "it all sounds like a romance, and I cannot understand it all."

"Why should you try, *Madame?*"

"But, tell me, why should your leader—why should you all—spend your money and risk your lives—for it is your lives you risk, *Messieurs*, when you set foot in France—and all for us French men and women, who are nothing to you?"

"Sport, *Madame la Comtesse*, sport," asserted Lord Antony, with his jovial, loud and pleasant voice; "we are a nation of sportsmen, you know, and just now it is the fashion to pull the hare from between the teeth of the hound."

"Ah, no, no, not sport only, *Monsieur* . . . you have a more noble motive, I am sure for the good work you do."

"Faith, *Madame*, I would like you to find it then . . . as for me, I vow, I love the game, for this is the finest sport I have yet encountered.—Hair-breath escapes—the devil's own risks!—Tally ho!—and away we go!"

But the *Comtesse* shook her head, still incredulously. To her it seemed preposterous that these young men and their great leader, all of them rich, probably wellborn, and young, should for no other motive than sport, run the terrible risks, which she knew they were constantly doing. Their nationality, once they had set foot in France, would be no safeguard to them. Anyone found harbouring or assisting suspected royalists would be ruthlessly condemned and summarily executed, whatever his nationality might be. And this band of young Englishmen had, to her own knowledge, bearded the implacable and bloodthirsty tribunal of the Revolution, within the very walls of Paris itself, and had snatched away condemned victims, almost from the very foot of the guillotine. With a shudder, she recalled the events of the last few days, her escape from Paris with her two children, all three of them hidden beneath the hood of a rickety cart, and lying amidst a heap of turnips and cabbages, not daring to breathe, whilst the mob howled, "Á *la lanterne les aristos!*" at the awful West Barricade.

It had all occurred in such a miraculous way; she and her husband had understood that they had been placed on the list of "suspected persons," which meant that their trial and death were but a matter of days—of hours, perhaps.

Then came the hope of salvation; the mysterious epistle, signed with the enigmatical scarlet device; the clear, peremptory directions; the parting from the Comte de Tournay, which had torn the poor wife's heart in two; the hope of reunion; the flight with her two children; the covered cart; that awful hag driving it, who looked like some horrible evil demon, with the ghastly trophy on her whip handle!

The *Comtesse* looked round at the quaint, old-fashioned English inn, the peace of this land of civil and religious liberty, and she closed her eyes to shut out the haunting vision of that West Barricade, and of the mob retreating panic-stricken when the old hag spoke of the plague.

Every moment under that cart she expected recognition, arrest, herself and her children tried and condemned, and these young Englishmen, under the guidance of their brave and mysterious leader, had risked their lives to save them all, as they had already saved scores of other innocent people.

And all only for sport? Impossible! Suzanne's eyes as she sought those of Sir Andrew plainly told him that she thought that *he* at any rate rescued his fellowmen from terrible and unmerited death, through a higher and nobler motive than his friend would have her believe.

"How many are there in your brave league, *Monsieur?*" she asked timidly.

"Twenty all told, *Mademoiselle*," he replied, "one to command, and nineteen to obey. All of us Englishmen, and all pledged to the same cause—to obey our leader and to rescue the innocent."

"May God protect you all, *Messieurs*," said the *Comtesse*, fervently.

"He had done that so far, *Madame*."

"It is wonderful to me, wonderful!—That you should all be so brave, so devoted to your fellowmen—yet you are English!—and in France treachery is rife—all in the name of liberty and fraternity."

"The women even, in France, have been more bitter against us aristocrats than the men," said the *Vicomte*, with a sigh.

"Ah, yes," added the *Comtesse*, while a look of haughty disdain and intense bitterness shot through her melancholy eyes, "There was that woman, Marguerite St. Just for instance. She denounced the Marquis de St. Cyr and all his family to the awful tribunal of the Terror."

"Marguerite St. Just?" said Lord Antony, as he shot a quick and apprehensive glance across at Sir Andrew.

"Marguerite St. Just?—Surely . . ."

"Yes!" replied the *Comtesse*, "surely you know her. She was a leading actress of the *Comédie Française*, and she married an Englishman lately. You must know her—"

"Know her?" said Lord Antony. "Know Lady Blakeney—the most fashionable woman in London—the wife of the richest man in England? Of course, we all know Lady Blakeney."

"She was a school-fellow of mine at the convent in Paris," interposed Suzanne, "and we came over to England together to learn your language. I was very fond of Marguerite, and I cannot believe that she ever did anything so wicked."

"It certainly seems incredible," said Sir Andrew. "You say that she actually denounced the Marquis de St. Cyr? Why should she have done such a thing? Surely there must be some mistake—"

"No mistake is possible, *Monsieur*," rejoined the *Comtesse*, coldly. "Marguerite St. Just's brother is a noted republican. There was some talk of a family feud between him and my cousin, the Marquis de St. Cyr. The St. Justs are quite plebeian, and the republican government employs many spies. I assure you there is no mistake—You had not heard this story?"

"Faith, *Madame*, I did hear some vague rumours of it, but in England no one would credit it—Sir Percy Blakeney, her husband, is a very wealthy man, of high social position, the intimate friend of the

Prince of Wales—and Lady Blakeney leads both fashion and society in London."

"That may be, *Monsieur*, and we shall, of course, lead a very quiet life in England, but I pray God that while I remain in this beautiful country, I may never meet Marguerite St. Just."

The proverbial wet-blanket seemed to have fallen over the merry little company gathered round the table. Suzanne looked sad and silent; Sir Andrew fidgeted uneasily with his fork, whilst the *Comtesse*, encased in the plate-armour of her aristocratic prejudices, sat, rigid and unbending, in her straight-backed chair. As for Lord Antony, he looked extremely uncomfortable, and glanced once or twice apprehensively towards Jellyband, who looked just as uncomfortable as himself.

"At what time do you expect Sir Percy and Lady Blakeney?" he contrived to whisper unobserved, to mine host.

"Any moment, my lord," whispered Jellyband in reply.

Even as he spoke, a distant clatter was heard of an approaching coach; louder and louder it grew, one or two shouts became distinguishable, then the rattle of horses' hoofs on the uneven cobble stones, and the next moment a stable boy had thrown open the coffee-room door and rushed in excitedly.

"Sir Percy Blakeney and my lady," he shouted at the top of his voice, "they're just arriving."

And with more shouting, jingling of harness, and iron hoofs upon the stones, a magnificent coach, drawn by four superb bays, had halted outside the porch of "The Fisherman's Rest."

Chapter 5

Marguerite

In a moment the pleasant oak-raftered coffee-room of the inn became the scene of hopeless confusion and discomfort. At the first announcement made by the stable boy, Lord Antony, with a fashionable oath, had jumped up from his seat and was now giving many and confused directions to poor bewildered Jellyband, who seemed at his wits' end what to do.

"For goodness' sake, man," admonished his lordship, "try to keep Lady Blakeney talking outside for a moment while the ladies withdraw. Zounds!" he added, with another more emphatic oath, "this is most unfortunate."

"Quick Sally! the candles!" shouted Jellyband, as hopping about from one leg to another, he ran hither and thither, adding to the general discomfort of everybody.

The *Comtesse*, too, had risen to her feet: rigid and erect, trying to hide her excitement beneath more becoming *sang-froid*, she repeated mechanically,—

"I will not see her!—I will not see her!"

Outside, the excitement attendant upon the arrival of very important guests grew apace.

"Good-day, Sir Percy!—Good-day to your ladyship! Your servant, Sir Percy!"—was heard in one long, continued chorus, with alternate more feeble tones of—"Remember the poor blind man! of your charity, lady and gentleman!"

Then suddenly a singularly sweet voice was heard through all the din.

"Let the poor man be—and give him some supper at my expense."

The voice was low and musical, with a slight sing-song in it, and a faint *soupcon* of foreign intonation in the pronunciation of the consonants.

Everyone in the coffee-room heard it and paused instinctively, listening to it for a moment. Sally was holding the candles by the opposite door, which led to the bedrooms upstairs, and the *Comtesse* was in the act of beating a hasty retreat before that enemy who owned such a sweet musical voice; Suzanne reluctantly was preparing to follow her mother, while casting regretful glances towards the door, where she hoped still to see her dearly-beloved, erstwhile school-fellow.

Then Jellyband threw open the door, still stupidly and blindly hoping to avert the catastrophe, which he felt was in the air, and the same low, musical voice said, with a merry laugh and mock consternation,—

"*B-r-r-r-r!* I am as wet as a herring! *Dieu*! has anyone ever seen such a contemptible climate?"

"Suzanne, come with me at once—I wish it," said the *Comtesse*, peremptorily.

"Oh! Mama!" pleaded Suzanne.

"My lady—er—h'm!—my lady!—" came in feeble accents from Jellyband, who stood clumsily trying to bar the way.

"*Pardieu*, my good man," said Lady Blakeney, with some impatience, "what are you standing in my way for, dancing about like a turkey with a sore foot? Let me get to the fire, I am perished with the cold."

And the next moment Lady Blakeney, gently pushing mine host on one side, had swept into the coffee-room.

There are many portraits and miniatures extant of Marguerite St. Just—Lady Blakeney as she was then—but it is doubtful if any of these really do her singular beauty justice. Tall, above the average, with magnificent presence and regal figure, it is small wonder that even the *Comtesse* paused for a moment in involuntary admiration before turning her back on so fascinating an apparition.

Marguerite Blakeney was then scarcely five-and-twenty, and her beauty was at its most dazzling stage. The large hat, with its undulating and waving plumes, threw a soft shadow across the classic brow with the aureole of auburn hair—free at the moment from any powder; the sweet, almost childlike mouth, the straight chiselled nose, round chin, and delicate throat, all seemed set off by the picturesque costume of the period. The rich blue velvet robe moulded in its every line the graceful contour of the figure, whilst one tiny hand held, with a dignity all its own, the tall stick adorned with a large bunch of ribbons which fashionable ladies of the period had taken to carrying recently.

With a quick glance all around the room, Marguerite Blakeney had taken stock of every one there. She nodded pleasantly to Sir Andrew Ffoulkes, whilst extending a hand to Lord Antony.

"Hello! my Lord Tony, why—what are *you* doing here in Dover?" she said merrily.

Then, without waiting for a reply, she turned and faced the *Comtesse* and Suzanne. Her whole face lighted up with additional brightness, as she stretched out both arms towards the young girl.

"Why! if that isn't my little Suzanne over there. *Pardieu*, little citizeness, how came you to be in England? And *Madame* too?"

She went up effusive to them both, with not a single touch of embarrassment in her manner or in her smile. Lord Tony and Sir Andrew watched the little scene with eager apprehension. English though they were, they had often been in France, and had mixed sufficiently with the French to realise the unbending *hauteur*, the bitter hatred with which the old *noblesse* of France viewed all those who had helped to contribute to their downfall. Armand St. Just, the brother of beautiful Lady Blakeney—though known to hold moderate and conciliatory views—was an ardent republican; his feud with the ancient family of St. Cyr—the rights and wrongs of which no outsider ever knew—had culminated in the downfall, the almost total extinction of the latter. In France, St. Just and his party had triumphed, and here in England, face to face with these three refugees driven from their country, flying for their lives, bereft of all which centuries of luxury had given them, there stood a fair scion of those same republican families which had hurled down a throne, and uprooted an aristocracy whose origin was lost in the dim and distant *vista* of bygone centuries.

She stood there before them, in all the unconscious insolence of beauty, and stretched out her dainty hand to them, as if she would, by that one act, bridge over the conflict and bloodshed of the past decade.

"Suzanne, I forbid you to speak to that woman," said the *Comtesse*, sternly, as she placed a restraining hand upon her daughter's arm.

She had spoken in English, so that all might hear and understand; the two young English gentlemen, as well as the common innkeeper and his daughter. The latter literally gasped with horror at this foreign insolence, this impudence before her ladyship—who was English, now that she was Sir Percy's wife, and a friend of the Princess of Wales to boot.

As for Lord Antony and Sir Andrew Ffoulkes, their very hearts seemed to stand still with horror at this gratuitous insult. One of them uttered an exclamation of appeal, the other one of warning, and instinctively both glanced hurriedly towards the door, whence a slow, drawly, not unpleasant voice had already been heard.

Alone among those present Marguerite Blakeney and the Comtesse de Tournay had remained seemingly unmoved. The latter, rigid, erect and defiant, with one hand still upon her daughter's arm, seemed the very personification of unbending pride. For the moment Marguerite's sweet face had become as white as the soft *fichu* which swathed her throat, and a very keen observer might have noted that the hand which held the tall, beribboned stick was clenched, and trembled somewhat.

But this was only momentary; the next instant the delicate eyebrows were raised slightly, the lips curved sarcastically upwards, the clear blue eyes looked straight at the rigid *Comtesse*, and with a slight shrug of the shoulders—

"Hoity-toity, citizeness," she said gaily, "what fly stings you, pray?"

"We are in England now, *Madame*," rejoined the *Comtesse*, coldly, "and I am at liberty to forbid my daughter to touch your hand in friendship. Come, Suzanne."

She beckoned to her daughter, and without another look at Marguerite Blakeney, but with a deep, old-fashioned curtsey to the two young men, she sailed majestically out of the room.

There was silence in the old inn parlour for a moment, as the rustle of the *Comtesse's* skirts died away down the passage. Marguerite, rigid as a statue followed with hard, set eyes the upright figure, as it disappeared through the doorway—but as little Suzanne, humble and obedient, was about to follow her mother, the hard, set expression suddenly vanished, and a wistful, almost pathetic and childlike look stole into Lady Blakeney's eyes.

Little Suzanne caught that look; the child's sweet nature went out to the beautiful woman, scarcely older than herself; filial obedience vanished before girlish sympathy; at the door she turned, ran back to Marguerite, and putting her arms round her, kissed her effusively; then only did she follow her mother, Sally bringing up the rear, with a final curtsey to my lady.

Suzanne's sweet and dainty impulse had relieved the unpleasant tension. Sir Andrew's eyes followed the pretty little figure, until it had quite disappeared, then they met Lady Blakeney's with unassumed merriment.

Marguerite, with dainty affection, had kissed her hand to the ladies, as they disappeared through the door, then a humorous smile began hovering round the corners of her mouth.

"So that's it, is it?" she said gaily. "La! Sir Andrew, did you ever see such an unpleasant person? I hope when I grow old I sha'n't look like that."

She gathered up her skirts and assuming a majestic gait, stalked towards the fireplace.

"Suzanne," she said, mimicking the *Comtesse's* voice, "I forbid you to speak to that woman!"

The laugh which accompanied this sally sounded perhaps a trifled forced and hard, but neither Sir Andrew nor Lord Tony were very keen observers. The mimicry was so perfect, the tone of the voice so accurately reproduced, that both the young men joined in a hearty cheerful "Bravo!"

"Ah! Lady Blakeney!" added Lord Tony, "how they must miss you at the *Comédie Française,* and how the Parisians must hate Sir Percy for having taken you away."

"Lud, man," rejoined Marguerite, with a shrug of her graceful shoulders, "'tis impossible to hate Sir Percy for anything; his witty sallies would disarm even *Madame la Comtesse* herself."

The young *Vicomte,* who had not elected to follow his mother in her dignified exit, now made a step forward, ready to champion the

Comtesse should Lady Blakeney aim any further shafts at her. But before he could utter a preliminary word of protest, a pleasant though distinctly inane laugh, was heard from outside, and the next moment an unusually tall and very richly dressed figure appeared in the doorway.

CHAPTER 6

An Exquisite of '92

Sir Percy Blakeney, as the chronicles of the time inform us, was in this year of grace 1792, still a year or two on the right side of thirty. Tall, above the average, even for an Englishman, broad-shouldered and massively built, he would have been called unusually good-looking, but for a certain lazy expression in his deep-set blue eyes, and that perpetual inane laugh which seemed to disfigure his strong, clearly-cut mouth.

It was nearly a year ago now that Sir Percy Blakeney, Bart., one of the richest men in England, leader of all the fashions, and intimate friend of the Prince of Wales, had astonished fashionable society in London and Bath by bringing home, from one of his journeys abroad, a beautiful, fascinating, clever, French wife. He, the sleepiest, dullest, most British Britisher that had ever set a pretty woman yawning, had secured a brilliant matrimonial prize for which, as all chroniclers aver, there had been many competitors.

Marguerite St. Just had first made her *début* in artistic Parisian circles, at the very moment when the greatest social upheaval the world has ever known was taking place within its very walls. Scarcely eighteen, lavishly gifted with beauty and talent, chaperoned only by a young and devoted brother, she had soon gathered round her, in her charming apartment in the Rue Richelieu, a coterie which was as brilliant as it was exclusive—exclusive, that is to say, only from one point of view. Marguerite St. Just was from principle and by conviction a republican—equality of birth was her motto—inequality of fortune was in her eyes a mere untoward accident, but the only inequality she admitted was that of talent. "Money and titles may be hereditary," she would say, "but brains are not," and thus her charming salon was reserved for originality and intellect, for brilliance and wit, for clever men and talented women, and the entrance into it was soon looked upon in the world of intellect—which even in those days and in those troublous times found its pivot in Paris—as the seal to an artistic career.

Clever men, distinguished men, and even men of exalted station formed a perpetual and brilliant court round the fascinating young actress of the *Comédie Française*, and she glided through republican, revolutionary, bloodthirsty Paris like a shining comet with a trail behind her of all that was most distinguished, most interesting, in intellectual Europe.

Then the climax came. Some smiled indulgently and called it an artistic eccentricity, others looked upon it as a wise provision, in view of the many events which were crowding thick and fast in Paris just then, but to all, the real motive of that climax remained a puzzle and a mystery. Anyway, Marguerite St. Just married Sir Percy Blakeney one fine day, just like that, without any warning to her friends, without a *soiree de contrat* or *diner de fiancailles* or other appurtenances of a fashionable French wedding.

How that stupid, dull Englishman ever came to be admitted within the intellectual circle which revolved round "the cleverest woman in Europe," as her friends unanimously called her, no one ventured to guess—golden key is said to open every door, asserted the more malignantly inclined.

Enough, she married him, and "the cleverest woman in Europe" had linked her fate to that "demmed idiot" Blakeney, and not even her most intimate friends could assign to this strange step any other motive than that of supreme eccentricity. Those friends who knew, laughed to scorn the idea that Marguerite St. Just had married a fool for the sake of the worldly advantages with which he might endow her. They knew, as a matter of fact, that Marguerite St. Just cared nothing about money, and still less about a title; moreover, there were at least half a dozen other men in the cosmopolitan world equally well-born, if not so wealthy as Blakeney, who would have been only too happy to give Marguerite St. Just any position she might choose to covet.

As for Sir Percy himself, he was universally voted to be totally unqualified for the onerous post he had taken upon himself. His chief qualifications for it seemed to consist in his blind adoration for her, his great wealth and the high favour in which he stood at the English court; but London society thought that, taking into consideration his own intellectual limitations, it would have been wiser on his part had he bestowed those worldly advantages upon a less brilliant and witty wife.

Although lately he had been so prominent a figure in fashionable English society, he had spent most of his early life abroad. His father, the late Sir Algernon Blakeney, had had the terrible misfortune of seeing an idolised young wife become hopelessly insane after two years of happy married life. Percy had just been born when the late Lady Blakeney fell prey to the terrible malady which in those days was looked upon as hopelessly incurable and nothing short of a curse of God upon the entire family. Sir Algernon took his afflicted young wife abroad, and there presumably Percy was educated, and grew up between an imbecile mother and a distracted father, until he attained his majority. The death of his parents following close upon one another left him a free man, and as Sir Algernon had led a forcibly simple and retired life, the large Blakeney fortune had increased tenfold.

Sir Percy Blakeney had travelled a great deal abroad, before he brought home his beautiful, young, French wife. The fashionable circles of the time were ready to receive them both with open arms; Sir Percy was rich, his wife was accomplished, the Prince of Wales took a very great liking to them both. Within six months they were the acknowledged leaders of fashion and of style. Sir Percy's coats were the talk of the town, his inanities were quoted, his foolish laugh copied by the gilded youth at Almack's or the Mall. Everyone knew that he was hopelessly stupid, but then that was scarcely to be wondered at, seeing that all the Blakeneys for generations had been notoriously dull, and that his mother died an imbecile.

Thus, society accepted him, petted him, made much of him, since his horses were the finest in the country, his *fêtes* and wines the most sought after. As for his marriage with "the cleverest woman in Europe," well! the inevitable came with sure and rapid footsteps. No one pitied him, since his fate was of his own making. There were plenty of young ladies in England, of high birth and good looks, who would have been quite willing to help him to spend the Blakeney fortune, whilst smiling indulgently at his inanities and his good-humoured foolishness. Moreover, Sir Percy got no pity, because he seemed to require none—he seemed very proud of his clever wife, and to care little that she took no pains to disguise that good-natured contempt which she evidently felt for him, and that she even amused herself by sharpening her ready wits at his expense.

But then Blakeney was really too stupid to notice the ridicule with which his wife covered him, and if his matrimonial relations with the fascinating Parisienne had not turned out all that his hopes and his dog-like devotion for her had pictured, society could never do more than vaguely guess at it.

In his beautiful house at Richmond he played second fiddle to his clever wife with imperturbable *bonhomie*; he lavished jewels and luxuries of all kinds upon her, which she took with inimitable grace, dispensing the hospitality of his superb mansion with the same graciousness with which she had welcomed the intellectual coterie of Paris.

Physically, Sir Percy Blakeney was undeniably handsome—always excepting the lazy, bored look which was habitual to him. He was always irreproachable dressed, and wore the exaggerated *Incroyable* fashions, which had just crept across from Paris to England, with the perfect good taste innate in an English gentleman. On this special afternoon in September, in spite of the long journey by coach, in spite of rain and mud, his coat set irreproachably across his fine shoulders, his hands looked almost femininely white, as they emerged through billowy frills of finest Mechline lace: the extravagantly short-waisted satin coat, wide-lapelled waistcoat, and tight-fitting striped breeches, set off his massive figure to perfection, and in repose one might have admired so fine a specimen of English manhood, until the foppish ways, the affected movements, the perpetual inane laugh, brought one's admiration of Sir Percy Blakeney to an abrupt close.

He had lolled into the old-fashioned inn parlour, shaking the wet off his fine overcoat; then putting up a gold-rimmed eye-glass to his lazy blue eye, he surveyed the company, upon whom an embarrassed silence had suddenly fallen.

"How do, Tony? How do, Ffoulkes?" he said, recognising the two young men and shaking them by the hand. "Zounds, my dear fellow," he added, smothering a slight yawn, "did you ever see such a beastly day? Demmed climate this."

With a quaint little laugh, half of embarrassment and half of sarcasm, Marguerite had turned towards her husband, and was surveying him from head to foot, with an amused little twinkle in her merry blue eyes.

"*La!*" said Sir Percy, after a moment or two's silence, as no one offered any comment, "how sheepish you all look—What's up?"

"Oh, nothing, Sir Percy," replied Marguerite, with a certain amount of gaiety, which, however, sounded somewhat forced, "nothing to disturb your equanimity—only an insult to your wife."

The laugh which accompanied this remark was evidently intended to reassure Sir Percy as to the gravity of the incident. It apparently succeeded in that, for echoing the laugh, he rejoined placidly—

"*La*, m'dear! you don't say so. Begad! who was the bold man who dared to tackle you—eh?"

Lord Tony tried to interpose, but had no time to do so, for the young *Vicomte* had already quickly stepped forward.

"*Monsieur*," he said, prefixing his little speech with an elaborate bow, and speaking in broken English, "my mother, the Comtesse de Tournay de Basserive, has offenced *Madame*, who, I see, is your wife. I cannot ask your pardon for my mother; what she does is right in my eyes. But I am ready to offer you the usual reparation between men of honour."

The young man drew up his slim stature to its full height and looked very enthusiastic, very proud, and very hot as he gazed at six foot odd of gorgeousness, as represented by Sir Percy Blakeney, Bart.

"Lud, Sir Andrew," said Marguerite, with one of her merry infectious laughs, "look on that pretty picture—the English turkey and the French bantam."

The simile was quite perfect, and the English turkey looked down with complete bewilderment upon the dainty little French bantam, which hovered quite threateningly around him.

"*La!* sir," said Sir Percy at last, putting up his eye glass and surveying the young Frenchman with undisguised wonderment, "where, in the cuckoo's name, did you learn to speak English?"

"*Monsieur!*" protested the *Vicomte*, somewhat abashed at the way his warlike attitude had been taken by the ponderous-looking Englishman.

"I protest 'tis marvellous!" continued Sir Percy, imperturbably, "demmed marvellous! Don't you think so, Tony—eh? I vow I can't speak the French lingo like that. What?"

"Nay, I'll vouch for that!" rejoined Marguerite, "Sir Percy has a British accent you could cut with a knife."

"*Monsieur*," interposed the *Vicomte* earnestly, and in still more broken English, "I fear you have not understand. I offer you the only posseeble reparation among gentlemen."

"What the devil is that?" asked Sir Percy, blandly.

"My sword, *Monsieur*," replied the *Vicomte*, who, though still bewildered, was beginning to lose his temper.

"You are a sportsman, Lord Tony," said Marguerite, merrily; "ten to one on the little bantam."

But Sir Percy was staring sleepily at the *Vicomte* for a moment or two, through his partly closed heavy lids, then he smothered another yawn, stretched his long limbs, and turned leisurely away.

"Lud love you, sir," he muttered good-humouredly, "demmit, young man, what's the good of your sword to me?"

What the *Vicomte* thought and felt at that moment, when that long-limbed Englishman treated him with such marked insolence, might fill volumes of sound reflections. . . . What he said resolved itself into a single articulate word, for all the others were choked in his throat by his surging wrath—

"A duel, *Monsieur*," he stammered.

Once more Blakeney turned, and from his high altitude looked down on the choleric little man before him; but not even for a second did he seem to lose his own imperturbable good-humour. He laughed his own pleasant and inane laugh, and burying his slender, long hands into the capacious pockets of his overcoat, he said leisurely—"a bloodthirsty young ruffian, Do you want to make a hole in a law-abiding man?—As for me, sir, I never fight duels," he added, as he placidly sat down and stretched his long, lazy legs out before him. "Demmed uncomfortable things, duels, ain't they, Tony?"

Now the *Vicomte* had no doubt vaguely heard that in England the fashion of duelling amongst gentlemen had been surpressed by the law with a very stern hand; still to him, a Frenchman, whose notions of bravery and honour were based upon a code that had centuries of tradition to back it, the spectacle of a gentleman actually refusing to fight a duel was a little short of an enormity. In his mind he vaguely pondered whether he should strike that long-legged Englishman in the face and call him a coward, or whether such conduct in a lady's presence might be deemed ungentlemanly, when Marguerite happily interposed.

"I pray you, Lord Tony," she said in that gentle, sweet, musical voice of hers, "I pray you play the peacemaker. The child is bursting with rage, and," she added with a *soupcon* of dry sarcasm, "might do Sir Percy an injury." She laughed a mocking little laugh, which, however, did not in the least disturb her husband's placid equanimity. "The British turkey has had the day," she said. "Sir Percy would provoke all the saints in the calendar and keep his temper the while."

But already Blakeney, good-humoured as ever, had joined in the laugh against himself.

"Demmed smart that now, wasn't it?" he said, turning pleasantly to the *Vicomte*. "Clever woman my wife, sir. . . . You will find *that* out if you live long enough in England."

"Sir Percy is right, *Vicomte*," here interposed Lord Antony, laying a friendly hand on the young Frenchman's shoulder. "It would hardly be fitting that you should commence your career in England by provoking him to a duel."

For a moment longer the *Vicomte* hesitated, then with a slight shrug of the shoulders directed against the extraordinary code of honour prevailing in this fog-ridden island, he said with becoming dignity,—

"Ah, well! if *Monsieur* is satisfied, I have no griefs. You mi'lor', are our protector. If I have done wrong, I withdraw myself."

"Aye, do!" rejoined Blakeney, with a long sigh of satisfaction, "withdraw yourself over there. Demmed excitable little puppy," he added under his breath, "Faith, Ffoulkes, if that's a specimen of the goods you and your friends bring over from France, my advice to you is, drop 'em 'mid Channel, my friend, or I shall have to see old Pitt about it, get him to clap on a prohibitive tariff, and put you in the stocks an you smuggle."

"*La*, Sir Percy, your chivalry misguides you," said Marguerite, coquettishly, "you forget that you yourself have imported one bundle of goods from France."

Blakeney slowly rose to his feet, and, making a deep and elaborate bow before his wife, he said with consummate gallantry,—

"I had the pick of the market, *Madame*, and my taste is unerring."

"More so than your chivalry, I fear," she retorted sarcastically.

"Odd's life, m'dear! be reasonable! Do you think I am going to allow my body to be made a pincushion of, by every little frog-eater who don't like the shape of your nose?"

"Lud, Sir Percy!" laughed Lady Blakeney as she bobbed him a quaint and pretty curtsey, "you need not be afraid! 'Tis not the *men* who dislike the shape of my nose."

"Afraid be demmed! Do you impugn my bravery, *Madame?* I don't patronise the ring for nothing, do I, Tony? I've put up the fists with Red Sam before now, and—and he didn't get it all his own way either—"

"S'faith, Sir Percy," said Marguerite, with a long and merry laugh, that went echoing along the old oak rafters of the parlour, "I would I had seen you then—ha! ha! ha! ha!—you must have looked a pretty picture—and—and to be afraid of a little French boy—ha! ha!—ha! ha!"

"Ha! ha! ha! he! he! he!" echoed Sir Percy, good-humouredly. "*La, Madame*, you honour me! Zooks! Ffoulkes, mark ye that! I have made my wife laugh!—The cleverest woman in Europe! . . . Odd's fish, we must have a bowl on that!" and he tapped vigorously on the table near him. "Hey! Jelly! Quick, man! Here, Jelly!"

Harmony was once more restored. Mr. Jellyband, with a mighty effort, recovered himself from the many emotions he had experienced within the last half hour. "A bowl of punch, Jelly, hot and strong, eh?" said Sir Percy. "The wits that have just made a clever woman laugh must be whetted! Ha! ha! ha! Hasten, my good Jelly!"

"Nay, there is no time, Sir Percy," interposed Marguerite. "The skipper will be here directly and my brother must get on board, or the *Daydream* will miss the tide."

"Time, m'dear? There is plenty of time for any gentleman to get drunk and get on board before the turn of the tide."

"I think, your ladyship," said Jellyband, respectfully, "that the young gentleman is coming along now with Sir Percy's skipper."

"That's right," said Blakeney, "then Armand can join us in the merry bowl. Think you, Tony," he added, turning towards the *Vicomte*, "that the jackanapes of yours will join us in a glass? Tell him that we drink in token of reconciliation."

"In fact, you are all such merry company," said Marguerite, "that I trust you will forgive me if I bid my brother goodbye in another room."

It would have been bad form to protest. Both Lord Antony and Sir Andrew felt that Lady Blakeney could not altogether be in tune with them at the moment. Her love for her brother, Armand St. Just, was deep and touching in the extreme. He had just spent a few weeks with her in her English home, and was going back to serve his country, at the moment when death was the usual reward for the most enduring devotion.

Sir Percy also made no attempt to detain his wife. With that perfect, somewhat affected gallantry which characterised his every movement, he opened the coffee-room door for her, and made her the most approved and elaborate bow, which the fashion of the time dictated, as she sailed out of the room without bestowing on him more than a passing, slightly contemptuous glance. Only Sir Andrew Ffoulkes, whose every thought since he had met Suzanne de Tournay seemed keener, more gentle, more innately sympathetic, noted the curious look of intense longing, of deep and hopeless passion, with which the inane and flippant Sir Percy followed the retreating figure of his brilliant wife.

Chapter 7

The Secret Orchard

Once outside the noisy coffee-room, alone in the dimly-lighted passage, Marguerite Blakeney seemed to breathe more freely. She heaved a deep sigh, like one who had long been oppressed with the heavy weight of constant self-control, and she allowed a few tears to fall unheeded down her cheeks.

Outside the rain had ceased, and through the swiftly passing clouds, the pale rays of an after-storm sun shone upon the beautiful white coast of Kent and the quaint, irregular houses that clustered round the Admiralty Pier. Marguerite Blakeney stepped on to the porch and looked out to sea. Silhouetted against the ever-changing sky, a graceful schooner, with white sails set, was gently dancing in the breeze. The *Daydream* it was, Sir Percy Blakeney's yacht, which was ready to take Armand St. Just back to France into the very midst of that seething, bloody Revolution which was overthrowing a monarchy, attacking a religion, destroying a society, in order to try and rebuild upon the ashes of tradition a new Utopia, of which a few men dreamed, but which none had the power to establish.

In the distance two figures were approaching "The Fisherman's Rest": one, an oldish man, with a curious fringe of grey hairs round a rotund and massive chin, and who walked with that peculiar rolling gait which invariably betrays the seafaring man: the other, a young, slight figure, neatly and becomingly dressed in a dark, many caped overcoat; he was clean-shaved, and his dark hair was taken well back over a clear and noble forehead.

"Armand!" said Marguerite Blakeney, as soon as she saw him approaching from the distance, and a happy smile shone on her sweet face, even through the tears.

A minute or two later brother and sister were locked in each other's arms, while the old skipper stood respectfully on one side.

"How much time have we got, Briggs?" asked Lady Blakeney, "before M. St. Just need go on board?"

"We ought to weigh anchor before half an hour, your ladyship," replied the old man, pulling at his grey forelock.

Linking her arm in his, Marguerite led her brother towards the cliffs.

"Half an hour," she said, looking wistfully out to sea, "half an hour more and you'll be far from me, Armand! Oh! I can't believe that you are going, dear! These last few days—whilst Percy has been away, and I've had you all to myself, have slipped by like a dream."

"I am not going far, sweet one," said the young man gently, "a narrow channel to cross—a few miles of road—I can soon come back."

"Nay, 'tis not the distance, Armand—but that awful Paris—just now—"

They had reached the edge of the cliff. The gentle sea-breeze blew Marguerite's hair about her face and sent the ends of her soft lace *fichu* waving round her, like a white and supple snake. She tried to pierce the distance far away, beyond which lay the shores of France: that relentless and stern France which was exacting her pound of flesh, the blood-tax from the noblest of her sons.

"Our own beautiful country, Marguerite," said Armand, who seemed to have divined her thoughts.

"They are going too far, Armand," she said vehemently. "You are a republican, so am I—we have the same thoughts, the same enthusiasm for liberty and equality—but even *you* must think that they are going too far—"

"Hush!—" said Armand, instinctively, as he threw a quick, apprehensive glance around him.

"Ah! you see: you don't think yourself that it is safe even to speak of these things—here in England!" She clung to him suddenly with strong, almost motherly, passion: "Don't go, Armand!" she begged; "don't go back! What should I do if—if—if—"

Her voice was choked in sobs, her eyes, tender, blue and loving, gazed appealingly at the young man, who in his turn looked steadfastly into hers.

"You would in any case be my own brave sister," he said gently, "who would remember that, when France is in peril, it is not for her sons to turn their backs on her."

Even as he spoke, that sweet childlike smile crept back into her face, pathetic in the extreme, for it seemed drowned in tears.

"Oh! Armand!" she said quaintly, "I sometimes wish you had not so many lofty virtues—I assure you little sins are far less dangerous and uncomfortable. But you *will* be prudent?" she added earnestly.

"As far as possible—I promise you."

"Remember, dear, I have only you—to—to care for me—"

"Nay, sweet one, you have other interests now. Percy cares for you—"

A look of strange wistfulness crept into her eyes as she murmured,—

"He did—once—"

"But surely—"

"There, there, dear, don't distress yourself on my account. Percy is very good—"

"Nay!" he interrupted energetically, "I will distress myself on your account, my Margot. Listen, dear, I have not spoken of these things to you before; something always seemed to stop me when I wished to question you. But, somehow, I feel as if I could not go away and leave you now without asking you one question—You need not answer it if you do not wish," he added, as he noted a sudden hard look, almost of apprehension, darting through her eyes.

"What is it?" she asked simply.

"Does Sir Percy Blakeney know that . . . I mean, does he know the part you played in the arrest of the Marquis de St. Cyr?"

She laughed—a mirthless, bitter, contemptuous laugh, which was like a jarring chord in the music of her voice.

"That I denounced the Marquis de St. Cyr, you mean, to the tribunal that ultimately sent him and all his family to the guillotine? Yes, he does know.—I told him after I married him—"

"You told him all the circumstances—which so completely exonerated you from any blame?"

"It was too late to talk of 'circumstances'; he heard the story from other sources; my confession came too tardily, it seems. I could no longer plead extenuating circumstances: I could not demean myself by trying to explain—"

"And?"

"And now I have the satisfaction, Armand, of knowing that the biggest fool in England has the most complete contempt for his wife."

She spoke with vehement bitterness this time, and Armand St. Just, who loved her so dearly, felt that he had placed a somewhat clumsy finger upon an aching wound.

"But Sir Percy loved you, Margot," he repeated gently.

"Loved me?—Well, Armand, I thought at one time that he did, or I should not have married him. I daresay," she added, speaking very rapidly, as if she were about to lay down a heavy burden, which had oppressed her for months, "I daresay that even you thought—as everybody else did—that I married Sir Percy because of his wealth—but I assure you, dear, that it was not so. He seemed to worship me with a curious intensity of concentrated passion, which went straight to my heart. I had never loved anyone before, as you know, and I was four-and-twenty then—so I naturally thought that it was not in my nature to love. But it has always seemed to me that it *must* be *heavenly* to be loved blindly, passionately, wholly—worshipped, in fact—and the very fact that Percy was slow and stupid was an attraction for me, as I thought he would love me all the more. A clever man would naturally have other interests, an ambitious man other hopes—I thought that a fool would worship and think of nothing else. And I was ready to respond, Armand; I would have allowed myself to be worshipped, and given infinite tenderness in return—"

She sighed—and there was a world of disillusionment in that sigh. Armand St. Just had allowed her to speak on without interruption: he listened to her, whilst allowing his own thoughts to run riot. It was terrible to see a young and beautiful woman—a girl in all but name—still standing almost at the threshold of her life, yet bereft of hope, bereft of illusions, bereft of all those golden and fantastic dreams, which should have made her youth one long, perpetual holiday.

Yet perhaps—though he loved his sister dearly—perhaps he understood: he had studied men in many countries, men of all ages, men of every grade of social and intellectual status, and inwardly he understood what Marguerite had left unsaid. Granted that Percy Blakeney was dull-witted, but in his slow-going mind, there would still be room for that ineradicable pride of a descendant of a long line of English gentlemen. A Blakeney had died on Bosworth field, another had sacrificed life and fortune for the sake of a treacherous Stuart: and that same pride—foolish and prejudiced as the republican Armand would call it—must have been stung to the quick on hearing of the sin which lay at Lady Blakeney's door. She had been young, misguided, ill-advised perhaps. Armand knew that: her impulses and imprudence, knew it still better; but Blakeney was slow-witted, he would not listen to "circumstances," he only clung to facts, and these had shown him Lady Blakeney denouncing a fellow man to a tribunal that knew no pardon: and the contempt he would feel for the deed she had done, however unwittingly, would kill that same love in him, in which sympathy and intellectuality could never have a part.

Yet even now, his own sister puzzled him. Life and love have such strange vagaries. Could it be that with the waning of her husband's love, Marguerite's heart had awakened with love for him? Strange extremes meet in love's pathway: this woman, who had had half intellectual Europe at her feet, might perhaps have set her affections on a fool. Marguerite was gazing out towards the sunset. Armand could not see her face, but presently it seemed to him that something which glittered for a moment in the golden evening light, fell from her eyes onto her dainty *fichu* of lace.

But he could not broach that subject with her. He knew her strange, passionate nature so well, and knew that reserve which lurked behind her frank, open ways. They had always been together, these two, for their parents had died when Armand was still a youth, and Marguerite but a child. He, some eight years her senior, had watched over her until her marriage; had chaperoned her during those brilliant years spent in the flat of the Rue de Richelieu, and had seen her enter upon this new life of hers, here in England, with much sorrow and some foreboding.

This was his first visit to England since her marriage, and the few months of separation had already seemed to have built up a slight, thin partition between brother and sister; the same deep, intense love was still there, on both sides, but each now seemed to have a secret orchard, into which the other dared not penetrate.

There was much Armand St. Just could not tell his sister; the political aspect of the revolution in France was changing almost every day; she might not understand how his own views and sympathies might become modified, even as the excesses, committed by those who had been his friends, grew in horror and in intensity. And Marguerite could not speak to her brother about the secrets of her heart; she hardly understood them herself, she only knew that, in the midst of luxury, she felt lonely and unhappy. And now Armand was going away; she feared for his safety, she longed for his presence. She would not spoil these last few sadly-sweet moments by speaking about herself. She led him gently along the cliffs, then down to the beach; their arms linked in one another's, they had still so much to say that lay just outside that secret orchard of theirs.

Chapter 8

The Accredited Agent

The afternoon was rapidly drawing to a close; and a long, chilly English summer's evening was throwing a misty pall over the green Kentish landscape.

The *Daydream* had set sail, and Marguerite Blakeney stood alone on the edge of the cliff over an hour, watching those white sails, which bore so swiftly away from her the only being who really cared for her, whom she dared to love, whom she knew she could trust.

Some little distance away to her left the lights from the coffee-room of "The Fisherman's Rest" glittered yellow in the gathering mist; from time to time it seemed to her aching nerves as if she could catch from thence the sound of merry-making and of jovial talk, or even that perpetual, senseless laugh of her husband's, which grated continually upon her sensitive ears.

Sir Percy had had the delicacy to leave her severely alone. She supposed that, in his own stupid, good-natured way, he may have understood that she would wish to remain alone, while those white sails disappeared into the vague horizon, so many miles away. He, whose notions of propriety and decorum were supersensitive, had not suggested even that an attendant should remain within call. Marguerite was grateful to her husband for all this; she always tried to be grateful to him for his thoughtfulness, which was constant, and for his generosity, which really was boundless. She tried even at times to curb the sarcastic, bitter thoughts of him, which made her—in spite of herself—say cruel, insulting things, which she vaguely hoped would wound him.

Yes! she often wished to wound him, to make him feel that she too held him in contempt, that she too had forgotten that she had almost loved him. Loved that inane fop! whose thoughts seemed unable to soar beyond the tying of a cravat or the new cut of a coat. Bah! And yet!—vague memories, that were sweet and ardent and attuned to this calm summer's evening, came wafted back to her memory, on the invisible wings of the light sea-breeze: the time when first he worshipped her; he seemed so devoted—a very slave—and there was a certain latent intensity in that love which had fascinated her.

Then suddenly that love, that devotion, which throughout his courtship she had looked upon as the slavish fidelity of a dog, seemed to vanish completely. Twenty-four hours after the simple little ceremony at old St. Roch, she had told him the story of how, inadvertently, she had spoken of certain matters connected with the Marquis de St. Cyr before some men—her friends—who had used this information against the unfortunate Marquis and sent him and his family to the guillotine.

She hated the Marquis. Years ago, Armand, her dear brother, loved Angele de St. Cyr, but St. Just was a plebeian, and the Marquis full of the pride and arrogant prejudices of his caste. One day Armand, the respectful, timid lover, ventured on sending a small poem—enthusiastic, ardent, passionate—to the idol of his dreams. The next night he was waylaid just outside Paris by the valets of Marquis de St. Cyr, and ignominiously thrashed—thrashed like a dog within an inch of his life—because he had dared to raise his eyes to the daughter of the aristocrat. The incident was one which, in those days, some two years before the great Revolution, was of almost daily occurrence in France; incidents of that type, in fact, led to bloody reprisals, which a few years later sent most of those haughty heads to the guillotine.

Marguerite remembered it all: what her brother must have suffered in his manhood and his pride must have been appalling; what she suffered through him and with him she never attempted even to analyse.

Then the day of retribution came. St. Cyr and his kin had found their masters, in those same plebeians whom they had despised. Armand and Marguerite, both intellectual, thinking beings, adopted with the enthusiasm of their years the Utopian doctrines of the Revolution, while the Marquis de St. Cyr and his family fought inch by inch for the retention of those privileges which had placed them socially above their fellow-men. Marguerite, impulsive, thoughtless, not calculating the purport of her words, still smarting under the terrible insult her brother had suffered at the Marquis' hands, happened to hear—amongst her own *coterie*—that the St. Cyrs were in treasonable correspondence with Austria, hoping to obtain the Emperor's support to quell the growing revolution in their own country.

In those days one denunciation was sufficient: Marguerite's few thoughtless words anent the Marquis de St. Cyr bore fruit within twenty-four hours. He was arrested. His papers were searched: letters from the Austrian Emperor, promising to send troops against the Paris populace, were found in his desk. He was arraigned for treason against the nation, and sent to the guillotine, whilst his family, his wife and his sons, shared in this awful fate.

Marguerite, horrified at the terrible consequences of her own thoughtlessness, was powerless to save the Marquis: his own coterie, the leaders of the revolutionary movement, all proclaimed her as a heroine: and when she married Sir Percy Blakeney, she did not perhaps altogether realise how severely he would look upon the sin, which she had so inadvertently committed, and which still lay heavily upon her soul. She made full confession of it to her husband, trusting his blind love for her, her boundless power over him, to soon make him forget what might have sounded unpleasant to an English ear.

Certainly, at the moment he seemed to take it very quietly; hardly, in fact, did he appear to understand the meaning of all she said; but what was more certain still, was that never after that could she detect the slightest sign of that love, which she once believed had been wholly hers. Now they had drifted quite apart, and Sir Percy seemed to have laid aside his love for her, as he would an ill-fitting glove. She tried to rouse him by sharpening her ready wit against his dull intellect; endeavouring to excite his jealousy, if she could not rouse his love; tried to goad him to self-assertion, but all in vain. He remained the same, always passive, drawling, sleepy, always courteous, invariably a gentleman: she had all that the world and a wealthy husband can give to a pretty woman, yet on this beautiful summer's evening, with the white sails of the *Daydream* finally hidden by the evening shadows, she felt more lonely than that poor tramp who plodded his way wearily along the rugged cliffs.

With another heavy sigh, Marguerite Blakeney turned her back upon the sea and cliffs and walked slowly back towards "The Fisherman's Rest." As she drew near, the sound of revelry, of gay, jovial laughter, grew louder and more distinct. She could distinguish Sir Andrew Ffoulkes' pleasant voice, Lord Tony's boisterous guffaws, her husband's occasional, drawly, sleepy comments; then realising the loneliness of the road and the fast gathering gloom round her, she quickened her steps—the next moment she perceived a stranger coming rapidly towards her. Marguerite did not look up: she was not the least nervous, and "The Fisherman's Rest" was now well within call.

The stranger paused when he saw Marguerite coming quickly towards him, and just as she was about to slip past him, he said very quietly:

"Citoyenne St. Just."

Marguerite uttered a little cry of astonishment, at thus hearing her own familiar maiden name uttered so close to her. She looked up at the stranger, and this time, with a cry of unfeigned pleasure, she put out both her hands effusively towards him.

"Chauvelin!" she exclaimed.

"Himself, *citoyenne*, at your service," said the stranger, gallantly kissing the tips of her fingers.

Marguerite said nothing for a moment or two, as she surveyed with obvious delight the not very prepossessing little figure before her. Chauvelin was then nearer forty than thirty—a clever, shrewd-looking personality, with a curious fox-like expression in the deep, sunken eyes. He was the same stranger who an hour or two previously had joined Mr. Jellyband in a friendly glass of wine.

"Chauvelin—my friend—" said Marguerite, with a pretty little sigh of satisfaction. "I am mightily pleased to see you."

No doubt poor Marguerite St. Just, lonely in the midst of her grandeur, and of her starchy friends, was happy to see a face that brought back memories of that happy time in Paris, when she reigned—a queen—over the intellectual coterie of the Rue de Richelieu. She did not notice the sarcastic little smile, however, that hovered round the thin lips of Chauvelin.

"But tell me," she added merrily, "what in the world, or whom in the world, are you doing here in England?"

"I might return the subtle compliment, fair lady," he said. "What of yourself?"

"Oh, I?" she said, with a shrug of the shoulders. "*Je m'ennuie, mon ami*, that is all."

They had reached the porch of "The Fisherman's Rest," but Marguerite seemed loth to go within. The evening air was lovely after the storm, and she had found a friend who exhaled the breath of Paris, who knew Armand well, who could talk of all the merry, brilliant friends whom she had left behind. So, she lingered on under the pretty porch, while through the gaily-lighted dormer-window of the coffee-room sounds of laughter, of calls for "Sally" and for beer, of tapping of mugs, and clinking of dice, mingled with Sir Percy Blakeney's inane and mirthless laugh. Chauvelin stood beside her, his shrewd, pale, yellow eyes fixed on the pretty face, which looked so sweet and childlike in this soft English summer twilight.

"You surprise me, *citoyenne*," he said quietly, as he took a pinch of snuff.

"Do I now?" she retorted gaily. "Faith, my little Chauvelin, I should have thought that, with your penetration, you would have guessed that an atmosphere composed of fogs and virtues would never suit Marguerite St. Just."

"Dear me! is it as bad as that?" he asked, in mock consternation.

"Quite," she retorted, "and worse."

"Strange! Now, I thought that a pretty woman would have found English country life peculiarly attractive."

"Yes! so did I," she said with a sigh, "Pretty women," she added meditatively, "ought to have a good time in England, since all the pleasant things are forbidden them—the very things they do every day."

"Quite so!"

"You'll hardly believe it, my little Chauvelin," she said earnestly, "but I often pass a whole day—a whole day—without encountering a single temptation."

"No wonder," retorted Chauvelin, gallantly, "that the cleverest woman in Europe is troubled with *ennui*."

She laughed one of her melodious, rippling, childlike laughs.

"It must be pretty bad, mustn't it?" she asked archly, "or I should not have been so pleased to see you."

"And this within a year of a romantic love match—that's just the difficulty—"

"Ah!—that idyllic folly," said Chauvelin, with quiet sarcasm, "did not then survive the lapse of—weeks?"

"Idyllic follies never last, my little Chauvelin—They come upon us like the measles—and are as easily cured."

Chauvelin took another pinch of snuff: he seemed very much addicted to that pernicious habit, so prevalent in those days; perhaps, too, he found the taking of snuff a convenient veil for disguising the quick, shrewd glances with which he strove to read the very souls of those with whom he came in contact.

"No wonder," he repeated, with the same gallantry, "that the most active brain in Europe is troubled with *ennui*."

"I was in hopes that you had a prescription against the malady, my little Chauvelin."

"How can I hope to succeed in that which Sir Percy Blakeney has failed to accomplish?"

"Shall we leave Sir Percy out of the question for the present, my dear friend?" she said drily.

"Ah! my dear lady, pardon me, but that is just what we cannot very well do," said Chauvelin, whilst once again his eyes, keen as those of a fox on the alert, darted a quick glance at Marguerite. "I have a most perfect prescription against the worst form of *ennui*, which I would have been happy to submit to you, but—"

"But what?"

"There *is* Sir Percy."

"What has he to do with it?"

"Quite a good deal, I am afraid. The prescription I would offer, fair lady, is called by a very plebeian name: Work!"

"Work?"

Chauvelin looked at Marguerite long and scrutinisingly. It seemed as if those keen, pale eyes of his were reading every one of her thoughts. They were alone together; the evening air was quite still, and their soft whispers were drowned in the noise which came from the coffee-room. Still, Chauvelin took a step or two from under the porch, looked quickly and keenly all round him, then seeing that indeed no one was within earshot, he once more came back close to Marguerite.

"Will you render France a small service, *citoyenne?*" he asked, with a sudden change of manner, which lent his thin, fox-like face a singular earnestness.

"*La*, man!" she replied flippantly, "how serious you look all of a sudden—Indeed, I do not know if I *would* render France a small service—at any rate, it depends upon the kind of service she—or you—want."

"Have you ever heard of the Scarlet Pimpernel, Citoyenne St. Just?" asked Chauvelin, abruptly.

"Heard of the Scarlet Pimpernel?" she retorted with a long and merry laugh, "Faith man! we talk of nothing else.—We have hats à *la Scarlet Pimpernel*; our horses are called 'Scarlet Pimpernel'; at the Prince of Wales' supper party the other night we had a *souffle à la Scarlet Pimpernel*—Lud!" she added gaily, "the other day I ordered at my milliner's a blue dress trimmed with green, and bless me, if she did not call that *à la Scarlet Pimpernel*."

Chauvelin had not moved while she prattled merrily along; he did not even attempt to stop her when her musical voice and her childlike laugh went echoing through the still evening air. But he remained serious and earnest whilst she laughed, and his voice, clear, incisive, and hard, was not raised above his breath as he said,—

"Then, as you have heard of that enigmatical personage, *citoyenne*, you must also have guessed, and know, that the man who hides his identity under that strange pseudonym, is the most bitter enemy of our republic, of France—of men like Armand St. Just."

"*La!*" she said, with a quaint little sigh, "I dare swear he is. . . . France has many bitter enemies these days."

"But you, *citoyenne*, are a daughter of France, and should be ready to help her in a moment of deadly peril."

"My brother Armand devotes his life to France," she retorted proudly; "as for me, I can do nothing—here in England.—"

"Yes, you—" he urged still more earnestly, whilst his thin fox-like face seemed suddenly to have grown impressive and full of dignity, "here, in England, *citoyenne*—you alone can help us—Listen!—I have been sent over here by the Republican Government as its representative: I present my credentials to Mr. Pitt in London tomorrow. One of my duties here is to find out all about this League of the Scarlet Pimpernel, which has become a standing menace to France, since it is pledged to help our cursed aristocrats—traitors to their country, and enemies of the people—to escape from the just punishment which they deserve. You know as well as I do, *citoyenne*, that once they are over here, those French *émigres* try to rouse public feeling against the Republic—They are ready to join issue with any enemy bold enough to attack France—Now, within the last month scores of these *émigres*, some only suspected of treason, others actually condemned by the Tribunal of Public Safety, have succeeded in crossing the Channel.

"Their escape in each instance was planned, organised and effected by this society of young English jackanapes, headed by a man whose brain seems as resourceful as his identity is mysterious. All the most strenuous efforts on the part of my spies have failed to discover who he is; whilst the others are the hands, he is the head, who beneath this strange anonymity calmly works at the destruction of France. I mean to strike at that head, and for this I want your help—through him afterwards I can reach the rest of the gang: he is a young buck in English society, of that I feel sure. Find that man for me, *citoyenne!*" he urged, "find him for France."

Marguerite had listened to Chauvelin's impassioned speech without uttering a word, scarce making a movement, hardly daring to breathe. She had told him before that this mysterious hero of romance was the talk of the smart set to which she belonged; already, before this, her heart and her imagination had been stirred by the thought of the brave man, who, unknown to fame, had rescued hundreds of lives from a terrible, often an unmerciful fate. She had but little real sympathy with those haughty French aristocrats, insolent in their pride of caste, of whom the Comtesse de Tournay de Basserive was so typical an example; but republican and liberal-minded though she was from principle, she hated and loathed the methods which the young Republic had chosen for establishing itself. She had not been in Paris for some months; the horrors and bloodshed of the Reign of Terror, culminating in the September massacres, had only come across the Channel to her as a faint echo. Robespierre, Danton, Marat, she had not known in their new guise of bloody judiciaries, merciless wielders of the guillotine. Her very soul recoiled in horror from these excesses, to which she feared her brother Armand—moderate republican as he was—might become one day the holocaust.

Then, when first she heard of this band of young English enthusiasts, who, for sheer love of their fellowmen, dragged women and children, old and young men, from a horrible death, her heart had glowed with pride for them, and now, as Chauvelin spoke, her very soul went out to the gallant and mysterious leader of the reckless little band, who risked his life daily, who gave it freely and without ostentation, for the sake of humanity.

Her eyes were moist when Chauvelin had finished speaking, the lace at her bosom rose and fell with her quick, excited breathing; she no longer heard the noise of drinking from the inn, she did not heed her husband's voice or his inane laugh, her thoughts had gone wandering in search of the mysterious hero! Ah! there was a man she might have loved, had he come her way: everything in him appealed to her romantic imagination; his personality, his strength, his bravery, the loyalty of those who served under him in that same noble cause, and, above all, that anonymity which crowned him, as if with a halo of romantic glory.

"Find him for France, *citoyenne!*"

Chauvelin's voice close to her ear roused her from her dreams. The mysterious hero had vanished, and, not twenty yards away from her, a man was drinking and laughing, to whom she had sworn faith and loyalty.

"*La!* man," she said with a return of her assumed flippancy, "you are astonishing. Where in the world am I to look for him?"

"You go everywhere, *citoyenne*," whispered Chauvelin, insinuatingly, "Lady Blakeney is the pivot of social London, so I am told—you see everything, you *hear* everything."

"Easy, my friend," retorted Marguerite, drawing herself up to her full height and looking down, with a slight thought of contempt on the small, thin figure before her. "Easy! you seem to forget that there are six feet of Sir Percy Blakeney, and a long line of ancestors to stand between Lady Blakeney and such a thing as you propose."

"For the sake of France, *citoyenne!*" reiterated Chauvelin, earnestly.

"Tush, man, you talk nonsense anyway; for even if you did know who this Scarlet Pimpernel is, you could do nothing to him—an Englishman!"

"I'd take my chance of that," said Chauvelin, with a dry, rasping little laugh. "At any rate we could send him to the guillotine first to cool his ardour, then, when there is a diplomatic fuss about it, we can apologise—humbly—to the British Government, and, if necessary, pay compensation to the bereaved family."

"What you propose is horrible, Chauvelin," she said, drawing away from him as from some noisome insect. "Whoever the man may be, he is brave and noble, and never—do you hear me?—never would I lend a hand to such villainy."

"You prefer to be insulted by every French aristocrat who comes to this country?"

Chauvelin had taken sure aim when he shot this tiny shaft. Marguerite's fresh young cheeks became a touch more pale and she bit her under lip, for she would not let him see that the shaft had struck home.

"That is beside the question," she said at last with indifference. "I can defend myself, but I refuse to do any dirty work for you—or for France. You have other means at your disposal; you must use them, my friend."

And without another look at Chauvelin, Marguerite Blakeney turned her back on him and walked straight into the inn.

"That is not your last word, *citoyenne*," said Chauvelin, as a flood of light from the passage illumined her elegant, richly-clad figure, "we meet in London, I hope!"

"We meet in London," she said, speaking over her shoulder at him, "but that is my last word."

She threw open the coffee-room door and disappeared from his view, but he remained under the porch for a moment or two, taking a pinch of snuff. He had received a rebuke and a snub, but his shrewd, fox-like face looked neither abashed nor disappointed; on the contrary, a curious smile, half sarcastic and wholly satisfied, played around the corners of his thin lips.

Chapter 9

The Outrage

A beautiful starlit night had followed on the day of incessant rain: a cool, balmy, late summer's night, essentially English in its suggestion of moisture and scent of wet earth and dripping leaves.

The magnificent coach, drawn by four of the finest thoroughbreds in England, had driven off along the London road, with Sir Percy Blakeney on the box, holding the reins in his slender feminine hands, and beside him Lady Blakeney wrapped in costly furs. A fifty-mile drive on a starlit summer's night! Marguerite had hailed the notion of it with delight. . . . Sir Percy was an enthusiastic whip; his four thoroughbreds, which had been sent down to Dover a couple of days before, were just sufficiently fresh and restive to add zest to the expedition and Marguerite revelled in anticipation of the few hours of solitude, with the soft night breeze fanning her cheeks, her thoughts wandering, whither away?

She knew from old experience that Sir Percy would speak little, if at all: he had often driven her on his beautiful coach for hours at night, from point to point, without making more than one or two casual remarks upon the weather or the state of the roads. He was very fond of driving by night, and she had very quickly adopted his fancy: as she sat next to him hour after hour, admiring the dexterous, certain way in which he handled the reins, she often wondered what went on in that slow-going head of his. He never told her, and she had never cared to ask.

At "The Fisherman's Rest" Mr. Jellyband was going the round, putting out the lights. His bar customers had all gone, but upstairs in the snug little bedrooms, Mr. Jellyband had quite a few important guests: the Comtesse de Tournay, with Suzannne, and the *Vicomte*, and there were two more bedrooms ready for Sir Andrew Ffoulkes and Lord Antony Dewhurst, if the two young men should elect to honour the ancient hostelry and stay the night.

For the moment these two young gallants were comfortably installed in the coffee-room, before the huge log-fire, which, in spite of the mildness of the evening, had been allowed to burn merrily.

"I say, Jelly, has everyone gone?" asked Lord Tony, as the worthy landlord still busied himself clearing away glasses and mugs.

"Everyone, as you see, my lord."

"And all your servants gone to bed?"

"All except the boy on duty in the bar, and," added Mr. Jellyband with a laugh, "I expect he'll be asleep afore long, the rascal."

"Then we can talk here undisturbed for half an hour?"

"At your service, my lord—I'll leave your candles on the dresser—and your rooms are quite ready—I sleep at the top of the house myself, but if your lordship'll only call loudly enough, I daresay I shall hear."

"All right, Jelly—and—I say, put the lamp out—the fire'll give us all the light we need—and we don't want to attract the passer-by."

"Al ri', my lord."

Mr. Jellyband did as he was bid—he turned out the quaint old lamp that hung from the raftered ceiling and blew out all the candles.

"Let's have a bottle of wine, Jelly," suggested Sir Andrew.

"Al ri', sir!"

Jellyband went off to fetch the wine. The room now was quite dark, save for the circle of ruddy and fitful light formed by the brightly blazing logs in the hearth.

"Is that all, gentlemen?" asked Jellyband, as he returned with a bottle of wine and a couple of glasses, which he placed on the table.

"That'll do nicely, thanks, Jelly!" said Lord Tony.

"Goodnight, my lord! Goodnight, sir!"

"Goodnight, Jelly!"

The two young men listened, whilst the heavy tread of Mr. Jellyband was heard echoing along the passage and staircase. Presently even that sound died out, and the whole of "The Fisherman's Rest" seemed wrapt in sleep, save the two young men drinking in silence beside the hearth.

For a while no sound was heard, even in the coffee-room, save the ticking of the old grandfather's clock and the crackling of the burning wood.

"All right again this time, Ffoulkes?" asked Lord Antony at last.

Sir Andrew had been dreaming evidently, gazing into the fire, and seeing therein, no doubt, a pretty, piquant face, with large brown eyes and a wealth of dark curls round a childish forehead.

"Yes!" he said, still musing, "all right!"

"No hitch?"

"None."

Lord Antony laughed pleasantly as he poured himself out another glass of wine.

"I need not ask, I suppose, whether you found the journey pleasant this time?"

"No, friend, you need not ask," replied Sir Andrew, gaily. "It was all right."

"Then here's to her very good health," said jovial Lord Tony. "She's a bonnie lass, though she *is* a French one. And here's to your courtship—may it flourish and prosper exceedingly."

He drained his glass to the last drop, then joined his friend beside the hearth.

"Well! you'll be doing the journey next, Tony, I expect," said Sir Andrew, rousing himself from his meditations, "you and Hastings, certainly; and I hope you may have as pleasant a task as I had, and as charming a travelling companion. You have no idea, Tony. . . ."

"No! I haven't," interrupted his friend pleasantly, "but I'll take your word for it. And now," he added, whilst a sudden earnestness crept over his jovial young face, "how about business?" The two young men drew their chairs closer together, and instinctively, though they were alone, their voices sank to a whisper.

"I saw the Scarlet Pimpernel alone, for a few moments in Calais," said Sir Andrew, "a day or two ago. He crossed over to England two days before we did. He had escorted the party all the way from Paris, dressed—you'll never credit it!—as an old market woman, and driving—until they were safely out of the city—the covered cart, under which the Comtesse de Tournay, Mlle. Suzanne, and the *Vicomte* lay concealed among the turnips and cabbages. They, themselves, of course, never suspected who their driver was. He drove them right through a line of soldiery and a yelling mob, who were screaming, '*À bas les aristos!*' But the market cart got through along with some others, and the Scarlet Pimpernel, in shawl, petticoat and hood, yelled '*À bas les aristos!*' louder than anybody. Faith!" added the young man, as his eyes glowed with enthusiasm for the beloved leader, "that man's a marvel! His cheek is preposterous, I vow!—and that's what carries him through."

Lord Antony, whose vocabulary was more limited than that of his friend, could only find an oath or two with which to show his admiration for his leader.

"He wants you and Hastings to meet him at Calais," said Sir Andrew, more quietly, "on the 2nd of next month. Let me see! that will be next Wednesday."

"Yes."

"It is, of course, the case of the Comte de Tournay, this time; a dangerous task, for the *Comte*, whose escape from his *château*, after he had been declared a 'suspect' by the Committee of Public Safety, was a masterpiece of the Scarlet Pimpernel's ingenuity, is now under sentence of death. It will be rare sport to get *him* out of France, and you will have a narrow escape, if you get through at all. St. Just has actually gone to meet him—of course, no one suspects St. Just as yet; but after that . . . to get them both out of the country! I'faith, 'twill be a tough job, and tax even the ingenuity of our chief. I hope I may yet have orders to be of the party."

"Have you any special instructions for me?"

"Yes! rather more precise ones than usual. It appears that the Republican Government have sent an accredited agent over to England, a man named Chauvelin, who is said to be terribly bitter against our league, and determined to discover the identity of our leader, so that he may have him kidnapped, the next time he attempts to set foot in France. This Chauvelin has brought a whole army of spies with him, and until the chief has sampled the lot, he thinks we should meet as seldom as possible on the business of the league, and on no account should talk to each other in public places for a time. When he wants to speak to us, he will contrive to let us know."

The two young men were both bending over the fire for the blaze had died down, and only a red glow from the dying embers cast a lurid light on a narrow semicircle in front of the hearth. The rest of the room lay buried in complete gloom; Sir Andrew had taken a pocket-book from his pocket, and drawn therefrom a paper, which he unfolded, and together they tried to read it by the dim red firelight. So intent were they upon this, so wrapt up in the cause, the business they had so much at heart, so precious was this document which came from the very hand of their adored leader, that they had eyes and ears only for that. They lost count of the sounds around them, of the dropping of the crisp ash from the grate, of the monotonous ticking of the clock, of the soft, almost imperceptible rustle of something on the floor close beside them. A figure had emerged from under one of the benches; with snake-like, noiseless movements it crept closer and closer to the two young men, not breathing, only gliding along the floor, in the inky blackness of the room.

"You are to read these instructions and commit them to memory," said Sir Andrew, "then destroy them."

He was about to replace the letter-case into his pocket, when a tiny slip of paper fluttered from it and fell on to the floor. Lord Antony stooped and picked it up.

"What's that?" he asked.

"I don't know," replied Sir Andrew.

"It dropped out of your pocket just now. It certainly does not seem to be with the other paper."

"Strange!—I wonder when it got there? It is from the chief," he added, glancing at the paper.

Both stooped to try and decipher this last tiny scrap of paper on which a few words had been hastily scrawled, when suddenly a slight noise attracted their attention, which seemed to come from the passage beyond.

"What's that?" said both instinctively. Lord Antony crossed the room towards the door, which he threw open quickly and suddenly; at that very moment he received a stunning blow between the eyes, which threw him back violently into the room. Simultaneously the crouching, snake-like figure in the gloom had jumped up and hurled itself from behind upon the unsuspecting Sir Andrew, felling him to the ground.

All this occurred within the short space of two or three seconds, and before either Lord Antony or Sir Andrew had time or chance to utter a cry or to make the faintest struggle. They were each seized by two men, a muffler was quickly tied round the mouth of each, and they were pinioned to one another back to back, their arms, hands, and legs securely fastened.

One man had in the meanwhile quietly shut the door; he wore a mask and now stood motionless while the others completed their work.

"All safe, *citoyen!*" said one of the men, as he took a final survey of the bonds which secured the two young men.

"Good!" replied the man at the door; "now search their pockets and give me all the papers you find."

This was promptly and quietly done. The masked man having taken possession of all the papers, listened for a moment or two if there were any sound within "The Fisherman's Rest." Evidently satisfied that this dastardly outrage had remained unheard, he once more opened the door and pointed peremptorily down the passage. The four men lifted Sir Andrew and Lord Antony from the ground, and as quietly, as noiselessly as they had come, they bore the two pinioned young gallants out of the inn and along the Dover Road into the gloom beyond.

In the coffee-room the masked leader of this daring attempt was quickly glancing through the stolen papers.

"Not a bad day's work on the whole," he muttered, as he quietly took off his mask, and his pale, fox-like eyes glittered in the red glow of the fire. "Not a bad day's work."

He opened one or two letters from Sir Andrew Ffoulkes' pocket-book, noted the tiny scrap of paper which the two young men had only just had time to read; but one letter specially, signed Armand St. Just, seemed to give him strange satisfaction.

"Armand St. Just a traitor after all," he murmured. "Now, fair Marguerite Blakeney," he added viciously between his clenched teeth, "I think that you will help me to find the Scarlet Pimpernel."

Chapter 10

In the Opera Box

It was one of the gala nights at Covent Garden Theatre, the first of the autumn season in this memorable year of grace 1792.

The house was packed, both in the smart orchestra boxes and in the pit, as well as in the more plebeian balconies and galleries above. Gluck's *Orpheus* made a strong appeal to the more intellectual portions of the house, whilst the fashionable women, the gaily-dressed and brilliant throng, spoke to the eye of those who cared but little for this "latest importation from Germany."

Selina Storace had been duly applauded after her grand *aria* by her numerous admirers; Benjamin Incledon, the acknowledged favourite of the ladies, had received special gracious recognition from the royal box; and now the curtain came down after the glorious finale to the second act, and the audience, which had hung spell-bound on the magic strains of the great maestro, seemed collectively to breathe a long sigh of satisfaction, previous to letting loose its hundreds of waggish and frivolous tongues. In the smart orchestra boxes many well-known faces were to be seen. Mr. Pitt, over-weighted with cares of state, was finding brief relaxation in tonight's musical treat; the Prince of Wales, jovial, rotund, somewhat coarse and commonplace in appearance, moved about from box to box, spending brief quarters of an hour with those of his more intimate friends.

In Lord Grenville's box, too, a curious, interesting personality attracted everyone's attention; a thin, small figure with shrewd, sarcastic face and deep-set eyes, attentive to the music, keenly critical of the audience, dressed in immaculate black, with dark hair free from any powder. Lord Grenville—Foreign Secretary of State—paid him marked, though frigid deference.

Here and there, dotted about among distinctly English types of beauty, one or two foreign faces stood out in marked contrast: the haughty aristocratic cast of countenance of the many French royalist émigres who, persecuted by the relentless, revolutionary faction of their country, had found a peaceful refuge in England. On these faces sorrow and care were deeply writ; the women especially paid but little heed, either to the music or to the brilliant audience; no doubt their thoughts were far away with husband, brother, son maybe, still in peril, or lately succumbed to a cruel fate.

Among these the Comtesse de Tournay de Basserive, but lately arrived from France, was a most conspicuous figure: dressed in deep, heavy black silk, with only a white lace kerchief to relieve the aspect of mourning about her person, she sat beside Lady Portarles, who was vainly trying by witty sallies and somewhat broad jokes, to bring a smile to the *Comtesse's* sad mouth. Behind her sat little Suzanne and the *Vicomte*, both silent and somewhat shy among so many strangers. Suzanne's eyes seemed wistful; when she first entered the crowded house, she had looked eagerly all around, scanning every face, scrutinised every box. Evidently the one face she wished to see was not there, for she settled herself quietly behind her mother, listened apathetically to the music, and took no further interest in the audience itself.

"Ah, Lord Grenville," said Lady Portarles, as following a discreet knock, the clever, interesting head of the Secretary of State appeared in the doorway of the box, "you could not arrive more *à propos*. Here is Madame la Comtesse de Tournay positively dying to hear the latest news from France."

The distinguished diplomat had come forward and was shaking hands with the ladies.

"Alas!" he said sadly, "it is of the very worst. The massacres continue; Paris literally reeks with blood; and the guillotine claims a hundred victims a day."

Pale and tearful, the *Comtesse* was leaning back in her chair, listening horror-struck to this brief and graphic account of what went on in her own misguided country.

"Ah, *monsieur!*" she said in broken English, "it is dreadful to hear all that—and my poor husband still in that awful country. It is terrible for me to be sitting here, in a theatre, all safe and in peace, whilst he is in such peril."

"Lud, *Madame!*" said honest, bluff Lady Portarles, "your sitting in a convent won't make your husband safe, and you have your children to consider: they are too young to be dosed with anxiety and premature mourning."

The *Comtesse* smiled through her tears at the vehemence of her friend. Lady Portarles, whose voice and manner would not have misfitted a jockey, had a heart of gold, and hid the most genuine sympathy and most gentle kindliness, beneath the somewhat coarse manners affected by some ladies at that time.

"Besides which, *Madame*," added Lord Grenville, "did you not tell me yesterday that the League of the Scarlet Pimpernel had pledged their honour to bring *M. le Comte* safely across the Channel?"

"Ah, yes!" replied the *Comtesse*, "and that is my only hope. I saw Lord Hastings yesterday—he reassured me again."

"Then I am sure you need have no fear. What the league have sworn, that they surely will accomplish. Ah!" added the old diplomat with a sigh, "if I were but a few years younger—"

"*La,* man!" interrupted honest Lady Portarles, "you are still young enough to turn your back on that French scarecrow that sits enthroned in your box tonight."

"I wish I could—but your ladyship must remember that in serving our country we must put prejudices aside. M. Chauvelin is the accredited agent of his Government—"

"Odd's fish, man!" she retorted, "you don't call those bloodthirsty ruffians over there a government, do you?"

"It has not been thought advisable as yet," said the Minister, guardedly, "for England to break off diplomatic relations with France, and we cannot therefore refuse to receive with courtesy the agent she wishes to send to us."

"Diplomatic relations be demmed, my lord! That sly little fox over there is nothing but a spy, I'll warrant, and you'll find—an I'm much mistaken, that he'll concern himself little with such diplomacy, beyond trying to do mischief to royalist refugees—to our heroic Scarlet Pimpernel and to the members of that brave little league."

"I am sure," said the *Comtesse*, pursing up her thin lips, "that if this Chauvelin wishes to do us mischief, he will find a faithful ally in Lady Blakeney."

"Bless the woman!" ejaculated Lady Portarles, "did ever anyone see such perversity? My Lord Grenville, you have the gift of gab, will you please explain to *Madame la Comtesse* that she is acting like a fool. In your position here in England, *Madame*," she added, turning a wrathful and resolute face towards the *Comtesse*, "you cannot afford to put on the hoity-toity airs you French aristocrats are so fond of. Lady Blakeney may or may not be in sympathy with those Ruffians in France; she may or may not have had anything to do with the arrest and condemnation of St. Cyr, or whatever the man's name is, but she is the leader of fashion in this country; Sir Percy Blakeney has more money than any half-dozen other men put together, he is hand and glove with royalty, and your trying to snub Lady Blakeney will not harm her, but will make you look a fool. Isn't that so, my Lord?"

But what Lord Grenville thought of this matter, or to what reflections this comely tirade of Lady Portarles' led the Comtesse de Tournay, remained unspoken, for the curtain had just risen on the third act of *Orpheus*, and admonishments to silence came from every part of the house.

Lord Grenville took a hasty farewell of the ladies and slipped back into his box, where M. Chauvelin had sat through this *entr'acte*, with his eternal snuff-box in his hand, and with his keen pale eyes intently fixed upon a box opposite him, where, with much *frou-frou* of silken skirts, much laughter and general stir of curiosity amongst the audience, Marguerite Blakeney had just entered, accompanied by her husband, and looking divinely pretty beneath the wealth of her golden, reddish curls, slightly besprinkled with powder, and tied back at the nape of her graceful neck with a gigantic black bow. Always dressed in the very latest vagary of fashion, Marguerite alone among the ladies that night had discarded the crossover *fichu* and broad-lapelled overdress, which had been in fashion for the last two or three years. She wore the short-waisted classical-shaped gown, which so soon was to become the approved mode in every country in Europe. It suited her graceful, regal figure to perfection, composed as it was of shimmering stuff which seemed a mass of rich gold embroidery.

As she entered, she leant for a moment out of the box, taking stock of all those present whom she knew. Many bowed to her as she did so, and from the royal box there came also a quick and gracious salute.

Chauvelin watched her intently all through the commencement of the third act, as she sat enthralled with the music, her exquisite little hand toying with a small jewelled fan, her regal head, her throat, arms and neck covered with magnificent diamonds and rare gems, the gift of the adoring husband who sprawled leisurely by her side.

Marguerite was passionately fond of music. *Orpheus* charmed her tonight. The very joy of living was writ plainly upon the sweet young face, it sparkled out of the merry blue eyes and lit up the smile that lurked around the lips. She was after all but five-and-twenty, in the heyday of youth, the darling of a brilliant throng, adored, *fêted*, petted, cherished. Two days ago, the *Daydream* had returned from Calais, bringing her news that her idolised brother had safely landed, that he thought of her, and would be prudent for her sake.

What wonder for the moment, and listening to Gluck's impassioned strains, that she forgot her disillusionments, forgot her vanished love-dreams, forgot even the lazy, good-humoured nonentity who had made up for his lack of spiritual attainments by lavishing worldly advantages upon her.

He had stayed beside her in the box just as long as convention demanded, making way for His Royal Highness, and for the host of admirers who in a continued procession came to pay homage to the queen of fashion. Sir Percy had strolled away, to talk to more congenial friends probably. Marguerite did not even wonder whither he had gone—she cared so little; she had had a little court round her, composed of the *jeunesse doree* of London, and had just dismissed them all, wishing to be alone with Gluck for a brief while.

A discreet knock at the door roused her from her enjoyment.

"Come in," she said with some impatience, without turning to look at the intruder.

Chauvelin, waiting for his opportunity, noted that she was alone, and now, without pausing for that impatient "Come in," he quietly slipped into the box, and the next moment was standing behind Marguerite's chair.

"A word with you, *citoyenne*," he said quietly.

Marguerite turned quickly, in alarm, which was not altogether feigned.

"Lud, man! you frightened me," she said with a forced little laugh, "your presence is entirely inopportune. I want to listen to Gluck and have no mind for talking."

"But this is my only opportunity," he said, as quietly, and without waiting for permission, he drew a chair close behind her—so close that he could whisper in her ear, without disturbing the audience, and without being seen, in the dark background of the box. "This is my only opportunity," he repeated, as she vouchsafed him no reply, "Lady Blakeney is always so surrounded, so *fêted* by her court, that a mere old friend has but very little chance."

"Faith, man!" she said impatiently, "you must seek for another opportunity then. I am going to Lord Grenville's ball tonight after the opera. So are you, probably. I'll give you five minutes then.—"

"Three minutes in the privacy of this box are quite sufficient for me," he rejoined placidly, "and I think that you will be wise to listen to me, Citoyenne St. Just."

Marguerite instinctively shivered. Chauvelin had not raised his voice above a whisper; he was now quietly taking a pinch of snuff, yet there was something in his attitude, something in those pale, foxy eyes, which seemed to freeze the blood in her veins, as would the sight of some deadly hitherto unguessed peril. "Is that a threat, *citoyen?*" she asked at last.

"Nay, fair lady," he said gallantly, "only an arrow shot into the air."

He paused a moment, like a cat which sees a mouse running heedlessly by, ready to spring, yet waiting with that feline sense of enjoyment of mischief about to be done. Then he said quietly—

"Your brother, St. Just, is in peril."

Not a muscle moved in the beautiful face before him. He could only see it in profile, for Marguerite seemed to be watching the stage intently, but Chauvelin was a keen observer; he noticed the sudden rigidity of the eyes, the hardening of the mouth, the sharp, almost paralysed tension of the beautiful, graceful figure.

"Lud, then," she said with affected merriment, "since 'tis one of your imaginary plots, you'd best go back to your own seat and leave me enjoy the music."

And with her hand she began to beat time nervously against the cushion of the box. Selina Storace was singing the "*Che faro*" to an audience that hung spellbound upon the prima donna's lips. Chauvelin did not move from his seat; he quietly watched that tiny nervous hand, the only indication that his shaft had indeed struck home.

"Well?" she said suddenly and irrelevantly, and with the same feigned unconcern.

"Well, *citoyenne?*" he rejoined placidly.

"About my brother?"

"I have news of him for you which, I think, will interest you, but first let me explain—May I?"

The question was unnecessary. He felt, though Marguerite still held her head steadily averted from him, that her every nerve was strained to hear what he had to say.

"The other day, *citoyenne*," he said, "I asked for your help.—France needed it, and I thought I could rely on you, but you gave me your answer—Since then the exigencies of my own affairs and your own social duties have kept us apart—although many things have happened—"

"To the point, I pray you, *citoyen*," she said lightly; "the music is entrancing, and the audience will get impatient of your talk."

"One moment, *citoyenne*. The day on which I had the honour of meeting you at Dover, and less than an hour after I had your final answer, I obtained possession of some papers, which revealed another of those subtle schemes for the escape of a batch of French aristocrats—that traitor de Tournay amongst others—all organised by that arch-meddler, the Scarlet Pimpernel. Some of the threads, too, of this mysterious organisation have come into my hands, but not all, and I want you—nay! you *must* help me to gather them together."

Marguerite seemed to have listened to him with marked impatience; she now shrugged her shoulders and said gaily—

"Bah! man. Have I not already told you that I care nought about your schemes or about the Scarlet Pimpernel. And had you not spoken about my brother—"

"A little patience, I entreat, *citoyenne*," he continued imperturbably. "Two gentlemen, Lord Antony Dewhurst and Sir Andrew Ffoulkes were at 'The Fisherman's Rest' at Dover that same night."

"I know. I saw them there."

"They were already known to my spies as members of that accursed league. It was Sir Andrew Ffoulkes who escorted the Comtesse de Tournay and her children across the Channel. When the two young men were alone, my spies forced their way into the coffee-room of the inn, gagged and pinioned the two gallants, seized their papers, and brought them to me."

In a moment she had guessed the danger. Papers?—Had Armand been imprudent?—The very thought struck her with nameless terror. Still she would not let this man see that she feared; she laughed gaily and lightly.

"Faith! and your impudence passes belief," she said merrily. "Robbery and violence!—in England!—in a crowded inn! Your men might have been caught in the act!"

"What if they had? They are children of France and have been trained by your humble servant. Had they been caught they would have gone to jail, or even to the gallows, without a word of protest or indiscretion; at any rate it was well worth the risk. A crowded inn is safer for these little operations than you think, and my men have experience."

"Well? And those papers?" she asked carelessly.

"Unfortunately, though they have given me cognisance of certain names—certain movements—enough, I think, to thwart their projected *coup* for the moment, it would only be for the moment, and still leaves me in ignorance of the identity of the Scarlet Pimpernel.

"*La!* my friend," she said, with the same assumed flippancy of manner, "then you are where you were before, aren't you? and you can let me enjoy the last strophe of the *aria*. Faith!" she added, ostentatiously smothering an imaginary yawn, "had you not spoken about my brother —"

"I am coming to him now, *citoyenne.* Among the papers there was a letter to Sir Andrew Ffoulkes, written by your brother, St. Just."

"Well? And?"

"That letter shows him to be not only in sympathy with the enemies of France, but actually a helper, if not a member, of the League of the Scarlet Pimpernel."

The blow had been struck at last. All along, Marguerite had been expecting it; she would not show fear, she was determined to seem unconcerned, flippant even. She wished, when the shock came, to be prepared for it, to have all her wits about her—those wits which had been nicknamed the keenest in Europe. Even now she did not flinch. She knew that Chauvelin had spoken the truth; the man was too earnest, too blindly devoted to the misguided cause he had at heart, too proud of his countrymen, of those makers of revolutions, to stoop to low, purposeless falsehoods.

That letter of Armand's—foolish, imprudent Armand—was in Chauvelin's hands. Marguerite knew that as if she had seen the letter with her own eyes; and Chauvelin would hold that letter for purposes of his own, until it suited him to destroy it or to make use of it against Armand. All that she knew, and yet she continued to laugh more gaily, more loudly than she had done before.

"*La,* man!" she said, speaking over her shoulder and looking him full and squarely in the face, "did I not say it was some imaginary plot—Armand in league with that enigmatic Scarlet Pimpernel!—Armand busy helping those French aristocrats whom he despises!—Faith, the tale does infinite credit to your imagination!"

"Let me make my point clear, *citoyenne,*" said Chauvelin, with the same unruffled calm, "I must assure you that St. Just is compromised beyond the slightest hope of pardon."

Inside the orchestra box all was silent for a moment or two. Marguerite sat, straight upright, rigid and inert, trying to think, trying to face the situation, to realise what had best be done.

In the house Storace had finished the *aria,* and was even now bowing in her classic garb, but in approved eighteenth-century fashion, to the enthusiastic audience, who cheered her to the echo.

"Chauvelin," said Marguerite Blakeney at last, quietly, and without that touch of bravado which had characterised her attitude all along, "Chauvelin, my friend, shall we try to understand one another. It seems that my wits have become rusty by contact with this damp climate. Now, tell me, you are very anxious to discover the identity of the Scarlet Pimpernel, isn't that so?"

"France's most bitter enemy, *citoyenne*—all the more dangerous, as he works in the dark."

"All the more noble, you mean—Well!—and you would now force me to do some spying work for you in exchange for my brother Armand's safety?—Is that it?"

"Fie! two very ugly words, fair lady," protested Chauvelin, urbanely. "There can be no question of force, and the service which I would ask of you, in the name of France, could never be called by the shocking name of spying."

"At any rate, that is what it is called over here," she said drily. "That is your intention, is it not?"

"My intention is, that you yourself win the free pardon for Armand St. Just by doing me a small service."

"What is it?"

"Only watch for me tonight, Citoyenne St. Just," he said eagerly. "Listen: among the papers which were found about the person of Sir Andrew Ffoulkes there was a tiny note. See!" he added, taking a tiny scrap of paper from his pocket-book and handing it to her.

It was the same scrap of paper which, four days ago, the two young men had been in the act of reading, at the very moment when they were attacked by Chauvelin's minions. Marguerite took it mechanically and stooped to read it. There were only two lines, written in a distorted, evidently disguised, handwriting; she read them half aloud—

> Remember we must not meet more often than is strictly necessary. You have all instructions for the 2nd. If you wish to speak to me again, I shall be at G.'s ball.

"What does it mean?" she asked.

"Look again, *citoyenne*, and you will understand."

"There is a device here in the corner, a small red flower—"

"Yes."

"The Scarlet Pimpernel," she said eagerly, "and G.'s ball means Grenville's ball.—He will be at my Lord Grenville's ball tonight."

"That is how I interpret the note, *citoyenne*," concluded Chauvelin, blandly. "Lord Antony Dewhurst and Sir Andrew Ffoulkes, after they were pinioned and searched by my spies, were carried by my orders to a lonely house in the Dover Road, which I had rented for the purpose: there they remained close prisoners until this morning. But having found this tiny scrap of paper, my intention was that they should be in London, in time to attend my Lord Grenville's ball. You see, do you not? that they must have a great deal to say to their chief—and thus they will have an opportunity of speaking to him tonight, just as he directed them to do. Therefore, this morning, those two young gallants found every bar and bolt open in that lonely house on the Dover Road, their jailers disappeared, and two good horses standing ready saddled and tethered in the yard. I have not seen them yet, but I think we may safely conclude that they did not draw rein until they reached London. Now you see how simple it all is, *citoyenne!*"

"It does seem simple, doesn't it?" she said, with a final bitter attempt at flippancy, "when you want to kill a chicken—you take hold of it—then you wring its neck—it's only the chicken who does not find it quite so simple. Now you hold a knife at my throat, and a hostage for my obedience—You find it simple—I don't."

"Nay, *citoyenne*, I offer you a chance of saving the brother you love from the consequences of his own folly."

Marguerite's face softened, her eyes at last grew moist, as she murmured, half to herself:

"The only being in the world who has loved me truly and constantly—But what do you want me to do, Chauvelin?" she said, with a world of despair in her tear-choked voice. "In my present position, it is well-nigh impossible!"

"Nay, *citoyenne*," he said drily and relentlessly, not heeding that despairing, childlike appeal, which might have melted a heart of stone, "as Lady Blakeney, no one suspects you, and with your help tonight I may—who knows?—succeed in finally establishing the identity of the Scarlet Pimpernel—You are going to the ball *anon*.—Watch for me there, *citoyenne*, watch and listen—You can tell me if you hear a chance word or whisper.—You can note everyone to whom Sir Andrew Ffoulkes or Lord Antony Dewhurst will speak. You are absolutely beyond suspicion now. The Scarlet Pimpernel will be at Lord Grenville's ball tonight. Find out who he is, and I will pledge the word of France that your brother shall be safe."

Chauvelin was putting the knife to her throat. Marguerite felt herself entangled in one of those webs, from which she could hope for no escape. A precious hostage was being held for her obedience: for she knew that this man would never make an empty threat. No doubt Armand was already signalled to the Committee of Public Safety as one of the "suspect"; he would not be allowed to leave France again, and would be ruthlessly struck, if she refused to obey Chauvelin. For a moment—woman-like—she still hoped to temporise. She held out her hand to this man, whom she now feared and hated.

"If I promise to help you in this matter, Chauvelin," she said pleasantly, "will you give me that letter of St. Just's?"

"If you render me useful service tonight, *citoyenne*," he replied with a sarcastic smile, "I will give you that letter—tomorrow."

"You do not trust me?"

"I trust you absolutely, dear lady, but St. Just's life is forfeit to his country—it rests with you to redeem it."

"I may be powerless to help you," she pleaded, "were I ever so willing."

"That would be terrible indeed," he said quietly, "for you—and for St. Just."

Marguerite shuddered. She felt that from this man she could expect no mercy. All-powerful, he held the beloved life in the hollow of his hand. She knew him too well not to know that, if he failed in gaining his own ends, he would be pitiless.

She felt cold in spite of the oppressive air of opera-house. The heart-appealing strains of the music seemed to reach her, as from a distant land. She drew her costly lace scarf up around her shoulders, and sat silently watching the brilliant scene, as if in a dream.

For a moment her thoughts wandered away from the loved one who was in danger, to that other man who also had a claim on her confidence and her affection. She felt lonely, frightened for Armand's sake; she longed to seek comfort and advice from someone who would know how to help and console. Sir Percy Blakeney had loved her once; he was her husband; why should she stand alone through this terrible ordeal? He had very little brains, it is true, but he had plenty of muscle: surely, if she provided the thought, and he the manly energy and pluck, together they could outwit the astute diplomatist, and save the hostage from his vengeful hands, without imperilling the life of the noble leader of that gallant little band of heroes. Sir Percy knew St. Just well—he seemed attached to him—she was sure that he could help.

Chauvelin was taking no further heed of her. He had said his cruel "Either—or—" and left her to decide. He, in his turn now, appeared to be absorbed in the sour-stirring melodies of *Orpheus*, and was beating time to the music with his sharp, ferret-like head.

A discreet rap at the door roused Marguerite from her thoughts.

It was Sir Percy Blakeney, tall, sleepy, good-humoured, and wearing that half-shy, half-inane smile, which just now seemed to irritate her every nerve.

"Er—your chair is outside—m'dear," he said, with his most exasperating drawl, "I suppose you will want to go to that demmed ball—Excuse me—er—Monsieur Chauvelin—I had not observed you—"

He extended two slender, white fingers toward Chauvelin, who had risen when Sir Percy entered the box.

"Are you coming, m'dear?"

"Hush! Sh! Sh!" came in angry remonstrance from different parts of the house. "Demmed impudence," commented Sir Percy with a good-natured smile.

Marguerite sighed impatiently. Her last hope seemed suddenly to have vanished away. She wrapped her cloak round her and without looking at her husband:

"I am ready to go," she said, taking his arm. At the door of the box she turned and looked straight at Chauvelin, who, with his *chapeau-bras* under his arm, and a curious smile round his thin lips, was preparing to follow the strangely ill-assorted couple.

"It is only *au revoir*, Chauvelin," she said pleasantly, "we shall meet at my Lord Grenville's ball, *anon*."

And in her eyes the astute Frenchman, read, no doubt, something which caused him profound satisfaction, for, with a sarcastic smile, he took a delicate pinch of snuff, then, having dusted his dainty lace *jabot*, he rubbed his thin, bony hands contentedly together.

Chapter 11

Lord Grenville's Ball

The historic ball given by the then Secretary of State for Foreign Affairs—Lord Grenville—was the most brilliant function of the year. Though the autumn season had only just begun, everybody who was anybody had contrived to be in London in time to be present there, and to shine at this ball, to the best of his or her respective ability.

His Royal Highness the Prince of Wales had promised to be present. He was coming on presently from the opera. Lord Grenville himself had listened to the two first acts of *Orpheus*, before preparing to receive his guests. At ten o'clock—an unusually late hour in those days—the grand rooms of the Foreign Office, exquisitely decorated with exotic palms and flowers, were filled to overflowing. One room had been set apart for dancing, and the dainty strains of the minuet made a soft accompaniment to the gay chatter, the merry laughter of the numerous and brilliant company.

In a smaller chamber, facing the top of the fine stairway, the distinguished host stood ready to receive his guests. Distinguished men, beautiful women, notabilities from every European country had already filed past him, had exchanged the elaborate bows and curtsies with him, which the extravagant fashion of the time demanded, and then, laughing and talking, had dispersed in the ball, reception, and card rooms beyond.

Not far from Lord Grenville's elbow, leaning against one of the console tables, Chauvelin, in his irreproachable black costume, was taking a quiet survey of the brilliant throng. He noted that Sir Percy and Lady Blakeney had not yet arrived, and his keen, pale eyes glanced quickly towards the door every time a newcomer appeared.

He stood somewhat isolated: the envoy of the Revolutionary Government of France was not likely to be very popular in England, at a time when the news of the awful September massacres, and of the Reign of Terror and Anarchy, had just begun to filtrate across the Channel.

In his official capacity he had been received courteously by his English colleagues: Mr. Pitt had shaken him by the hand; Lord Grenville had entertained him more than once; but the more intimate circles of London society ignored him altogether; the women openly turned their backs upon him; the men who held no official position refused to shake his hand.

But Chauvelin was not the man to trouble himself about these social amenities, which he called mere incidents in his diplomatic career. He was blindly enthusiastic for the revolutionary cause, he despised all social inequalities, and he had a burning love for his own country: these three sentiments made him supremely indifferent to the snubs he received in this fog-ridden, loyalist, old-fashioned England.

But, above all, Chauvelin had a purpose at heart. He firmly believed that the French aristocrat was the most bitter enemy of France; he would have wished to see every one of them annihilated: he was one of those who, during this awful Reign of Terror, had been the first to utter the historic and ferocious desire "that aristocrats might have but one head between them, so that it might be cut off with a single stroke of the guillotine." And thus, he looked upon every French aristocrat, who had succeeded in escaping from France, as so much prey of which the guillotine had been unwarrantably cheated.

There is no doubt that those royalist *émigres*, once they had managed to cross the frontier, did their very best to stir up foreign indignation against France. Plots without end were hatched in England, in Belgium, in Holland, to try and induce some great power to send troops into revolutionary Paris, to free King Louis, and to summarily hang the bloodthirsty leaders of that monster republic.

Small wonder, therefore, that the romantic and mysterious personality of the Scarlet Pimpernel was a source of bitter hatred to Chauvelin. He and the few young jackanapes under his command, well furnished with money, armed with boundless daring, and acute cunning, had succeeded in rescuing hundreds of aristocrats from France. Nine-tenths of the *émigres*, who were *fêted* at the English court, owed their safety to that man and to his league.

Chauvelin had sworn to his colleagues in Paris that he would discover the identity of that meddlesome Englishman, entice him over to France, and then—Chauvelin drew a deep breath of satisfaction at the very thought of seeing that enigmatic head falling under the knife of the guillotine, as easily as that of any other man.

Suddenly there was a great stir on the handsome staircase, all conversation stopped for a moment as the *major-domo's* voice outside announced,—

"His Royal Highness the Prince of Wales and suite, Sir Percy Blakeney, Lady Blakeney."

Lord Grenville went quickly to the door to receive his exalted guest.

The Prince of Wales, dressed in a magnificent court suit of salmon-coloured velvet richly embroidered with gold, entered with Marguerite Blakeney on his arm; and on his left Sir Percy, in gorgeous shimmering cream satin, cut in the extravagant *Incroyable* style, his fair hair free from powder, priceless lace at his neck and wrists, and the flat *chapeau-bras* under his arm.

After the few conventional words of deferential greeting, Lord Grenville said to his royal guest,—

"Will your Highness permit me to introduce M. Chauvelin, the accredited agent of the French Government?"

Chauvelin, immediately the prince entered, had stepped forward, expecting this introduction. He bowed very low, whilst the prince returned his salute with a curt nod of the head.

"*Monsieur*," said His Royal Highness coldly, "we will try to forget the government that sent you and look upon you merely as our guest—a private gentleman from France. As such you are welcome, *Monsieur*."

"*Monseigneur*," rejoined Chauvelin, bowing once again. "*Madame*," he added, bowing ceremoniously before Marguerite.

"Ah! my little Chauvelin!" she said with unconcerned gaiety, and extending her tiny hand to him. "*Monsieur* and I are old friends, your Royal Highness."

"Ah, then," said the prince, this time very graciously, "you are doubly welcome, *Monsieur*."

"There is someone else I would crave permission to present to your Royal Highness," here interposed Lord Grenville.

"Ah! who is it?" asked the prince.

"Madame la Comtesse de Tournay de Basserive and her family, who have but recently come from France."

"By all means!—They are among the lucky ones then!"

Lord Grenville turned in search of the *Comtesse*, who sat at the further end of the room.

"Lud love me!" whispered his Royal Highness to Marguerite, as soon as he had caught sight of the rigid figure of the old lady; "Lud love me! she looks very virtuous and very melancholy."

"Faith, your Royal Highness," she rejoined with a smile, "virtue is like precious odours, most fragrant when it is crushed."

"Virtue, alas!" sighed the prince, "is mostly unbecoming to your charming sex, *Madame*."

"Madame la Comtesse de Tournay de Basserive," said Lord Grenville, introducing the lady.

"This is a pleasure, *Madame*; my royal father, as you know, is ever glad to welcome those of your compatriots whom France has driven from her shores."

"Your Royal Highness is ever gracious," replied the *Comtesse* with becoming dignity. Then, indicating her daughter, who stood timidly by her side: "My daughter Suzanne, *Monseigneur*," she said.

"Ah! charming!—charming!" said the prince, "and now allow me, *Comtesse*, to introduce you, Lady Blakeney, who honours us with her friendship. You and she will have much to say to one another, I vow. Every compatriot of Lady Blakeney's is doubly welcome for her sake—her friends are our friends—her enemies, the enemies of England."

Marguerite's blue eyes had twinkled with merriment at this gracious speech from her exalted friend. The Comtesse de Tournay, who lately had so flagrantly insulted her, was here receiving a public lesson, at which Marguerite could not help but rejoice. But the *Comtesse*, for whom respect of royalty amounted almost to a religion, was too well-schooled in courtly etiquette to show the slightest sign of embarrassment, as the two ladies curtsied ceremoniously to one another.

"His Royal Highness is ever gracious, *Madame*," said Marguerite, demurely, and with a wealth of mischief in her twinkling blue eyes, "but there is no need for his kind of mediation—Your amiable reception of me at our last meeting still dwells pleasantly in my memory."

"We poor exiles, *Madame*," rejoined the *Comtesse*, frigidly, "show our gratitude to England by devotion to the wishes of *Monseigneur*."

"*Madame!*" said Marguerite, with another ceremonious curtsey.

"*Madame*," responded the *Comtesse* with equal dignity.

The prince in the meanwhile was saying a few gracious words to the young *Vicomte*.

"I am happy to know you, *Monsieur le Vicomte*," he said. "I knew your father well when he was ambassador in London."

"Ah, *Monseigneur!*" replied the *Vicomte*, "I was a leetle boy then—and now I owe the honour of this meeting to our protector, the Scarlet Pimpernel."

"Hush!" said the prince, earnestly and quickly, as he indicated Chauvelin, who had stood a little on one side throughout the whole of this little scene, watching Marguerite and the *Comtesse* with an amused, sarcastic little smile around his thin lips.

"Nay, *Monseigneur*," he said now, as if in direct response to the prince's challenge, "pray do not check this gentleman's display of gratitude; the name of that interesting red flower is well known to me—and to France."

The prince looked at him keenly for a moment or two.

"Faith, then, *Monsieur*," he said, "perhaps you know more about our national hero than we do ourselves . . . perchance you know who he is—See!" he added, turning to the groups round the room, "the ladies hang upon your lips—you would render yourself popular among the fair sex if you were to gratify their curiosity."

"Ah, *Monseigneur*," said Chauvelin, significantly, "rumour has it in France that your Highness could—an you would—give the truest account of that enigmatical wayside flower."

He looked quickly and keenly at Marguerite as he spoke; but she betrayed no emotion, and her eyes met his quite fearlessly.

"Nay, man," replied the prince, "my lips are sealed! and the members of the league jealously guard the secret of their chief—so his fair adorers have to be content with worshipping a shadow. Here in England, *Monsieur*," he added, with wonderful charm and dignity, "we but name the Scarlet Pimpernel, and every fair cheek is suffused with a blush of enthusiasm. None have seen him save his faithful lieutenants. We know not if he be tall or short, fair or dark, handsome or ill-formed; but we know that he is the bravest gentleman in all the world, and we all feel a little proud, *Monsieur*, when we remember that he is an Englishman.

"Ah, Monsieur Chauvelin," added Marguerite, looking almost with defiance across at the placid, sphinx-like face of the Frenchman, "His Royal Highness should add that we ladies think of him as of a hero of old—we worship him—we wear his badge—we tremble for him when he is in danger, and exult with him in the hour of his victory."

Chauvelin did no more than bow placidly both to the prince and to Marguerite; he felt that both speeches were intended—each in their way—to convey contempt or defiance. The pleasure-loving, idle prince he despised: the beautiful woman, who in her golden hair wore a spray of small red flowers composed of rubies and diamonds—her he held in the hollow of his hand: he could afford to remain silent and to wait events.

A long, jovial, inane laugh broke the sudden silence which had fallen over everyone. "And we poor husbands," came in slow, affected accents from gorgeous Sir Percy, "we have to stand by—while they worship a demmed shadow."

Everyone laughed—the prince more loudly than anyone. The tension of subdued excitement was relieved, and the next moment everyone was laughing and chatting merrily as the gay crowd broke up and dispersed in the adjoining rooms.

Chapter 12

The Scrap of Paper

Marguerite suffered intensely. Though she laughed and chatted, though she was more admired, more surrounded, more *fêted* than any woman there, she felt like one condemned to death, living her last day upon this earth.

Her nerves were in a state of painful tension, which had increased a hundredfold during that brief hour which she had spent in her husband's company, between the opera and the ball. The short ray of hope—that she might find in this good-natured, lazy individual a valuable friend and adviser—had vanished as quickly as it had come, the moment she found herself alone with him. The same feeling of good-humoured contempt which one feels for an animal or a faithful servant, made her turn away with a smile from the man who should have been her moral support in this heart-rending crisis through which she was passing: who should have been her cool-headed adviser, when feminine sympathy and sentiment tossed her hither and thither, between her love for her brother, who was far away and in mortal peril, and horror of the awful service which Chauvelin had exacted from her, in exchange for Armand's safety.

There he stood, the moral support, the cool-headed adviser, surrounded by a crowd of brainless, empty-headed young fops, who were even now repeating from mouth to mouth, and with every sign of the keenest enjoyment, a doggerel quatrain which he had just given forth. Everywhere the absurd, silly words met her: people seemed to have little else to speak about, even the prince had asked her, with a little laugh, whether she appreciated her husband's latest poetic efforts.

"All done in the tying of a cravat," Sir Percy had declared to his clique of admirers.

We seek him here, we seek him there,
Those Frenchies seek him everywhere.
Is he in heaven?—Is he in hell?
That demmed, elusive Pimpernel"

Sir Percy's *bon mot* had gone the round of the brilliant reception-rooms. The prince was enchanted. He vowed that life without Blakeney would be but a dreary desert. Then, taking him by the arm, had led him to the card-room, and engaged him in a long game of hazard.

Sir Percy, whose chief interest in most social gatherings seemed to centre round the card-table, usually allowed his wife to flirt, dance, to amuse or bore herself as much as she liked. And tonight, having delivered himself of his *bon mot*, he had left Marguerite surrounded by a crowd of admirers of all ages, all anxious and willing to help her to forget that somewhere in the spacious reception rooms, there was a long, lazy being who had been fool enough to suppose that the cleverest woman in Europe would settle down to the prosaic bonds of English matrimony.

Her still overwrought nerves, her excitement and agitation, lent beautiful Marguerite Blakeney much additional charm: escorted by a veritable bevy of men of all ages and of most nationalities, she called forth many exclamations of admiration from everyone as she passed.

She would not allow herself any more time to think. Her early, somewhat Bohemian training had made her something of a fatalist. She felt that events would shape themselves, that the directing of them was not in her hands. From Chauvelin she knew that she could expect no mercy. He had set a price on Armand's head, and left it to her to pay or not, as she chose.

Later on, in the evening she caught sight of Sir Andrew Ffoulkes and Lord Antony Dewhurst, who seemingly had just arrived. She noticed at once that Sir Andrew immediately made for little Suzanne de Tournay, and that the two young people soon managed to isolate themselves in one of the deep embrasures of the mullioned windows, there to carry on a long conversation, which seemed very earnest and very pleasant on both sides.

Both the young men looked a little haggard and anxious, but otherwise they were irreproachably dressed, and there was not the slightest sign, about their courtly demeanour, of the terrible catastrophe, which they must have felt hovering round them and round their chief.

That the League of the Scarlet Pimpernel had no intention of abandoning its cause, she had gathered through little Suzanne herself, who spoke openly of the assurance she and her mother had had that the Comte de Tournay would be rescued from France by the league, within the next few days. Vaguely she began to wonder, as she looked at the brilliant and fashionable in the gaily-lighted ballroom, which of these worldly men round her was the mysterious "Scarlet Pimpernel," who held the threads of such daring plots, and the fate of valuable lives in his hands.

A burning curiosity seized her to know him: although for months she had heard of him and had accepted his anonymity, as everyone else in society had done; but now she longed to know—quite impersonally, quite apart from Armand, and oh! quite apart from Chauvelin—only for her own sake, for the sake of the enthusiastic admiration she had always bestowed on his bravery and cunning.

He was at the ball, of course, somewhere, since Sir Andrew Ffoulkes and Lord Antony Dewhurst were here, evidently expecting to meet their chief—and perhaps to get a fresh *mot d'ordre* from him.

Marguerite looked round at everyone, at the aristocratic high-typed Norman faces, the squarely-built, fair-haired Saxon, the more gentle, humorous caste of the Celt, wondering which of these betrayed the power, the energy, the cunning which had imposed its will and its leadership upon a number of high-born English gentlemen, among whom rumour asserted was His Royal Highness himself.

Sir Andrew Ffoulkes? Surely not, with his gentle blue eyes, which were looking so tenderly and longingly after little Suzanne, who was being led away from the pleasant *tête-à-tête* by her stern mother. Marguerite watched him across the room, as he finally turned away with a sigh, and seemed to stand, aimless and lonely, now that Suzanne's dainty little figure had disappeared in the crowd.

She watched him as he strolled towards the doorway, which led to a small *boudoir* beyond, then paused and leaned against the framework of it, looking still anxiously all round him.

Marguerite contrived for the moment to evade her present attentive cavalier, and she skirted the fashionable crowd, drawing nearer to the doorway, against which Sir Andrew was leaning. Why she wished to get closer to him, she could not have said: perhaps she was impelled by an all-powerful fatality, which so often seems to rule the destinies of men.

Suddenly she stopped: her very heart seemed to stand still, her eyes, large and excited, flashed for a moment towards that doorway, then as quickly were turned away again. Sir Andrew Ffoulkes was still in the same listless position by the door, but Marguerite had distinctly seen that Lord Hastings—a young buck, a friend of her husband's and one of the prince's set—had, as he quickly brushed past him, slipped something into his hand.

For one moment longer—oh! it was the merest flash—Marguerite paused: the next she had, with admirably played unconcern, resumed her walk across the room—but this time more quickly towards that doorway whence Sir Andrew had now disappeared.

All this, from the moment that Marguerite had caught sight of Sir Andrew leaning against the doorway, until she followed him into the little boudoir beyond, had occurred in less than a minute. Fate is usually swift when she deals a blow.

Now Lady Blakeney had suddenly ceased to exist. It was Marguerite St. Just who was there only: Marguerite St. Just who had passed her childhood, her early youth, in the protecting arms of her brother Armand. She had forgotten everything else—her rank, her dignity, her secret enthusiasms—everything save that Armand stood in peril of his life, and that there, not twenty feet away from her, in the small *boudoir* which was quite deserted, in the very hands of Sir Andrew Ffoulkes, might be the talisman which would save her brother's life.

Barely another thirty seconds had elapsed between the moment when Lord Hastings slipped the mysterious "something" into Sir Andrew's hand, and the one when she, in her turn, reached the deserted *boudoir.* Sir Andrew was standing with his back to her and close to a table upon which stood a massive silver candelabra. A slip of paper was in his hand, and he was in the very act of perusing its contents.

Unperceived, her soft clinging robe making not the slightest sound upon the heavy carpet, not daring to breathe until she had accomplished her purpose, Marguerite slipped close behind him.—At that moment he looked round and saw her; she uttered a groan, passed her hand across her forehead, and murmured faintly:

"The heat in the room was terrible—I felt so faint —Ah!—"

She tottered almost as if she would fall, and Sir Andrew, quickly recovering himself, and crumpling in his hand the tiny note he had been reading, was only apparently, just in time to support her.

"You are ill, Lady Blakeney?" he asked with much concern, "Let me . . ."

"No, no, nothing—" she interrupted quickly. "A chair—quick."

She sank into a chair close to the table, and throwing back her head, closing her eyes.

"There!" she murmured, still faintly; "the giddiness is passing off—. Do not heed me, Sir Andrew; I assure you I already feel better."

At moments like these there is no doubt—and psychologists actually assert it—that there is in us a sense which has absolutely nothing to do with the other five: it is not that we see, it is not that we hear or touch, yet we seem to do all three at once. Marguerite sat there with her eyes apparently closed. Sir Andrew was immediately behind her, and on her right was the table with the five-armed candelabra upon it. Before her mental vision there was absolutely nothing but Armand's face. Armand, whose life was in the most imminent danger, and who seemed to be looking at her from a background upon which were dimly painted the seething crowd of Paris, the bare walls of the Tribunal of Public Safety, with Foucquier-Tinville, the Public Prosecutor, demanding Armand's life in the name of the people of France, and the lurid guillotine with its stained knife waiting for another victim—Armand!—.

For one moment there was dead silence in the little *boudoir.* Beyond, from the brilliant ballroom, the sweet notes of the gavotte, the *frou-frou* of rich dresses, the talk and laughter of a large and merry crowd, came as a strange, weird accompaniment to the drama which was being enacted here. Sir Andrew had not uttered another word.

Then it was that that extra sense became potent in Marguerite Blakeney. She could not see, for her two eyes were closed, she could not hear, for the noise from the ballroom drowned the soft rustle of that momentous scrap of paper; nevertheless, she knew—as if she had both seen and heard—that Sir Andrew was even now holding the paper to the flame of one of the candles.

At the exact moment that it began to catch fire, she opened her eyes, raised her hand and, with two dainty fingers, had taken the burning scrap of paper from the young man's hand. Then she blew out the flame and held the paper to her nostril with perfect unconcern.

"How thoughtful of you, Sir Andrew," she said gaily, "surely 'twas your grandmother who taught you that the smell of burnt paper was a sovereign remedy against giddiness."

She sighed with satisfaction, holding the paper tightly between her jewelled fingers; that talisman which perhaps would save her brother Armand's life. Sir Andrew was staring at her, too dazed for the moment to realise what had actually happened; he had been taken so completely by surprise, that he seemed quite unable to grasp the fact that the slip of paper, which she held in her dainty hand, was one perhaps on which the life of his comrade might depend.

Marguerite burst into a long, merry peal of laughter.

"Why do you stare at me like that?" she said playfully. "I assure you I feel much better; your remedy has proved most effectual. This room is most delightedly cool," she added, with the same perfect composure, "and the sound of the gavotte from the ballroom is fascinating and soothing."

She was prattling on in the most unconcerned and pleasant way, whilst Sir Andrew, in an agony of mind, was racking his brains as to the quickest method he could employ to get that bit of paper out of that beautiful woman's hand. Instinctively, vague and tumultuous thoughts rushed through his mind: he suddenly remembered her nationality, and worst of all, recollected that horrible tale anent the Marquis de St. Cyr, which in England no one had credited, for the sake of Sir Percy, as well as for her own.

"What? Still dreaming and staring?" she said, with a merry laugh, "you are most ungallant, Sir Andrew; and now I come to think of it, you seemed more startled than pleased when you saw me just now. I do believe, after all, that it was not concern for my health, nor yet a remedy taught you by your grandmother that caused you to burn this tiny scrap of paper.—I vow it must have been your lady love's last cruel epistle you were trying to destroy. Now confess!" she added, playfully holding up the scrap of paper, "does this contain her final *conge*, or a last appeal to kiss and make friends?"

"Whichever it is, Lady Blakeney," said Sir Andrew, who was gradually recovering his self-possession, "this little note is undoubtedly mine, and—" Not caring whether his action was one that would be styled ill-bred towards a lady, the young man had made a bold dash for the note; but Marguerite's thoughts flew quicker than his own; her actions under pressure of this intense excitement, were swifter and more sure. She was tall and strong; she took a quick step backwards and knocked over the small Sheraton table which was already top-heavy, and which fell down with a crash, together with the massive candelabra upon it.

She gave a quick cry of alarm:

"The candles, Sir Andrew—quick!"

There was not much damage done; one or two of the candles had blown out as the candelabra fell; others had merely sent some grease upon the valuable carpet; one had ignited the paper shade over it. Sir Andrew quickly and dexterously put out the flames and replaced the candelabra upon the table; but this had taken him a few seconds to do, and those seconds had been all that Marguerite needed to cast a quick glance at the paper, and to note its contents—a dozen words in the same distorted handwriting she had seen before, and bearing the same device—a star-shaped flower drawn in red ink.

When Sir Andrew once more looked at her, he only saw upon her face alarm at the untoward accident and relief at its happy issue; whilst the tiny and momentous note had apparently fluttered to the ground. Eagerly the young man picked it up, and his face looked much relieved, as his fingers closed tightly over it.

"For shame, Sir Andrew," she said, shaking her head with a playful sigh, "making havoc in the heart of some impressionable duchess, whilst conquering the affections of my sweet little Suzanne. Well, well! I do believe it was Cupid himself who stood by you and threatened the entire Foreign Office with destruction by fire, just on purpose to make me drop love's message, before it had been polluted by my indiscreet eyes. To think that, a moment longer, and I might have known the secrets of an erring duchess."

"You will forgive me, Lady Blakeney," said Sir Andrew, now as calm as she was herself, "if I resume the interesting occupation which you have interrupted?"

"By all means, Sir Andrew! How should I venture to thwart the love-god again? Perhaps he would mete out some terrible chastisement against my presumption. Burn your love-token, by all means!"

Sir Andrew had already twisted the paper into a long spill and was once again holding it to the flame of the candle, which had remained alight. He did not notice the strange smile on the face of his fair *vis-à-vis*, so intent was he on the work of destruction; perhaps, had he done so, the look of relief would have faded from his face. He watched the fateful note, as it curled under the flame. Soon the last fragment fell on the floor, and he placed his heel upon the ashes.

"And now, Sir Andrew," said Marguerite Blakeney, with the pretty nonchalance peculiar to herself, and with the most winning of smiles, "will you venture to excite the jealousy of your fair lady by asking me to dance the minuet?"

Chapter 13

Either—Or?

The few words which Marguerite Blakeney had managed to read on the half-scorched piece of paper, seemed literally to be the words of Fate. "Start myself tomorrow.—" This she had read quite distinctly; then came a blur caused by the smoke of the candle, which obliterated the next few words; but, right at the bottom, there was another sentence, like letters of fire, before her mental vision, "If you wish to speak to me again I shall be in the supper-room at one o'clock precisely." The whole was signed with the hastily-scrawled little device—a tiny star-shaped flower, which had become so familiar to her.

One o'clock precisely! It was now close upon eleven, the last minuet was being danced, with Sir Andrew Ffoulkes and beautiful Lady Blakeney leading the couples, through its delicate and intricate figures.

Close upon eleven! the hands of the handsome Louis XV. clock upon its ormolu bracket seemed to move along with maddening rapidity. Two hours more, and her fate and that of Armand would be sealed. In two hours she must make up her mind whether she will keep the knowledge so cunningly gained to herself, and leave her brother to his fate, or whether she will wilfully betray a brave man, whose life was devoted to his fellow-men, who was noble, generous, and above all, unsuspecting. It seemed a horrible thing to do. But then, there was Armand! Armand, too, was noble and brave, Armand, too, was unsuspecting. And Armand loved her, would have willingly trusted his life in her hands, and now, when she could save him from death, she hesitated. Oh! it was monstrous; her brother's kind, gentle face, so full of love for her, seemed to be looking reproachfully at her. "You might have saved me, Margot!" he seemed to say to her, "and you chose the life of a stranger, a man you do not know, whom you have never seen, and preferred that he should be safe, whilst you sent me to the guillotine!"

All these conflicting thoughts raged through Marguerite's brain, while, with a smile upon her lips, she glided through the graceful mazes of the minuet. She noted—with that acute sense of hers—that she had succeeded in completely allaying Sir Andrew's fears. Her self-control had been absolutely perfect—she was a finer actress at this moment, and throughout the whole of this minuet, than she had ever been upon the boards of the *Comédie Française*; but then, a beloved brother's life had not depended upon her histrionic powers.

She was too clever to overdo her part and made no further allusions to the supposed *billet doux*, which had caused Sir Andrew Ffoulkes such an agonising five minutes. She watched his anxiety melting away under her sunny smile, and soon perceived that, whatever doubt may have crossed his mind at the moment, she had, by the time the last bars of the minuet had been played, succeeded in completely dispelling it; he never realised in what a fever of excitement she was, what effort it cost her to keep up a constant ripple of *banal* conversation.

When the minuet was over, she asked Sir Andrew to take her into the next room.

"I have promised to go down to supper with His Royal Highness," she said, "but before we part, tell me—am I forgiven?"

"Forgiven?"

"Yes! Confess, I gave you a fright just now.—But remember, I am not an English woman, and I do not look upon the exchanging of *billet doux* as a crime, and I vow I'll not tell my little Suzanne. But now, tell me, shall I welcome you at my water-party on Wednesday?"

"I am not sure, Lady Blakeney," he replied evasively. "I may have to leave London tomorrow."

"I would not do that, if I were you," she said earnestly; then seeing the anxious look reappearing in his eyes, she added gaily; "No one can throw a ball better than you can, Sir Andrew, we should so miss you on the bowling-green."

He had led her across the room, to one beyond, where already His Royal Highness was waiting for the beautiful Lady Blakeney.

"*Madame*, supper awaits us," said the prince, offering his arm to Marguerite, "and I am full of hope. The goddess Fortune has frowned so persistently on me at hazard, that I look with confidence for the smiles of the goddess of Beauty."

"Your Highness has been unfortunate at the card tables?" asked Marguerite, as she took the prince's arm.

"Aye! most unfortunate. Blakeney, not content with being the richest among my father's subjects, has also the most outrageous luck. By the way, where is that inimitable wit? I vow, Madam, that this life would be but a dreary desert without your smiles and his sallies."

Chapter 14

One O'Clock Precisely!

Supper had been extremely gay. All those present declared that never had Lady Blakeney been more adorable, nor that "demmed idiot" Sir Percy more amusing.

His Royal Highness had laughed until the tears streamed down his cheeks at Blakeney's foolish yet funny repartees. His doggerel verse, "We seek him here, we seek him there," etc., was sung to the tune of "Ho! Merry Britons!" and to the accompaniment of glasses knocked loudly against the table. Lord Grenville, moreover, had a most perfect cook—some wags asserted that he was a scion of the old French *noblesse*, who having lost his fortune, had come to seek it in the *cuisine* of the Foreign Office.

Marguerite Blakeney was in her most brilliant mood, and surely not a soul in that crowded supper-room had even an inkling of the terrible struggle which was raging within her heart.

The clock was ticking so mercilessly on. It was long past midnight, and even the Prince of Wales was thinking of leaving the supper-table. Within the next half-hour the destinies of two brave men would be pitted against one another—the dearly-beloved brother and he, the unknown hero.

Marguerite had not tried to see Chauvelin during this last hour; she knew that his keen, fox-like eyes would terrify her at once, and incline the balance of her decision towards Armand. Whilst she did not see him, there still lingered in her heart of hearts a vague, undefined hope that "something" would occur, something big, enormous, epoch-making, which would shift from her young, weak shoulders this terrible burden of responsibility, of having to choose between two such cruel alternatives.

But the minutes ticked on with that dull monotony which they invariably seem to assume when our very nerves ache with their incessant ticking.

After supper, dancing was resumed. His Royal Highness had left, and there was general talk of departing among the older guests; the young were indefatigable and had started on a new *gavotte*, which would fill the next quarter of an hour.

Marguerite did not feel equal to another dance; there is a limit to the most enduring of self-control. Escorted by a Cabinet Minister, she had once more found her way to the tiny *boudoir*, still the most deserted among all the rooms. She knew that Chauvelin must be lying in wait for her somewhere, ready to seize the first possible opportunity for a *tête-à-tête*. His eyes had met hers for a moment after the 'fore-supper minuet, and she knew that the keen diplomat, with those searching pale eyes of his, had divined that her work was accomplished.

Fate had willed it so. Marguerite, torn by the most terrible conflict heart of woman can ever know, had resigned herself to its decrees. But Armand must be saved at any cost; he, first of all, for he was her brother, had been mother, father, friend to her ever since she, a tiny babe, had lost both her parents. To think of Armand dying a traitor's death on the guillotine was too horrible even to dwell upon—impossible in fact. That could never be, never—As for the stranger, the hero—well! there, let Fate decide. Marguerite would redeem her brother's life at the hands of the relentless enemy, then let that cunning Scarlet Pimpernel extricate himself after that.

Perhaps—vaguely—Marguerite hoped that the daring plotter, who for so many months had baffled an army of spies, would still manage to evade Chauvelin and remain immune to the end.

She thought of all this, as she sat listening to the witty discourse of the Cabinet Minister, who, no doubt, felt that he had found in Lady Blakeney a most perfect listener. Suddenly she saw the keen, fox-like face of Chauvelin peeping through the curtained doorway.

"Lord Fancourt," she said to the Minister, "will you do me a service?"

"I am entirely at your ladyship's service," he replied gallantly.

"Will you see if my husband is still in the card-room? And if he is, will you tell him that I am very tired, and would be glad to go home soon."

The commands of a beautiful woman are binding on all mankind, even on Cabinet Ministers. Lord Fancourt prepared to obey instantly.

"I do not like to leave your ladyship alone," he said.

"Never fear. I shall be quite safe here—and, I think, undisturbed—but I am really tired. You know Sir Percy will drive back to Richmond. It is a long way, and we shall not—an' we do not hurry—get home before daybreak."

Lord Fancourt had perforce to go.

The moment he had disappeared, Chauvelin slipped into the room, and the next instant stood calm and impassive by her side.

"You have news for me?" he said.

An icy mantle seemed to have suddenly settled round Marguerite's shoulders; though her cheeks glowed with fire, she felt chilled and numbed. Oh, Armand! will you ever know the terrible sacrifice of pride, of dignity, of womanliness a devoted sister is making for your sake?

"Nothing of importance," she said, staring mechanically before her, "but it might prove a clue. I contrived—no matter how—to detect Sir Andrew Ffoulkes in the very act of burning a paper at one of these candles, in this very room. That paper I succeeded in holding between my fingers for the space of two minutes, and to cast my eyes on it for that of ten seconds."

"Time enough to learn its contents?" asked Chauvelin, quietly.

She nodded. Then continued in the same even, mechanical tone of voice—

"In the corner of the paper there was the usual rough device of a small star-shaped flower. Above it I read two lines, everything else was scorched and blackened by the flame."

"And what were the two lines?"

Her throat seemed suddenly to have contracted. For an instant she felt that she could not speak the words, which might send a brave man to his death.

"It is lucky that the whole paper was not burned," added Chauvelin, with dry sarcasm, "for it might have fared ill with Armand St. Just. What were the two lines *citoyenne?*"

"One was, 'I start myself tomorrow,'" she said quietly, "the other—'If you wish to speak to me, I shall be in the supper-room at one o'clock precisely.'"

Chauvelin looked up at the clock just above the mantelpiece.

"Then I have plenty of time," he said placidly.

"What are you going to do?" she asked.

She was pale as a statue, her hands were icy cold, her head and heart throbbed with the awful strain upon her nerves. Oh, this was cruel! cruel! What had she done to have deserved all this? Her choice was made: had she done a vile action or one that was sublime? The recording angel, who writes in the book of gold, alone could give an answer.

"What are you going to do?" she repeated mechanically.

"Oh, nothing for the present. After that it will depend."

"On what?"

"On whom I shall see in the supper-room at one o'clock precisely."

"You will see the Scarlet Pimpernel, of course. But you do not know him."

"No. But I shall presently."

"Sir Andrew will have warned him."

"I think not. When you parted from him after the minuet he stood and watched you, for a moment or two, with a look which gave me to understand that something had happened between you. It was only natural, was it not? that I should make a shrewd guess as to the nature of that 'something.' I thereupon engaged the young man in a long and animated conversation—we discussed Herr Gluck's singular success in London—until a lady claimed his arm for supper."

"Since then?"

"I did not lose sight of him through supper. When we all came upstairs again, Lady Portarles buttonholed him and started on the subject of pretty Mlle. Suzanne de Tournay. I knew he would not move until Lady Portarles had exhausted on the subject, which will not be for another quarter of an hour at least, and it is five minutes to one now."

He was preparing to go, and went up to the doorway where, drawing aside the curtain, he stood for a moment pointing out to Marguerite the distant figure of Sir Andrew Ffoulkes in close conversation with Lady Portarles.

"I think," he said, with a triumphant smile, "that I may safely expect to find the person I seek in the dining-room, fair lady."

"There may be more than one."

"Whoever is there, as the clock strikes one, will be shadowed by one of my men; of these, one, or perhaps two, or even three, will leave for France tomorrow. *One* of these will be the 'Scarlet Pimpernel.'"

"Yes?—And?"

"I also, fair lady, will leave for France tomorrow. The papers found at Dover upon the person of Sir Andrew Ffoulkes speak of the neighbourhood of Calais, of an inn which I know well, called 'Le Chat

Gris,' of a lonely place somewhere on the coast—the Père Blanchard's hut—which I must endeavour to find. All these places are given as the point where this meddlesome Englishman has bidden the traitor de Tournay and others to meet his emissaries. But it seems that he has decided not to send his emissaries, that 'he will start himself tomorrow.' Now, one of these persons whom I shall see anon in the supper-room, will be journeying to Calais, and I shall follow that person, until I have tracked him to where those fugitive aristocrats await him; for that person, fair lady, will be the man whom I have sought for, for nearly a year, the man whose energies has outdone me, whose ingenuity has baffled me, whose audacity has set me wondering—yes! me!—who have seen a trick or two in my time—the mysterious and elusive Scarlet Pimpernel."

"And Armand?" she pleaded.

"Have I ever broken my word? I promise you that the day the Scarlet Pimpernel and I start for France, I will send you that imprudent letter of his by special courier. More than that, I will pledge you the word of France, that the day I lay hands on that meddlesome Englishman, St. Just will be here in England, safe in the arms of his charming sister."

And with a deep and elaborate bow and another look at the clock, Chauvelin glided out of the room.

It seemed to Marguerite that through all the noise, all the din of music, dancing, and laughter, she could hear his cat-like tread, gliding through the vast reception-rooms; that she could hear him go down the massive staircase, reach the dining-room and open the door. Fate *had* decided, had made her speak, had made her do a vile and abominable thing, for the sake of the brother she loved. She lay back in her chair, passive and still, seeing the figure of her relentless enemy ever present before her aching eyes.

When Chauvelin reached the supper-room it was quite deserted. It had that woebegone, forsaken, tawdry appearance, which reminds one so much of a ball-dress, the morning after.

Half-empty glasses littered the table, unfolded napkins lay about, the chairs—turned towards one another in groups of twos and threes—very close to one another—in the far corners of the room, which spoke of recent whispered flirtations, over cold game-pie and champagne; there were sets of three and four chairs, that recalled pleasant, animated discussions over the latest scandal; there were chairs straight up in a row that still looked starchy, critical, acid, like antiquated dowagers; there were a few isolated, single chairs, close to the table, that spoke of gourmands intent on the most *recherche* dishes, and others overturned on the floor, that spoke volumes on the subject of my Lord Grenville's cellars.

It was a ghostlike replica, in fact, of that fashionable gathering upstairs; a ghost that haunts every house where balls and good suppers are given; a picture drawn with white chalk on grey cardboard, dull and colourless, now that the bright silk dresses and gorgeously embroidered coats were no longer there to fill in the foreground, and now that the candles flickered sleepily in their sockets.

Chauvelin smiled benignly, and rubbing his long, thin hands together, he looked round the deserted supper-room, whence even the last flunkey had retired in order to join his friends in the hall below. All was silence in the dimly-lighted room, whilst the sound of the gavotte, the hum of distant talk and laughter, and the rumble of an occasional coach outside, only seemed to reach this palace of the Sleeping Beauty as the murmur of some flitting spooks far away.

It all looked so peaceful, so luxurious, and so still, that the keenest observer—a veritable prophet—could never have guessed that, at this present moment, that deserted supper-room was nothing but a trap laid for the capture of the most cunning and audacious plotter those stirring times had ever seen.

Chauvelin pondered and tried to peer into the immediate future. What would this man be like, whom he and the leaders of the whole revolution had sworn to bring to his death? Everything about him was weird and mysterious; his personality, which he so cunningly concealed, the power he wielded over nineteen English gentlemen who seemed to obey his every command blindly and enthusiastically, the passionate love and submission he had roused in his little trained band, and, above all, his marvellous audacity, the boundless impudence which had caused him to beard his most implacable enemies, within the very walls of Paris.

No wonder that in France the *sobriquet* of the mysterious Englishman roused in the people a superstitious shudder. Chauvelin himself as he gazed round the deserted room, where presently the weird hero would appear, felt a strange feeling of awe creeping all down his spine.

But his plans were well laid. He felt sure that the Scarlet Pimpernel had not been warned and felt equally sure that Marguerite Blakeney had not played him false. If she had—a cruel look, that would have made her shudder, gleamed in Chauvelin's keen, pale eyes. If she had played him a trick, Armand St. Just would suffer the extreme penalty.

But no, no! of course she had not played him false!

Fortunately, the supper-room was deserted: this would make Chauvelin's task all the easier, when presently that unsuspecting enigma would enter it alone. No one was here now save Chauvelin himself.

Stay! as he surveyed with a satisfied smile the solitude of the room, the cunning agent of the French Government became aware of the peaceful, monotonous breathing of some one of my Lord Grenville's guests, who, no doubt, had supped both wisely and well, and was enjoying a quiet sleep, away from the din of the dancing above.

Chauvelin looked round once more, and there in the corner of a sofa, in the dark angle of the room, his mouth open, his eyes shut, the sweet sounds of peaceful slumbers proceedings from his nostrils, reclined the gorgeously-apparelled, long-limbed husband of the cleverest woman in Europe.

Chauvelin looked at him as he lay there, placid, unconscious, at peace with all the world and himself, after the best of suppers, and a smile, that was almost one of pity, softened for a moment the hard lines of the Frenchman's face and the sarcastic twinkle of his pale eyes.

Evidently the slumberer, deep in dreamless sleep, would not interfere with Chauvelin's trap for catching that cunning Scarlet Pimpernel. Again, he rubbed his hands together, and, following the example of Sir Percy Blakeney, he too, stretched himself out in the corner of another sofa, shut his eyes, opened his mouth, gave forth sounds of peaceful breathing, and—waited!

CHAPTER 14

Doubt

Marguerite Blakeney had watched the slight sable-clad figure of Chauvelin, as he worked his way through the ballroom. Then perforce she had had to wait, while her nerves tingled with excitement.

Listlessly she sat in the small, still deserted *boudoir*, looking out through the curtained doorway on the dancing couples beyond: looking at them, yet seeing nothing, hearing the music, yet conscious of naught save a feeling of expectancy, of anxious, weary waiting.

Her mind conjured up before her the vision of what was, perhaps at this very moment, passing downstairs. The half-deserted dining-room, the fateful hour—Chauvelin on the watch!—then, precise to the moment, the entrance of a man, he, the Scarlet Pimpernel, the mysterious leader, who to Marguerite had become almost unreal, so strange, so weird was this hidden identity.

She wished she were in the supper-room, too, at this moment, watching him as he entered; she knew that her woman's penetration would at once recognise in the stranger's face—whoever he might be—that strong individuality which belongs to a leader of men—to a hero: to the mighty, high-soaring eagle, whose daring wings were becoming entangled in the ferret's trap.

Woman-like, she thought of him with unmixed sadness; the irony of that fate seemed so cruel which allowed the fearless lion to succumb to the gnawing of a rat! Ah! had Armand's life not been at stake! . . .

"Faith! your ladyship must have thought me very remiss," said a voice suddenly, close to her elbow. "I had a deal of difficulty in delivering your message, for I could not find Blakeney anywhere at first . . ."

Marguerite had forgotten all about her husband and her message to him; his very name, as spoken by Lord Fancourt, sounded strange and unfamiliar to her, so completely had she in the last five minutes lived her old life in the Rue de Richelieu again, with Armand always near her to love and protect her, to guard her from the many subtle intrigues which were forever raging in Paris in those days.

"I did find him at last," continued Lord Fancourt, "and gave him your message. He said that he would give orders at once for the horses to be put to."

"Ah!" she said, still very absently, "you found my husband, and gave him my message?"

"Yes; he was in the dining-room fast asleep. I could not manage to wake him up at first."

"Thank you very much," she said mechanically, trying to collect her thoughts.

"Will your ladyship honour me with the *contredanse* until your coach is ready?" asked Lord Fancourt.

"No, I thank you, my lord, but—and you will forgive me—I really am too tired, and the heat in the ballroom has become oppressive."

"The conservatory is deliciously cool; let me take you there, and then get you something. You seem ailing, Lady Blakeney."

"I am only very tired," she repeated wearily, as she allowed Lord Fancourt to lead her, where subdued lights and green plants lent coolness to the air. He got her a chair, into which she sank. This long interval of waiting was intolerable. Why did not Chauvelin come and tell her the result of his watch?

Lord Fancourt was very attentive. She scarcely heard what he said, and suddenly startled him by asking abruptly,—

"Lord Fancourt, did you perceive who was in the dining-room just now besides Sir Percy Blakeney?"

"Only the agent of the French Government, M. Chauvelin, equally fast asleep in another corner," he said. "Why does your ladyship ask?"

"I know not—I—Did you notice the time when you were there?"

"It must have been about five or ten minutes past one—I wonder what your ladyship is thinking about," he added, for evidently the fair lady's thoughts were very far away, and she had not been listening to his intellectual conversation.

But indeed, her thoughts were not very far away: only one storey below, in this same house, in the dining-room where sat Chauvelin still on the watch. Had he failed? For one instant that possibility rose before as a hope—the hope that the Scarlet Pimpernel had been warned by Sir Andrew, and that Chauvelin's trap had failed to catch his bird; but that hope soon gave way to fear. Had he failed? But then—Armand!

Lord Fancourt had given up talking since he found that he had no listener. He wanted an opportunity for slipping away; for sitting opposite to a lady, however fair, who is evidently not heeding the most vigorous efforts made for her entertainment, is not exhilarating, even to a Cabinet Minister.

"Shall I find out if your ladyship's coach is ready," he said at last, tentatively.

"Oh, thank you—thank you—if you would be so kind—I fear I am but sorry company—but I am really tired—and, perhaps, would be best alone."

But Lord Fancourt went, and still Chauvelin did not come. Oh! what had happened? She felt Armand's fate trembling in the balance—she feared—now with a deadly fear that Chauvelin *had* failed, and that the mysterious Scarlet Pimpernel had proved elusive once more; then she knew that she need hope for no pity, no mercy, from him.

He had pronounced his "Either—or—" and nothing less would content him: he was very spiteful and would affect the belief that she had wilfully misled him, and having failed to trap the eagle once again, his revengeful mind would be content with the humble prey—Armand!

Yet she had done her best; had strained every nerve for Armand's sake. She could not bear to think that all had failed. She could not sit still; she wanted to go and hear the worst at once; she wondered even that Chauvelin had not come yet, to vent his wrath and satire upon her.

Lord Grenville himself came presently to tell her that her coach was ready, and that Sir Percy was already waiting for her—ribbons in hand. Marguerite said "Farewell" to her distinguished host; many of her friends stopped her, as she crossed the rooms, to talk to her, and exchange pleasant *au revoirs*.

The Minister only took final leave of beautiful Lady Blakeney on the top of the stairs; below, on the landing, a veritable army of gallant gentlemen were waiting to bid "Goodbye" to the queen of beauty and fashion, whilst outside, under the massive portico, Sir Percy's magnificent bays were impatient pawing the ground.

At the top of the stairs, just after she had taken final leave of her host, she suddenly saw Chauvelin; he was coming up the stairs slowly and rubbing his thin hands very softly together.

There was a curious look on his mobile face, partly amused and wholly puzzled, as his keen eyes met Marguerite's they became strangely sarcastic.

"M. Chauvelin," she said, as he stopped on the top of the stairs, bowing elaborately before her, "my coach is outside; may I claim your arm?"

As gallant as ever, he offered her his arm and led her downstairs. The crowd was very great, some of the Minister's guests were departing, others were leaning against the banisters watching the throng as it filed up and down the wide staircase.

"Chauvelin," she said at last desperately, "I must know what has happened."

"What has happened, dear lady?" he said, with affected surprise. "Where? When?"

"You are torturing me, Chauvelin. I have helped you tonight—surely I have the right to know. What happened in the dining-room at one o'clock just now?"

She spoke in a whisper, trusting that in the general hubbub of the crowd her words would remain unheeded by all, save the man at her side.

"Quiet and peace reigned supreme, fair lady; at that hour I was asleep in one corner of one sofa and Sir Percy Blakeney in another."

"Nobody came into the room at all?"

"Nobody."

"Then we have failed, you and I?"

"Yes! we have failed—perhaps—"

"But Armand?" she pleaded.

"Ah! Armand St. Just's chances hang on a thread—pray heaven, dear lady, that that thread may not snap."

"Chauvelin, I worked for you, sincerely, earnestly—remember—"

"I remember my promise," he said quietly. "The day that the Scarlet Pimpernel and I meet on French soil, St. Just will be in the arms of his charming sister."

"Which means that a brave man's blood will be on my hands," she said, with a shudder.

"His blood, or that of your brother. Surely at the present moment you must hope, as I do, that the enigmatical Scarlet Pimpernel will start for Calais today—"

"I am only conscious of one hope, *citoyen*."

"And that is?"

"That Satan, your master, will have need of you elsewhere, before the sun rises today."

"You flatter me, *citoyenne*."

She had detained him for a while, mid-way down the stairs, trying to get at the thoughts which lay beyond that thin, fox-like mask. But Chauvelin remained urbane, sarcastic, mysterious; not a line betrayed to the poor, anxious woman whether she need fear or whether she dared to hope.

Downstairs on the landing she was soon surrounded. Lady Blakeney never stepped from any house into her coach, without an escort of fluttering human moths around the dazzling light of her beauty. But before she finally turned away from Chauvelin, she held out a tiny hand to him, with that pretty gesture of childish appeal which was essentially her own. "Give me some hope, my little Chauvelin," she pleaded.

With perfect gallantry he bowed over that tiny hand, which looked so dainty and white through the delicately transparent black lace mitten, and kissing the tips of the rosy fingers:—

"Pray heaven that the thread may not snap," he repeated, with his enigmatic smile.

And stepping aside, he allowed the moths to flutter more closely round the candle, and the brilliant throng of the *jeunesse doree*, eagerly attentive to Lady Blakeney's every movement, hid the keen, fox-like face from her view.

Chapter 16

Richmond

A few minutes later she was sitting, wrapped in cosy furs, near Sir Percy Blakeney on the box-seat of his magnificent coach, and the four splendid bays had thundered down the quiet street.

The night was warm in spite of the gentle breeze which fanned Marguerite's burning cheeks. Soon London houses were left behind, and rattling over old Hammersmith Bridge, Sir Percy was driving his bays rapidly towards Richmond.

The river wound in and out in its pretty delicate curves, looking like a silver serpent beneath the glittering rays of the moon. Long shadows from overhanging trees spread occasional deep palls right across the road. The bays were rushing along at breakneck speed, held but slightly back by Sir Percy's strong, unerring hands.

These nightly drives after balls and suppers in London were a source of perpetual delight to Marguerite, and she appreciated her husband's eccentricity keenly, which caused him to adopt this mode of taking her home every night, to their beautiful home by the river, instead of living in a stuffy London house. He loved driving his spirited horses along the lonely, moonlit roads, and she loved to sit on the box-seat, with the soft air of an English late summer's night fanning her face after the hot atmosphere of a ball or supper-party. The drive was not a long one—less than an hour, sometimes, when the bays were very fresh, and Sir Percy gave them full rein.

Tonight, he seemed to have a very devil in his fingers, and the coach seemed to fly along the road, beside the river. As usual, he did not speak to her, but stared straight in front of him, the ribbons seeming to lie quite loosely in his slender, white hands. Marguerite looked at him tentatively once or twice; she could see his handsome profile, and one lazy eye, with its straight fine brow and drooping heavy lid.

The face in the moonlight looked singularly earnest and recalled to Marguerite's aching heart those happy days of courtship, before he had become the lazy nincompoop, the effete fop, whose life seemed spent in card and supper rooms.

But now, in the moonlight, she could not catch the expression of the lazy blue eyes; she could only see the outline of the firm chin, the corner of the strong mouth, the well-cut massive shape of the forehead; truly, nature had meant well by Sir Percy; his faults must all be laid at the door of that poor, half-crazy mother, and of the distracted heartbroken father, neither of whom had cared for the young life which was sprouting up between them, and which, perhaps, their very carelessness was already beginning to wreck.

Marguerite suddenly felt intense sympathy for her husband. The moral crisis she had just gone through made her feel indulgent towards the faults, the delinquencies, of others.

How thoroughly a human being can be buffeted and overmastered by Fate, had been borne in upon her with appalling force. Had anyone told her a week ago that she would stoop to spy upon her friends, that she would betray a brave and unsuspecting man into the hands of a relentless enemy, she would have laughed the idea to scorn.

Yet she had done these things; anon, perhaps the death of that brave man would be at her door, just as two years ago the Marquis de St. Cyr had perished through a thoughtless words of hers; but in that case she was morally innocent—she had meant no serious harm—fate merely had stepped in. But this time she had done a thing that obviously was base, had done it deliberately, for a motive which, perhaps, high moralists would not even appreciate.

As she felt her husband's strong arm beside her, she also felt how much more he would dislike and despise her, if he knew of this night's work. Thus, human beings judge of one another, with but little reason, and no charity. She despised her husband for his inanities and vulgar, unintellectual occupations; and he, she felt, would despise her still worse, because she had not been strong enough to do right for right's sake, and to sacrifice her brother to the dictates of her conscience.

Buried in her thoughts, Marguerite had found this hour in the breezy summer night all too brief; and it was with a feeling of keen disappointment, that she suddenly realised that the bays had turned into the massive gates of her beautiful English home.

Sir Percy Blakeney's house on the river has become a historic one: palatial in its dimensions, it stands in the midst of exquisitely laid-out gardens, with a picturesque terrace and frontage to the river. Built in Tudor days, the old red brick of the walls looks eminently picturesque in the midst of a bower of green, the beautiful lawn, with its old sundial, adding the true note of harmony to its foregrounds, and now, on this warm early autumn night, the leaves slightly turned to russets and gold, the old garden looked singularly poetic and peaceful in the moonlight.

With unerring precision, Sir Percy had brought the four bays to a standstill immediately in front of the fine Elizabethan entrance hall;

in spite of the late hour, an army of grooms seemed to have emerged from the very ground, as the coach had thundered up, and were standing respectfully round.

Sir Percy jumped down quickly, then helped Marguerite to alight. She lingered outside a moment, whilst he gave a few orders to one of his men. She skirted the house, and stepped on to the lawn, looking out dreamily into the silvery landscape. Nature seemed exquisitely at peace, in comparison with the tumultuous emotions she had gone through: she could faintly hear the ripple of the river and the occasional soft and ghostlike fall of a dead leaf from a tree.

All else was quiet round her. She had heard the horses prancing as they were being led away to their distant stables, the hurrying of servant's feet as they had all gone within to rest: the house also was quite still. In two separate suites of apartments, just above the magnificent reception-rooms, lights were still burning, they were her rooms, and his, well divided from each other by the whole width of the house, as far apart as their own lives had become. Involuntarily she sighed—at that moment she could really not have told why.

She was suffering from unconquerable heartache. Deeply and achingly she was sorry for herself. Never had she felt so pitiably lonely, so bitterly in want of comfort and of sympathy. With another sigh she turned away from the river towards the house, vaguely wondering if, after such a night, she could ever find rest and sleep.

Suddenly, before she reached the terrace, she heard a firm step upon the crisp gravel, and the next moment her husband's figure emerged out of the shadow. He too, had skirted the house, and was wandering along the lawn, towards the river. He still wore his heavy driving coat with the numerous lapels and collars he himself had set in fashion, but he had thrown it well back, burying his hands as was his wont, in the deep pockets of his satin breeches: the gorgeous white costume he had worn at Lord Grenville's ball, with its jabot of priceless lace, looked strangely ghostly against the dark background of the house.

He apparently did not notice her, for, after a few moments pause, he presently turned back towards the house, and walked straight up to the terrace.

"Sir Percy!"

He already had one foot on the lowest of the terrace steps, but at her voice he started, and paused, then looked searchingly into the shadows whence she had called to him.

She came forward quickly into the moonlight, and, as soon as he saw her, he said, with that air of consummate gallantry he always wore when speaking to her,—

"At your service, *Madame!*" But his foot was still on the step, and in his whole attitude there was a remote suggestion, distinctly visible to her, that he wished to go, and had no desire for a midnight interview.

"The air is deliciously cool," she said, "the moonlight peaceful and poetic, and the garden inviting. Will you not stay in it awhile; the hour is not yet late, or is my company so distasteful to you, that you are in a hurry to rid yourself of it?"

"Nay, *Madame*," he rejoined placidly, "but 'tis on the other foot the shoe happens to be, and I'll warrant you'll find the midnight air more poetic without my company: no doubt the sooner I remove the obstruction the better your ladyship will like it."

He turned once more to go.

"I protest you mistake me, Sir Percy," she said hurriedly, and drawing a little closer to him; "the estrangement, which alas! has arisen between us, was none of my making, remember."

"Begad! you must pardon me there, *Madame!*" he protested coldly, "my memory was always of the shortest."

He looked her straight in the eyes, with that lazy nonchalance which had become second nature to him. She returned his gaze for a moment, then her eyes softened, as she came up quite close to him, to the foot of the terrace steps.

"Of the shortest, Sir Percy! Faith! how it must have altered! Was it three years ago or four that you saw me for one hour in Paris, on your way to the East? When you came back two years later you had not forgotten me."

She looked divinely pretty as she stood there in the moonlight, with the fur-cloak sliding off her beautiful shoulders, the gold embroidery on her dress shimmering around her, her childlike blue eyes turned up fully at him.

He stood for a moment, rigid and still, but for the clenching of his hand against the stone balustrade of the terrace.

"You desired my presence, *Madame*," he said frigidly. "I take it that it was not with the view to indulging in tender reminiscences."

His voice certainly was cold and uncompromising: his attitude before her, stiff and unbending. Womanly decorum would have suggested Marguerite should return coldness for coldness, and should sweep past him without another word, only with a curt nod of her head: but womanly instinct suggested that she should remain—that keen instinct, which makes a beautiful woman conscious of her powers long to bring to her knees the one man who pays her no homage. She stretched out her hand to him.

"Nay, Sir Percy, why not? the present is not so glorious but that I should not wish to dwell a little in the past."

He bent his tall figure and taking hold of the extreme tip of the fingers which she still held out to him, he kissed them ceremoniously.

"I' faith, *Madame*," he said, "then you will pardon me, if my dull wits cannot accompany you there."

Once again, he attempted to go, once more her voice, sweet, child-like, almost tender, called him back.

"Sir Percy."

"Your servant, *Madame*."

"Is it possible that love can die?" she said with sudden, unreasoning vehemence. "Methought that the passion which you once felt for me would outlast the span of human life. Is there nothing left of that love, Percy—which might help you—to bridge over that sad estrangement?"

His massive figure seemed, while she spoke thus to him, to stiffen still more, the strong mouth hardened, a look of relentless obstinacy crept into the habitually lazy blue eyes.

"With what object, I pray you, *Madame?*" he asked coldly.

"I do not understand you."

"Yet 'tis simple enough," he said with sudden bitterness, which seemed literally to surge through his words, though he was making visible efforts to suppress it, "I humbly put the question to you, for my slow wits are unable to grasp the cause of this, your ladyship's sudden new mood. Is it that you have the taste to renew the devilish sport which you played so successfully last year? Do you wish to see me once more a love-sick suppliant at your feet, so that you might again have the pleasure of kicking me aside, like a troublesome lap-dog?"

She had succeeded in rousing him for the moment: and again, she looked straight at him, for it was thus she remembered him a year ago.

"Percy! I entreat you!" she whispered, "can we not bury the past?"

"Pardon me, *Madame*, but I understood you to say that your desire was to dwell in it."

"Nay! I spoke not of *that* past, Percy!" she said, while a tone of tenderness crept into her voice. "Rather did I speak of a time when you loved me still! and I—oh! I was vain and frivolous; your wealth and position allured me: I married you, hoping in my heart that your great love for me would beget in me a love for you—but, alas!—"

The moon had sunk low down behind a bank of clouds. In the east a soft grey light was beginning to chase away the heavy mantle of the night. He could only see her graceful outline now, the small queenly head, with its wealth of reddish golden curls, and the glittering gems forming the small, star-shaped, red flower which she wore as a diadem in her hair.

"Twenty-four hours after our marriage, *Madame*, the Marquis de St. Cyr and all his family perished on the guillotine, and the popular rumour reached me that it was the wife of Sir Percy Blakeney who helped to send them there."

"Nay! I myself told you the truth of that odious tale."

"Not till after it had been recounted to me by strangers, with all its horrible details."

"And you believed them then and there," she said with great vehemence, "without a proof or question—you believed that I, whom you vowed you loved more than life, whom you professed you worshipped, that *I* could do a thing so base as these *strangers* chose to recount. You thought I meant to deceive you about it all—that I ought to have spoken before I married you: yet, had you listened, I would have told you that up to the very morning on which St. Cyr went to the guillotine, I was straining every nerve, using every influence I possessed, to save him and his family. But my pride sealed my lips, when your love seemed to perish, as if under the knife of that same guillotine. Yet I would have told you how I was duped! Aye! I, whom that same popular rumour had endowed with the sharpest wits in France! I was tricked into doing this thing, by men who knew how to play upon my love for an only brother, and my desire for revenge. Was it unnatural?"

Her voice became choked with tears. She paused for a moment or two, trying to regain some sort of composure. She looked appealingly at him, almost as if he were her judge. He had allowed her to speak on in her own vehement, impassioned way, offering no comment, no word of sympathy: and now, while she paused, trying to swallow down the hot tears that gushed to her eyes, he waited, impassive and still. The dim, grey light of early dawn seemed to make his tall form look taller and more rigid. The lazy, good-natured face looked strangely altered. Marguerite, excited, as she was, could see that the eyes were no longer languid, the mouth no longer good-humoured and inane. A curious look of intense passion seemed to glow from beneath his drooping lids, the mouth was tightly closed, the lips compressed, as if the will alone held that surging passion in check.

Marguerite Blakeney was, above all, a woman, with all a woman's fascinating foibles, all a woman's most lovable sins. She knew in a moment that for the past few months she had been mistaken: that this man who stood here before her, cold as a statue, when her musical voice struck upon his ear, loved her, as he had loved her a year ago: that his passion might have been dormant, but that it was there, as strong, as intense, as overwhelming, as when first her lips met his in one long, maddening kiss. Pride had kept him from her, and, woman-like, she meant to win back that conquest which had been hers before. Suddenly it seemed to her that the only happiness life could ever hold for her again would be in feeling that man's kiss once more upon her lips.

"Listen to the tale, Sir Percy," she said, and her voice was low, sweet, infinitely tender. "Armand was all in all to me! We had no parents and brought one another up. He was my little father, and I, his tiny mother; we loved one another so. Then one day—do you mind me, Sir Percy? the Marquis de St. Cyr had my brother Armand thrashed—thrashed by his lacqueys—that brother whom I loved better than all the world! And his offence? That he, a plebeian, had dared to love the daughter of the aristocrat; for that he was waylaid and thrashed . . . thrashed like a dog within an inch of his life! Oh, how I suffered! his humiliation had eaten into my very soul! When the opportunity occurred, and I was able to take my revenge, I took it. But I only thought to bring that proud marquis to trouble and humiliation. He plotted with Austria against his own country. Chance gave me knowledge of this; I spoke of it, but I did not know—how could I guess?—they trapped and duped me. When I realised what I had done, it was too late."

"It is perhaps a little difficult, *Madame*," said Sir Percy, after a moment of silence between them, "to go back over the past. I have confessed to you that my memory is short, but the thought certainly lingered in my mind that, at the time of the marquis' death, I entreated you for an explanation of those same noisome popular rumours. If that same memory does not, even now, play me a trick, I fancy that you refused me *all* explanation then, and demanded of my love a humiliating allegiance it was not prepared to give."

"I wished to test your love for me, and it did not bear the test. You used to tell me that you drew the very breath of life but for me, and for love of me."

"And to probe that love, you demanded that I should forfeit mine honour," he said, whilst gradually his impassiveness seemed to leave him, his rigidity to relax; "that I should accept without murmur or question, as a dumb and submissive slave, every action of my mistress. My heart overflowing with love and passion, I *asked* for no explanation—I *waited* for one, not doubting—only hoping. Had you spoken but one word, from you I would have accepted any explanation and believed it. But you left me without a word, beyond a bald confession of the actual horrible facts; proudly you returned to your brother's house and left me alone—for weeks—not knowing, now, in whom to believe, since the shrine, which contained my one illusion, lay shattered to earth at my feet."

She need not complain now that he was cold and impassive; his very voice shook with an intensity of passion, which he was making superhuman efforts to keep in check.

"Aye! the madness of my pride!" she said sadly. "Hardly had I gone, already I had repented. But when I returned, I found you, oh, so altered! wearing already that mask of somnolent indifference which you have never laid aside until—until now."

She was so close to him that her soft, loose hair was wafted against his cheek; her eyes, glowing with tears, maddened him, the music in her voice sent fire through his veins. But he would not yield to the magic charm of this woman whom he had so deeply loved, and at whose hands his pride had suffered so bitterly. He closed his eyes to shut out the dainty vision of that sweet face, of that snow-white neck and graceful figure, round which the faint rosy light of dawn was just beginning to hover playfully.

"Nay, *Madame*, it is no mask," he said icily; "I swore to you—once, that my life was yours. For months now, it has been your plaything—it has served its purpose."

But now she knew that the very coldness was a mask. The trouble, the sorrow she had gone through last night, suddenly came back into her mind, but no longer with bitterness, rather with a feeling that this man who loved her, would help her bear the burden.

"Sir Percy," she said impulsively, "Heaven knows you have been at pains to make the task, which I had set to myself, difficult to accomplish. You spoke of my mood just now; well! we will call it that, if you will. I wished to speak to you—because—because I was in trouble—and had need—of your sympathy."

"It is yours to command, *Madame*."

"How cold you are!" she sighed. "Faith! I can scarce believe that but a few months ago one tear in my eye had set you well-nigh crazy. Now I come to you—with a half-broken heart—and—and—"

"I pray you, *Madame*," he said, whilst his voice shook almost as much as hers, "in what way can I serve you?"

"Percy!—Armand is in deadly danger. A letter of his—rash, impetuous, as were all his actions, and written to Sir Andrew Ffoulkes, has fallen into the hands of a fanatic. Armand is hopelessly compromised—tomorrow, perhaps he will be arrested—after that the guillotine—unless—oh! it is horrible!"—she said, with a sudden wail of anguish, as all the events of the past night came rushing back to her mind, "horrible!—and you do not understand—you cannot—and I have no one to whom I can turn—for help—or even for sympathy—"

Tears now refused to be held back. All her trouble, her struggles, the awful uncertainty of Armand's fate overwhelmed her. She tottered, ready to fall, and leaning against the tone balustrade, she buried her face in her hands and sobbed bitterly.

At first mention of Armand St. Just's name and of the peril in which he stood, Sir Percy's face had become a shade more pale; and the look of determination and obstinacy appeared more marked than ever between his eyes. However, he said nothing for the moment, but watched her, as her delicate frame was shaken with sobs, watched her until unconsciously his face softened, and what looked almost like tears seemed to glisten in his eyes.

"And so," he said with bitter sarcasm, "the murderous dog of the revolution is turning upon the very hands that fed it?—Begad, *Madame*," he added very gently, as Marguerite continued to sob hysterically, "will you dry your tears?—I never could bear to see a pretty woman cry, and I—"

Instinctively, with sudden overmastering passion at the sight of her helplessness and of her grief, he stretched out his arms, and the next, would have seized her and held her to him, protected from every evil with his very life, his very heart's blood—But pride had the better of it in this struggle once again; he restrained himself with a tremendous effort of will, and said coldly, though still very gently,—

"Will you not turn to me, *Madame*, and tell me in what way I may have the honour to serve you?"

She made a violent effort to control herself, and turning her tear-stained face to him, she once more held out her hand, which he kissed with the same punctilious gallantry; but Marguerite's fingers, this time, lingered in his hand for a second or two longer than was absolutely necessary, and this was because she had felt that his hand trembled perceptibly and was burning hot, whilst his lips felt as cold as marble.

"Can you do aught for Armand?" she said sweetly and simply. "You have so much influence at court—so many friends—"

"Nay, *Madame*, should you not seek the influence of your French friend, M. Chauvelin? His extends, if I mistake not, even as far as the Republican Government of France."

"I cannot ask him, Percy—Oh! I wish I dared to tell you—but—but—he has put a price on my brother's head, which—"

She would have given worlds if she had felt the courage then to tell him everything . . . all she had done that night—how she had suffered and how her hand had been forced. But she dared not give way to that impulse . . . not now, when she was just beginning to feel that he still loved her, when she hoped that she could win him back. She dared not make another confession to him. After all, he might not understand; he might not sympathise with her struggles and temptation. His love still dormant might sleep the sleep of death.

Perhaps he divined what was passing in her mind. His whole attitude was one of intense longing—a veritable prayer for that confidence, which her foolish pride withheld from him. When she remained silent he sighed, and said with marked coldness—

"Faith, *Madame*, since it distresses you, we will not speak of it—As for Armand, I pray you have no fear. I pledge you my word that he shall be safe. Now, have I your permission to go? The hour is getting late, and—"

"You will at least accept my gratitude?" she said, as she drew quite close to him, and speaking with real tenderness.

With a quick, almost involuntary effort he would have taken her then in his arms, for her eyes were swimming in tears, which he longed to kiss away; but she had lured him once, just like this, then cast him aside like an ill-fitting glove. He thought this was but a mood, a caprice, and he was too proud to lend himself to it once again.

"It is too soon, *Madame!*" he said quietly; "I have done nothing as yet. The hour is late, and you must be fatigued. Your women will be waiting for you upstairs."

He stood aside to allow her to pass. She sighed, a quick sigh of disappointment. His pride and her beauty had been in direct conflict, and his pride had remained the conqueror. Perhaps, after all, she had been deceived just now; what she took to be the light of love in his eyes might only have been the passion of pride or, who knows, of hatred instead of love. She stood looking at him for a moment or two longer. He was again as rigid, as impassive, as before. Pride had conquered, and he cared naught for her. The grey light of dawn was gradually yielding to the rosy light of the rising sun. Birds began to twitter; Nature awakened, smiling in happy response to the warmth of this glorious October morning. Only between these two hearts there lay a strong, impassable barrier, built up of pride on both sides, which neither of them cared to be the first to demolish.

He had bent his tall figure in a low ceremonious bow, as she finally, with another bitter little sigh, began to mount the terrace steps.

The long train of her gold-embroidered gown swept the dead leaves off the steps, making a faint harmonious *sh—sh—sh* as she glided up, with one hand resting on the balustrade, the rosy light of dawn making an aureole of gold round her hair, and causing the rubies on her head and arms to sparkle. She reached the tall glass doors which led into the house. Before entering, she paused once again to look at him, hoping against hope to see his arms stretched out to her, and to hear his voice calling her back. But he had not moved; his massive figure looked the very personification of unbending pride, of fierce obstinacy.

Hot tears again surged to her eyes, as she would not let him see them, she turned quickly within, and ran as fast as she could up to her own rooms.

Had she but turned back then and looked out once more on to the rose-lit garden, she would have seen that which would have made her own sufferings seem but light and easy to bear—a strong man, overwhelmed with his own passion and his own despair. Pride had given way at last, obstinacy was gone: the will was powerless. He was but a man madly, blindly, passionately in love, and as soon as her light footsteps had died away within the house, he knelt down upon the terrace steps, and in the very madness of his love he kissed one by one the places where her small foot had trodden, and the stone balustrade there, where her tiny hand had rested last.

Chapter 17

Farewell

When Marguerite reached her room, she found her maid terribly anxious about her.

"Your ladyship will be so tired," said the poor woman, whose own eyes were half closed with sleep. "It is past five o'clock."

"Ah, yes, Louise, I daresay I shall be tired presently," said Marguerite, kindly; "but you are very tired now, so go to bed at once. I'll get into bed alone."

"But, my lady—"

"Now, don't argue, Louise, but go to bed. Give me a wrap and leave me alone."

Louise was only too glad to obey. She took off her mistress's gorgeous ball-dress and wrapped her up in a soft billowy gown.

"Does your ladyship wish for anything else?" she asked, when that was done.

"No, nothing more. Put out the lights as you go out."

"Yes, my lady. Goodnight, my lady."

"Goodnight, Louise."

When the maid was gone, Marguerite drew aside the curtains and threw open the windows. The garden and the river beyond were flooded with rosy light. Far away to the east, the rays of the rising sun had changed the rose into vivid gold. The lawn was deserted now, and Marguerite looked down upon the terrace where she had stood a few moments ago trying in vain to win back a man's love, which once had been so wholly hers.

It was strange that through all her troubles, all her anxiety for Armand, she was mostly conscious at the present moment of a keen and bitter heartache.

Her very limbs seemed to ache with longing for the love of a man who had spurned her, who had resisted her tenderness, remained cold to her appeals, and had not responded to the glow of passion, which had caused her to feel and hope that those happy olden days in Paris were not all dead and forgotten.

How strange it all was! She loved him still. And now that she looked back upon the last few months of misunderstandings and of loneliness, she realised that she had never ceased to love him; that deep down in her heart she had always vaguely felt that his foolish inanities, his empty laugh, his lazy nonchalance were nothing but a mask; that the real man, strong, passionate, wilful, was there still—the man she had loved, whose intensity had fascinated her, whose personality attracted her, since she always felt that behind his apparently slow wits there was a certain something, which he kept hidden from all the world, and most especially from her.

A woman's heart is such a complex problem—the owner thereof is often most incompetent to find the solution of this puzzle.

Did Marguerite Blakeney, "the cleverest woman in Europe," really love a fool? Was it love that she had felt for him a year ago when she married him? Was it love she felt for him now that she realised that he still loved her, but that he would not become her slave, her passionate, ardent lover once again? Nay! Marguerite herself could not have told that. Not at this moment at any rate; perhaps her pride had sealed her mind against a better understanding of her own heart. But this she did know—that she meant to capture that obstinate heart back again. That she would conquer once more—and then, that she would never lose him—She would keep him, keep his love, deserve it, and cherish it; for this much was certain, that there was no longer any happiness possible for her without that one man's love.

Thus, the most contradictory thoughts and emotions rushed madly through her mind. Absorbed in them, she had allowed time to slip by; perhaps, tired out with long excitement, she had actually closed her eyes and sunk into a troubled sleep, wherein quickly fleeting dreams seemed but the continuation of her anxious thoughts—when suddenly she was roused, from dream or meditation, by the noise of footsteps outside her door.

Nervously she jumped up and listened; the house itself was as still as ever; the footsteps had retreated. Through her wide-open window the brilliant rays of the morning sun were flooding her room with light. She looked up at the clock; it was half-past six—too early for any of the household to be already astir.

She certainly must have dropped asleep, quite unconsciously. The noise of the footsteps, also of hushed subdued voices had awakened her—what could they be?

Gently, on tip-toe, she crossed the room and opened the door to listen; not a sound—that peculiar stillness of the early morning when sleep with all mankind is at its heaviest. But the noise had made her nervous, and when, suddenly, at her feet, on the very doorstep, she saw something white lying there—a letter evidently—she hardly dared touch it. It seemed so ghostlike. It certainly was not there when she came upstairs; had Louise dropped it? or was some tantalising spook at play, showing her fairy letters where none existed?

At last she stooped to pick it up, and, amazed, puzzled beyond measure, she saw that the letter was addressed to herself in her husband's large, businesslike-looking hand. What could he have to say to her, in the middle of the night, which could not be put off until the morning?

She tore open the envelope and read:—

A most unforeseen circumstance forces me to leave for the North immediately, so I beg your ladyship's pardon if I do not avail myself of the honour of bidding you goodbye. My business may keep me employed for about a week, so I shall not have the privilege of being present at your ladyship's water-party on Wednesday. I remain your ladyship's most humble and most obedient servant, Percy Blakeney.

Marguerite must suddenly have been imbued with her husband's slowness of intellect, for she had perforce to read the few simple lines over and over again, before she could fully grasp their meaning.

She stood on the landing, turning over and over in her hand this curt and mysterious epistle, her mind a blank, her nerves strained with agitation and a presentiment she could not very well have explained.

Sir Percy owned considerable property in the North, certainly, and he had often before gone there alone and stayed away a week at a time; but it seemed so very strange that circumstances should have arisen between five and six o'clock in the morning that compelled him to start in this extreme hurry.

Vainly she tried to shake off an unaccustomed feeling of nervousness: she was trembling from head to foot. A wild, unconquerable desire seized her to see her husband again, at once, if only he had not already started.

Forgetting the fact that she was only very lightly clad in a morning wrap, and that her hair lay loosely about her shoulders, she flew down the stairs, right through the hall towards the front door.

It was as usual barred and bolted, for the indoor servants were not yet up; but her keen ears had detected the sound of voices and the pawing of a horse's hoof against the flag-stones.

With nervous, trembling fingers Marguerite undid the bolts one by one, bruising her hands, hurting her nails, for the locks were heavy and stiff. But she did not care; her whole frame shook with anxiety at the very thought that she might be too late; that he might have gone without her seeing him and bidding him "God-speed!"

At last, she had turned the key and thrown open the door. Her ears had not deceived her. A groom was standing close by holding a couple of horses; one of these was Sultan, Sir Percy's favourite and swiftest horse, saddled ready for a journey.

The next moment Sir Percy himself appeared round the further corner of the house and came quickly towards the horses. He had changed his gorgeous ball costume but was as usual irreproachably and richly apparelled in a suit of fine cloth, with lace *jabot* and ruffles, high top-boots, and riding breeches.

Marguerite went forward a few steps. He looked up and saw her. A slight frown appeared between his eyes.

"You are going?" she said quickly and feverishly. "Whither?"

"As I have had the honour of informing your ladyship, urgent, most unexpected business calls me to the North this morning," he said, in his usual cold, drawly manner.

"But—your guests tomorrow—"

"I have prayed your ladyship to offer my humble excuses to His Royal Highness. You are such a perfect hostess, I do not think I shall be missed."

"But surely you might have waited for your journey—until after our water-party—" she said, still speaking quickly and nervously. "Surely this business is not so urgent—and you said nothing about it—just now."

"My business, as I had the honour to tell you, *Madame*, is as unexpected as it is urgent—May I therefore crave your permission to go—Can I do aught for you in town?—on my way back?"

"No—no—thanks—nothing—But you will be back soon?"

"Very soon."

"Before the end of the week?"

"I cannot say."

He was evidently trying to get away, whilst she was straining every nerve to keep him back for a moment or two.

"Percy," she said, "will you not tell me why you go today? Surely, I, as your wife, have the right to know. You have *not* been called away to the North. I know it. There were no letters, no couriers from there before we left for the opera last night, and nothing was waiting for you when we returned from the ball—You are *not* going to the North, I feel convinced—There is some mystery—and—"

"Nay, there is no mystery, *Madame*," he replied, with a slight tone of impatience. "My business has to do with Armand—there! Now, have I your leave to depart?"

"With Armand?—But you will run no danger?"

"Danger? I?—Nay, *Madame*, your solicitude does me honour. As you say, I have some influence; my intention is to exert it before it be too late."

"Will you allow me to thank you at least?"

"Nay, *Madame*," he said coldly, "there is no need for that. My life is at your service, and I am already more than repaid."

"And mine will be at yours, Sir Percy, if you will but accept it, in exchange for what you do for Armand," she said, as, impulsively, she stretched out both her hands to him. "There! I will not detain you—my thoughts go with you—Farewell!—"

How lovely she looked in this morning sunlight, with her ardent hair streaming around her shoulders. He bowed very low and kissed her hand; she felt the burning kiss and her heart thrilled with joy and hope.

"You will come back?" she said tenderly.

"Very soon!" he replied, looking longingly into her blue eyes.

"And—you will remember?—" she asked as her eyes, in response to his look, gave him an infinity of promise.

"I will always remember, *Madame*, that you have honoured me by commanding my services."

The words were cold and formal, but they did not chill her this time. Her woman's heart had read his, beneath the impassive mask his pride still forced him to wear.

He bowed to her again, then begged her leave to depart. She stood on one side whilst he jumped on to Sultan's back, then, as he galloped out of the gates, she waved him a final "*Adieu*."

A bend in the road soon hid him from view; his confidential groom had some difficulty in keeping pace with him, for Sultan flew along in response to his master's excited mood. Marguerite, with a sigh that was almost a happy one, turned and went within. She went back to her room, for suddenly, like a tired child, she felt quite sleepy.

Her heart seemed all at once to be in complete peace, and, though it still ached with undefined longing, a vague and delicious hope soothed it as with a balm.

She felt no longer anxious about Armand. The man who had just ridden away, bent on helping her brother, inspired her with complete confidence in his strength and in his power. She marvelled at herself for having ever looked upon him as an inane fool; of course, *that* was a mask worn to hide the bitter wound she had dealt to his faith and to his love. His passion would have overmastered him, and he would not let her see how much he still cared and how deeply he suffered.

But now all would be well: she would crush her own pride, humble it before him, tell him everything, trust him in everything; and those happy days would come back, when they used to wander off together in the forests of Fontainebleau, when they spoke little—for he was always a silent man—but when she felt that against that strong heart she would always find rest and happiness.

The more she thought of the events of the past night, the less fear had she of Chauvelin and his schemes. He had failed to discover the identity of the Scarlet Pimpernel, of that she felt sure. Both Lord Fancourt and Chauvelin himself had assured her that no one had been in the dining-room at one o'clock except the Frenchman himself and Percy—Yes!—Percy! she might have asked him, had she thought of it! Anyway, she had no fears that the unknown and brave hero would fall in Chauvelin's trap; his death at any rate would not be at her door.

Armand certainly was still in danger, but Percy had pledged his word that Armand would be safe, and somehow, as Marguerite had seen him riding away, the possibility that he could fail in whatever he undertook never even remotely crossed her mind. When Armand was safely over in England she would not allow him to go back to France.

She felt almost happy now, and, drawing the curtains closely together again to shut out the piercing sun, she went to bed at last, laid her head upon the pillow, and, like a wearied child, soon fell into a peaceful and dreamless sleep.

Chapter 13

The Mysterious Device

The day was well advanced when Marguerite woke, refreshed by her long sleep. Louise had brought her some fresh milk and a dish of fruit, and she partook of this frugal breakfast with hearty appetite.

Thoughts crowded thick and fast in her mind as she munched her grapes; most of them went galloping away after the tall, erect figure of her husband, whom she had watched riding out of sight more than five hours ago.

In answer to her eager inquiries, Louise brought back the news that the groom had come home with Sultan, having left Sir Percy in London. The groom thought that his master was about to get on board his schooner, which was lying off just below London Bridge. Sir Percy had ridden thus far, had then met Briggs, the skipper of the *Daydream*, and had sent the groom back to Richmond with Sultan and the empty saddle.

This news puzzled Marguerite more than ever. Where could Sir Percy be going just now in the *Daydream?* On Armand's behalf, he had said. Well! Sir Percy had influential friends everywhere. Perhaps he was going to Greenwich, or—but Marguerite ceased to conjecture; all would be explained *anon*: he said that he would come back, and that he would remember. A long, idle day lay before Marguerite. She was expecting a visit of her old school-fellow, little Suzanne de Tournay. With all the merry mischief at her command, she had tendered her request for Suzanne's company to the *Comtesse* in the Presence of the Prince of Wales last night. His Royal Highness had loudly applauded the notion and declared that he would give himself the pleasure of calling on the two ladies in the course of the afternoon. The *Comtesse* had not dared to refuse, and then and there was entrapped into a promise to send little Suzanne to spend a long and happy day at Richmond with her friend.

Marguerite expected her eagerly; she longed for a chat about old school-days with the child; she felt that she would prefer Suzanne's company to that of anyone else, and together they would roam through the fine old garden and rich deer park or stroll along the river.

But Suzanne had not come yet, and Marguerite being dressed, prepared to go downstairs. She looked quite a girl this morning in her simple muslin frock, with a broad blue sash round her slim waist, and the dainty cross-over *fichu* into which, at her bosom, she had fastened a few late crimson roses.

She crossed the landing outside her own suite of apartments and stood still for a moment at the head of the fine oak staircase, which led to the lower floor. On her left were her husband's apartments, a suite of rooms which she practically never entered.

They consisted of bedroom, dressing and reception room, and at the extreme end of the landing, of a small study, which, when Sir Percy did not use it, was always kept locked. His own special and confidential valet, Frank, had charge of this room. No one was ever allowed to go inside. My lady had never cared to do so, and the other servants, had, of course, not dared to break this hard-and-fast rule.

Marguerite had often, with that good-natured contempt which she had recently adopted towards her husband, chaffed him about this secrecy which surrounded his private study. Laughingly she had always declared that he strictly excluded all prying eyes from his *sanctum* for fear they should detect how very little "study" went on within its four walls: a comfortable armchair for Sir Percy's sweet slumbers was, no doubt, its most conspicuous piece of furniture.

Marguerite thought of all this on this bright October morning as she glanced along the corridor. Frank was evidently busy with his master's rooms, for most of the doors stood open, that of the study amongst the others.

A sudden burning, childish curiosity seized her to have a peep at Sir Percy's *sanctum*. This restriction, of course, did not apply to her, and Frank would, of course, not dare to oppose her. Still, she hoped that the valet would be busy in one of the other rooms, that she might have that one quick peep in secret, and unmolested.

Gently, on tip-toe, she crossed the landing and, like Blue Beard's wife, trembling half with excitement and wonder, she paused a moment on the threshold, strangely perturbed and irresolute.

The door was ajar, and she could not see anything within. She pushed it open tentatively: there was no sound: Frank was evidently not there, and she walked boldly in.

At once she was struck by the severe simplicity of everything around her: the dark and heavy hangings, the massive oak furniture, the one or two maps on the wall, in no way recalled to her mind the lazy man about town, the lover of race-courses, the dandified leader of fashion, that was the outward representation of Sir Percy Blakeney.

There was no sign here, at any rate, of hurried departure. Everything was in its place, not a scrap of paper littered the floor, not a cupboard or drawer was left open. The curtains were drawn aside, and through the open window the fresh morning air was streaming in.

Facing the window, and well into the centre of the room, stood a ponderous business-like desk, which looked as if it had seen much service. On the wall to the left of the desk, reaching almost from floor to ceiling, was a large full-length portrait of a woman, magnificently framed, exquisitely painted, and signed with the name of Boucher. It was Percy's mother.

Marguerite knew very little about her, except that she had died abroad, ailing in body as well as in mind, while Percy was still a lad. She must have been a very beautiful woman once, when Boucher painted her, and as Marguerite looked at the portrait, she could not but be struck by the extraordinary resemblance which must have existed between mother and son. There was the same low, square forehead, crowned with thick, fair hair, smooth and heavy; the same deep-set, somewhat lazy blue eyes beneath firmly marked, straight brows; and in those eyes there was the same intensity behind that apparent laziness, the same latent passion which used to light up Percy's face in the olden days before his marriage, and which Marguerite had again noted, last night at dawn, when she had come quite close to him, and had allowed a note of tenderness to creep into her voice.

Marguerite studied the portrait, for it interested her: after that she turned and looked again at the ponderous desk. It was covered with a mass of papers, all neatly tied and docketed, which looked like accounts and receipts arrayed with perfect method. It had never before struck Marguerite—nor had she, alas! found it worthwhile to inquire—as to how Sir Percy, whom all the world had credited with a total lack of brains, administered the vast fortune which his father had left him.

Since she had entered this neat, orderly room, she had been taken so much by surprise, that this obvious proof of her husband's strong business capacities did not cause her more than a passing thought of wonder. But it also strengthened her in the now certain knowledge that, with his worldly inanities, his foppish ways, and foolish talk, he was not only wearing a mask, but was playing a deliberate and studied part.

Marguerite wondered again. Why should he take all this trouble? Why should he—who was obviously a serious, earnest man—wish to appear before his fellow-men as an empty-headed nincompoop?

He may have wished to hide his love for a wife who held him in contempt—but surely such an object could have been gained at less sacrifice, and with far less trouble than constant incessant acting of an unnatural part.

She looked round her quite aimlessly now: she was horribly puzzled, and a nameless dread, before all this strange, unaccountable mystery, had begun to seize upon her. She felt cold and uncomfortable suddenly in this severe and dark room. There were no pictures on the wall, save the fine Boucher portrait, only a couple of maps, both of parts of France, one of the North coast and the other of the environs of Paris. What did Sir Percy want with those, she wondered?

Her head began to ache, she turned away from this strange Blue Beard's chamber, which she had entered, and which she did not understand. She did not wish Frank to find her here, and with a fast look round, she once more turned to the door. As she did so, her foot knocked against a small object, which had apparently been lying close to the desk, on the carpet, and which now went rolling, right across the room.

She stooped to pick it up. It was a solid gold ring, with a flat shield, on which was engraved a small device.

Marguerite turned it over in her fingers, and then studied the engraving on the shield. It represented a small star-shaped flower, of a shape she had seen so distinctly twice before: once at the opera, and once at Lord Grenville's ball.

CHAPTER 19

The Scarlet Pimpernel

At what particular moment the strange doubt first crept into Marguerite's mind, she could not herself have said. With the ring tightly clutched in her hand, she had run out of the room, down the stairs, and out into the garden, where, in complete seclusion, alone with the flowers, and the river and the birds, she could look again at the ring, and study that device more closely.

Stupidly, senselessly, now, sitting beneath the shade of an overhanging sycamore, she was looking at the plain gold shield, with the star-shaped little flower engraved upon it.

Bah! It was ridiculous! she was dreaming! her nerves were overwrought, and she saw signs and mysteries in the most trivial coincidences. Had not everybody about town recently made a point of affecting the device of that mysterious and heroic Scarlet Pimpernel?

Did she herself wear it embroidered on her gowns? set in gems and enamel in her hair? What was there strange in the fact that Sir Percy should have chosen to use the device as a seal-ring? He might easily have done that—yes—quite easily—and—besides—what connection could there be between her exquisite dandy of a husband, with his fine clothes and refined, lazy ways, and the daring plotter who rescued French victims from beneath the very eyes of the leaders of a bloodthirsty revolution?

Her thoughts were in a whirl—her mind a blank—She did not see anything that was going on around her and was quite startled when a fresh young voice called to her across the garden.

"*Chérie!—Chérie!* where are you?" and little Suzanne, fresh as a rosebud, with eyes dancing with glee, and brown curls fluttering in the soft morning breeze, came running across the lawn.

"They told me you were in the garden," she went on prattling merrily, and throwing herself with a pretty, girlish impulse into Marguerite's arms, "so I ran out to give you a surprise. You did not expect me quite so soon, did you, my darling little Margot *chérie?*"

Marguerite, who had hastily concealed the ring in the folds of her kerchief, tried to respond gaily and unconcernedly to the young girl's impulsiveness.

"Indeed, sweet one," she said with a smile, "it is delightful to have you all to myself, and for a nice whole long day.—You won't be bored?"

"Oh! bored! Margot, how *can* you say such a wicked thing. Why! when we were in the dear old convent together, we were always happy when we were allowed to be alone together."

"And to talk secrets."

The two young girls had linked their arms in one another's and began wandering round the garden.

"Oh! how lovely your home is, Margot, darling," said little Suzanne, enthusiastically, "and how happy you must be!"

"Aye, indeed! I ought to be happy—oughtn't I, sweet one?" said Marguerite, with a wistful little sigh.

"How sadly you say it, *chérie*—Ah, well, I suppose now that you are a married woman you won't care to talk secrets with me any longer. Oh! what lots and lots of secrets we used to have at school! Do you remember?—some we did not even confide to Sister Theresa of the Holy Angels—though she was such a dear."

"And now you have one all-important secret, eh, little one?" said Marguerite, merrily, "which you are forthwith going to confide in me. Nay, you need not blush, *chérie*." she added, as she saw Suzanne's pretty little face crimson with blushes. "Faith, there's naught to be ashamed of! He is a noble and true man, and one to be proud of as a lover, and —as a husband."

"Indeed, *chérie*, I am not ashamed," rejoined Suzanne, softly; "and it makes me very, very proud to hear you speak so well of him. I think *maman* will consent," she added thoughtfully, "and I shall be—oh! so happy—but, of course, nothing is to be thought of until papa is safe—"

Marguerite started. Suzanne's father! the Comte de Tournay!—one of those whose life would be jeopardised if Chauvelin succeeded in establishing the identity of the Scarlet Pimpernel.

She had understood all along from the *Comtesse*, and also from one or two of the members of the league, that their mysterious leader had pledged his honour to bring the fugitive Comte de Tournay safely out of France. Whilst little Suzanne—unconscious of all—save her own all-important little secret, went prattling on, Marguerite's thoughts went back to the events of the past night.

Armand's peril, Chauvelin's threat, his cruel "Either—or—" which she had accepted.

And then her own work in the matter, which should have culminated at one o'clock in Lord Grenville's dining-room, when the relentless agent of the French Government would finally learn who was this mysterious Scarlet Pimpernel, who so openly defied an army of spies and placed himself so boldly, and for mere sport, on the side of the enemies of France.

Since then she had heard nothing from Chauvelin. She had concluded that he had failed, and yet, she had not felt anxious about Armand, because her husband had promised her that Armand would be safe.

But now, suddenly, as Suzanne prattled merrily along, an awful horror came upon her for what she had done. Chauvelin had told her nothing, it was true; but she remembered how sarcastic and evil he looked when she took final leave of him after the ball. Had he discovered something then? Had he already laid his plans for catching the daring plotter, red-handed, in France, and sending him to the guillotine without compunction or delay?

Marguerite turned sick with horror, and her hand convulsively clutched the ring in her dress.

"You are not listening, *chérie*," said Suzanne, reproachfully, as she paused in her long, highly interesting narrative.

"Yes, yes, darling—indeed I am," said Marguerite with an effort, forcing herself to smile. "I love to hear you talking—and your happiness makes me so very glad—Have no fear, we will manage to propitiate *maman*. Sir Andrew Ffoulkes is a noble English gentleman; he has money and position, the *Comtesse* will not refuse her consent—But—now, little one—tell me—what is the latest news about your father?"

"Oh!" said Suzanne with mad glee, "the best we could possibly hear. My Lord Hastings came to see *maman* early this morning. He said that all is now well with dear papa, and we may safely expect him here in England in less than four days."

"Yes," said Marguerite, whose glowing eyes were fastened on Suzanne's lips, as she continued merrily:

"Oh, we have no fear now! You don't know, *chérie*, that that great and noble Scarlet Pimpernel himself has gone to save papa. He has gone, *chérie*—actually gone—" added Suzanne excitedly, "he was in London this morning; he will be in Calais, perhaps, tomorrow—where he will meet papa—and then—and then—"

The blow had fallen. She had expected it all along, though she had tried for the last half-hour to delude herself and to cheat her fears.

He had gone to Calais, had been in London this morning—he—the Scarlet Pimpernel—Percy Blakeney—her husband—whom she had betrayed last night to Chauvelin.

Percy—Percy—her husband—the Scarlet Pimpernel—Oh! how could she have been so blind? She understood it all now—all at once—that part he played—the mask he wore—in order to throw dust in everybody's eyes.

And all for the sheer sport and devilry of course!—saving men, women and children from death, as other men destroy and kill animals for the excitement, the love of the thing. The idle, rich man wanted some aim in life—he, and the few young bucks he enrolled under his banner, had amused themselves for months in risking their lives for the sake of an innocent few.

Perhaps he had meant to tell her when they were first married; and then the story of the Marquis de St. Cyr had come to his ears, and he had suddenly turned from her, thinking, no doubt, that she might someday betray him and his comrades, who had sworn to follow him; and so he had tricked her, as he tricked all others, whilst hundreds now owed their lives to him, and many families owed him both life and happiness.

The mask of an inane fop had been a good one, and the part consummately well played. No wonder that Chauvelin's spies had failed to detect, in the apparently brainless nincompoop, the man whose reckless daring and resourceful ingenuity had baffled the keenest French spies, both in France and in England. Even last night when Chauvelin went to Lord Grenville's dining-room to seek that daring Scarlet Pimpernel, he only saw that inane Sir Percy Blakeney fast asleep in a corner of the sofa.

Had his astute mind guessed the secret, then? Here lay the whole awful, horrible, amazing puzzle. In betraying a nameless stranger to his fate in order to save her brother, had Marguerite Blakeney sent her husband to his death?

No! no! no! a thousand times no! Surely Fate could not deal a blow like that: Nature itself would rise in revolt: her hand, when it held that tiny scrap of paper last night, would have surely have been struck numb ere it committed a deed so appalling and so terrible.

"But what is it, *chérie*?" said little Suzanne, now genuinely alarmed, for Marguerite's colour had become dull and ashen. "Are you ill, Marguerite? What is it?"

"Nothing, nothing, child," she murmured, as in a dream. "Wait a moment—let me think—think!—You said—the Scarlet Pimpernel had gone today—?"

"Marguerite, *chérie*, what is it? You frighten me—"

"It is nothing, child, I tell you—nothing—I must be alone a minute—and—dear one—I may have to curtail our time together today—I may have to go away—you'll understand?"

"I understand that something has happened, *chérie*, and that you want to be alone. I won't be a hindrance to you. Don't think of me. My maid, Lucile, has not yet gone—we will go back together—don't think of me."

She threw her arms impulsively round Marguerite. Child as she was, she felt the poignancy of her friend's grief, and with the infinite tact of her girlish tenderness, she did not try to pry into it, but was ready to efface herself.

She kissed Marguerite again and again, then walked sadly back across the lawn. Marguerite did not move, she remained there, thinking—wondering what was to be done.

Just as little Suzanne was about to mount the terrace steps, a groom came running round the house towards his mistress. He carried a sealed letter in his hand. Suzanne instinctively turned back; her heart told her that here perhaps was further ill news for her friend, and she felt that poor Margot was not in a fit state to bear any more.

The groom stood respectfully beside his mistress, then he handed her the sealed letter.

"What is that?" asked Marguerite.

"Just come by runner, my lady."

Marguerite took the letter mechanically and turned it over in her trembling fingers.

"Who sent it?" she said.

"The runner said, my lady," replied the groom, "that his orders were to deliver this, and that your ladyship would understand from whom it came."

Marguerite tore open the envelope. Already her instinct told her what it contained, and her eyes only glanced at it mechanically.

It was a letter by Armand St. Just to Sir Andrew Ffoulkes—the letter which Chauvelin's spies had stolen at "The Fisherman's Rest," and which Chauvelin had held as a rod over her to enforce her obedience.

Now he had kept his word—he had sent her back St. Just's compromising letter—for he was on the track of the Scarlet Pimpernel.

Marguerite's senses reeled, her very soul seemed to be leaving her body; she tottered and would have fallen but for Suzanne's arm round her waist. With superhuman effort she regained control over herself—there was yet much to be done.

"Bring that runner here to me," she said to the servant, with much calm. "He has not gone?"

"No, my lady."

The groom went, and Marguerite turned to Suzanne.

"And you, child, run within. Tell Lucile to get ready. I fear that I must send you home, child. And—stay, tell one of the maids to prepare a travelling dress and cloak for me."

Suzanne made no reply. She kissed Marguerite tenderly and obeyed without a word; the child was overawed by the terrible, nameless misery in her friend's face.

A minute later the groom returned, followed by the runner who had brought the letter.

"Who gave you this packet?" asked Marguerite.

"A gentleman, my lady," replied the man, "at 'The Rose and Thistle' inn opposite Charing Cross. He said you would understand."

"At 'The Rose and Thistle'? What was he doing?"

"He was waiting for the coach, your ladyship, which he had ordered."

"The coach?"

"Yes, my lady. A special coach he had ordered. I understood from his man that he was posting straight to Dover."

"That's enough. You may go." Then she turned to the groom: "My coach and the four swiftest horses in the stables, to be ready at once."

The groom and runner both went quickly off to obey. Marguerite remained standing for a moment on the lawn quite alone. Her graceful figure was as rigid as a statue, her eyes were fixed, her hands were tightly clasped across her breast; her lips moved as they murmured with pathetic heart-breaking persistence,—

"What's to be done? What's to be done? Where to find him?—Oh, God! grant me light."

But this was not the moment for remorse and despair. She had done—unwittingly—an awful and terrible thing—the very worst crime, in her eyes, that woman ever committed—she saw it in all its horror. Her very blindness in not having guessed her husband's secret seemed now to her another deadly sin. She ought to have known! she ought to have known!

How could she imagine that a man who could love with so much intensity as Percy Blakeney had loved her from the first—how could such a man be the brainless idiot he chose to appear? She, at least, ought to have known that he was wearing a mask, and having found that out, she should have torn it from his face, whenever they were alone together.

Her love for him had been paltry and weak, easily crushed by her own pride; and she, too, had worn a mask in assuming a contempt for him, whilst, as a matter of fact, she completely misunderstood him.

But there was no time now to go over the past. By her own blindness she had sinned; now she must repay, not by empty remorse, but by prompt and useful action.

Percy had started for Calais, utterly unconscious of the fact that his most relentless enemy was on his heels. He had set sail early that morning from London Bridge. Provided he had a favourable wind, he would no doubt be in France within twenty-four hours; no doubt he had reckoned on the wind and chosen this route.

Chauvelin, on the other hand, would post to Dover, charter a vessel there, and undoubtedly reach Calais much about the same time. Once in Calais, Percy would meet all those who were eagerly waiting for the noble and brave Scarlet Pimpernel, who had come to rescue them from horrible and unmerited death. With Chauvelin's eyes now fixed upon his every movement, Percy would thus not only be endangering his own life, but that of Suzanne's father, the old Comte de Tournay, and of those other fugitives who were waiting for him and trusting in him. There was also Armand, who had gone to meet de Tournay, secure in the knowledge that the Scarlet Pimpernel was watching over his safety.

All these lives and that of her husband, lay in Marguerite's hands; these she must save, if human pluck and ingenuity were equal to the task.

Unfortunately, she could not do all this quite alone. Once in Calais she would not know where to find her husband, whilst Chauvelin, in stealing the papers at Dover, had obtained the whole itinerary. Above everything, she wished to warn Percy.

She knew enough about him by now to understand that he would never abandon those who trusted in him, that he would not turn his back from danger, and leave the Comte de Tournay to fall into the bloodthirsty hands that knew of no mercy. But if he were warned, he might form new plans, be more wary, more prudent. Unconsciously, he might fall into a cunning trap, but—once warned—he might yet succeed.

And if he failed—if indeed Fate, and Chauvelin, with all the resources at his command, proved too strong for the daring plotter after all—then at least she would be there by his side, to comfort, love and cherish, to cheat death perhaps at the last by making it seem sweet, if they died both together, locked in each other's arms, with the supreme happiness of knowing that passion had responded to passion, and that all misunderstandings were at an end.

Her whole body stiffened as with a great and firm resolution. This she meant to do, if God gave her wits and strength. Her eyes lost their fixed look; they glowed with inward fire at the thought of meeting him again so soon, in the very midst of most deadly perils; they sparkled with the joy of sharing these dangers with him—of helping him perhaps—of being with him at the last—if she failed.

The childlike sweet face had become hard and set, the curved mouth was closed tightly over her clenched teeth. She meant to do or die, with him and for his sake. A frown, which spoke of an iron will and unbending resolution, appeared between the two straight brows; already her plans were formed. She would go and find Sir Andrew Ffoulkes first; he was Percy's best friend, and Marguerite remembered, with a thrill, with what blind enthusiasm the young man always spoke of his mysterious leader.

He would help her where she needed help; her coach was ready. A change of raiment, and a farewell to little Suzanne, and she could be on her way.

Without haste, but without hesitation, she walked quietly into the house.

Chapter 20

The Friend

Less than half an hour later, Marguerite, buried in thoughts, sat inside her coach, which was bearing her swiftly to London.

She had taken an affectionate farewell of little Suzanne, and seen the child safely started with her maid, and in her own coach, back to town. She had sent one courier with a respectful letter of excuse to His Royal Highness, begging for a postponement of the august visit on account of pressing and urgent business, and another on ahead to bespeak a fresh relay of horses at Faversham.

Then she had changed her muslin frock for a dark travelling costume and mantle, had provided herself with money—which her husband's lavishness always placed fully at her disposal—and had started on her way.

She did not attempt to delude herself with any vain and futile hopes; the safety of her brother Armand was to have been conditional on the imminent capture of the Scarlet Pimpernel. As Chauvelin had sent her back Armand's compromising letter, there was no doubt that he was quite satisfied in his own mind that Percy Blakeney was the man whose death he had sworn to bring about.

No! there was no room for any fond delusions! Percy, the husband whom she loved with all the ardour which her admiration for his bravery had kindled, was in immediate, deadly peril, through her hand. She had betrayed him to his enemy—unwittingly 'tis true—but she *had* betrayed him, and if Chauvelin succeeded in trapping him, who so far was unaware of his danger, then his death would be at her door. His death! when with her very heart's blood, she would have defended him and given willingly her life for his.

She had ordered her coach to drive her to the "Crown" inn; once there, she told her coachman to give the horses food and rest. Then she ordered a chair and had herself carried to the house in Pall Mall where Sir Andrew Ffoulkes lived.

Among all Percy's friends who were enrolled under his daring banner, she felt that she would prefer to confide in Sir Andrew Ffoulkes. He had always been her friend, and now his love for little Suzanne had brought him closer to her still. Had he been away from home, gone on the mad errand with Percy, perhaps, then she would have called on Lord Hastings or Lord Tony—for she wanted the help of one of these young men, or she would indeed be powerless to save her husband.

Sir Andrew Ffoulkes, however, was at home, and his servant introduced her ladyship immediately. She went upstairs to the young man's comfortable bachelor's chambers, and was shown into a small, though luxuriously furnished, dining-room. A moment or two later Sir Andrew himself appeared.

He had evidently been much startled when he heard who his lady visitor was, for he looked anxiously—even suspiciously—at Marguerite, whilst performing the elaborate bows before her, which the rigid etiquette of the time demanded.

Marguerite had laid aside every vestige of nervousness; she was perfectly calm, and having returned the young man's elaborate salute, she began very calmly,—

"Sir Andrew, I have no desire to waste valuable time in much talk.

You must take certain things I am going to tell you for granted. These will be of no importance. What is important is that your leader and comrade, the Scarlet Pimpernel—my husband—Percy Blakeney—is in deadly peril."

Had she the remotest doubt of the correctness of her deductions, she would have had them confirmed now, for Sir Andrew, completely taken by surprise, had grown very pale, and was quite incapable of making the slightest attempt at clever parrying.

"No matter how I know this, Sir Andrew," she continued quietly, "thank God that I do, and that perhaps it is not too late to save him. Unfortunately, I cannot do this quite alone, and therefore have come to you for help."

"Lady Blakeney," said the young man, trying to recover himself, "I—"

"Will you hear me first?" she interrupted. "This is how the matter stands. When the agent of the French Government stole your papers that night in Dover, he found amongst them certain plans, which you or your leader meant to carry out for the rescue of the Comte de Tournay and others. The Scarlet Pimpernel—Percy, my husband—has gone on this errand himself today. Chauvelin knows that the Scarlet Pimpernel and Percy Blakeney are one and the same person. He will follow him to Calais, and there will lay hands on him. You know as well as I do the fate that awaits him at the hands of the Revolutionary Government of France.

"No interference from England—from King George himself—would save him. Robespierre and his gang would see to it that the interference came too late. But not only that, the much-trusted leader will also have been unconsciously the means of revealing the hiding-place of the Comte de Tournay and of all those who, even now, are placing their hopes in him."

She had spoken quietly, dispassionately, and with firm, unbending resolution. Her purpose was to make that young man trust and help her, for she could do nothing without him.

"I do not understand," he repeated, trying to gain time, to think what was best to be done.

"Aye! but I think you do, Sir Andrew. You must know that I am speaking the truth. Look these facts straight in the face. Percy has sailed for Calais, I presume for some lonely part of the coast, and Chauvelin is on his track. *He* has posted for Dover and will cross the Channel probably tonight. What do you think will happen?"

The young man was silent.

"Percy will arrive at his destination: unconscious of being followed he will seek out de Tournay and the others—among these is Armand St. Just my brother—he will seek them out, one after another, probably, not knowing that the sharpest eyes in the world are watching his every movement. When he has thus unconsciously betrayed those who blindly trust in him, when nothing can be gained from him, and he is ready to come back to England, with those whom he has gone so bravely to save, the doors of the trap will close upon him, and he will be sent to end his noble life upon the guillotine."

Still Sir Andrew was silent.

"You do not trust me," she said passionately. "Oh God! cannot you see that I am in deadly earnest? Man, man," she added, while, with her tiny hands she seized the young man suddenly by the shoulders, forcing him to look straight at her, "tell me, do I look like that vilest thing on earth—a woman who would betray her own husband?"

"God forbid, Lady Blakeney," said the young man at last, "that I should attribute such evil motives to you, but—"

"But what?—tell me—Quick, man!—the very seconds are precious!"

"Will you tell me," he asked resolutely, and looking searchingly into her blue eyes, "whose hand helped to guide M. Chauvelin to the knowledge which you say he possesses?"

"Mine," she said quietly, "I own it—I will not lie to you, for I wish you to trust me absolutely. But I had no idea—how *could* I have?—of the identity of the Scarlet Pimpernel—and my brother's safety was to be my prize if I succeeded."

"In helping Chauvelin to track the Scarlet Pimpernel?"

She nodded.

"It is no use telling you how he forced my hand. Armand is more than a brother to me, and—and . . . how *could* I guess?—But we waste time, Sir Andrew—every second is precious—in the name of God!—my husband is in peril—your friend!—your comrade!—Help me to save him."

Sir Andrew felt his position to be a very awkward one. The oath he had taken before his leader and comrade was one of obedience and secrecy; and yet the beautiful woman, who was asking him to trust her, was undoubtedly in earnest; his friend and leader was equally undoubtedly in imminent danger and—

"Lady Blakeney," he said at last, "God knows you have perplexed me, so that I do not know which way my duty lies. Tell me what you wish me to do. There are nineteen of us ready to lay down our lives for the Scarlet Pimpernel if he is in danger."

"There is no need for lives just now, my friend," she said drily; "my wits and four swift horses will serve the necessary purpose. But I must know where to find him. See," she added, while her eyes filled with tears, "I have humbled myself before you, I have owned my fault to you; shall I also confess my weakness?—My husband and I have been estranged, because he did not trust me, and because I was too blind to understand. You must confess that the bandage which he put over my eyes was a very thick one. Is it small wonder that I did not see through it? But last night, after I led him unwittingly into such deadly peril, it suddenly fell from my eyes. If you will not help me, Sir Andrew, I would still strive to save my husband. I would still exert every faculty I possess for his sake; but I might be powerless, for I might arrive too late, and nothing would be left for you but lifelong remorse, and—and—for me, a broken heart."

"But, Lady Blakeney," said the young man, touched by the gentle earnestness of this exquisitely beautiful woman, "do you know that what you propose doing is man's work?—you cannot possibly journey to Calais alone. You would be running the greatest possible risks to yourself, and your chances of finding your husband now—were I to direct you ever so carefully—are infinitely remote.

"Oh, I hope there are risks!" she murmured softly, "I hope there are dangers, too!—I have so much to atone for. But I fear you are mistaken. Chauvelin's eyes are fixed upon you all, he will scarce notice me. Quick, Sir Andrew!—the coach is ready, and there is not a moment to be lost.—I *must* get to him! I *must!*" she repeated with almost savage energy, "to warn him that that man is on his track—Can't you see—can't you see, that I *must* get to him—even—even if it be too late to save him—at least—to be by his side—at the least."

"Faith, *Madame*, you must command me. Gladly would I or any of my comrades lay down our lives for your husband. If you *will* go yourself—"

"Nay, friend, do you not see that I would go mad if I let you go without me?" She stretched out her hand to him. "You *will* trust me?"

"I await your orders," he said simply.

"Listen, then. My coach is ready to take me to Dover. Do you follow me, as swiftly as horses will take you. We meet at nightfall at 'The Fisherman's Rest.' Chauvelin would avoid it, as he is known there, and I think it would be the safest. I will gladly accept your escort to Calais—as you say, I might miss Sir Percy were you to direct me ever so carefully. We'll charter a schooner at Dover and cross over during the night. Disguised, if you will agree to it, as my lacquey, you will, I think, escape detection."

"I am entirely at your service, *Madame*," rejoined the young man earnestly. "I trust to God that you will sight the *Daydream* before we reach Calais. With Chauvelin at his heels, every step the Scarlet Pimpernel takes on French soil is fraught with danger."

"God grant it, Sir Andrew. But now, farewell. We meet tonight at Dover! It will be a race between Chauvelin and me across the Channel tonight—and the prize—the life of the Scarlet Pimpernel."

He kissed her hand, and then escorted her to her chair. A quarter of an hour later she was back at the "Crown" inn, where her coach and horses were ready and waiting for her. The next moment they thundered along the London streets, and then straight on to the Dover road at maddening speed.

She had no time for despair now. She was up and doing and had no leisure to think. With Sir Andrew Ffoulkes as her companion and ally, hope had once again revived in her heart.

God would be merciful. He would not allow so appalling a crime to be committed, as the death of a brave man, through the hand of a woman who loved him, and worshipped him, and who would gladly have died for his sake.

Marguerite's thoughts flew back to him, the mysterious hero, whom she had always unconsciously loved, when his identity was still unknown to her. Laughingly, in the olden days, she used to call him the shadowy king of her heart, and now she had suddenly found that this enigmatic personality whom she had worshipped, and the man who loved her so passionately, were one and the same: what wonder that one or two happier visions began to force their way before her mind. She vaguely wondered what she would say to him when first they would stand face to face.

She had had so many anxieties, so much excitement during the past few hours, that she allowed herself the luxury of nursing these few more hopeful, brighter thoughts. Gradually the rumble of the coach wheels, with its incessant monotony, acted soothingly on her nerves: her eyes, aching with fatigue and many shed and unshed tears, closed involuntarily, and she fell into a troubled sleep.

Chapter 21

Suspense

It was late into the night when she at last reached "The Fisherman's Rest." She had done the whole journey in less than eight hours, thanks to innumerable changes of horses at the various coaching stations, for which she always paid lavishly, thus obtaining the very best and swiftest that could be had.

Her coachman, too, had been indefatigable; the promise of special and rich reward had no doubt helped to keep him up, and he had literally burned the ground beneath his mistress' coach wheels.

The arrival of Lady Blakeney in the middle of the night caused a considerable flutter at "The Fisherman's Rest." Sally jumped hastily out of bed, and Mr. Jellyband was at great pains how to make his important guest comfortable.

Both of these good folk were far too well drilled in the manners appertaining to innkeepers, to exhibit the slightest surprise at Lady Blakeney's arrival, alone, at this extraordinary hour. No doubt they thought all the more, but Marguerite was far too absorbed in the importance—the deadly earnestness—of her journey, to stop and ponder over trifles of that sort.

The coffee-room—the scene lately of the dastardly outrage on two English gentlemen—was quite deserted. Mr. Jellyband hastily relit the lamp, rekindled a cheerful bit of fire in the great hearth, and then wheeled a comfortable chair by it, into which Marguerite gratefully sank.

"Will your ladyship stay the night?" asked pretty Miss Sally, who was already busy laying a snow-white cloth on the table, preparatory to providing a simple supper for her ladyship.

"No! not the whole night," replied Marguerite. "At any rate, I shall not want any room but this, if I can have it to myself for an hour or two."

"It is at your ladyship's service," said honest Jellyband, whose rubicund face was set in its tightest folds, lest it should betray before "the quality" that boundless astonishment which the very worthy fellow had begun to feel.

"I shall be crossing over at the first turn of the tide," said Marguerite, "and in the first schooner I can get. But my coachman and men will stay the night, and probably several days longer, so I hope you will make them comfortable."

"Yes, my lady; I'll look after them. Shall Sally bring your ladyship some supper?"

"Yes, please. Put something cold on the table, and as soon as Sir Andrew Ffoulkes comes, show him in here."

"Yes, my lady."

Honest Jellyband's face now expressed distress in spite of himself. He had great regard for Sir Percy Blakeney and did not like to see his lady running away with young Sir Andrew. Of course, it was no business of his, and Mr. Jellyband was no gossip. Still, in his heart, he recollected that her ladyship was after all only one of them "furriners"; what wonder that she was immoral like the rest of them?

"Don't sit up, honest Jellyband," continued Marguerite kindly, "nor you either, Mistress Sally. Sir Andrew may be late."

Jellyband was only too willing that Sally should go to bed. He was beginning not to like these goings-on at all. Still, Lady Blakeney would pay handsomely for the accommodation, and it certainly was no business of his.

Sally arranged a simple supper of cold meat, wine, and fruit on the table, then with a respectful curtsey, she retired, wondering in her little mind why her ladyship looked so serious, when she was about to elope with her gallant.

Then commenced a period of weary waiting for Marguerite. She knew that Sir Andrew—who would have to provide himself with clothes befitting a lacquey—could not possibly reach Dover for at least a couple of hours. He was a splendid horseman of course and would make light in such an emergency of the seventy odd miles between London and Dover. He would, too, literally burn the ground beneath his horse's hoofs, but he might not always get very good remounts, and in any case, he could not have started from London until at least an hour after she did.

She had seen nothing of Chauvelin on the road. Her coachman, whom she questioned, had not seen anyone answering the description his mistress gave him of the wizened figure of the little Frenchman.

Evidently, therefore, he had been ahead of her all the time. She had not dared to question the people at the various inns, where they had stopped to change horses. She feared that Chauvelin had spies all along the route, who might overhear her questions, then outdistance her and warn her enemy of her approach.

Now she wondered at what inn he might be stopping, or whether he had had the good luck of chartering a vessel already and was now himself on the way to France. That thought gripped her at the heart as with an iron vice. If indeed she should not be too late already!

The loneliness of the room overwhelmed her; everything within was so horribly still; the ticking of the grandfather's clock—dreadfully slow and measured—was the only sound which broke this awful loneliness.

Marguerite had need of all her energy, all her steadfastness of purpose, to keep up her courage through this weary midnight waiting.

Everyone else in the house but herself must have been asleep. She had heard Sally go upstairs. Mr. Jellyband had gone to see to her coachman and men, and then had returned and taken up a position under the porch outside, just where Marguerite had first met Chauvelin about a week ago. He evidently meant to wait up for Sir Andrew Ffoulkes, but was soon overcome by sweet slumbers, for presently—in addition to the slow ticking of the clock—Marguerite could hear the monotonous and dulcet tones of the worthy fellow's breathing.

For some time now, she had realised that the beautiful warm October's day, so happily begun, had turned into a rough and cold night. She had felt very chilly and was glad of the cheerful blaze in the hearth: but gradually, as time wore on, the weather became more rough, and the sound of the great breakers against the Admiralty Pier, though some distance from the inn, came to her as the noise of muffled thunder.

The wind was becoming boisterous, rattling the leaded windows and the massive doors of the old-fashioned house: it shook the trees outside and roared down the vast chimney. Marguerite wondered if the wind would be favourable for her journey. She had no fear of the storm and would have braved worse risks sooner than delay the crossing by an hour.

A sudden commotion outside roused her from her meditations. Evidently it was Sir Andrew Ffoulkes, just arrived in mad haste, for she heard his horse's hoofs thundering on the flag-stones outside, then Mr. Jellyband's sleepy, yet cheerful tones bidding him welcome.

For a moment, then, the awkwardness of her position struck Marguerite; alone at this hour, in a place where she was well known, and having made an assignation with a young cavalier equally well known, and who arrived in disguise! What food for gossip to those mischievously inclined.

The idea struck Marguerite chiefly from its humorous side: there was such quaint contrast between the seriousness of her errand, and the construction which would naturally be put on her actions by honest Mr. Jellyband, that, for the first time since many hours, a little smile began playing round the corners of her childlike mouth, and when, presently, Sir Andrew, almost unrecognisable in his lacquey-like garb, entered the coffee-room, she was able to greet him with quite a merry laugh.

"Faith! *Monsieur*, my lacquey," she said, "I am satisfied with your appearance!"

Mr. Jellyband had followed Sir Andrew, looking strangely perplexed. The young gallant's disguise had confirmed his worst suspicions. Without a smile upon his jovial face, he drew the cork from the bottle of wine, set the chairs ready, and prepared to wait.

"Thanks, honest friend," said Marguerite, who was still smiling at the thought of what the worthy fellow must be thinking at that very moment, "we shall require nothing more; and here's for all the trouble you have been put to on our account."

She handed two or three gold pieces to Jellyband, who took them respectfully, and with becoming gratitude.

"Stay, Lady Blakeney," interposed Sir Andrew, as Jellyband was about to retire, "I am afraid we shall require something more of my friend Jelly's hospitality. I am sorry to say we cannot cross over tonight."

"Not cross over tonight?" she repeated in amazement. "But we must, Sir Andrew, we must! There can be no question of cannot, and whatever it may cost, we must get a vessel tonight."

But the young man shook his head sadly.

"I am afraid it is not a question of cost, Lady Blakeney. There is a nasty storm blowing from France, the wind is dead against us, we cannot possibly sail until it has changed."

Marguerite became deadly pale. She had not foreseen this. Nature herself was playing her a horrible, cruel trick. Percy was in danger, and she could not go to him, because the wind happened to blow from the coast of France.

"But we must go!—we must!" she repeated with strange, persistent energy, "you know, we must go!—can't you find a way?"

"I have been down to the shore already," he said, "and had a talk to one or two skippers. It is quite impossible to set sail tonight, so every sailor assured me. No one," he added, looking significantly at Marguerite, "*No one* could possibly put out of Dover tonight."

Marguerite at once understood what he meant. *No one* included

Chauvelin as well as herself. She nodded pleasantly to Jellyband.

"Well, then, I must resign myself," she said to him. "Have you a room for me?"

"Oh, yes, your ladyship. A nice, bright, airy room. I'll see to it at once.—And there is another one for Sir Andrew—both quite ready."

"That's brave now, mine honest Jelly," said Sir Andrew, gaily, and clapping his worth host vigorously on the back. "You unlock both those rooms and leave our candles here on the dresser. I vow you are dead with sleep, and her ladyship must have some supper before she retires. There, have no fear, friend of the rueful countenance, her ladyship's visit, though at this unusual hour, is a great honour to thy house, and Sir Percy Blakeney will reward thee doubly, if thou seest well to her privacy and comfort."

Sir Andrew had no doubt guessed the many conflicting doubts and fears which raged in honest Jellyband's head; and, as he was a gallant gentleman, he tried by this brave hint to allay some of the worthy innkeeper's suspicions. He had the satisfaction of seeing that he had partially succeeded. Jellyband's rubicund countenance brightened somewhat, at the mention of Sir Percy's name.

"I'll go and see to it at once, sir," he said with alacrity, and with less frigidity in his manner. "Has her ladyship everything she wants for supper?"

"Everything, thanks, honest friend, and as I am famished and dead with fatigue, I pray you see to the rooms."

"Now tell me," she said eagerly, as soon as Jellyband had gone from the room, "tell me all your news."

"There is nothing else much to tell you, Lady Blakeney," replied the young man. "The storm makes it quite impossible for any vessel to put out of Dover this tide. But, what seems to you at first a terrible calamity is really a blessing in disguise. If we cannot cross over to France tonight, Chauvelin is in the same quandary.

"He may have left before the storm broke out."

"God grant he may," said Sir Andrew, merrily, "for very likely then he'll have been driven out of his course! Who knows? He may now even be lying at the bottom of the sea, for there is a furious storm raging, and it will fare ill with all small craft which happen to be out. But I fear me we cannot build our hopes upon the shipwreck of that cunning devil, and of all his murderous plans. The sailors I spoke to, all assured me that no schooner had put out of Dover for several hours: on the other hand, I ascertained that a stranger had arrived by coach this afternoon, and had, like myself, made some inquiries about crossing over to France.

"Then Chauvelin is still in Dover?"

"Undoubtedly. Shall I go waylay him and run my sword through him? That were indeed the quickest way out of the difficulty."

"Nay! Sir Andrew, do not jest! Alas! I have often since last night caught myself wishing for that fiend's death. But what you suggest is impossible! The laws of this country do not permit of murder! It is only in our beautiful France that wholesale slaughter is done lawfully, in the name of Liberty and of brotherly love."

Sir Andrew had persuaded her to sit down to the table, to partake of some supper and to drink a little wine. This enforced rest of at least twelve hours, until the next tide, was sure to be terribly difficult to bear in the state of intense excitement in which she was. Obedient in these small matters like a child, Marguerite tried to eat and drink.

Sir Andrew, with that profound sympathy born in all those who are in love, made her almost happy by talking to her about her husband. He recounted to her some of the daring escapes the brave Scarlet Pimpernel had contrived for the poor French fugitives, whom a relentless and bloody revolution was driving out of their country. He made her eyes glow with enthusiasm by telling her of his bravery, his ingenuity, his resourcefulness, when it meant snatching the lives of men, women, and even children from beneath the very edge of that murderous, ever-ready guillotine.

He even made her smile quite merrily by telling her of the Scarlet Pimpernel's quaint and many disguises, through which he had baffled the strictest watch set against him at the barricades of Paris. This last time, the escape of the Comtesse de Tournay and her children had been a veritable masterpiece—Blakeney disguised as a hideous old market-woman, in filthy cap and straggling grey locks, was a sight fit to make the gods laugh.

Marguerite laughed heartily as Sir Andrew tried to describe Blakeney's appearance, whose gravest difficulty always consisted in his great height, which in France made disguise doubly difficult.

Thus, an hour wore on. There were many more to spend in enforced inactivity in Dover. Marguerite rose from the table with an impatient sigh. She looked forward with dread to the night in the bed upstairs, with terribly anxious thoughts to keep her company, and the howling of the storm to help chase sleep away.

She wondered where Percy was now. The *Daydream* was a strong, well-built sea-going yacht. Sir Andrew had expressed the opinion that no doubt she had got in the lee of the wind before the storm broke out, or else perhaps had not ventured into the open at all but was lying quietly at Gravesend.

Briggs was an expert skipper, and Sir Percy handled a schooner as well as any master mariner. There was no danger for them from the storm.

It was long past midnight when at last Marguerite retired to rest. As she had feared, sleep sedulously avoided her eyes. Her thoughts were of the blackest during these long, weary hours, whilst that incessant storm raged which was keeping her away from Percy. The sound of the distant breakers made her heart ache with melancholy. She was in the mood when the sea has a saddening effect upon the nerves. It is only when we are very happy, that we can bear to gaze merrily upon the vast and limitless expanse of water, rolling on and on with such persistent, irritating monotony, to the accompaniment of our thoughts, whether grave or gay. When they are gay, the waves echo their gaiety; but when they are sad, then every breaker, as it rolls, seems to bring additional sadness, and to speak to us of hopelessness and of the pettiness of all our joys.

Chapter 22
Calais

The weariest nights, the longest days, sooner or later must perforce come to an end.

Marguerite had spent over fifteen hours in such acute mental torture as well-nigh drove her crazy. After a sleepless night, she rose early, wild with excitement, dying to start on her journey, terrified lest further obstacles lay in her way. She rose before anyone else in the house was astir, so frightened was she, lest she should miss the one golden opportunity of making a start.

When she came downstairs, she found Sir Andrew Ffoulkes sitting in the coffee-room. He had been out half an hour earlier, and had gone to the Admiralty Pier, only to find that neither the French packet nor any privately chartered vessel could put out of Dover yet. The storm was then at its fullest, and the tide was on the turn. If the wind did not abate or change, they would perforce have to wait another ten or twelve hours until the next tide, before a start could be made. And the storm had not abated, the wind had not changed, and the tide was rapidly drawing out.

Marguerite felt the sickness of despair when she heard this melancholy news. Only the most firm resolution kept her from totally breaking down, and thus adding to the young man's anxiety, which evidently had become very keen.

Though he tried to hide it, Marguerite could see that Sir Andrew was just as anxious as she was to reach his comrade and friend. This enforced inactivity was terrible to them both.

How they spent that wearisome day at Dover, Marguerite could never afterwards say. She was in terror of showing herself, lest Chauvelin's spies happened to be about, so she had a private sitting-room, and she and Sir Andrew sat there hour after hour, trying to take, at long intervals, some perfunctory meals, which little Sally would bring them, with nothing to do but to think, to conjecture, and only occasionally to hope.

The storm had abated just too late; the tide was by then too far out to allow a vessel to put off to sea. The wind had changed and was settling down to a comfortable north-westerly breeze—a veritable godsend for a speedy passage across to France.

And there those two waited, wondering if the hour would ever come when they could finally make a start. There had been one happy interval in this long weary day, and that was when Sir Andrew went down once again to the pier, and presently came back to tell Marguerite that he had chartered a quick schooner, whose skipper was ready to put to sea the moment the tide was favourable.

From that moment the hours seemed less wearisome; there was less hopelessness in the waiting; and at last, at five o'clock in the afternoon, Marguerite, closely veiled and followed by Sir Andrew Ffoulkes, who, in the guise of her lacquey, was carrying a number of impedimenta, found her way down to the pier.

Once on board, the keen, fresh sea-air revived her, the breeze was just strong enough to nicely swell the sails of the *Foam Crest*, as she cut her way merrily towards the open.

The sunset was glorious after the storm, and Marguerite, as she watched the white cliffs of Dover gradually disappearing from view, felt more at peace and once more almost hopeful.

Sir Andrew was full of kind attentions, and she felt how lucky she had been to have him by her side in this, her great trouble.

Gradually the grey coast of France began to emerge from the fast-gathering evening mists. One or two lights could be seen flickering, and the spires of several churches to rise out of the surrounding haze.

Half an hour later Marguerite had landed upon French shore. She was back in that country where at this very moment men slaughtered their fellow-creatures by the hundreds and sent innocent women and children in thousands to the block.

The very aspect of the country and its people, even in this remote sea-coast town, spoke of that seething revolution, three hundred miles away, in beautiful Paris, now rendered hideous by the constant flow of the blood of her noblest sons, by the wailing of the widows, and the cries of fatherless children.

The men all wore red caps—in various stages of cleanliness—but all with the tricolour cockade pinned on the left-side. Marguerite noticed with a shudder that, instead of the laughing, merry countenance habitual to her own countrymen, their faces now invariably wore a look of sly distrust.

Every man nowadays was a spy upon his fellows: the most innocent word uttered in jest might at any time be brought up as a proof of aristocratic tendencies, or of treachery against the people. Even the women went about with a curious look of fear and of hate lurking in their brown eyes; and all watched Marguerite as she stepped on shore, followed by Sir Andrew, and murmured as she passed along: "*Sacrées Aristos!*" or else "*Sacrées Anglais!*"

Otherwise their presence excited no further comment. Calais, even in those days, was in constant business communication with England, and English merchants were often seen on this coast. It was well known that in view of the heavy duties in England, a vast deal of French wines and brandies were smuggled across. This pleased the French *bourgeois* immensely; he liked to see the English Government and the English king, both of whom he hated, cheated out of their revenues; and an English smuggler was always a welcome guest at the tumble-down taverns of Calais and Boulogne.

So, perhaps, as Sir Andrew gradually directed Marguerite through the tortuous streets of Calais, many of the population, who turned with an oath to look at the strangers clad in English fashion, thought that they were bent on purchasing dutiable articles for their own fog-ridden country, and gave them no more than a passing thought.

Marguerite, however, wondered how her husband's tall, massive figure could have passed through Calais unobserved: she marvelled what disguise he assumed to do his noble work, without exciting too much attention.

Without exchanging more than a few words, Sir Andrew was leading her right across the town, to the other side from that where they had landed, and the way towards Cap Gris Nez. The streets were narrow, tortuous, and mostly evil-smelling, with a mixture of stale fish and damp cellar odours. There had been heavy rain here during the storm last night, and sometimes Marguerite sank ankle-deep in the mud, for the roads were not lighted save by the occasional glimmer from a lamp inside a house.

But she did not heed any of these petty discomforts: "We may meet Blakeney at the 'Chat Gris,'" Sir Andrew had said, when they landed, and she was walking as if on a carpet of rose-leaves, for she was going to meet him almost at once.

At last they reached their destination. Sir Andrew evidently knew the road, for he had walked unerringly in the dark, and had not asked his way from anyone. It was too dark then for Marguerite to notice the outside aspect of this house. The "Chat Gris," as Sir Andrew had called it, was evidently a small wayside inn on the outskirts of Calais, and on the way to Gris Nez. It lay some little distance from the coast, for the sound of the sea seemed to come from afar.

Sir Andrew knocked at the door with the knob of his cane, and from within Marguerite heard a sort of grunt and the muttering of a number of oaths. Sir Andrew knocked again, this time more peremptorily: more oaths were heard, and then shuffling steps seemed to draw near the door. Presently this was thrown open, and Marguerite found herself on the threshold of the most dilapidated, most squalid room she had ever seen in all her life.

The paper, such as it was, was hanging from the walls in strips; there did not seem to be a single piece of furniture in the room that could, by the wildest stretch of imagination, be called "whole." Most of the chairs had broken backs, others had no seats to them, one corner of the table was propped up with a bundle of faggots, there where the fourth leg had been broken.

In one corner of the room there was a huge hearth, over which hung a stock-pot, with a not altogether unpalatable odour of hot soup emanating therefrom. On one side of the room, high up in the wall, there was a species of loft, before which hung a tattered blue-and-white checked curtain. A rickety set of steps led up to this loft.

On the great bare walls, with their colourless paper, all stained with varied filth, there were chalked up at intervals in great bold characters, the words: "*Liberté—Egalité—Fraternité*."

The whole of this sordid abode was dimly lighted by an evil-smelling oil-lamp, which hung from the rickety rafters of the ceiling. It all looked so horribly squalid, so dirty and uninviting, that Marguerite hardly dared to cross the threshold.

Sir Andrew, however, had stepped unhesitatingly forward.

"English travellers, *citoyen*!" he said boldly, and speaking in French.

The individual who had come to the door in response to Sir Andrew's knock, and who, presumably, was the owner of this squalid abode, was an elderly, heavily built peasant, dressed in a dirty blue blouse, heavy sabots, from which wisps of straw protruded all round, shabby blue trousers, and the inevitable red cap with the tricolour cockade, that proclaimed his momentary political views. He carried a short wooden pipe, from which the odour of rank tobacco emanated. He looked with some suspicion and a great deal of contempt at the two travellers, muttering "*Sacrées Anglais!*" and spat upon the ground to further show his independence of spirit, but, nevertheless, he stood aside to let them enter, no doubt well aware that these same *Sacrées Anglais* always had well-filled purses.

"Oh, lud!" said Marguerite, as she advanced into the room, holding her handkerchief to her dainty nose, "what a dreadful hole! Are you sure this is the place?"

"Aye! 'tis the place, sure enough," replied the young man as, with his lace-edged, fashionable handkerchief, he dusted a chair for Marguerite to sit on; "but I vow I never saw a more villainous hole."

"Faith!" she said, looking round with some curiosity and a great deal of horror at the dilapidated walls, the broken chairs, the rickety table, "it certainly does not look inviting."

The landlord of the "Chat Gris"—by name, Brogard—had taken no further notice of his guests; he concluded that presently they would order supper, and in the meanwhile it was not for a free citizen to show deference, or even courtesy, to anyone, however smartly they might be dressed.

By the hearth sat a huddled-up figure clad, seemingly, mostly in rags: that figure was apparently a woman, although even that would have been hard to distinguish, except for the cap, which had once been white, and for what looked like the semblance of a petticoat. She was sitting mumbling to herself, and from time to time stirring the brew in her stock-pot.

"Hey, my friend!" said Sir Andrew at last, "we should like some supper—The *citoyenne* there," he added, "is concocting some delicious soup, I'll warrant, and my mistress has not tasted food for several hours."

It took Brogard some few minutes to consider the question. A free citizen does not respond too readily to the wishes of those who happen to require something of him.

"*Sacrées Aristos!*" he murmured, and once more spat upon the ground.

Then he went very slowly up to a dresser which stood in a corner of the room; from this he took an old pewter soup-tureen and slowly, and without a word, he handed it to his better-half, who, in the same silence, began filling the tureen with the soup out of her stock-pot.

Marguerite had watched all these preparations with absolute horror; were it not for the earnestness of her purpose, she would incontinently have fled from this abode of dirt and evil smells.

"Faith! our host and hostess are not cheerful people," said Sir Andrew, seeing the look of horror on Marguerite's face. "I would I could offer you a more hearty and more appetising meal—but I think you will find the soup eatable and the wine good; these people wallow in dirt, but live well as a rule."

"Nay! I pray you, Sir Andrew," she said gently, "be not anxious about me. My mind is scarce inclined to dwell on thoughts of supper."

Brogard was slowly pursuing his gruesome preparations; he had placed a couple of spoons, also two glasses on the table, both of which Sir Andrew took the precaution of wiping carefully.

Brogard had also produced a bottle of wine and some bread, and Marguerite made an effort to draw her chair to the table and to make some pretence at eating. Sir Andrew, as befitting his *rôle* of lacquey, stood behind her chair.

"Nay, *Madame*, I pray you," he said, seeing that Marguerite seemed quite unable to eat, "I beg of you to try and swallow some food—remember you have need of all your strength."

The soup certainly was not bad; it smelt and tasted good. Marguerite might have enjoyed it, but for the horrible surroundings. She broke the bread, however, and drank some of the wine.

"Nay, Sir Andrew," she said, "I do not like to see you standing. You have need of food just as much as I have. This creature will only think that I am an eccentric Englishwoman eloping with her lacquey, if you'll sit down and partake of this semblance of supper beside me."

Indeed, Brogard having placed what was strictly necessary upon the table, seemed not to trouble himself any further about his guests. The Mére Brogard had quietly shuffled out of the room, and the man stood and lounged about, smoking his evil-smelling pipe, sometimes under Marguerite's very nose, as any free-born citizen who was anybody's equal should do.

"Confound the brute!" said Sir Andrew, with native British wrath, as Brogard leant up against the table, smoking and looking down superciliously at these two *Sacrées Anglais.*

"In Heaven's name, man," admonished Marguerite, hurriedly, seeing that Sir Andrew, with British-born instinct, was ominously clenching his fist, "remember that you are in France, and that in this year of grace this is the temper of the people."

"I'd like to scrag the brute!" muttered Sir Andrew, savagely.

He had taken Marguerite's advice and sat next to her at table, and they were both making noble efforts to deceive one another, by pretending to eat and drink.

"I pray you," said Marguerite, "keep the creature in a good temper, so that he may answer the questions we must put to him."

"I'll do my best, but, begad! I'd sooner scrag him than question him. Hey! my friend," he said pleasantly in French, and tapping Brogard lightly on the shoulder, "do you see many of our quality along these parts? Many English travellers, I mean?"

Brogard looked round at him, over his near shoulder, puffed away at his pipe for a moment or two as he was in no hurry, then muttered,—

"*Heu!*—sometimes!"

"Ah!" said Sir Andrew, carelessly, "English travellers always know where they can get good wine, eh! my friend?—Now, tell me, my lady was desiring to know if by any chance you happen to have seen a great friend of hers, an English gentleman, who often comes to Calais on business; he is tall, and recently was on his way to Paris—my lady hoped to have met him in Calais."

Marguerite tried not to look at Brogard, lest she should betray before him the burning anxiety with which she waited for his reply. But a free-born French citizen is never in any hurry to answer questions: Brogard took his time, then he said very slowly,—

"Tall Englishman?—Today!—Yes."

"Yes, today," muttered Brogard, sullenly. Then he quietly took Sir Andrew's hat from a chair close by, put it on his own head, tugged at his dirty blouse, and generally tried to express in pantomime that the individual in question wore very fine clothes. "*Sacrée Aristo!*" he muttered, "that tall Englishman!"

Marguerite could scarce repress a scream.

"It's Sir Percy right enough," she murmured, "and not even in disguise!"

She smiled, in the midst of all her anxiety and through her gathering tears, at the thought of "the ruling passion strong in death"; of Percy running into the wildest, maddest dangers, with the latest-cut coat upon his back, and the laces of his jabot unruffled.

"Oh! the foolhardiness of it!" she sighed. "Quick, Sir Andrew! ask the man when he went."

"Ah yes, my friend," said Sir Andrew, addressing Brogard, with the same assumption of carelessness, "my lord always wears beautiful clothes; the tall Englishman you saw, was certainly my lady's friend. And he has gone, you say?"

"He went—yes—but he's coming back—here—he ordered supper—"

Sir Andrew put his hand with a quick gesture of warning upon Marguerite's arm; it came none too soon, for the next moment her wild, mad joy would have betrayed her. He was safe and well, was coming back here presently, she would see him in a few moments perhaps—Oh! the wildness of her joy seemed almost more than she could bear.

"Here!" she said to Brogard, who seemed suddenly to have been transformed in her eyes into some heaven-born messenger of bliss. "Here!—did you say the English gentleman was coming back here?"

The heaven-born messenger of bliss spat upon the floor, to express his contempt for all and sundry *aristos*, who chose to haunt the "Chat Gris."

"*Heu!*" he muttered, "he ordered supper—he will come back . . . *Sacrées Anglais!*" he added, by way of protest against all this fuss for a mere Englishman.

"But where is he now?—Do you know?" she asked eagerly, placing her dainty white hand upon the dirty sleeve of his blue blouse.

"He went to get a horse and cart," said Brogard, laconically, as with a surly gesture, he shook off from his arm that pretty hand which princes had been proud to kiss.

"At what time did he go?"

But Brogard had evidently had enough of these questionings. He did not think that it was fitting for a citizen—who was the equal of anybody—to be thus catechised by these *Sacrées Aristos*, even though they were rich English ones. It was distinctly more fitting to his new-born dignity to be as rude as possible; it was a sure sign of servility to meekly reply to civil questions.

"I don't know," he said surlily. "I have said enough, *voyons, les aristos!* —He came today. He ordered supper. He went out.—He'll come back. *Voila!*"

And with this parting assertion of his rights as a citizen and a free man, to be as rude as he well pleased, Brogard shuffled out of the room, banging the door after him.

CHAPTER 23

Hope

"Faith, *Madame!*" said Sir Andrew, seeing that Marguerite seemed desirous to call her surly host back again, "I think we'd better leave him alone. We shall not get anything more out of him, and we might arouse his suspicions. One never knows what spies may be lurking around these God-forsaken places."

"What care I?" she replied lightly, "now I know that my husband is safe, and that I shall see him almost directly!"

"Hush!" he said in genuine alarm, for she had talked quite loudly, in the fulness of her glee, "the very walls have ears in France, these days."

He rose quickly from the table, and walked round the bare, squalid room, listening attentively at the door, through which Brogard has just disappeared, and whence only muttered oaths and shuffling footsteps could be heard. He also ran up the rickety steps that led to the attic, to assure himself that there were no spies of Chauvelin's about the place.

"Are we alone, *Monsieur*, my lacquey?" said Marguerite, gaily, as the young man once more sat down beside her. "May we talk?"

"As cautiously as possible!" he entreated.

"Faith, man! but you wear a glum face! As for me, I could dance with joy! Surely there is no longer any cause for fear. Our boat is on the beach, the *Foam Crest* not two miles out at sea, and my husband will be here, under this very roof, within the next half hour perhaps. Sure! there is naught to hinder us. Chauvelin and his gang have not yet arrived."

"Nay, madam! that I fear we do not know."

"What do you mean?"

"He was at Dover at the same time that we were."

"Held up by the same storm, which kept us from starting."

"Exactly. But—I did not speak of it before, for I feared to alarm you—I saw him on the beach not five minutes before we embarked. At least, I swore to myself at the time that it was himself; he was disguised as a *curé*, so that Satan, his own guardian, would scarce have known him. But I heard him then, bargaining for a vessel to take him swiftly to Calais; and he must have set sail less than an hour after we did."

Marguerite's face had quickly lost its look of joy. The terrible danger in which Percy stood, now that he was actually on French soil, became suddenly and horribly clear to her. Chauvelin was close upon his heels; here in Calais, the astute diplomatist was all-powerful; a word from him and Percy could be tracked and arrested and—

Every drop of blood seemed to freeze in her veins; not even during the moments of her wildest anguish in England had she so completely realised the imminence of the peril in which her husband stood. Chauvelin had sworn to bring the Scarlet Pimpernel to the guillotine, and now the daring plotter, whose anonymity hitherto had been his safeguard, stood revealed through her own hand, to his most bitter, most relentless enemy.

Chauvelin—when he waylaid Lord Tony and Sir Andrew Ffoulkes in the coffee-room of "The Fisherman's Rest"—had obtained possession of all the plans of this latest expedition. Armand St. Just, the Comte de Tournay and other fugitive royalists were to have met the Scarlet Pimpernel—or rather, as it had been originally arranged, two of his emissaries—on this day, the 2nd of October, at a place evidently known to the league, and vaguely alluded to as the "Père Blanchard's hut."

Armand, whose connection with the Scarlet Pimpernel and disavowal of the brutal policy of the Reign of Terror was still unknown to his countryman, had left England a little more than a week ago, carrying with him the necessary instructions, which would enable him to meet the other fugitives and to convey them to this place of safety.

This much Marguerite had fully understood from the first, and Sir Andrew Ffoulkes had confirmed her surmises. She knew, too, that when Sir Percy realised that his own plans and his directions to his lieutenants had been stolen by Chauvelin, it was too late to communicate with Armand, or to send fresh instructions to the fugitives.

They would, of necessity, be at the appointed time and place, not knowing how grave was the danger which now awaited their brave rescuer.

Blakeney, who as usual had planned and organised the whole expedition, would not allow any of his younger comrades to run the risk of almost certain capture. Hence his hurried note to them at Lord Grenville's ball—

"Start myself tomorrow—alone."

And now with his identity known to his most bitter enemy, his every step would be dogged, the moment he set foot in France. He would be tracked by Chauvelin's emissaries, followed until he reached that mysterious hut where the fugitives were waiting for him, and there the trap would be closed on him and on them.

There was but one hour—the hour's start which Marguerite and Sir Andrew had of their enemy—in which to warn Percy of the imminence of his danger, and to persuade him to give up the foolhardy expedition, which could only end in his own death.

But there *was* that one hour.

"Chauvelin knows of this inn, from the papers he stole," said Sir Andrew, earnestly, "and on landing will make straight for it."

"He has not landed yet," she said, "we have an hour's start on him, and Percy will be here directly. We shall be mid-Channel ere Chauvelin has realised that we have slipped through his fingers."

She spoke excitedly and eagerly, wishing to infuse into her young friend some of that buoyant hope which still clung to her heart. But he shook his head sadly.

"Silent again, Sir Andrew?" she said with some impatience. "Why do you shake your head and look so glum?"

"Faith, Madame," he replied, "'tis only because in making your rose-coloured plans, you are forgetting the most important factor."

"What in the world do you mean?—I am forgetting nothing. . . . What factor do you mean?" she added with more impatience.

"It stands six foot odd high," replied Sir Andrew, quietly, "and hath name Percy Blakeney."

"I don't understand," she murmured.

"Do you think that Blakeney would leave Calais without having accomplished what he set out to do?"

"You mean—?"

"There's the old Comte de Tournay—"

"The *Comte*—?" she murmured.

"And St. Just—and others—"

"My brother!" she said with a heart-broken sob of anguish. "Heaven help me, but I fear I had forgotten."

"Fugitives as they are, these men at this moment await with perfect confidence and unshaken faith the arrival of the Scarlet Pimpernel, who has pledged his honour to take them safely across the Channel."

Indeed, she had forgotten! With the sublime selfishness of a woman who loves with her whole heart, she had in the last twenty-four hours had no thought save for him. His precious, noble life, his danger—he, the loved one, the brave hero, he alone dwelt in her mind.

"My brother!" she murmured, as one by one the heavy tears gathered in her eyes, as memory came back to her of Armand, the companion and darling of her childhood, the man for whom she had committed the deadly sin, which had so hopelessly imperilled her brave husband's life.

"Sir Percy Blakeney would not be the trusted, honoured leader of a score of English gentlemen," said Sir Andrew, proudly, "if he abandoned those who placed their trust in him. As for breaking his word, the very thought is preposterous!"

There was silence for a moment or two. Marguerite had buried her face in her hands and was letting the tears slowly trickle through her trembling fingers. The young man said nothing; his heart ached for this beautiful woman in her awful grief. All along he had felt the terrible *impasse* in which her own rash act had plunged them all. He knew his friend and leader so well, with his reckless daring, his mad bravery, his worship of his own word of honour. Sir Andrew knew that Blakeney would brave any danger, run the wildest risks sooner than break it, and with Chauvelin at his very heels, would make a final attempt, however desperate, to rescue those who trusted in him.

"Faith, Sir Andrew," said Marguerite at last, making brave efforts to dry her tears, "you are right, and I would not now shame myself by trying to dissuade him from doing his duty. As you say, I should plead in vain. God grant him strength and ability," she added fervently and resolutely, "to outwit his pursuers. He will not refuse to take you with him, perhaps, when he starts on his noble work; between you, you will have cunning as well as valour! God guard you both! In the meanwhile, I think we should lose no time. I still believe that his safety depends upon his knowing that Chauvelin is on his track."

"Undoubtedly. He has wonderful resources at his command. As soon as he is aware of his danger he will exercise more caution: his ingenuity is a veritable miracle."

"Then, what say you to a voyage of reconnaissance in the village whilst I wait here against his coming!—You might come across Percy's track and thus save valuable time. If you find him, tell him to beware!—his bitterest enemy is on his heels!"

"But this is such a villainous hole for you to wait in."

"Nay, that I do not mind!—But you might ask our surly host if he could let me wait in another room, where I could be safer from the prying eyes of any chance traveller. Offer him some ready money, so that he should not fail to give me word the moment the tall Englishman returns."

She spoke quite calmly, even cheerfully now, thinking out her plans, ready for the worst if need be; she would show no more weakness, she would prove herself worthy of him, who was about to give his life for the sake of his fellow-men.

Sir Andrew obeyed her without further comment. Instinctively he felt that hers now was the stronger mind; he was willing to give himself over to her guidance, to become the hand, whilst she was the directing hand.

He went to the door of the inner room, through which Brogard and his wife had disappeared before, and knocked; as usual, he was answered by a salvo of muttered oaths.

"Hey! friend Brogard!" said the man peremptorily, "my lady friend would wish to rest here awhile. Could you give her the use of another room? She would wish to be alone."

He took some money out of his pocket and allowed it to jingle significantly in his hand. Brogard had opened the door, and listened, with his usual surly apathy, to the young man's request. At the sight of the gold, however, his lazy attitude relaxed slightly; he took his pipe from his mouth and shuffled into the room.

He then pointed over his shoulder at the attic up in the wall.

"She can wait up there!" he said with a grunt. "It's comfortable, and I have no other room."

"Nothing could be better," said Marguerite in English; she at once realised the advantages such a position hidden from view would give her. "Give him the money, Sir Andrew; I shall be quite happy up there and can see everything without being seen."

She nodded to Brogard, who condescended to go up to the attic, and to shake up the straw that lay on the floor.

"May I entreat you, madam, to do nothing rash," said Sir Andrew, as Marguerite prepared in her turn to ascend the rickety flight of steps. "Remember this place is infested with spies. Do not, I beg of you, reveal yourself to Sir Percy, unless you are absolutely certain that you are alone with him."

Even as he spoke, he felt how unnecessary was this caution: Marguerite was as calm, as clear-headed as any man. There was no fear of her doing anything that was rash.

"Nay," she said with a slight attempt at cheerfulness, "that I can faithfully promise you. I would not jeopardise my husband's life, nor yet his plans, by speaking to him before strangers. Have no fear, I will watch my opportunity, and serve him in the manner I think he needs it most."

Brogard had come down the steps again, and Marguerite was ready to go up to her safe retreat.

"I dare not kiss your hand, madam," said Sir Andrew, as she began to mount the steps, "since I am your lacquey, but I pray you be of good cheer. If I do not come across Blakeney in half an hour, I shall return, expecting to find him here."

"Yes, that will be best. We can afford to wait for half an hour. Chauvelin cannot possibly be here before that. God grant that either you or I may have seen Percy by then. Good luck to you, friend! Have no fear for me."

Lightly she mounted the rickety wooden steps that led to the attic. Brogard was taking no further heed of her. She could make herself comfortable there or not as she chose. Sir Andrew watched her until she had reached the curtains across, and the young man noted that she was singularly well placed there, for seeing and hearing, whilst remaining unobserved.

He had paid Brogard well; the surly old innkeeper would have no object in betraying her. Then Sir Andrew prepared to go. At the door he turned once again and looked up at the loft. Through the ragged curtains Marguerite's sweet face was peeping down at him, and the young man rejoiced to see that it looked serene, and even gently smiling. With a final nod of farewell to her, he walked out into the night.

Chapter 24

The Death-Trap

The next quarter of an hour went by swiftly and noiselessly. In the room downstairs, Brogard had for a while busied himself with clearing the table and re-arranging it for another guest.

It was because she watched these preparations that Marguerite found the time slipping by more pleasantly. It was for Percy that this semblance of supper was being got ready. Evidently Brogard had a certain amount of respect for the tall Englishman, as he seemed to take some trouble in making the place look a trifle less uninviting than it had done before.

He even produced, from some hidden recess in the old dresser, what actually looked like a table-cloth; and when he spread it out, and saw it was full of holes, he shook his head dubiously for a while, then was at much pains so to spread it over the table as to hide most of its blemishes.

Then he got out a serviette, also old and ragged, but possessing some measure of cleanliness, and with this he carefully wiped the glasses, spoons and plates, which he put on the table.

Marguerite could not help smiling to herself as she watched all these preparations, which Brogard accomplished to an accompaniment of muttered oaths. Clearly the great height and bulk of the Englishman, or perhaps the weight of his fist, had overawed this free-born citizen of France, or he would never have been at such trouble for any *Sacré aristo*.

When the table was set—such as it was—Brogard surveyed it with evident satisfaction. He then dusted one of the chairs with the corner of his blouse, gave a stir to the stock-pot, threw a fresh bundle of faggots on to the fire, and slouched out of the room.

Marguerite was left alone with her reflections. She had spread her travelling cloak over the straw, and was sitting fairly comfortably, as the straw was fresh, and the evil odours from below came up to her only in a modified form.

But, momentarily, she was almost happy; happy because, when she peeped through the tattered curtains, she could see a rickety chair, a torn table-cloth, a glass, a plate and a spoon; that was all. But those mute and ugly things seemed to say to her that they were waiting for Percy; that soon, very soon, he would be here, that the squalid room being still empty, they would be alone together.

That thought was so heavenly, that Marguerite closed her eyes in order to shut out everything but that. In a few minutes she would be alone with him; she would run down the ladder and let him see her; then he would take her in his arms, and she would let him see that, after that, she would gladly die for him, and with him, for earth could hold no greater happiness than that.

And then what would happen? She could not even remotely conjecture. She knew, of course, that Sir Andrew was right, that Percy would do everything he had set out to accomplish; that she—now she was here—could do nothing, beyond warning him to be cautious, since Chauvelin himself was on his track. After having cautioned him, she would perforce have to see him go off upon the terrible and daring mission; she could not even with a word or look, attempt to keep him back. She would have to obey, whatever he told her to do, even perhaps have to efface herself, and wait, in indescribable agony, whilst he, perhaps, went to his death.

But even that seemed less terrible to bear than the thought that he should never know how much she loved him—that at any rate would be spared her; the squalid room itself, which seemed to be waiting for him, told her that he would be here soon.

Suddenly her over-sensitive ears caught the sound of distant footsteps drawing near; her heart gave a wild leap of joy! Was it Percy at last? No! the step did not seem quite as long, nor quite as firm as his; she also thought that she could hear two distinct sets of footsteps. Yes! that was it! two men were coming this way. Two strangers perhaps, to get a drink, or . . .

But she had not time to conjecture, for presently there was a peremptory call at the door, and the next moment it was violently open from the outside, whilst a rough, commanding voice shouted,—

"Hey! Citoyen Brogard! *Hola!*"

Marguerite could not see the newcomers, but, through a hole in one of the curtains, she could observe one portion of the room below.

She heard Brogard's shuffling footsteps, as he came out of the inner room, muttering his usual string of oaths. On seeing the strangers, however, he paused in the middle of the room, well within range of Marguerite's vision, looked at them, with even more withering contempt than he had bestowed upon his former guests, and muttered, "*Sacrées Soutane!*"

Marguerite's heart seemed all at once to stop beating; her eyes, large and dilated, had fastened on one of the newcomers, who, at this point, had taken a quick step forward towards Brogard. He was dressed in the soutane, broad-brimmed hat and buckled shoes habitual to the French *curé*, but as he stood opposite the innkeeper, he threw open his *soutane* for a moment, displaying the tri-colour scarf of officialism, which sight immediately had the effect of transforming Brogard's attitude of contempt, into one of cringing obsequiousness.

It was the sight of this French *curé*, which seemed to freeze the very blood in Marguerite's veins. She could not see his face, which was shaded by his broad-brimmed hat, but she recognised the thin, bony hands, the slight stoop, the whole gait of the man! It was Chauvelin!

The horror of the situation struck her as with a physical blow; the awful disappointment, the dread of what was to come, made her very senses reel, and she needed almost superhuman effort, not to fall senseless beneath it all.

"A plate of soup and a bottle of wine," said Chauvelin imperiously to Brogard, "then clear out of here—understand? I want to be alone."

Silently, and without any muttering this time, Brogard obeyed. Chauvelin sat down at the table, which had been prepared for the tall Englishman, and the innkeeper busied himself obsequiously round him, dishing up the soup and pouring out the wine. The man who had entered with Chauvelin and whom Marguerite could not see, stood waiting close by the door.

At a brusque sign from Chauvelin, Brogard had hurried back to the inner room, and the former now beckoned to the man who had accompanied him.

In him Marguerite at once recognised Desgas, Chauvelin's secretary and confidential factotum, whom she had often seen in Paris, in days gone by. He crossed the room, and for a moment or two listened attentively at the Brogards' door. "Not listening?" asked Chauvelin, curtly.

"No, *citoyen*."

For a moment Marguerite dreaded lest Chauvelin should order Desgas to search the place; what would happen if she were to be discovered, she hardly dared to imagine. Fortunately, however, Chauvelin seemed more impatient to talk to his secretary than afraid of spies, for he called Desgas quickly back to his side.

"The English schooner?" he asked.

"She was lost sight of at sundown, *citoyen*," replied Desgas, "but was then making west, towards Cap Gris Nez."

"Ah!—good!—" muttered Chauvelin, "and now, about Captain Jutley?—what did he say?"

"He assured me that all the orders you sent him last week have been implicitly obeyed. All the roads which converge to this place have been patrolled night and day ever since: and the beach and cliffs have been most rigorously searched and guarded."

"Does he know where this 'Père Blanchard's' hut is?"

"No, *citoyen*, nobody seems to know of it by that name. There are any amount of fisherman's huts all along the course . . . but . . ."

"That'll do. Now about tonight?" interrupted Chauvelin, impatiently.

"The roads and the beach are patrolled as usual, *citoyen*, and Captain Jutley awaits further orders."

"Go back to him at once, then. Tell him to send reinforcements to the various patrols; and especially to those along the beach—you understand?"

Chauvelin spoke curtly and to the point, and every word he uttered struck at Marguerite's heart like the death-knell of her fondest hopes.

"The men," he continued, "are to keep the sharpest possible lookout for any stranger who may be walking, riding, or driving, along the road or the beach, more especially for a tall stranger, whom I need not describe further, as probably he will be disguised; but he cannot very well conceal his height, except by stooping. You understand?"

"Perfectly, *citoyen*," replied Desgas.

"As soon as any of the men have sighted a stranger, two of them are to keep him in view. The man who loses sight of the tall stranger, after he is once seen, will pay for his negligence with his life; but one man is to ride straight back here and report to me. Is that clear?"

"Absolutely clear, *citoyen*."

"Very well, then. Go and see Jutley at once. See the reinforcements start off for the patrol duty, then ask the captain to let you have a half-a-dozen more men and bring them here with you. You can be back in ten minutes. Go—"

Desgas saluted and went to the door.

As Marguerite, sick with horror, listened to Chauvelin's directions to his underling, the whole of the plan for the capture of the Scarlet Pimpernel became appallingly clear to her. Chauvelin wished that the fugitives should be left in false security waiting in their hidden retreat until Percy joined them. Then the daring plotter was to be surrounded and caught red-handed, in the very act of aiding and abetting royalists, who were traitors to the republic. Thus, if his capture were noised abroad, even the British Government could not legally protest in his favour; having plotted with the enemies of the French Government, France had the right to put him to death.

Escape for him and them would be impossible. All the roads patrolled and watched, the trap well set, the net, wide at present, but drawing together tighter and tighter, until it closed upon the daring plotter, whose superhuman cunning even could not rescue him from its meshes now.

Desgas was about to go, but Chauvelin once more called him back.

Marguerite vaguely wondered what further devilish plans he could have formed, in order to entrap one brave man, alone, against two-score of others. She looked at him as he turned to speak to Desgas; she could just see his face beneath the broad-brimmed, *curé's* hat. There was at that moment so much deadly hatred, such fiendish malice in the thin face and pale, small eyes, that Marguerite's last hope died in her heart, for she felt that from this man she could expect no mercy.

"I had forgotten," repeated Chauvelin, with a weird chuckle, as he rubbed his bony, talon-like hands one against the other, with a gesture of fiendish satisfaction. "The tall stranger may show fight. In any case no shooting, remember, except as a last resort. I want that tall stranger alive—if possible."

He laughed, as Dante has told us that the devils laugh at the sight of the torture of the damned. Marguerite had thought that by now she had lived through the whole gamut of horror and anguish that human heart could bear; yet now, when Desgas left the house, and she remained alone in this lonely, squalid room, with that fiend for company, she felt as if all that she had suffered was nothing compared with this. He continued to laugh and chuckle to himself for a while, rubbing his hands together in anticipation of his triumph.

His plans were well laid, and he might well triumph! Not a loop-hole was left, through which the bravest, the most cunning man might escape. Every road guarded, every corner watched, and in that lonely hut somewhere on the coast, a small band of fugitives waiting for their rescuer, and leading him to his death—nay! to worse than death. That fiend there, in a holy man's garb, was too much of a devil to allow a brave man to die the quick, sudden death of a soldier at the post of duty.

He, above all, longed to have the cunning enemy, who had so long baffled him, helpless in his power; he wished to gloat over him, to enjoy his downfall, to inflict upon him what moral and mental torture a deadly hatred alone can devise. The brave eagle, captured, and with noble wings clipped, was doomed to endure the gnawing of the rat. And she, his wife, who loved him, and who had brought him to this, could do nothing to help him.

Nothing, save to hope for death by his side, and for one brief moment in which to tell him that her love—whole, true and passionate—was entirely his.

Chauvelin was now sitting close to the table; he had taken off his hat, and Marguerite could just see the outline of his thin profile and pointed chin, as he bent over his meagre supper. He was evidently quite contented, and awaited events with perfect calm; he even seemed to enjoy Brogard's unsavoury fare. Marguerite wondered how so much hatred could lurk in one human being against another.

Suddenly, as she watched Chauvelin, a sound caught her ear, which turned her very heart to stone. And yet that sound was not calculated to inspire anyone with horror, for it was merely the cheerful sound of a gay, fresh voice singing lustily, "God save the King!"

Chapter 25

The Eagle and the Fox

Marguerite's breath stopped short; she seemed to feel her very life standing still momentarily whilst she listened to that voice and to that song. In the singer she had recognised her husband. Chauvelin, too, had heard it, for he darted a quick glance towards the door, then hurriedly took up his broad-brimmed hat and clapped it over his head.

The voice drew nearer; for one brief second, the wild desire seized Marguerite to rush down the steps and fly across the room, to stop that song at any cost, to beg the cheerful singer to fly—fly for his life, before it be too late. She checked the impulse just in time. Chauvelin would stop her before she reached the door, and, moreover, she had no idea if he had any soldiers posted within his call. Her impetuous act might prove the death-signal of the man she would have died to save.

"Long to reign over us, God save the King!"

sang the voice more lustily than ever. The next moment the door was thrown open and there was dead silence for a second or so.

Marguerite could not see the door; she held her breath, trying to imagine what was happening.

Percy Blakeney on entering had, of course, at once caught sight of the *curé* at the table; his hesitation lasted less than five seconds, the next moment, Marguerite saw his tall figure crossing the room, whilst he called in a loud, cheerful voice,—

"Hello, there! no one about? Where's that fool Brogard?"

He wore the magnificent coat and riding-suit which he had on when Marguerite last saw him at Richmond, so many hours ago. As usual, his get-up was absolutely irreproachable, the fine Mechlin lace at his neck and wrists were immaculate and white, his fair hair was carefully brushed, and he carried his eyeglass with his usual affected gesture. In fact, at this moment, Sir Percy Blakeney, Bart., might have been on his way to a garden-party at the Prince of Wales', instead of deliberately, cold-bloodedly running his head in a trap, set for him by his deadliest enemy.

He stood for a moment in the middle of the room, whilst Marguerite, absolutely paralysed with horror, seemed unable even to breathe.

Every moment she expected that Chauvelin would give a signal, that the place would fill with soldiers, that she would rush down and help Percy to sell his life dearly. As he stood there, suavely unconscious, she very nearly screamed out to him,—

"Fly, Percy!—'tis your deadly enemy!—fly before it be too late!"

But she had not time even to do that, for the next moment Blakeney quietly walked to the table, and, jovially clapped the *curé* on the back, said in his own drawly, affected way,—

"Odds's fish!—er—M. Chauvelin—I vow I never thought of meeting you here."

Chauvelin, who had been in the very act of conveying soup to his mouth, fairly choked. His thin face became absolutely purple, and a violent fit of coughing saved this cunning representative of France from betraying the most boundless surprise he had ever experienced. There was no doubt that this bold move on the part of the enemy had been wholly unexpected, as far as he was concerned: and the daring impudence of it completely nonplussed him for the moment.

Obviously, he had not taken the precaution of having the inn surrounded with soldiers. Blakeney had evidently guessed that much, and no doubt his resourceful brain had already formed some plan by which he could turn this unexpected interview to account.

Marguerite up in the loft had not moved. She had made a solemn promise to Sir Andrew not to speak to her husband before strangers, and she had sufficient self-control not to throw herself unreasoningly and impulsively across his plans. To sit still and watch these two men together was a terrible trial of fortitude. Marguerite had heard Chauvelin give the orders for the patrolling of all the roads. She knew that if Percy now left the "Chat Gris"—in whatever direction he happened to go—he could not go far without being sighted by some of Captain Jutley's men on patrol. On the other hand, if he stayed, then Desgas would have time to come back with the dozen men Chauvelin had specially ordered.

The trap was closing in, and Marguerite could do nothing but watch and wonder. The two men looked such a strange contrast, and of the two it was Chauvelin who exhibited a slight touch of fear. Marguerite knew him well enough to guess what was passing in his mind. He had no fear for his own person, although he certainly was alone in a lonely inn with a man who was powerfully built, and who was daring and reckless beyond the bounds of probability. She knew that Chauvelin would willingly have braved perilous encounters for the sake of the cause he had at heart, but what he did fear was that this impudent Englishman would, by knocking him down, double his own chances of escape; his underlings might not succeed so well in capturing the Scarlet Pimpernel, when not directed by the cunning hand and the shrewd brain, which had deadly hate for an incentive.

Evidently, however, the representative of the French Government had nothing to fear for the moment, at the hands of his powerful adversary. Blakeney, with his most inane laugh and pleasant good-nature, was solemnly patting him on the back.

"I am so demmed sorry—" he was saying cheerfully, "so very sorry —I seem to have upset you—eating soup, too—nasty, awkward thing, soup—er—Begad!—a friend of mine died once—er—choked—just like you—with a spoonful of soup."

And he smiled shyly, good-humouredly, down at Chauvelin.

"Odd's life!" he continued, as soon as the latter had somewhat recovered himself, "beastly hole this—ain't it now? *La!* you don't mind?" he added, apologetically, as he sat down on a chair close to the table and drew the soup tureen towards him. "That fool Brogard seems to be asleep or something."

There was a second plate on the table, and he calmly helped himself to soup, then poured himself out a glass of wine.

For a moment Marguerite wondered what Chauvelin would do. His disguise was so good that perhaps he meant, on recovering himself, to deny his identity: but Chauvelin was too astute to make such an obviously false and childish move, and already he too had stretched out his hand and said pleasantly,—

"I am indeed charmed to see you Sir Percy. You must excuse me—h'm—I thought you the other side of the Channel. Sudden surprise almost took my breath away."

"La!" said Sir Percy, with a good-humoured grin, "it did that quite, didn't it—er—M.—er—Chaubertin?"

"Pardon me—Chauvelin."

"I beg pardon—a thousand times. Yes—Chauvelin of course—Er—I never could cotton to foreign names—"

He was calmly eating his soup, laughing with pleasant good-humour, as if he had come all the way to Calais for the express purpose of enjoying supper at this filthy inn, in the company of his arch-enemy.

For the moment Marguerite wondered why Percy did not knock the little Frenchman down then and there—and no doubt something of the sort must have darted through his mind, for every now and then his lazy eyes seemed to flash ominously, as they rested on the slight figure of Chauvelin, who had now quite recovered himself and was also calmly eating his soup.

But the keen brain, which had planned and carried through so many daring plots, was too far-seeing to take unnecessary risks. This place, after all, might be infested with spies; the innkeeper might be in Chauvelin's pay. One call on Chauvelin's part might bring twenty men about Blakeney's ears for aught he knew, and he might be caught and trapped before he could help, or, at least, warn the fugitives. This he would not risk; he meant to help the others, to get *them* safely away; for he had pledged his word to them, and his word he *would* keep. And whilst he ate and chatted, he thought and planned, whilst, up in the loft, the poor, anxious woman racked her brain as to what she should do, and endured agonies of longing to rush down to him, yet not daring to move for fear of upsetting his plans.

"I didn't know," Blakeney was saying jovially, "that you—er—were in holy orders."

"I—er—hem—" stammered Chauvelin. The calm impudence of his antagonist had evidently thrown him off his usual balance.

"But, *la!* I should have known you anywhere," continued Sir Percy, placidly, as he poured himself out another glass of wine, "although the wig and hat have changed you a bit."

"Do you think so?"

"Lud! they alter a man so—but—begad! I hope you don't mind my having made the remark?—Demmed bad form making remarks—I hope you don't mind?"

"No, no, not at all—hem! I hope Lady Blakeney is well," said Chauvelin, hurriedly changing the topic of conversation.

Blakeney, with much deliberation, finished his plate of soup, drank his glass of wine, and, momentarily, it seemed to Marguerite as if he glanced all round the room. "Quite well, thank you," he said at last, drily. There was a pause, during which Marguerite could watch these two antagonists who, evidently in their minds, were measuring themselves against one another. She could see Percy almost full face where he sat at the table not ten yards from where she herself was crouching, puzzled, not knowing what to do, or what she should think. She had quite controlled her impulse now of rushing down and disclosing herself to her husband. A man capable of acting a part, in the way he was doing at the present moment, did not need a woman's word to warn him to be cautious.

Marguerite indulged in the luxury, dear to every tender woman's heart, of looking at the man she loved. She looked through the tattered curtain, across at the handsome face of her husband, in whose lazy blue eyes, and behind whose inane smile, she could now so plainly see the strength, energy, and resourcefulness which had caused the Scarlet Pimpernel to be reverenced and trusted by his followers. "There are nineteen of us ready to lay down our lives for your husband, Lady Blakeney," Sir Andrew had said to her; and as she looked at the forehead, low, but square and broad, the eyes, blue, yet deep-set and intense, the whole aspect of the man, of indomitable energy, hiding, behind a perfectly acted comedy, his almost superhuman strength of will and marvellous ingenuity, she understood the fascination which he exercised over his followers, for had he not also cast his spells over her heart and her imagination?

Chauvelin, who was trying to conceal his impatience beneath his usual urbane manner, took a quick look at his watch. Desgas should not be long: another two or three minutes, and this impudent Englishman would be secure in the keeping of half a dozen of Captain Jutley's most trusted men.

"You are on your way to Paris, Sir Percy?" he asked carelessly.

"Odd's life, no," replied Blakeney, with a laugh. "Only as far as Lille—not Paris for me—beastly uncomfortable place Paris, just now—eh, Monsieur Chaubertin—beg pardon—Chauvelin!"

"Not for an English gentleman like yourself, Sir Percy," rejoined Chauvelin, sarcastically, "who takes no interest in the conflict that is raging there."

"*La!* you see it's no business of mine, and our demmed government is all on your side of the business. Old Pitt daren't say 'Bo' to a goose. You are in a hurry, sir," he added, as Chauvelin once again took out his watch; "an appointment, perhaps—I pray you take no heed of me—My time's my own."

He rose from the table and dragged a chair to the hearth. Once more Marguerite was terribly tempted to go to him, for time was getting on; Desgas might be back at any moment with his men. Percy did not know that and—oh! how horrible it all was—and how helpless she felt.

"I am in no hurry," continued Percy, pleasantly, "but, *la!* I don't want to spend any more time than I can help in this God-forsaken hole! But, begad! sir," he added, as Chauvelin had surreptitiously looked at his watch for the third time, "that watch of yours won't go any faster for all the looking you give it. You are expecting a friend, maybe?"

"Aye—a friend!"

"Not a lady—I trust, *Monsieur l'Abbé*," laughed Blakeney; "surely the holy church does not allow?—eh?—what! But, I say, come by the fire—it's getting demmed cold."

He kicked the fire with the heel of his boot, making the logs blaze in the old hearth. He seemed in no hurry to go, and apparently was quite unconscious of his immediate danger. He dragged another chair to the fire, and Chauvelin, whose impatience was by now quite beyond control, sat down beside the hearth, in such a way as to command a view of the door. Desgas had been gone nearly a quarter of an hour. It was quite plain to Marguerite's aching senses that as soon as he arrived, Chauvelin would abandon all his other plans with regard to the fugitives and capture this impudent Scarlet Pimpernel at once.

"Hey, M. Chauvelin," the latter was saying airily, "tell me, I pray you, is your friend pretty? Demmed smart these little French women sometimes—what? But I protest I need not ask," he added, as he carelessly strode back towards the supper-table. "In matters of taste the Church has never been backward—Eh?"

But Chauvelin was not listening. His every faculty was now concentrated on that door through which presently Desgas would enter. Marguerite's thoughts, too, were centred there, for her ears had suddenly caught, through the stillness of the night, the sound of numerous and measured treads some distance away.

It was Desgas and his men. Another three minutes and they would be here! Another three minutes and the awful thing would have occurred: the brave eagle would have fallen in the ferret's trap! She would have moved now and screamed, but she dared not; for whilst she heard the soldiers approaching, she was looking at Percy and watching his every movement. He was standing by the table whereon the remnants of the supper, plates, glasses, spoons, salt and pepper-pots were scattered pell-mell. His back was turned to Chauvelin and he was still prattling along in his own affected and inane way, but from his pocket he had taken his snuff-box, and quickly and suddenly he emptied the contents of the pepper-pot into it.

Then he again turned with an inane laugh to Chauvelin,—

"Eh? Did you speak, sir?"

Chauvelin had been too intent on listening to the sound of those approaching footsteps, to notice what his cunning adversary had been doing. He now pulled himself together, trying to look unconcerned in the very midst of his anticipated triumph. "No," he said presently, "that is—as you were saying, Sir Percy—?"

"I was saying," said Blakeney, going up to Chauvelin, by the fire, "that the Jew in Piccadilly has sold me better snuff this time than I have ever tasted. Will you honour me, *Monsieur l'Abbé?*"

He stood close to Chauvelin in his own careless, *debonnaire* way, holding out his snuff-box to his arch-enemy.

Chauvelin, who, as he told Marguerite once, had seen a trick or two in his day, had never dreamed of this one. With one ear fixed on those fast-approaching footsteps, one eye turned to that door where Desgas and his men would presently appear, lulled into false security by the impudent Englishman's airy manner, he never even remotely guessed the trick which was being played upon him.

He took a pinch of snuff.

Only he, who has ever by accident sniffed vigorously a dose of pepper, can have the faintest conception of the hopeless condition in which such a sniff would reduce any human being.

Chauvelin felt as if his head would burst—sneeze after sneeze seemed nearly to choke him; he was blind, deaf, and dumb for the moment, and during that moment Blakeney quietly, without the slightest haste, took up his hat, took some money out of his pocket, which he left on the table, then calmly stalked out of the room!

Chapter 26

The Jew

It took Marguerite some time to collect her scattered senses; the whole of this last short episode had taken place in less than a minute, and Desgas and the soldiers were still about two hundred yards away from the "Chat Gris."

When she realised what had happened, a curious mixture of joy and wonder filled her heart. It all was so neat, so ingenious. Chauvelin was still absolutely helpless, far more so than he could even have been under a blow from the fist, for now he could neither see, nor hear, nor speak, whilst his cunning adversary had quietly slipped through his fingers.

Blakeney was gone, obviously to try and join the fugitives at the Père Blanchard's hut. For the moment, true, Chauvelin was helpless; for the moment the daring Scarlet Pimpernel had not been caught by Desgas and his men. But all the roads and the beach were patrolled. Every place was watched, and every stranger kept in sight. How far could Percy go, thus arrayed in his gorgeous clothes, without being sighted and followed? Now she blamed herself terribly for not having gone down to him sooner and given him that word of warning and of love which, perhaps, after all, he needed. He could not know of the orders which Chauvelin had given for his capture, and even now, perhaps—

But before all these horrible thoughts had taken concrete form in her brain, she heard the grounding of arms outside, close to the door, and Desgas' voice shouting "Halt!" to his men.

Chauvelin had partially recovered; his sneezing had become less violent, and he had struggled to his feet. He managed to reach the door just as Desgas' knock was heard on the outside.

Chauvelin threw open the door, and before his secretary could say a word, he had managed to stammer between two sneezes—

"The tall stranger—quick!—did any of you see him?"

"Where, *citoyen?*" asked Desgas, in surprise.

"Here, man! through that door! not five minutes ago."

"We saw nothing, *citoyen!* The moon is not yet up, and . . ."

"And you are just five minutes too late, my friend," said Chauvelin, with concentrated fury.

"*Citoyen*—I—"

"You did what I ordered you to do," said Chauvelin, with impatience. "I know that, but you were a precious long time about it. Fortunately, there's not much harm done, or it had fared ill with you, Citoyen Desgas."

Desgas turned a little pale. There was so much rage and hatred in his superior's whole attitude.

"The tall stranger, *citoyen*—" he stammered.

"Was here, in this room, five minutes ago, having supper at that table. Damn his impudence! For obvious reasons, I dared not tackle him alone. Brogard is too big a fool, and that cursed Englishman appears to have the strength of a bullock, and so he slipped away under your very nose."

"He cannot go far without being sighted, *citoyen*."

"Ah?"

"Captain Jutley sent forty men as reinforcements for the patrol duty: twenty went down to the beach. He again assured me that the watch had been constant all day, and that no stranger could possibly get to the beach, or reach a boat, without being sighted."

"That's good.—Do the men know their work?"

"They have had very clear orders, *citoyen*: and I myself spoke to those who were about to start. They are to shadow—as secretly as possible—any stranger they may see, especially if he be tall, or stoop as if he would disguise his height."

"In no case to detain such a person, of course," said Chauvelin, eagerly. "That impudent Scarlet Pimpernel would slip through clumsy fingers. We must let him get to the Père Blanchard's hut now; there surround and capture him."

"The men understand that, *citoyen*, and also that, as soon as a tall stranger has been sighted, he must be shadowed, whilst one man is to turn straight back and report to you."

"That is right," said Chauvelin, rubbing his hands, well pleased.

"I have further news for you, *citoyen*."

"What is it?"

"A tall Englishman had a long conversation about three-quarters of an hour ago with a Jew, Reuben by name, who lives not ten paces from here."

"Yes—and?" queried Chauvelin, impatiently.

"The conversation was all about a horse and cart, which the tall Englishman wished to hire, and which was to have been ready for him by eleven o'clock."

"It is past that now. Where does that Reuben live?"

"A few minutes' walk from this door."

"Send one of the men to find out if the stranger has driven off in Reuben's cart."

"Yes, *citoyen*."

Desgas went to give the necessary orders to one of the men. Not a word of this conversation between him and Chauvelin had escaped Marguerite, and every word they had spoken seemed to strike at her heart, with terrible hopelessness and dark foreboding.

She had come all this way, and with such high hopes and firm determination to help her husband, and so far, she had been able to do nothing, but to watch, with a heart breaking with anguish, the meshes of the deadly net closing round the daring Scarlet Pimpernel.

He could not now advance many steps, without spying eyes to track and denounce him. Her own helplessness struck her with the terrible sense of utter disappointment. The possibility of being the slightest use to her husband had become almost *nil*, and her only hope rested in being allowed to share his fate, whatever it might ultimately be.

For the moment, even her chance of ever seeing the man she loved again, had become a remote one. Still, she was determined to keep a close watch over his enemy, and a vague hope filled her heart, that whilst she kept Chauvelin in sight, Percy's fate might still be hanging in the balance.

Desgas left Chauvelin moodily pacing up and down the room, whilst he himself waited outside for the return of the man whom he had sent in search of Reuben. Thus, several minutes went by. Chauvelin was evidently devoured with impatience. Apparently, he trusted no one: this last trick played upon him by the daring Scarlet Pimpernel had made him suddenly doubtful of success, unless he himself was there to watch, direct and superintend the capture of this impudent Englishman.

About five minutes later, Desgas returned, followed by an elderly Jew, in a dirty, threadbare gaberdine, worn greasy across the shoulders. His red hair, which he wore after the fashion of the Polish Jews, with the corkscrew curls each side of his face, was plentifully sprinkled with grey—a general coating of grime, about his cheeks and his chin, gave him a peculiarly dirty and loathsome appearance. He had the habitual stoop, those of his race affected in mock humility in past centuries, before the dawn of equality and freedom in matters of faith, and he walked behind Desgas with the peculiar shuffling gait which has remained the characteristic of the Jew trader in continental Europe to this day.

Chauvelin, who had all the Frenchman's prejudice against the despised race, motioned to the fellow to keep at a respectful distance. The group of the three men were standing just underneath the hanging oil-lamp, and Marguerite had a clear view of them all.

"Is this the man?" asked Chauvelin.

"No, *citoyen*," replied Desgas, "Reuben could not be found, so presumably his cart has gone with the stranger; but this man here seems to know something, which he is willing to sell for a consideration."

"Ah!" said Chauvelin, turning away with disgust from the loathsome specimen of humanity before him.

The Jew, with characteristic patience, stood humbly on one side, leaning on the knotted staff, his greasy, broad-brimmed hat casting a deep shadow over his grimy face, waiting for the noble Excellency to deign to put some questions to him.

"The *citoyen* tells me," said Chauvelin peremptorily to him, "that you know something of my friend, the tall Englishman, whom I desire to meet—*morbleu!* keep your distance, man," he added hurriedly, as the Jew took a quick and eager step forward.

"Yes, your Excellency," replied the Jew, who spoke the language with that peculiar lisp which denotes Eastern origin, "I and Reuben Goldstein met a tall Englishman, on the road, close by here this evening."

"Did you speak to him?"

"He spoke to us, your Excellency. He wanted to know if he could hire a horse and cart to go down along the St. Martin road, to a place he wanted to reach tonight."

"What did you say?"

"I did not say anything," said the Jew in an injured tone, "Reuben Goldstein, that accursed traitor, that son of Belial—"

"Cut that short, man," interrupted Chauvelin, roughly, "and go on with your story."

"He took the words out of my mouth, your Excellency: when I was about to offer the wealthy Englishman my horse and cart, to take him wheresoever he chose, Reuben had already spoken, and offered his half-starved nag, and his broken-down cart."

"And what did the Englishman do?"

"He listened to Reuben Goldstein, your Excellency, and put his hand in his pocket then and there, and took out a handful of gold, which he showed to that descendant of Beelzebub, telling him that all that would be his, if the horse and cart were ready for him by eleven o'clock."

"And, of course, the horse and cart were ready?"

"Well! they were ready for him in a manner, so to speak, your Excellency. Reuben's nag was lame as usual; she refused to budge at first. It was only after a time and with plenty of kicks, that she at last could be made to move," said the Jew with a malicious chuckle.

"Then they started?"

"Yes, they started about five minutes ago. I was disgusted with that stranger's folly. An Englishman too!—He ought to have known Reuben's nag was not fit to drive."

"But if he had no choice?"

"No choice, your Excellency?" protested the Jew, in a rasping voice, "did I not repeat to him a dozen times, that my horse and cart would take him quicker, and more comfortably than Reuben's bag of bones. He would not listen. Reuben is such a liar and has such insinuating ways. The stranger was deceived. If he was in a hurry, he would have had better value for his money by taking my cart."

"You have a horse and cart too, then?" asked Chauvelin, peremptorily.

"Aye! that I have, your Excellency, and if your Excellency wants to drive . . ."

"Do you happen to know which way my friend went in Reuben Goldstein's cart?"

Thoughtfully the Jew rubbed his dirty chin. Marguerite's heart was beating well-nigh to bursting. She had heard the peremptory question; she looked anxiously at the Jew but could not read his face beneath the shadow of his broad-brimmed hat. Vaguely she felt somehow as if he held Percy's fate in his long dirty hands.

There was a long pause, whilst Chauvelin frowned impatiently at the stooping figure before him: at last the Jew slowly put his hand in his breast pocket and drew out from its capacious depths a number of silver coins. He gazed at them thoughtfully, then remarked, in a quiet tone of voice,—

"This is what the tall stranger gave me, when he drove away with Reuben, for holding my tongue about him, and his doings."

Chauvelin shrugged his shoulders impatiently.

"How much is there there?" he asked.

"Twenty *francs*, your Excellency," replied the Jew, "and I have been an honest man all my life."

Chauvelin without further comment took a few pieces of gold out of his own pocket, and leaving them in the palm of his hand, he allowed them to jingle as he held them out towards the Jew.

"How many gold pieces are there in the palm of my hand?" he asked quietly.

Evidently, he had no desire to terrorise the man, but to conciliate him, for his own purposes, for his manner was pleasant and suave. No doubt he feared that threats of the guillotine, and various other persuasive methods of that type, might addle the old man's brains, and that he would be more likely to be useful through greed of gain, than through terror of death.

The eyes of the Jew shot a quick, keen glance at the gold in his interlocutor's hand.

"At least five, I should say, your Excellency," he replied obsequiously.

"Enough, do you think, to loosen that honest tongue of yours?"

"What does your Excellency wish to know?"

"Whether your horse and cart can take me to where I can find my friend the tall stranger, who has driven off in Reuben Goldstein's cart?"

"My horse and cart can take your Honour there, where you please."

"To a place called the Père Blanchard's hut?"

"Your Honour has guessed?" said the Jew in astonishment.

"You know the place? Which road leads to it?"

"The St. Martin Road, your Honour, then a footpath from there to the cliffs."

"You know the road?" repeated Chauvelin, roughly.

"Every stone, every blade of grass, your Honour," replied the Jew quietly.

Chauvelin without another word threw the five pieces of gold one by one before the Jew, who knelt down, and on his hands and knees struggled to collect them. One rolled away, and he had some trouble to get it, for it had lodged underneath the dresser. Chauvelin quietly waited while the old man scrambled on the floor, to find the piece of gold.

When the Jew was again on his feet, Chauvelin said,—

"How soon can your horse and cart be ready?"

"They are ready now, your Honour."

"Where?"

"Not ten metres from this door. Will your Excellency deign to look?"

"I don't want to see it. How far can you drive me in it?"

"As far as the Père Blanchard's hut, your Honour, and further than Reuben's nag took your friend. I am sure that, not two leagues from here, we shall come across that wily Reuben, his nag, his cart and the tall stranger all in a heap in the middle of the road."

"How far is the nearest village from here?"

"On the road which the Englishman took, Miquelon is the nearest village, not two leagues from here."

"There he could get fresh conveyance, if he wanted to go further?"

"He could—if he ever got so far."

"Can you?"

"Will your Excellency try?" said the Jew simply.

"That is my intention," said Chauvelin very quietly, "but remember, if you have deceived me, I shall tell off two of my most stalwart soldiers to give you such a beating, that your breath will perhaps leave your ugly body for ever. But if we find my friend the tall Englishman, either on the road or at the Père Blanchard's hut, there will be ten more gold pieces for you. Do you accept the bargain?"

The Jew again thoughtfully rubbed his chin. He looked at the money in his hand, then at this stern interlocutor, and at Desgas, who had stood silently behind him all this while. After a moment's pause, he said deliberately,—

"I accept."

"Go and wait outside then," said Chauvelin, "and remember to stick to your bargain, or by Heaven, I will keep to mine."

With a final, most abject and cringing bow, the old Jew shuffled out of the room. Chauvelin seemed pleased with his interview, for he rubbed his hands together, with that usual gesture of his, of malignant satisfaction.

"My coat and boots," he said to Desgas at last.

Desgas went to the door, and apparently gave the necessary orders, for presently a soldier entered, carrying Chauvelin's coat, boots, and hat.

He took off his *soutane*, beneath which he was wearing close-fitting breeches and a cloth waistcoat and began changing his attire.

"You, *citoyen*, in the meanwhile," he said to Desgas, "go back to Captain Jutley as fast as you can and tell him to let you have another dozen men, and bring them with you along the St. Martin Road, where I daresay you will soon overtake the Jew's cart with myself in it. There will be hot work presently, if I mistake not, in the Père Blanchard's hut. We shall corner our game there, I'll warrant, for this impudent Scarlet Pimpernel has had the audacity—or the stupidity, I hardly know which—to adhere to his original plans. He has gone to meet de Tournay, St. Just and the other traitors, which for the moment, I thought, perhaps, he did not intend to do. When we find them, there will be a band of desperate men at bay. Some of our men will, I presume, be put *hors de combat*. These royalists are good swordsmen, and the Englishman is devilish cunning, and looks very powerful. Still, we shall be five against one at least. You can follow the cart closely with your men, all along the St. Martin Road, through Miquelon. The

Englishman is ahead of us, and not likely to look behind him."

Whilst he gave these curt and concise orders, he had completed his change of attire. The priest's costume had been laid aside, and he was once more dressed in his usual dark, tight-fitting clothes. At last he took up his hat.

"I shall have an interesting prisoner to deliver into your hands," he said with a chuckle, as with unwonted familiarity he took Desgas' arm, and led him towards the door. "We won't kill him outright, eh, friend Desgas? The Père Blanchard's hut is—an I mistake not—a lonely spot upon the beach, and our men will enjoy a bit of rough sport there with the wounded fox. Choose your men well, friend Desgas . . . of the sort who would enjoy that type of sport—eh? We must see that Scarlet Pimpernel wither a bit—what?—shrink and tremble, eh? . . . before we finally . . ." He made an expressive gesture, whilst he laughed a low, evil laugh, which filled Marguerite's soul with sickening horror.

"Choose your men well, Citoyen Desgas," he said once more, as he led his secretary finally out of the room.

Chapter 27

On the Track

Never for a moment did Marguerite Blakeney hesitate. The last sounds outside the "Chat Gris" had died away in the night. She had heard Desgas giving orders to his men, and then starting off towards the fort, to get a reinforcement of a dozen more men: six were not thought sufficient to capture the cunning Englishman, whose resourceful brain was even more dangerous than his valour and his strength.

Then a few minutes later, she heard the Jew's husky voice again, evidently shouting to his nag, then the rumble of wheels, and noise of a rickety cart bumping over the rough road.

Inside the inn, everything was still. Brogard and his wife, terrified of Chauvelin, had given no sign of life; they hoped to be forgotten, and at any rate to remain unperceived: Marguerite could not even hear their usual volleys of muttered oaths.

She waited a moment or two longer, then she quietly slipped down the broken stairs, wrapped her dark cloak closely round her and slipped out of the inn.

The night was fairly dark, sufficiently so at any rate to hide her dark figure from view, whilst her keen ears kept count of the sound of the cart going on ahead. She hoped by keeping well within the shadow of the ditches which lined the road, that she would not be seen by Desgas' men, when they approached, or by the patrols, which she concluded were still on duty.

Thus, she started to do this, the last stage of her weary journey, alone, at night, and on foot. Nearly three leagues to Miquelon, and then on to the Père Blanchard's hut, wherever that fatal spot might be, probably over rough roads: she cared not.

The Jew's nag could not get on very fast, and though she was weary with mental fatigue and nerve strain, she knew that she could easily keep up with it, on a hilly road, where the poor beast, who was sure to be half-starved, would have to be allowed long and frequent rests. The road lay some distance from the sea, bordered on either side by shrubs and stunted trees, sparsely covered with meagre foliage, all turning away from the North, with their branches looking in the semi-darkness, like stiff, ghostly hair, blown by a perpetual wind.

Fortunately, the moon showed no desire to peep between the clouds, and Marguerite hugging the edge of the road, and keeping close to the low line of shrubs, was fairly safe from view. Everything around her was so still: only from far, very far away, there came like a long soft moan, the sound of the distant sea.

The air was keen and full of brine; after that enforced period of inactivity, inside the evil-smelling, squalid inn, Marguerite would have enjoyed the sweet scent of this autumnal night, and the distant melancholy rumble of the autumnal night, and the distant melancholy rumble of the waves; she would have revelled in the calm and stillness of this lonely spot, a calm, broken only at intervals by the strident and mournful cry of some distant gull, and by the creaking of the wheels, some way down the road: she would have loved the cool atmosphere, the peaceful immensity of Nature, in this lonely part of the coast: but her heart was too full of cruel foreboding, of a great ache and longing for a being who had become infinitely dear to her.

Her feet slipped on the grassy bank, for she thought it safest not to walk near the centre of the road, and she found it difficult to keep up a sharp pace along the muddy incline. She even thought it best not to keep too near to the cart; everything was so still, that the rumble of the wheels could not fail to be a safe guide.

The loneliness was absolute. Already the few dim lights of Calais lay far behind, and on this road, there was not a sign of human habitation, not even the hut of a fisherman or of a woodcutter anywhere near; far away on her right was the edge of the cliff, below it the rough beach, against which the incoming tide was dashing itself with its constant, distant murmur. And ahead the rumble of the wheels, bearing an implacable enemy to his triumph.

Marguerite wondered at what particular spot, on this lonely coast, Percy could be at this moment. Not very far surely, for he had had less than a quarter of an hour's start of Chauvelin. She wondered if he knew that in this cool, ocean-scented bit of France, there lurked many spies, all eager to sight his tall figure, to track him to where his unsuspecting friends waited for him, and then, to close the net over him and them.

Chauvelin, on ahead, jolted and jostled in the Jew's vehicle, was nursing comfortable thoughts. He rubbed his hands together, with content, as he thought of the web which he had woven, and through which that ubiquitous and daring Englishman could not hope to escape. As the time went on, and the old Jew drove him leisurely but surely along the dark road, he felt more and more eager for the grand finale of this exciting chase after the mysterious Scarlet Pimpernel. The capture of the audacious plotter would be the finest leaf in Citoyen Chauvelin's wreath of glory. Caught, red-handed, on the spot, in the very act of aiding and abetting the traitors against the Republic of France, the Englishman could claim no protection from his own country. Chauvelin had, in any case, fully made up his mind that all intervention should come too late.

Never for a moment did the slightest remorse enter his heart, as to the terrible position in which he had placed the unfortunate wife, who had unconsciously betrayed her husband. As a matter of fact, Chauvelin had ceased even to think of her: she had been a useful tool, that was all.

The Jew's lean nag did little more than walk. She was going along at a slow jog trot, and her driver had to give her long and frequent halts.

"Are we a long way yet from Miquelon?" asked Chauvelin from time to time.

"Not very far, your Honour," was the uniform placid reply.

"We have not yet come across your friend and mine, lying in a heap in the roadway," was Chauvelin's sarcastic comment.

"Patience, noble Excellency," rejoined the son of Moses, "they are ahead of us. I can see the imprint of the cart wheels, driven by that traitor, that son of the Amalekite."

"You are sure of the road?"

"As sure as I am of the presence of those ten gold pieces in the noble Excellency's pockets, which I trust will presently be mine."

"As soon as I have shaken hands with my friend the tall stranger, they will certainly be yours."

"Hark, what was that?" said the Jew suddenly.

Through the stillness, which had been absolute, there could now be heard distinctly the sound of horses' hoofs on the muddy road.

"They are soldiers," he added in an awed whisper.

"Stop a moment, I want to hear," said Chauvelin.

Marguerite had also heard the sound of galloping hoofs, coming towards the cart and towards herself. For some time, she had been on the alert thinking that Desgas and his squad would soon overtake them, but these came from the opposite direction, presumably from Miquelon. The darkness lent her sufficient cover. She had perceived that the cart had stopped, and with utmost caution, treading noiselessly on the soft road, she crept a little nearer.

Her heart was beating fast, she was trembling in every limb; already she had guessed what news these mounted men would bring. "Every stranger on these roads or on the beach must be shadowed, especially if he be tall or stoops as if he would disguise his height; when sighted a mounted messenger must at once ride back and report." Those had been Chauvelin's orders. Had then the tall stranger been sighted, and was this the mounted messenger, come to bring the great news, that the hunted hare had run its head into the noose at last?

Marguerite, realising that the cart had come to a standstill, managed to slip nearer to it in the darkness; she crept close up, hoping to get within earshot, to hear what the messenger had to say.

She heard the quick words of challenge—

"*Liberté, Fraternité, Egalité!*" then Chauvelin's quick query:—

"What news?"

Two men on horseback had halted beside the vehicle.

Marguerite could see them silhouetted against the midnight sky. She could hear their voices, and the snorting of their horses, and now, behind her, some little distance off, the regular and measured tread of a body of advancing men: Desgas and his soldiers.

There had been a long pause, during which, no doubt, Chauvelin satisfied the men as to his identity, for presently, questions and answers followed each other in quick succession.

"You have seen the stranger?" asked Chauvelin, eagerly.

"No, *citoyen*, we have seen no tall stranger; we came by the edge of the cliff."

"Then?"

"Less than a quarter of a league beyond Miquelon, we came across a rough construction of wood, which looked like the hut of a fisherman, where he might keep his tools and nets. When we first sighted it, it seemed to be empty, and, at first, we thought that there was nothing suspicious about, until we saw some smoke issuing through an aperture at the side. I dismounted and crept close to it. It was then empty, but in one corner of the hut, there was a charcoal fire, and a couple of stools were also in the hut. I consulted with my comrades, and we decided that they should take cover with the horses, well out of sight, and that I should remain on the watch, which I did."

"Well! and did you see anything?"

"About half an hour later, I heard voices, *citoyen*, and presently, two men came along towards the edge of the cliff; they seemed to me to have come from the Lille Road. One was young, the other quite old. They were talking in a whisper, to one another, and I could not hear what they said." One was young, and the other quite old. Marguerite's aching heart almost stopped beating as she listened: was the young one Armand?—her brother?—and the old one de Tournay—were they the two fugitives who, unconsciously, were used as a decoy, to entrap their fearless and noble rescuer.

"The two men presently went into the hut," continued the soldier, whilst Marguerite's aching nerves seemed to catch the sound of Chauvelin's triumphant chuckle, "and I crept nearer to it then. The hut is very roughly built, and I caught snatches of their conversation."

"Yes?—Quick!—What did you hear?"

"The old man asked the young one if he were sure that was right place. 'Oh, yes,' he replied, ''tis the place sure enough,' and by the light of the charcoal fire he showed to his companion a paper, which he carried. 'Here is the plan,' he said, 'which he gave me before I left London. We were to adhere strictly to that plan, unless I had contrary orders, and I have had none. Here is the road we followed, see—here the fork—here we cut across the St. Martin Road—and here is the footpath which brought us to the edge of the cliff.' I must have made a slight noise then, for the young man came to the door of the hut and peered anxiously all round him. When he again joined his companion, they whispered so low, that I could no longer hear them."

"Well?—and?" asked Chauvelin, impatiently.

"There were six of us altogether, patrolling that part of the beach, so we consulted together, and thought it best that four should remain behind and keep the hut in sight, and I and my comrade rode back at once to make report of what we had seen."

"You saw nothing of the tall stranger?"

"Nothing, *citoyen*."

"If your comrades see him, what would they do?"

"Not lose sight of him for a moment, and if he showed signs of escape, or any boat came in sight, they would close in on him, and, if necessary, they would shoot: the firing would bring the rest of the patrol to the spot. In any case they would not let the stranger go."

"Aye! but I did not want the stranger hurt—not just yet," murmured Chauvelin, savagely, "but there, you've done your best. The Fates grant that I may not be too late—"

"We met half a dozen men just now, who have been patrolling this road for several hours."

"Well?"

"They have seen no stranger either."

"Yet he is on ahead somewhere, in a cart or else . . . Here! there is not a moment to lose. How far is that hut from here?"

"About a couple of leagues, *citoyen*."

"You can find it again?—at once?—without hesitation?"

"I have absolutely no doubt, *citoyen*."

"The footpath, to the edge of the cliff?—Even in the dark?"

"It is not a dark night, *citoyen*, and I know I can find my way," repeated the soldier firmly.

"Fall in behind then. Let your comrade take both your horses back to Calais. You won't want them. Keep beside the cart, and direct the Jew to drive straight ahead; then stop him, within a quarter of a league of the footpath; see that he takes the most direct road."

Whilst Chauvelin spoke, Desgas and his men were fast approaching, and Marguerite could hear their footsteps within a hundred yards behind her now. She thought it unsafe to stay where she was, and unnecessary too, as she had heard enough. She seemed suddenly to have lost all faculty even for suffering: her heart, her nerves, her brain seemed to have become numb after all these hours of ceaseless anguish, culminating in this awful despair.

For now, there was absolutely not the faintest hope. Within two short leagues of this spot, the fugitives were waiting for their brave deliverer. He was on his way, somewhere on this lonely road, and presently he would join them; then the well-laid trap would close, two dozen men, led by one whose hatred was as deadly as his cunning was malicious, would close round the small band of fugitives, and their daring leader. They would all be captured. Armand, according to Chauvelin's pledged word would be restored to her, but her husband, Percy, whom with every breath she drew she seemed to love and worship more and more, he would fall into the hands of a remorseless enemy, who had no pity for a brave heart, no admiration for the courage of a noble soul, who would show nothing but hatred for the cunning antagonist, who had baffled him so long.

She heard the soldier giving a few brief directions to the Jew, then she retired quickly to the edge of the road, and cowered behind some low shrubs, whilst Desgas and his men came up.

All fell in noiselessly behind the cart, and slowly they all started down the dark road. Marguerite waited until she reckoned that they were well outside the range of earshot, then, she too in the darkness, which suddenly seemed to have become more intense, crept noiselessly along.

Chapter 28

The Père Blanchard's Hut

As in a dream, Marguerite followed on; the web was drawing more and more tightly every moment round the beloved life, which had become dearer than all. To see her husband once again, to tell him how she had suffered, how much she had wronged, and how little understood him, had become now her only aim. She had abandoned all hope of saving him: she saw him gradually hemmed in on all sides, and, in despair, she gazed round her into the darkness, and wondered whence he would presently come, to fall into the death-trap which his relentless enemy had prepared for him.

The distant roar of the waves now made her shudder; the occasional dismal cry of an owl, or a sea-gull, filled her with unspeakable horror. She thought of the ravenous beasts—in human shape—who lay in wait for their prey, and destroyed them, as mercilessly as any hungry wolf, for the satisfaction of their own appetite of hate. Marguerite was not afraid of the darkness, she only feared that man, on ahead, who was sitting at the bottom of a rough wooden cart, nursing thoughts of vengeance, which would have made the very demons in hell chuckle with delight.

Her feet were sore. Her knees shook under her, from sheer bodily fatigue. For days now, she had lived in a wild turmoil of excitement;

she had not had a quiet rest for three nights; now, she had walked on a slippery road for nearly two hours, and yet her determination never swerved for a moment. She would see her husband, tell him all, and, if he was ready to forgive the crime, which she had committed in her blind ignorance, she would yet have the happiness of dying by his side.

She must have walked on almost in a trance, instinct alone keeping her up, and guiding her in the wake of the enemy, when suddenly her ears, attuned to the slightest sound, by that same blind instinct, told her that the cart had stopped, and that the soldiers had halted. They had come to their destination. No doubt on the right, somewhere close ahead, was the footpath that led to the edge of the cliff and to the hut.

Heedless of any risks, she crept up quite close up to where Chauvelin stood, surrounded by his little troop: he had descended from the cart, and was giving some orders to the men. These she wanted to hear: what little chance she yet had, of being useful to Percy, consisted in hearing absolutely every word of his enemy's plans.

The spot where all the party had halted must have lain some eight hundred metres from the coast; the sound of the sea came only very faintly, as from a distance. Chauvelin and Desgas, followed by the soldiers, had turned off sharply to the right of the road, apparently on to the footpath, which led to the cliffs. The Jew had remained on the road, with his cart and nag.

Marguerite, with infinite caution, and literally crawling on her hands and knees, had also turned off to the right: to accomplish this she had to creep through the rough, low shrubs, trying to make as little noise as possible as she went along, tearing her face and hands against the dry twigs, intent only upon hearing without being seen or heard. Fortunately—as is usual in this part of France—the footpath was bordered by a low rough hedge, beyond which was a dry ditch, filled with coarse grass. In this Marguerite managed to find shelter; she was quite hidden from view yet could contrive to get within three yards of where Chauvelin stood, giving orders to his men.

"Now," he was saying in a low and peremptory whisper, "where is the Père Blanchard's hut?"

"About eight hundred metres from here, along the footpath," said the soldier who had lately been directing the party, "and half-way down the cliff."

"Very good. You shall lead us. Before we begin to descend the cliff, you shall creep down to the hut, as noiselessly as possible, and ascertain if the traitor royalists are there? Do you understand?"

"I understand, *citoyen*."

"Now listen very attentively, all of you," continued Chauvelin, impressively, and addressing the soldiers collectively, "for after this we may not be able to exchange another word, so remember every syllable I utter, as if your very lives depended on your memory. Perhaps they do," he added drily.

"We listen, *citoyen*," said Desgas, "and a soldier of the Republic never forgets an order."

"You, who have crept up to the hut, will try to peep inside. If an Englishman is there with those traitors, a man who is tall above the average, or who stoops as if he would disguise his height, then give a sharp, quick whistle as a signal to your comrades. All of you," he added, once more speaking to the soldiers collectively, "then quickly surround and rush into the hut, and each seize one of the men there, before they have time to draw their firearms; if any of them struggle, shoot at their legs or arms, but on no account kill the tall man. Do you understand?"

"We understand, *citoyen*."

"The man who is tall above the average is probably also strong above the average; it will take four or five of you at least to overpower him."

There was a little pause, then Chauvelin continued,—

"If the royalist traitors are still alone, which is more than likely to be the case, then warn your comrades who are lying in wait there, and all of you creep and take cover behind the rocks and boulders round the hut, and wait there, in dead silence, until the tall Englishman arrives; then only rush the hut, when he is safely within its doors. But remember that you must be as silent as the wolf is at night, when he prowls around the pens. I do not wish those royalists to be on the alert—the firing of a pistol, a shriek or call on their part would be sufficient, perhaps, to warn the tall personage to keep clear of the cliffs, and of the hut, and," he added emphatically, "it is the tall Englishman whom it is your duty to capture tonight."

"You shall be implicitly obeyed, *citoyen*."

"Then get along as noiselessly as possible, and I will follow you."

"What about the Jew, *citoyen?*" asked Desgas, as silently like noiseless shadows, one by one the soldiers began to creep along the rough and narrow footpath.

"Ah, yes; I had forgotten about the Jew," said Chauvelin, and, turning towards the Jew, he called him peremptorily.

"Here, you—Aaron, Moses, Abraham, or whatever your confounded name may be," he said to the old man, who had quietly stood beside his lean nag, as far away from the soldiers as possible.

"Benjamin Rosenbaum, so it please your Honour," he replied humbly.

"It does not please me to hear your voice, but it does please me to give you certain orders, which you will find it wise to obey."

"So, it please your Honour—"

"Hold your confounded tongue. You shall stay here, do you hear? with your horse and cart until our return. You are on no account to utter the faintest sound, or to even breathe louder than you can help; nor are you, on any consideration whatever, to leave your post, until I give you orders to do so. Do you understand?"

"But your Honour—" protested the Jew pitiably.

"There is no question of 'but' or of any argument," said Chauvelin, in a tone that made the timid old man tremble from head to foot. "If, when I return, I do not find you here, I most solemnly assure you that, wherever you may try to hide yourself, I can find you, and that punishment swift, sure and terrible, will sooner or later overtake you. Do you hear me?"

"But your Excellency—"

"I said, do you hear me?"

The soldiers had all crept away; the three men stood alone together in the dark and lonely road, with Marguerite there, behind the hedge, listening to Chauvelin's orders, as she would to her own death sentence.

"I heard your Honour," protested the Jew again, while he tried to draw nearer to Chauvelin, "and I swear by Abraham, Isaac and Jacob that I would obey your Honour most absolutely, and that I would not move from this place until your Honour once more deigned to shed the light of your countenance upon your humble servant; but remember, your Honour, I am a poor man; my nerves are not as strong as those of a young soldier. If midnight marauders should come prowling round this lonely road, I might scream or run in my fright! And is my life to be forfeit, is some terrible punishment to come on my poor old head for that which I cannot help?"

The Jew seemed in real distress; he was shaking from head to foot. Clearly, he was not the man to be left by himself on this lonely road. The man spoke truly; he might unwittingly, in sheer terror, utter the shriek that might prove a warning to the wily Scarlet Pimpernel.

Chauvelin reflected for a moment.

"Will your horse and cart be safe alone, here, do you think?" he asked roughly.

"I fancy, *citoyen*," here interposed Desgas, "that they will be safer without that dirty, cowardly Jew than with him. There seems no doubt that, if he gets scared, he will either make a bolt of it, or shriek his head off."

"But what am I to do with the brute?"

"Will you send him back to Calais*, citoyen?*"

"No, for we shall want him to drive back the wounded presently," said Chauvelin, with grim significance.

There was a pause again—Desgas waiting for the decision of his chief, and the old Jew whining beside his nag.

"Well, you lazy, lumbering old coward," said Chauvelin at last, "you had better shuffle along behind us. Here, Citoyen Desgas, tie this handkerchief tightly round the fellow's mouth."

Chauvelin handed a scarf to Desgas, who solemnly began winding it round the Jew's mouth. Meekly Benjamin Rosenbaum allowed himself to be gagged; he, evidently, preferred this uncomfortable state to that of being left alone, on the dark St. Martin Road. Then the three men fell in line.

"Quick!" said Chauvelin, impatiently, "we have already wasted much valuable time."

And the firm footsteps of Chauvelin and Desgas, the shuffling gait of the old Jew, soon died away along the footpath.

Marguerite had not lost a single one of Chauvelin's words of command. Her every nerve was strained to completely grasp the situation first, then to make a final appeal to those wits which had so often been called the sharpest in Europe, and which alone might be of service now.

Certainly, the situation was desperate enough; a tiny band of unsuspecting men, quietly awaiting the arrival of their rescuer, who was equally unconscious of the trap laid for them all. It seemed so horrible, this net, as it were drawn in a circle, at dead of night, on a lonely beach, round a few defenceless men, defenceless because they were tricked and unsuspecting; of these one was the husband she idolised, another the brother she loved. She vaguely wondered who the others were, who were also calmly waiting for the Scarlet Pimpernel, while death lurked behind every boulder of the cliffs.

For the moment she could do nothing but follow the soldiers and

Chauvelin. She feared to lose her way, or she would have rushed forward and found that wooden hut, and perhaps been in time to warn the fugitives and their brave deliverer yet.

For a second, the thought flashed through her mind of uttering the piercing shrieks, which Chauvelin seemed to dread, as a possible warning to the Scarlet Pimpernel and his friends—in the wild hope that they would hear and have yet time to escape before it was too late. But she did not know if her shrieks would reach the ears of the doomed men. Her effort might be premature, and she would never be allowed to make another. Her mouth would be securely gagged, like that of the Jew, and she, a helpless prisoner in the hands of Chauvelin's men.

Like a ghost she flitted noiselessly behind that hedge: she had taken her shoes off, and her stockings were by now torn off her feet. She felt neither soreness nor weariness; indomitable will to reach her husband in spite of adverse Fate, and of a cunning enemy, killed all sense of bodily pain within her, and rendered her instincts doubly acute.

She heard nothing save the soft and measured footsteps of Percy's enemies on in front; she saw nothing but—in her mind's eye—that wooden hut, and he, her husband, walking blindly to his doom.

Suddenly, those same keen instincts within her made her pause in her mad haste and cower still further within the shadow of the hedge. The moon, which had proved a friend to her by remaining hidden behind a bank of clouds, now emerged in all the glory of an early autumn night, and in a moment flooded the weird and lonely landscape with a rush of brilliant light.

There, not two hundred metres ahead, was the edge of the cliff, and below, stretching far away to free and happy England, the sea rolled on smoothly and peaceably. Marguerite's gaze rested for an instant on the brilliant, silvery waters; and as she gazed, her heart, which had been numb with pain for all these hours, seemed to soften and distend, and her eyes filled with hot tears: not three miles away, with white sails set, a graceful schooner lay in wait.

Marguerite had guessed rather than recognised her. It was the *Daydream*, Percy's favourite yacht, and all her crew of British sailors: her white sails, glistening in the moonlight, seemed to convey a message to Marguerite of joy and hope, which yet she feared could never be. She waited there, out at sea, waited for her master, like a beautiful white bird all ready to take flight, and he would never reach her, never see her smooth deck again, never gaze any more on the white cliffs of

England, the land of liberty and of hope.

The sight of the schooner seemed to infuse into the poor, wearied woman the superhuman strength of despair. There was the edge of the cliff, and some way below was the hut, where presently, her husband would meet his death. But the moon was out: she could see her way now: she would see the hut from a distance, run to it, rouse them all, warn them at any rate to be prepared and to sell their lives dearly, rather than be caught like so many rats in a hole.

She stumbled on behind the hedge in the low, thick grass of the ditch. She must have run on very fast, and had outdistanced Chauvelin and Desgas, for presently she reached the edge of the cliff, and heard their footsteps distinctly behind her. But only a very few yards away, and now the moonlight was full upon her, her figure must have been distinctly silhouetted against the silvery background of the sea.

Only for a moment, though; the next she had cowered, like some animal doubled up within itself. She peeped down the great rugged cliffs—the descent would be easy enough, as they were not precipitous, and the great boulders afforded plenty of foothold. Suddenly, as she gazed, she saw at some little distance on her left, and about midway down the cliffs, a rough wooden construction, through the wall of which a tiny red light glimmered like a beacon. Her very heart seemed to stand still, the eagerness of joy was so great that it felt like an awful pain.

She could not gauge how distant the hut was, but without hesitation she began the steep descent, creeping from boulder to boulder, caring nothing for the enemy behind, or for the soldiers, who evidently had all taken cover since the tall Englishman had not yet appeared.

On she pressed, forgetting the deadly foe on her track, running, stumbling, foot-sore, half-dazed, but still on—When, suddenly, a crevice, or stone, or slippery bit of rock, threw her violently to the ground. She struggled again to her feet and started running forward once more to give them that timely warning, to beg them to flee before he came, and to tell him to keep away—away from this death-trap—away from this awful doom. But now she realised that other steps, quicker than her own, were already close at her heels. The next instant a hand dragged at her skirt, and she was down on her knees again, whilst something was wound round her mouth to prevent her uttering a scream.

Bewildered, half frantic with the bitterness of disappointment, she looked round her helplessly, and, bending down quite close to her, she saw through the mist, which seemed to gather round her, a pair of keen, malicious eyes, which appeared to her excited brain to have a weird, supernatural green light in them. She lay in the shadow of a great boulder; Chauvelin could not see her features, but he passed his thin, white fingers over her face.

"A woman!" he whispered, "by all the saints in the calendar."

"We cannot let her loose, that's certain," he muttered to himself. "I wonder now—"

Suddenly he paused, after a few moments of deadly silence, he gave forth a long, low, curious chuckle, while once again Marguerite felt, with a horrible shudder, his thin fingers wandering over her face.

"Dear me! dear me!" he whispered, with affected gallantry, "this is indeed a charming surprise," and Marguerite felt her resistless hand raised to Chauvelin's thin, mocking lips.

The situation was indeed grotesque, had it not been at the same time so fearfully tragic: the poor, weary woman, broken in spirit, and half frantic with the bitterness of her disappointment, receiving on her knees the *banal* gallantries of her deadly enemy.

Her senses were leaving her; half choked with the tight grip round her mouth, she had no strength to move or to utter the faintest sound. The excitement which all along had kept up her delicate body seemed at once to have subsided, and the feeling of blank despair to have completely paralyzed her brain and nerves.

Chauvelin must have given some directions, which she was too dazed to hear, for she felt herself lifted from off her feet: the bandage round her mouth was made more secure, and a pair of strong arms carried her towards that tiny, red light, on ahead, which she had looked upon as a beacon and the last faint glimmer of hope.

Chapter 29

Trapped

She did not know how long she was thus carried along, she had lost all notion of time and space, and for a few seconds tired nature, mercifully, deprived her of consciousness.

When she once more realised her state, she felt that she was placed with some degree of comfort upon a man's coat, with her back resting against a fragment of rock. The moon was hidden again behind some clouds, and the darkness seemed in comparison more intense. The sea was roaring some two hundred feet below her, and on looking all round she could no longer see any vestige of the tiny glimmer of red light.

That the end of the journey had been reached, she gathered from the fact that she heard rapid questions and answers spoken in a whisper quite close to her.

"There are four men in there, *citoyen*; they are sitting by the fire, and seem to be waiting quietly."

"The hour?"

"Nearly two o'clock."

"The tide?"

"Coming in quickly."

"The schooner?"

"Obviously an English one, lying some three kilometres out. But we cannot see her boat."

"Have the men taken cover?"

"Yes, *citoyen*."

"They will not blunder?"

"They will not stir until the tall Englishman comes, then they will surround and overpower the five men."

"Right. And the lady?"

"Still dazed, I fancy. She's close beside you, *citoyen*."

"And the Jew?"

"He's gagged, and his legs strapped together. He cannot move or scream."

"Good. Then have your gun ready, in case you want it. Get close to the hut and leave me to look after the lady."

Desgas evidently obeyed, for Marguerite heard him creeping away along the stony cliff, then she felt that a pair of warm, thin, talon-like hands took hold of both her own and held them in a grip of steel.

"Before that handkerchief is removed from your pretty mouth, fair lady," whispered Chauvelin close to her ear, "I think it right to give you one small word of warning. What has procured me the honour of being followed across the Channel by so charming a companion, I cannot, of course, conceive, but, if I mistake it not, the purpose of this flattering attention is not one that would commend itself to my vanity and I think that I am right in surmising, moreover, that the first sound which your pretty lips would utter, as soon as the cruel gag is removed, would be one that would prove a warning to the cunning fox, which I have been at such pains to track to his lair."

He paused a moment, while the steel-like grasp seemed to tighten round her wrist; then he resumed in the same hurried whisper:—

"Inside that hut, if again I am not mistaken, your brother, Armand St. Just, waits with that traitor de Tournay, and two other men unknown to you, for the arrival of the mysterious rescuer, whose identity has for so long puzzled our Committee of Public Safety—the audacious Scarlet Pimpernel. No doubt if you scream, if there is a scuffle here, if shots are fired, it is more than likely that the same long legs that brought this scarlet enigma here, will as quickly take him to some place of safety. The purpose then, for which I have travelled all these miles, will remain unaccomplished. On the other hand, it only rests with yourself that your brother—Armand—shall be free to go off with you tonight if you like, to England, or any other place of safety."

Marguerite could not utter a sound, as the handkerchief was would very tightly round her mouth, but Chauvelin was peering through the darkness very closely into her face; no doubt too her hand gave a responsive appeal to his last suggestion, for presently he continued:—

"What I want you to do to ensure Armand's safety is a very simple thing, dear lady."

"What is it?" Marguerite's hand seemed to convey to his, in response.

"To remain—on this spot, without uttering a sound, until I give you leave to speak. Ah! but I think you will obey," he added, with that funny dry chuckle of his as Marguerite's whole figure seemed to stiffen, in defiance of this order, "for let me tell you that if you scream, nay! if you utter one sound, or attempt to move from here, my men—there are thirty of them about—will seize St. Just, de Tournay, and their two friends, and shoot them here—by my orders—before your eyes."

Marguerite had listened to her implacable enemy's speech with ever-increasing terror. Numbed with physical pain, she yet had sufficient mental vitality in her to realise the full horror of this terrible "either—or" he was once more putting before her; "either—or" ten thousand times more appalling and horrible than the one he had suggested to her that fatal night at the ball.

This time it meant that she should keep still and allow the husband she worshipped to walk unconsciously to his death, or that she should, by trying to give him a word of warning, which perhaps might even be unavailing, actually give the signal for her own brother's death, and that of three other unsuspecting men.

She could not see Chauvelin, but she could almost feel those keen, pale eyes of his fixed maliciously upon her helpless form, and his hurried, whispered words reached her ear, as the death-knell of her last faint, lingering hope.

"Nay, fair lady," he added urbanely, "you can have no interest in anyone save in St. Just, and all you need do for his safety is to remain where you are, and to keep silent. My men have strict orders to spare him in every way. As for that enigmatic Scarlet Pimpernel, what is he to you? Believe me, no warning from you could possibly save him. And now dear lady, let me remove this unpleasant coercion, which has been placed before your pretty mouth. You see I wish you to be perfectly free, in the choice which you are about to make."

Her thoughts in a whirl, her temples aching, her nerves paralyzed, her body numb with pain, Marguerite sat there, in the darkness which surrounded her as with a pall. From where she sat she could not see the sea, but she heard the incessant mournful murmur of the incoming tide, which spoke of her dead hopes, her lost love, the husband she had with her own hand betrayed, and sent to his death.

Chauvelin removed the handkerchief from her mouth. She certainly did not scream: at that moment, she had no strength to do anything but barely to hold herself upright, and to force herself to think.

Oh! think! think! think! of what she should do. The minutes flew on; in this awful stillness she could not tell how fast or how slowly; she heard nothing, she saw nothing: she did not feel the sweet-smelling autumn air, scented with the briny odour of the sea, she no longer heard the murmur of the waves, the occasional rattling of a pebble, as it rolled down some steep incline. More and more unreal did the whole situation seem. It was impossible that she, Marguerite Blakeney, the queen of London society, should actually be sitting here on this bit of lonely coast, in the middle of the night, side by side with a most bitter enemy; and oh! it was not possible that somewhere, not many hundred feet away perhaps, from where she stood, the being she had once despised, but who now, in every moment of this weird, dream-like life, became more and more dear—it was not possible that *he* was unconsciously, even now walking to his doom, whilst she did nothing to save him.

Why did she not with unearthly screams, that would re-echo from one end of the lonely beach to the other, send out a warning to him to desist, to retrace his steps, for death lurked here whilst he advanced? Once or twice the screams rose to her throat—as if by instinct: then, before her eyes there stood the awful alternative: her brother and those three men shot before her eyes, practically by her orders: she their murderer.

Oh! that fiend in human shape, next to her, knew human—female—nature well. He had played upon her feelings as a skilful musician plays upon an instrument. He had gauged her very thoughts to a nicety.

She could not give that signal—for she was weak, and she was a woman. How could she deliberately order Armand to be shot before her eyes, to have his dear blood upon her head, he dying perhaps with a curse on her, upon his lips. And little Suzanne's father, too! he, an old man; and the others!—oh! it was all too, too horrible.

Wait! wait! wait! how long? The early morning hours sped on, and yet it was not dawn: the sea continued its incessant mournful murmur, the autumnal breeze sighed gently in the night: the lonely beach was silent, even as the grave.

Suddenly from somewhere, not very far away, a cheerful, strong voice was heard singing "God save the King!"

Chapter 30

The Schooner

Marguerite's aching heart stood still. She felt, more than she heard, the men on the watch preparing for the fight. Her senses told her that each, with sword in hand, was crouching, ready for the spring.

The voice came nearer and nearer; in the vast immensity of these lonely cliffs, with the loud murmur of the sea below, it was impossible to say how near, or how far, nor yet from which direction came that cheerful singer, who sang to God to save his King, whilst he himself was in such deadly danger. Faint at first, the voice grew louder and louder; from time to time a small pebble detached itself apparently from beneath the firm tread of the singer and went rolling down the rocky cliffs to the beach below.

Marguerite as she heard, felt that her very life was slipping away, as if when that voice drew nearer, when that singer became entrapped . . .

She distinctly heard the click of Desgas' gun close to her—.

No! no! no! no! Oh, God in heaven! this cannot be! let Armand's blood then be on her own head! let her be branded as his murderer! let even he, whom she loved, despise and loathe her for this, but God! oh God! save him at any cost!

With a wild shriek, she sprang to her feet, and darted round the rock, against which she had been cowering; she saw the little red gleam through the chinks of the hut; she ran up to it and fell against its wooden walls, which she began to hammer with clenched fists in an almost maniacal frenzy, while she shouted,—

"Armand! Armand! for God's sake fire! your leader is near! he is coming! he is betrayed! Armand! Armand! fire in Heaven's name!"

She was seized and thrown to the ground. She lay there moaning, bruised, not caring, but still half-sobbing, half-shrieking,—

"Percy, my husband, for God's sake fly! Armand! Armand! why don't you fire?"

"One of you stop that woman screaming," hissed Chauvelin, who hardly could refrain from striking her.

Something was thrown over her face; she could not breathe, and perforce she was silent.

The bold singer, too, had become silent, warned, no doubt, of his impending danger by Marguerite's frantic shrieks. The men had sprung to their feet, there was no need for further silence on their part; the very cliffs echoed the poor, heart-broken woman's screams.

Chauvelin, with a muttered oath, which boded no good to her, who had dared to upset his most cherished plans, had hastily shouted the word of command,—

"Into it, my men, and let no one escape from that hut alive!"

The moon had once more emerged from between the clouds: the darkness on the cliffs had gone, giving place once more to brilliant, silvery light. Some of the soldiers had rushed to the rough, wooden door of the hut, whilst one of them kept guard over Marguerite.

The door was partially open; one of the soldiers pushed it further, but within all was darkness, the charcoal fire only lighting with a dim, red light the furthest corner of the hut. The soldiers paused automatically at the door, like machines waiting for further orders.

Chauvelin, who was prepared for a violent onslaught from within, and for a vigorous resistance from the four fugitives, under cover of the darkness, was for the moment paralyzed with astonishment when he saw the soldiers standing there at attention, like sentries on guard, whilst not a sound proceeded from the hut.

Filled with strange, anxious foreboding, he, too, went to the door of the hut, and peering into the gloom, he asked quickly,—

"What is the meaning of this?"

"I think, *citoyen*, that there is no one there now," replied one of the soldiers imperturbably.

"You have not let those four men go?" thundered Chauvelin, menacingly. "I ordered you to let no man escape alive!—Quick, after them all of you! Quick, in every direction!"

The men, obedient as machines, rushed down the rocky incline towards the beach, some going off to right and left, as fast as their feet could carry them.

"You and your men will pay with your lives for this blunder, *citoyen* sergeant," said Chauvelin viciously to the sergeant who had been in charge of the men; "and you, too, *citoyen*," he added turning with a snarl to Desgas, "for disobeying my orders."

"You ordered us to wait, *citoyen*, until the tall Englishman arrived and joined the four men in the hut. No one came," said the sergeant sullenly.

"But I ordered you just now, when the woman screamed, to rush in and let no one escape."

"But, *citoyen*, the four men who were there before had been gone some time, I think—"

"You think?—You?—" said Chauvelin, almost choking with fury, "and you let them go—"

"You ordered us to wait, *citoyen*," protested the sergeant, "and to implicitly obey your commands on pain of death. We waited."

"I heard the men creep out of the hut, not many minutes after we took cover, and long before the woman screamed," he added, as Chauvelin seemed still quite speechless with rage.

"Hark!" said Desgas suddenly.

In the distance the sound of repeated firing was heard. Chauvelin tried to peer along the beach below, but as luck would have it, the fitful moon once more hid her light behind a bank of clouds, and he could see nothing.

"One of you go into the hut and strike a light," he stammered at last.

Stolidly the sergeant obeyed: he went up to the charcoal fire and lit the small lantern he carried in his belt; it was evident that the hut was quite empty.

"Which way did they go?" asked Chauvelin.

"I could not tell, *citoyen*," said the sergeant; "they went straight down the cliff first, then disappeared behind some boulders."

"Hush! what was that?"

All three men listened attentively. In the far, very far distance, could be heard faintly echoing and already dying away, the quick, sharp splash of half a dozen oars. Chauvelin took out his handkerchief and wiped the perspiration from his forehead.

"The schooner's boat!" was all he gasped.

Evidently Armand St. Just and his three companions had managed to creep along the side of the cliffs, whilst the men, like true soldiers of the well-drilled Republican Army, had with blind obedience, and in fear of their own lives, implicitly obeyed Chauvelin's orders—to wait for the tall Englishman, who was the important capture.

They had no doubt reached one of the creeks which jut far out to sea on this coast at intervals; behind this, the boat of the *Daydream* must have been on the lookout for them, and they were by now safely on board the British schooner.

As if to confirm this last supposition, the dull boom of a gun was heard from out at sea.

"The schooner, *citoyen*," said Desgas, quietly; "she's off."

It needed all Chauvelin's nerve and presence of mind not to give way to a useless and undignified access of rage. There was no doubt now, that once again, that accursed British head had completely outwitted him. How he had contrived to reach the hut, without being seen by one of the thirty soldiers who guarded the spot, was more than Chauvelin could conceive. That he had done so before the thirty men had arrived on the cliff was, of course, fairly clear, but how he had come over in Reuben Goldstein's cart, all the way from Calais, without being sighted by the various patrols on duty was impossible of explanation. It really seemed as if some potent Fate watched over that daring Scarlet Pimpernel, and his astute enemy almost felt a superstitious shudder pass through him, as he looked round at the towering cliffs, and the loneliness of this outlying coast.

But surely this was reality! and the year of grace 1792: there were no fairies and hobgoblins about. Chauvelin and his thirty men had all heard with their own ears that accursed voice singing "God save the King," fully twenty minutes *after* they had all taken cover around the hut; by that time the four fugitives must have reached the creek, and got into the boat, and the nearest creek was more than a mile from the hut.

Where had that daring singer got to? Unless Satan himself had lent him wings, he could not have covered that mile on a rocky cliff in the space of two minutes; and only two minutes had elapsed between his song and the sound of the boat's oars away at sea. He must have remained behind and was even now hiding somewhere about the cliffs; the patrols were still about, he would still be sighted, no doubt. Chauvelin felt hopeful once again.

One or two of the men, who had run after the fugitives, were now slowly working their way up the cliff: one of them reached Chauvelin's side, at the very moment that this hope arose in the astute diplomatist's heart.

"We were too late, *citoyen*," the soldier said, "we reached the beach just before the moon was hidden by that bank of clouds. The boat had undoubtedly been on the look-out behind that first creek, a mile off, but she had shoved off some time ago, when we got to the beach, and was already some way out to sea. We fired after her, but of course, it was no good. She was making straight and quickly for the schooner. We saw her very clearly in the moonlight."

"Yes," said Chauvelin, with eager impatience, "she had shoved off some time ago, you said, and the nearest creek is a mile further on."

"Yes, *citoyen!* I ran all the way, straight to the beach, though I guessed the boat would have waited somewhere near the creek, as the tide would reach there earliest. The boat must have shoved off some minutes before the woman began to scream."

"Bring the light in here!" he commanded eagerly, as he once more entered the hut.

The sergeant brought his lantern, and together the two men explored the little place: with a rapid glance Chauvelin noted its contents: the cauldron placed close under an aperture in the wall, and containing the last few dying embers of burned charcoal, a couple of stools, overturned as if in the haste of sudden departure, then the fisherman's tools and his nets lying in one corner, and beside them, something small and white.

"Pick that up," said Chauvelin to the sergeant, pointing to this white scrap, "and bring it to me."

It was a crumpled piece of paper, evidently forgotten there by the fugitives, in their hurry to get away. The sergeant, much awed by the *citoyen's* obvious rage and impatience, picked the paper up and handed it respectfully to Chauvelin.

"Read it, sergeant," said the latter curtly.

"It is almost illegible, *citoyen*—a fearful scrawl—"

"I ordered you to read it," repeated Chauvelin, viciously.

The sergeant, by the light of his lantern, began deciphering the few hastily scrawled words.

"I cannot quite reach you, without risking your lives and endangering the success of your rescue. When you receive this, wait two minutes, then creep out of the hut one by one, turn to your left sharply, and creep cautiously down the cliff; keep to the left all the time, till you reach the first rock, which you see jutting far out to sea—behind it in the creek the boat is on the look-out for you—give a long, sharp whistle—she will come up—get into her—my men will row you to the schooner, and thence to England and safety—once on board the *Daydream* send the boat back for me, tell my men that I shall be at the creek, which is in a direct line opposite the 'Chat Gris' near Calais. They know it. I shall be there as soon as possible—they must wait for me at a safe distance out at sea, till they hear the usual signal. Do not delay—and obey these instructions implicitly."

"Then there is the signature, *citoyen*," added the sergeant, as he handed the paper back to Chauvelin.

But the latter had not waited an instant. One phrase of the momentous scrawl had caught his ear. "I shall be at the creek which is in a direct line opposite the 'Chat Gris' near Calais": that phrase might yet mean victory for him. "Which of you knows this coast well?" he shouted to his men who now one by one all returned from their fruitless run and were all assembled once more round the hut.

"I do, *citoyen*," said one of them, "I was born in Calais, and know every stone of these cliffs."

"There is a creek in a direct line from the 'Chat Gris'?"

"There is, *citoyen*. I know it well."

"The Englishman is hoping to reach that creek. He does *not* know every stone of these cliffs, he may go there by the longest way round, and in any case he will proceed cautiously for fear of the patrols. At any rate, there is a chance to get him yet. A thousand *francs* to each man who gets to that creek before that long-legged Englishman."

"I know of a short cut across the cliffs," said the soldier, and with an enthusiastic shout, he rushed forward, followed closely by his comrades.

Within a few minutes their running footsteps had died away in the distance. Chauvelin listened to them for a moment; the promise of the reward was lending spurs to the soldiers of the Republic. The gleam of hate and anticipated triumph was once more apparent on his face.

Close to him Desgas still stood mute and impassive, waiting for further orders, whilst two soldiers were kneeling beside the prostrate form of Marguerite. Chauvelin gave his secretary a vicious look. His well-laid plan had failed, its sequel was problematical; there was still a great chance now that the Scarlet Pimpernel might yet escape, and Chauvelin, with that unreasoning fury, which sometimes assails a strong nature, was longing to vent his rage on somebody.

The soldiers were holding Marguerite pinioned to the ground, though, she, poor soul, was not making the faintest struggle. Overwrought nature had at last peremptorily asserted herself, and she lay there in a dead swoon: her eyes circled by deep purple lines, that told of long, sleepless nights, her hair matted and damp round her forehead, her lips parted in a sharp curve that spoke of physical pain.

The cleverest woman in Europe, the elegant and fashionable Lady Blakeney, who had dazzled London society with her beauty, her wit and her extravagances, presented a very pathetic picture of tired-out, suffering womanhood, which would have appealed to any, but the hard, vengeful heart of her baffled enemy.

"It is no use mounting guard over a woman who is half dead," he said spitefully to the soldiers, "when you have allowed five men who were very much alive to escape."

Obediently the soldiers rose to their feet.

"You'd better try and find that footpath again for me, and that broken-down cart we left on the road."

Then suddenly a bright idea seemed to strike him.

"Ah! by-the-bye! where is the Jew?"

"Close by here, *citoyen*," said Desgas; "I gagged him and tied his legs together as you commanded."

From the immediate vicinity, a plaintive moan reached Chauvelin's ears. He followed his secretary, who led the way to the other side of the hut, where, fallen into an absolute heap of dejection, with his legs tightly pinioned together and his mouth gagged, lay the unfortunate descendant of Israel.

His face in the silvery light of the moon looked positively ghastly with terror: his eyes were wide open and almost glassy, and his whole body was trembling, as if with ague, while a piteous wail escaped his bloodless lips. The rope which had originally been wound round his shoulders and arms had evidently given way, for it lay in a tangle about his body, but he seemed quite unconscious of this, for he had not made the slightest attempt to move from the place where Desgas had originally put him: like a terrified chicken which looks upon a line of white chalk, drawn on a table, as on a string which paralyzes its movements.

"Bring the cowardly brute here," commanded Chauvelin.

He certainly felt exceedingly vicious, and since he had no reasonable grounds for venting his ill-humour on the soldiers who had but too punctually obeyed his orders, he felt that the son of the despised race would prove an excellent butt. With true French contempt of the Jew, which has survived the lapse of centuries even to this day, he would not go too near him, but said with biting sarcasm, as the wretched old man was brought in full light of the moon by the two soldiers,—

"I suppose now, that being a Jew, you have a good memory for bargains?"

"Answer!" he again commanded, as the Jew with trembling lips seemed too frightened to speak.

"Yes, your Honour," stammered the poor wretch.

"You remember, then, the one you and I made together in Calais, when you undertook to overtake Reuben Goldstein, his nag and my friend the tall stranger? Eh?"

"B—b—but—your Honour—"

"There is no 'but.' I said, do you remember?"

"Y—y—y—yes—your Honour!"

"What was the bargain?"

There was dead silence. The unfortunate man looked round at the great cliffs, the moon above, the stolid faces of the soldiers, and even at the poor, prostate, inanimate woman close by, but said nothing.

"Will you speak?" thundered Chauvelin, menacingly.

He did try, poor wretch, but, obviously, he could not. There was no doubt, however, that he knew what to expect from the stern man before him.

"Your Honour—" he ventured imploringly.

"Since your terror seems to have paralyzed your tongue," said Chauvelin sarcastically, "I must needs refresh your memory. It was agreed between us, that if we overtook my friend the tall stranger, before he reached this place, you were to have ten pieces of gold."

A low moan escaped from the Jew's trembling lips.

"But," added Chauvelin, with slow emphasis, "if you deceived me in your promise, you were to have a sound beating, one that would teach you not to tell lies."

"I did not, your Honour; I swear it by Abraham—"

"And by all the other patriarchs, I know. Unfortunately, they are still in Hades, I believe, according to your creed, and cannot help you much in your present trouble. Now, you did not fulfil your share of the bargain, but I am ready to fulfil mine. Here," he added, turning to the soldiers, "the buckle-end of your two belts to this confounded Jew."

As the soldiers obediently unbuckled their heavy leather belts, the Jew set up a howl that surely would have been enough to bring all the patriarchs out of Hades and elsewhere, to defend their descendant from the brutality of this French official.

"I think I can rely on you, *citoyen* soldiers," laughed Chauvelin, maliciously, "to give this old liar the best and soundest beating he has ever experienced. But don't kill him," he added drily.

"We will obey, *citoyen*," replied the soldiers as imperturbably as ever.

He did not wait to see his orders carried out: he knew that he could trust these soldiers—who were still smarting under his rebuke—not to mince matters, when given a free hand to belabour a third party.

"When that lumbering coward has had his punishment," he said to Desgas, "the men can guide us as far as the cart, and one of them can drive us in it back to Calais. The Jew and the woman can look after each other," he added roughly, "until we can send somebody for them in the morning. They can't run away very far, in their present condition, and we cannot be troubled with them just now."

Chauvelin had not given up all hope. His men, he knew, were spurred on by the hope of the reward. That enigmatic and audacious Scarlet Pimpernel, alone and with thirty men at his heels, could not reasonably be expected to escape a second time.

But he felt less sure now: the Englishman's audacity had baffled him once, whilst the wooden-headed stupidity of the soldiers, and the interference of a woman had turned his hand, which held all the trumps, into a losing one. If Marguerite had not taken up his time, if the soldiers had had a grain of intelligence, if—it was a long "if," and Chauvelin stood for a moment quite still, and enrolled thirty odd people in one long, overwhelming anathema. Nature, poetic, silent, balmy, the bright moon, the calm, silvery sea spoke of beauty and of rest, and Chauvelin cursed nature, cursed man and woman, and above all, he cursed all long-legged, meddlesome British enigmas with one gigantic curse.

The howls of the Jew behind him, undergoing his punishment sent a balm through his heart, overburdened as it was with revengeful malice. He smiled. It eased his mind to think that some human being at least was, like himself, not altogether at peace with mankind.

He turned and took a last look at the lonely bit of coast, where stood the wooden hut, now bathed in moonlight, the scene of the greatest discomfiture ever experienced by a leading member of the Committee of Public Safety.

Against a rock, on a hard bed of stone, lay the unconscious figure of Marguerite Blakeney, while some few paces further on, the unfortunate Jew was receiving on his broad back the blows of two stout leather belts, wielded by the stolid arms of two sturdy soldiers of the Republic. The howls of Benjamin Rosenbaum were fit to make the dead rise from their graves. They must have wakened all the gulls from sleep and made them look down with great interest at the doings of the lords of the creation.

"That will do," commanded Chauvelin, as the Jew's moans became more feeble, and the poor wretch seemed to have fainted away, "we don't want to kill him."

Obediently the soldiers buckled on their belts, one of them viciously kicking the Jew to one side.

"Leave him there," said Chauvelin, "and lead the way now quickly to the cart. I'll follow."

He walked up to where Marguerite lay and looked down into her face. She had evidently recovered consciousness and was making feeble efforts to raise herself. Her large, blue eyes were looking at the moonlit scene round her with a scared and terrified look; they rested with a mixture of horror and pity on the Jew, whose luckless fate and wild howls had been the first signs that struck her, with her returning senses; then she caught sight of Chauvelin, in his neat, dark clothes, which seemed hardly crumpled after the stirring events of the last few hours. He was smiling sarcastically, and his pale eyes peered down at her with a look of intense malice.

With mock gallantry, he stooped and raised her icy-cold hand to his lips, which sent a thrill of indescribable loathing through Marguerite's weary frame.

"I much regret, fair lady," he said in his most suave tones, "that circumstances, over which I have no control, compel me to leave you here for the moment. But I go away, secure in the knowledge that I do not leave you unprotected. Our friend Benjamin here, though a trifle the worse for wear at the present moment, will prove a gallant defender of your fair person, I have no doubt. At dawn I will send an escort for you; until then, I feel sure that you will find him devoted, though perhaps a trifle slow."

Marguerite only had the strength to turn her head away. Her heart was broken with cruel anguish. One awful thought had returned to her mind, together with gathering consciousness: "What had become of Percy?—What of Armand?"

She knew nothing of what had happened after she heard the cheerful song, "God save the King," which she believed to be the signal of death.

"I, myself," concluded Chauvelin, "must now very reluctantly leave you. *Au revoir*, fair lady. We meet, I hope, soon in London. Shall I see you at the Prince of Wales' garden party?—No?—Ah, well, *au revoir!*—Remember me, I pray, to Sir Percy Blakeney."

And, with a last ironical smile and bow, he once more kissed her hand, and disappeared down the footpath in the wake of the soldiers and followed by the imperturbable Desgas.

Chapter 31

The Escape

Marguerite listened—half-dazed as she was—to the fast-retreating, firm footsteps of the four men.

All nature was so still that she, lying with her ear close to the ground, could distinctly trace the sound of their tread, as they ultimately turned into the road, and presently the faint echo of the old cart-wheels, the halting gait of the lean nag, told her that her enemy was a quarter of a league away. How long she lay there she knew not. She had lost count of time; dreamily she looked up at the moonlit sky and listened to the monotonous roll of the waves.

The invigorating scent of the sea was nectar to her wearied body, the immensity of the lonely cliffs was silent and dreamlike. Her brain only remained conscious of its ceaseless, its intolerable torture of uncertainty.

She did not know!—

She did not know whether Percy was even now, at this moment, in the hands of the soldiers of the Republic, enduring—as she had done herself—the gibes and jeers of his malicious enemy. She did not know, on the other hand, whether Armand's lifeless body did not lie there, in the hut, whilst Percy had escaped, only to hear that his wife's hands had guided the human bloodhounds to the murder of Armand and his friends.

The physical pain of utter weariness was so great, that she hoped confidently her tired body could rest here for ever, after all the turmoil, the passion, and the intrigues of the last few days—here, beneath that clear sky, within sound of the sea, and with this balmy autumn breeze whispering to her a last lullaby. All was so solitary, so silent, like unto dreamland. Even the last faint echo of the distant cart had long ago died away, afar.

Suddenly . . . a sound . . . the strangest, undoubtedly, that these lonely cliffs of France had ever heard, broke the silent solemnity of the shore.

So strange a sound was it that the gentle breeze ceased to murmur, the tiny pebbles to roll down the steep incline! So strange, that Marguerite, wearied, overwrought as she was, thought that the beneficial unconsciousness of the approach of death was playing her half-sleeping senses a weird and elusive trick.

It was the sound of a good, solid, absolutely British "Damn!"

The sea gulls in their nests awoke and looked round in astonishment; a distant and solitary owl set up a midnight hoot, the tall cliffs frowned down majestically at the strange, unheard-of sacrilege.

Marguerite did not trust her ears. Half-raising herself on her hands, she strained every sense to see or hear, to know the meaning of this very earthly sound.

All was still again for the space of a few seconds; the same silence once more fell upon the great and lonely vastness.

Then Marguerite, who had listened as in a trance, who felt she must be dreaming with that cool, magnetic moonlight overhead, heard again; and this time her heart stood still, her eyes large and dilated, looked round her, not daring to trust her other sense.

"Odd's life! but I wish those demmed fellows had not hit quite so hard!"

This time it was quite unmistakable, only one particular pair of essentially British lips could have uttered those words, in sleepy, drawly, affected tones.

"Damn!" repeated those same British lips, emphatically. "Zounds! but I'm as weak as a rat!"

In a moment Marguerite was on her feet.

Was she dreaming? Were those great, stony cliffs the gates of paradise? Was the fragrant breath of the breeze suddenly caused by the flutter of angels' wings, bringing tidings of unearthly joys to her, after all her suffering, or—faint and ill—was she the prey of delirium?

She listened again, and once again she heard the same very earthly sounds of good, honest British language, not the least akin to whisperings from paradise or flutter of angels' wings.

She looked round her eagerly at the tall cliffs, the lonely hut, the great stretch of rocky beach. Somewhere there, above or below her, behind a boulder or inside a crevice, but still hidden from her longing, feverish eyes, must be the owner of that voice, which once used to irritate her, but now would make her the happiest woman in Europe, if only she could locate it.

"Percy! Percy!" she shrieked hysterically, tortured between doubt and hope, "I am here! Come to me! Where are you? Percy! Percy!—"

"It's all very well calling me, m'dear!" said the same sleepy, drawly voice, "but odd's life, I cannot come to you: those demmed frog-eaters have trussed me like a goose on a spit, and I am weak as a mouse—I cannot get away."

And still Marguerite did not understand. She did not realise for at least another ten seconds whence came that voice, so drawly, so dear, but alas! with a strange accent of weakness and of suffering. There was no one within sight—except by that rock—Great God!—the Jew!—Was she mad or dreaming?—

His back was against the pale moonlight, he was half crouching, trying vainly to raise himself with his arms tightly pinioned. Marguerite ran up to him, took his head in both her hands—and look straight into a pair of blue eyes, good-natured, even a trifle amused—shining out of the weird and distorted mask of the Jew.

"Percy!—Percy!—my husband!" she gasped, faint with the fulness of her joy. "Thank God! Thank God!"

"*La!* m'dear," he rejoined good-humouredly, "we will both do that *anon*, an' you think you can loosen these demmed ropes and release me from my inelegant attitude."

She had no knife, her fingers were numb and weak, but she worked away with her teeth, while great welcome tears poured from her eyes, onto those poor, pinioned hands.

"Odd's life!" he said, when at last, after frantic efforts on her part, the ropes seemed at last to be giving way, "but I marvel whether it has ever happened before, that an English gentleman allowed himself to be licked by a demmed foreigner and made no attempt to give as good as he got."

It was very obvious that he was exhausted from sheer physical pain, and when at last the rope gave way, he fell in a heap against the rock.

Marguerite looked helplessly round her.

"Oh! for a drop of water on this awful beach!" she cried in agony, seeing that he was ready to faint again.

"Nay, m'dear," he murmured with his good-humoured smile, "personally I should prefer a drop of good French brandy! an you'll dive in the pocket of this dirty old garment, you'll find my flask. . . . I am demmed if I can move."

When he had drunk some brandy, he forced Marguerite to do likewise.

"*La!* that's better now! Eh! little woman?" he said, with a sigh of satisfaction. "Heigh-ho! but this is a queer rig-up for Sir Percy Blakeney, Bart., to be found in by his lady, and no mistake. Begad!" he added, passing his hand over his chin, "I haven't been shaved for nearly twenty hours: I must look a disgusting object. As for these curls—"

And laughingly he took off the disfiguring wig and curls, and stretched out his long limbs, which were cramped from many hours' stooping. Then he bent forward and looked long and searchingly into his wife's blue eyes.

"Percy," she whispered, while a deep blush suffused her delicate cheeks and neck, "if you only knew—"

"I do know, dear—everything," he said with infinite gentleness.

"And can you ever forgive?"

"I have naught to forgive, sweetheart; your heroism, your devotion, which I, alas! so little deserved, have more than atoned for that unfortunate episode at the ball."

"Then you knew?—" she whispered, "all the time—"

"Yes!" he replied tenderly, "I knew—all the time—But, begad! had I but known what a noble heart yours was, my Margot, I should have trusted you, as you deserved to be trusted, and you would not have had to undergo the terrible sufferings of the past few hours, in order to run after a husband, who has done so much that needs forgiveness."

They were sitting side by side, leaning up against a rock, and he had rested his aching head on her shoulder. She certainly now deserved the name of "the happiest woman in Europe."

"It is a case of the blind leading the lame, sweetheart, is it not?" he said with his good-natured smile of old. "Odd's life! but I do not know which are the more sore, my shoulders or your little feet."

He bent forward to kiss them, for they peeped out through her torn stockings, and bore pathetic witness to her endurance and devotion.

"But Armand—" she said with sudden terror and remorse, as in the midst of her happiness the image of the beloved brother, for whose sake she had so deeply sinned, rose now before her mind.

"Oh! have no fear for Armand, sweetheart," he said tenderly, "did I not pledge you my word that he should be safe? He with de Tournay and the others are even now on board the *Daydream*."

"But how?" she gasped, "I do not understand."

"Yet, 'tis simple enough, m'dear," he said with that funny, half-shy, half-inane laugh of his, "you see! when I found that that brute Chauvelin meant to stick to me like a leech, I thought the best thing I could do, as I could not shake him off, was to take him along with me. I had to get to Armand and the others somehow, and all the roads were patrolled, and everyone on the look-out for your humble servant. I knew that when I slipped through Chauvelin's fingers at the 'Chat Gris,' that he would lie in wait for me here, whichever way I took. I wanted to keep an eye on him and his doings, and a British head is as good as a French one any day."

Indeed, it had proved to be infinitely better, and Marguerite's heart was filled with joy and marvel, as he continued to recount to her the daring manner in which he had snatched the fugitives away, right from under Chauvelin's very nose.

"Dressed as the dirty old Jew," he said gaily, "I knew I should not be recognised. I had met Reuben Goldstein in Calais earlier in the evening. For a few gold pieces he supplied me with this rig-out and undertook to bury himself out of sight of everybody, whilst he lent me his cart and nag."

"But if Chauvelin had discovered you," she gasped excitedly, "your disguise was good—but he is so sharp."

"Odd's fish!" he rejoined quietly, "then certainly the game would have been up. I could but take the risk. I know human nature pretty well by now," he added, with a note of sadness in his cheery, young voice, "and I know these Frenchmen out and out. They so loathe a Jew, that they never come nearer than a couple of yards of him, and begad! I fancy that I contrived to make myself look about as loathsome an object as it is possible to conceive."

"Yes!—and then?" she asked eagerly.

"Zooks!—then I carried out my little plan: that is to say, at first I only determined to leave everything to chance, but when I heard Chauvelin giving his orders to the soldiers, I thought that Fate and I were going to work together after all. I reckoned on the blind obedience of the soldiers. Chauvelin had ordered them on pain of death not to stir until the tall Englishman came. Desgas had thrown me down in a heap quite close to the hut; the soldiers took no notice of the Jew, who had driven Citoyen Chauvelin to this spot. I managed to free my hands from the ropes, with which the brute had trussed me; I always carry pencil and paper with me wherever I go, and I hastily scrawled a few important instructions on a scrap of paper; then I looked about me. I crawled up to the hut, under the very noses of the soldiers, who lay under cover without stirring, just as Chauvelin had ordered them to do, then I dropped my little note into the hut through a chink in the wall and waited. In this note I told the fugitives to walk noiselessly out of the hut, creep down the cliffs, keep to the left until they came to the first creek, to give a certain signal, when the boat of the *Day-dream*, which lay in wait not far out to sea, would pick them up. They obeyed implicitly, fortunately for them and for me. The soldiers who saw them were equally obedient to Chauvelin's orders. They did not stir! I waited for nearly half an hour; when I knew that the fugitives were safe I gave the signal, which caused so much stir."

And that was the whole story. It seemed so simple! and Marguerite could but marvel at the wonderful ingenuity, the boundless pluck and audacity which had evolved and helped to carry out this daring plan.

"But those brutes struck you!" she gasped in horror, at the bare recollection of the fearful indignity.

"Well! that could not be helped," he said gently, "whilst my little wife's fate was so uncertain, I had to remain here by her side. Odd's life!" he added merrily, "never fear! Chauvelin will lose nothing by waiting, I warrant! Wait till I get him back to England!—*La!* he shall pay for the thrashing he gave me with compound interest, I promise you."

Marguerite laughed. It was so good to be beside him, to hear his cheery voice, to watch that good-humoured twinkle in his blue eyes, as he stretched out his strong arms, in longing for that foe, and anticipation of his well-deserved punishment.

Suddenly, however, she started: the happy blush left her cheek, the light of joy died out of her eyes: she had heard a stealthy footfall overhead, and a stone had rolled down from the top of the cliffs right down to the beach below.

"What's that?" she whispered in horror and alarm.

"Oh! nothing, m'dear," he muttered with a pleasant laugh, "only a trifle you happened to have forgotten—my friend, Ffoulkes—"

"Sir Andrew!" she gasped.

Indeed, she had wholly forgotten the devoted friend and companion, who had trusted and stood by her during all these hours of anxiety and suffering. She remembered him now, tardily and with a pang of remorse.

"Aye! you had forgotten him, hadn't you, m'dear?" said Sir Percy merrily. "Fortunately, I met him, not far from the 'Chat Gris.' before I had that interesting supper party, with my friend Chauvelin. . . . Odd's life! but I have a score to settle with that young reprobate!—but in the meanwhile, I told him of a very long, very circuitous road which Chauvelin's men would never suspect, just about the time when we are ready for him, eh, little woman?"

"And he obeyed?" asked Marguerite, in utter astonishment.

"Without word or question. See, here he comes. He was not in the way when I did not want him, and now he arrives in the nick of time. Ah! he will make pretty little Suzanne a most admirable and methodical husband."

In the meanwhile, Sir Andrew Ffoulkes had cautiously worked his way down the cliffs: he stopped once or twice, pausing to listen for whispered words, which would guide him to Blakeney's hiding-place.

"Blakeney!" he ventured to say at last cautiously, "Blakeney! are you there?"

The next moment he rounded the rock against which Sir Percy and Marguerite were leaning, and seeing the weird figure still clad in the Jew's long gaberdine, he paused in sudden, complete bewilderment.

But already Blakeney had struggled to his feet.

"Here I am, friend," he said with his funny, inane laugh, "all alive! though I do look a begad scarecrow in these demmed things."

"Zooks!" ejaculated Sir Andrew in boundless astonishment as he recognised his leader, "of all the—"

The young man had seen Marguerite, and happily checked the forcible language that rose to his lips, at sight of the exquisite Sir Percy in this weird and dirty garb.

"Yes!" said Blakeney, calmly, "of all the—hem!—My friend!—I have not yet had time to ask you what you were doing in France, when I ordered you to remain in London? Insubordination? What? Wait till my shoulders are less sore, and, by God, see the punishment you'll get."

"Odd's fish! I'll bear it," said Sir Andrew with a merry laugh, "seeing that you are alive to give it—Would you have had me allow Lady Blakeney to do the journey alone? But, in the name of heaven, man, where did you get these extraordinary clothes?"

"Lud! they are a bit quaint, ain't they?" laughed Sir Percy, jovially, "But, odd's fish!" he added, with sudden earnestness and authority, "now you are here, Ffoulkes, we must lose no more time: that brute

Chauvelin may send someone to look after us."

Marguerite was so happy, she could have stayed here for ever, hearing his voice, asking a hundred questions. But at mention of Chauvelin's name she started in quick alarm, afraid for the dear life she would have died to save.

"But how can we get back?" she gasped; "the roads are full of soldiers between here and Calais, and—"

"We are not going back to Calais, sweetheart," he said, "but just the other side of Gris Nez, not half a league from here. The boat of the *Daydream* will meet us there."

"The boat of the *Daydream?*"

"Yes!" he said, with a merry laugh; "another little trick of mine. I should have told you before that when I slipped that note into the hut, I also added another for Armand, which I directed him to leave behind, and which has sent Chauvelin and his men running full tilt back to the 'Chat Gris' after me; but the first little note contained my real instructions, including those to old Briggs. He had my orders to go out further to sea, and then towards the west. When well out of sight of Calais, he will send the galley to a little creek he and I know of, just beyond Gris Nez. The men will look out for me—we have a preconcerted signal, and we will all be safely aboard, whilst Chauvelin and his men solemnly sit and watch the creek which is 'just opposite the "Chat Gris."'"

"The other side of Gris Nez? But I—I cannot walk, Percy," she moaned helplessly as, trying to struggle to her tired feet, she found herself unable even to stand.

"I will carry you, dear," he said simply; "the blind leading the lame, you know."

Sir Andrew was ready, too, to help with the precious burden, but Sir Percy would not entrust his beloved to any arms but his own.

"When you and she are both safely on board the *Daydream*," he said to his young comrade, "and I feel that Mlle. Suzanne's eyes will not greet me in England with reproachful looks, then it will be my turn to rest."

And his arms, still vigorous in spite of fatigue and suffering, closed round Marguerite's poor, weary body, and lifted her as gently as if she had been a feather.

Then, as Sir Andrew discreetly kept out of earshot, there were many things said, or rather whispered, which even the autumn breeze did not catch, for it had gone to rest.

All his fatigue was forgotten; his shoulders must have been very sore, for the soldiers had hit hard, but the man's muscles seemed made of steel, and his energy was almost supernatural. It was a weary tramp, half a league along the stony side of the cliffs, but never for a moment did his courage give way or his muscles yield to fatigue. On he tramped, with firm footstep, his vigorous arms encircling the precious burden, and—no doubt, as she lay, quiet and happy, at times lulled to momentary drowsiness, at others watching, through the slowly gathering morning light, the pleasant face with the lazy, drooping blue eyes, ever cheerful, ever illumined with a good-humoured smile, she whispered many things, which helped to shorten the weary road, and acted as a soothing balsam to his aching sinews.

The many-hued light of dawn was breaking in the east, when at last they reached the creek beyond Gris Nez. The galley lay in wait: in answer to a signal from Sir Percy, she drew near, and two sturdy British sailors had the honour of carrying my lady into the boat.

Half an hour later, they were on board the *Daydream*. The crew, who of necessity were in their master's secrets, and who were devoted to him heart and soul, were not surprised to see him arriving in so extraordinary a disguise.

Armand St. Just and the other fugitives were eagerly awaiting the advent of their brave rescuer; he would not stay to hear the expressions of their gratitude but found the way to his private cabin as quickly as he could, leaving Marguerite quite happy in the arms of her brother.

Everything on board the *Daydream* was fitted with that exquisite luxury, so dear to Sir Percy Blakeney's heart, and by the time they all landed at Dover he had found time to get into some of the sumptuous clothes which he loved, and of which he always kept a supply on board his yacht.

The difficulty was to provide Marguerite with a pair of shoes, and great was the little middy's joy when my lady found that she could put foot on English shore in his best pair.

The rest is silence!—silence and joy for those who had endured so much suffering, yet found at last a great and lasting happiness.

But it is on record that at the brilliant wedding of Sir Andrew Ffoulkes, Bart., with Mlle. Suzanne de Tournay de Basserive, a function at which H. R. H. the Prince of Wales and all the *élite* of fashionable society were present, the most beautiful woman there was unquestionably Lady Blakeney, whilst the clothes of Sir Percy Blakeney were the talk of the *jeunesse doree* of London for many days.

It is also a fact that M. Chauvelin, the accredited agent of the French Republican Government, was not present at that or any other social function in London, after that memorable evening at Lord Grenville's ball.

I Will Repay

Contents

Prologue: Paris 1783

1

"Coward! Coward! Coward!"

The words rang out, clear, strident, passionate, in a *crescendo* of agonised humiliation.

The boy, quivering with rage, had sprung to his feet, and, losing his balance, he fell forward clutching at the table, whilst with a convulsive movement of the lids, he tried in vain to suppress the tears of shame which were blinding him.

"Coward!" He tried to shout the insult so that all might hear, but his parched throat refused him service, his trembling hand sought the scattered cards upon the table, he collected them together, quickly, nervously, fingering them with feverish energy, then he hurled them at the man opposite, whilst with a final effort he still contrived to mutter: "Coward!"

The older men tried to interpose, but the young ones only laughed, quite prepared for the adventure which must inevitably ensue, the only possible ending to a quarrel such as this.

Conciliation or arbitration was out of the question. Déroulède should have known better than to speak disrespectfully of Adèle de Montchéri, when the little Vicomte de Marny's infatuation for the notorious beauty had been the talk of Paris and Versailles these many months past.

Adèle was very lovely and a veritable tower of greed and egotism. The Marnys were rich and the little Vicomte very young, and just now the brightly-plumaged hawk was busy plucking the latest pigeon, newly arrived from its ancestral cote.

The boy was still in the initial stage of his infatuation. To him Adèle was a paragon of all the virtues, and he would have done battle on her behalf against the entire aristocracy of France, in a vain endeavour to justify his own exalted opinion of one of the most dissolute women of the epoch. He was a first-rate swordsman too, and his friends had already learned that it was best to avoid all allusions to Adèle's beauty and weaknesses.

But Déroulède was a noted blunderer. He was little versed in the manners and tones of that high society in which, somehow, he still seemed and intruder. But for his great wealth, no doubt, he never would have been admitted within the intimate circle of aristocratic France. His ancestry was somewhat doubtful and his coat-of-arms unadorned with quarterings.

But little was known of his family or the origin of its wealth; it was only known that his father had suddenly become the late king's dearest friend, and commonly surmised that Déroulède gold had on more than one occasion filled the emptied coffers of the First Gentleman of France.

Déroulède had not sought the present quarrel. He had merely blundered in that clumsy way of his, which was no doubt a part of the inheritance bequeathed to him by his *bourgeois* ancestry.

He knew nothing of the little *Vicomte's* private affairs, still less of his relationship with Adèle, but he knew enough of the world and enough of Paris to be acquainted with the lady's reputation. He hated at all times to speak of women. He was not what in those days would be termed a ladies' man and was even somewhat unpopular with the sex. But in this instance the conversation had drifted in that direction, and when Adèle's name was mentioned, every one became silent, save the little *Vicomte*, who waxed enthusiastic.

A shrug of the shoulders on Déroulède's part had aroused the boy's ire, then a few casual words, and, without further warning, the insult had been hurled and the cards thrown in the older man's face.

Déroulède did not move from his seat. He sat erect and placid, one knee crossed over the other, his serious, rather swarthy face perhaps a shade paler than usual: otherwise it seemed as if the insult had never reached his ears, or the cards struck his cheek.

He had perceived his blunder, just twenty seconds too late. Now he was sorry for the boy and angered with himself, but it was too late to draw back. To avoid a conflict, he would at this moment have sacrificed half his fortune, but not one particle of his dignity.

He knew and respected the old Duc de Marny, a feeble old man now, almost a dotard whose hitherto spotless *blason*, the young *Vicomte*, his son, was doing his best to besmirch.

When the boy fell forward, blind and drunk with rage, Déroulède leant towards him automatically, quite kindly, and helped him to his feet. He would have asked the lad's pardon for his own thoughtlessness, had that been possible: but the stilted code of so-called honour forbade so logical a proceeding. It would have done no good and could but imperil his own reputation without averting the traditional sequel.

The panelled walls of the celebrated gaming saloon had often witnessed scenes such as this. All those present acted by routine. The etiquette of duelling prescribed certain formalities, and these were strictly but rapidly adhered to.

The young *Vicomte* was quickly surrounded by a close circle of friends. His great name, his wealth, his father's influence, had opened for him every door in Versailles and Paris. At this moment he might have had an army of seconds to support him in the coming conflict.

Déroulède for a while was left alone near the card table, where the unsnuffed candles began smouldering in their sockets. He had risen to his feet, somewhat bewildered at the rapid turn of events. His dark, restless eyes wandered for a moment round the room, as if in quick search for a friend.

But where the *Vicomte* was at home by right, Déroulède had only been admitted by reason of his wealth. His acquaintances and sycophants were many, but his friends very few.

For the first time this fact was brought home to him. Everyone in the room must have known and realised that he had not wilfully sought this quarrel, that throughout he had borne himself as any gentleman would, yet now, when the issue was so close at hand, no one came forward to stand by him.

"For form's sake, *monsieur*, will you choose your seconds?"

It was the young Marquis de Villefranche who spoke, a little haughtily, with a certain ironical condescension towards the rich *parvenu*, who was about to have the honour of crossing swords with one of the noblest gentlemen in France.

"I pray you, *Monsieur le Marquis*," rejoined Déroulède coldly, "to make the choice for me. You see, I have few friends in Paris."

The Marquis bowed, and gracefully flourished his lace handkerchief. He was accustomed to being appealed to in all matters pertaining to etiquette, to the toilet, to the latest cut in coats, and the procedure in duels. Good-natured, foppish, and idle, he felt quite happy and, in his element, thus to be made chief organiser of the tragic farce, about to be enacted on the parquet floor of the gaming saloon.

He looked about the room for a while, scrutinising the faces of those around him. The gilded youth was crowding round De Marny;

a few older men stood in a group at the farther end of the room: to these the Marquis turned, and addressing one of them, an elderly man with a military bearing and a shabby brown coat:

"*Mon* Colonel," he said, with another flourishing bow; "I am deputed by M. Déroulède to provide him with seconds for this affair of honour, may I call upon you to—"

"Certainly, certainly," replied the Colonel. "I am not intimately acquainted with M. Déroulède, but since you stand sponsor, *M. le Marquis*—"

"Oh!" rejoined the Marquis, lightly, "a mere matter of form, you know. M. Déroulède belongs to the entourage of Her Majesty. He is a man of honour. But I am not his sponsor. Marny is my friend, and if you prefer not to—"

"Indeed, I am entirely at M. Déroulède's service," said the Colonel, who had thrown a quick, scrutinising glance at the isolated figure near the card table, "if he will accept my services.—"

"He will be very glad to accept, my dear Colonel," whispered the Marquis with an ironical twist of his aristocratic lips. "He has no friends in our set, and if you and De Quettare will honour him, I think he should be grateful."

M. de Quettare, adjutant to *M. le Colonel*, was ready to follow in the footsteps of his chief, and the two men, after the prescribed salutations to M. le Marquis de Villefranche, went across to speak to Déroulède.

"If you will accept our services, *monsieur*," began the Colonel abruptly, "mine, and my adjutant's, M. de Quettare, we place ourselves entirely at your disposal."

"I thank you, *messieurs*," rejoined Déroulède. "The whole thing is a farce, and that young man is a fool; but I have been in the wrong and—"

"You would wish to apologise?" queried the Colonel icily.

The worthy soldier had heard something of Déroulède's reputed *bourgeois* ancestry. This suggestion of an apology was no doubt in accordance with the customs of the middle-classes, but the Colonel literally gasped at the unworthiness of the proceeding. An apology? Bah! Disgusting! cowardly! beneath the dignity of any gentleman, however wrong he might be. How could two soldiers of His Majesty's army identify themselves with such doings?

But Déroulède seemed unconscious of the enormity of his suggestion.

"If I could avoid a conflict," he said, "I would tell the *Vicomte* that

I had no knowledge of his admiration for the lady we were discussing and—"

"Are you so very much afraid of getting a sword scratch, *monsieur?*" interrupted the Colonel impatiently, whilst M. de Quettare elevated a pair of aristocratic eyebrows in bewilderment at such an extraordinary display of *bourgeois* cowardice.

"You mean, *Monsieur le Colonel?*"—queried Déroulède.

"That you must either fight the Vicomte de Marny tonight or clear out of Paris tomorrow. Your position in our set would become untenable," retorted the Colonel, not unkindly, for in spite of Déroulède's extraordinary attitude, there was nothing in his bearing or his appearance that suggested cowardice or fear.

"I bow to your superior knowledge of your friends, *M. le Colonel,*" responded Déroulède, as he silently drew his sword from its sheath.

The centre of the saloon was quickly cleared. The seconds measured the length of the swords and then stood behind the antagonists, slightly in advance of the groups of spectators, who stood massed all round the room.

They represented the flower of what France had of the best and noblest in name, in lineage, in chivalry, in that year of grace 1783. The storm-cloud which a few years hence was destined to break over their heads, sweeping them from their palaces to the prison and the guillotine, was only gathering very slowly in the dim horizon of squalid, starving Paris: for the next half-dozen years they would still dance and gamble, fight and flirt, surround a tottering throne, and hoodwink a weak monarch.

The Fates' avenging sword still rested in its sheath; the relentless, ceaseless wheel still bore them up in their whirl of pleasure; the downward movement had only just begun: the cry of the oppressed children of France had not yet been heard above the din of dance music and lovers' serenades.

The young Duc de Châteaudun was there, he who, nine years later, went to the guillotine on that cold September morning, his hair dressed in the latest fashion, the finest Mechlin lace around his wrists, playing a final game of piquet with his younger brother, as the tumbril bore them along through the hooting, yelling crowd of the half-naked starvelings of Paris.

There was the Vicomte de Mirepoix, who, a few years later, standing on the platform of the guillotine, laid a bet with M. de Miranges that his own blood would flow bluer than that of any other head cut off that day in France. Citizen Samson heard the bet made, and when De Mirepoix's head fell into the basket, the headsman lifted it up for M. de Miranges to see. The latter laughed.

"Mirepoix was always a braggart," he said lightly, as he laid his head upon the block.

"Who'll take my bet that my blood turns out to be bluer than his?"

But of all these comedies, these *tragico*-farces of later years, none who were present on that night, when the Vicomte de Marny fought Paul Déroulède, had as yet any presentiment.

They watched the two men fighting, with the same casual interest, at first, which they would have bestowed on the dancing of a new movement in the minuet.

De Marny came of a race that had wielded the sword of many centuries, but he was hot, excited, not a little addled with wine and rage. Déroulède was lucky; he would come out of the affair with a slight scratch.

A good swordsman too, that wealthy parvenu. It was interesting to watch his sword-play: very quiet at first, no feint or parry, scarcely a riposte, only *en garde*, always *en garde* very carefully, steadily, ready for his antagonist at every turn and in every circumstance.

Gradually the circle round the combatants narrowed. A few discreet exclamations of admiration greeted Déroulède's most successful parry. De Marny was getting more and more excited, the older man more and more sober and reserved.

A thoughtless lunge placed the little *Vicomte* at his opponent's mercy. The next instant he was disarmed, and the seconds were pressing forward to end the conflict.

Honour was satisfied: the *parvenu* and the scion of the ancient race had crossed swords over the reputation of one of the most dissolute women in France. Déroulède's moderation was a lesson to all the hotheaded young bloods who toyed with their lives, their honour, their reputation as lightly as they did with their lace-edged handkerchiefs and gold snuff-boxes.

Already Déroulède had drawn back. With the gentle tact peculiar to kindly people, he avoided looking at his disarmed antagonist. But something in the older man's attitude seemed to further nettle the over-stimulated sensibility of the young *Vicomte*.

"This is no child's play, *monsieur*," he said excitedly. "I demand full satisfaction."

"And are you not satisfied?" queried Déroulède. "You have borne yourself bravely, you have fought in honour of your liege lady. I, on the other hand—"

"You," shouted the boy hoarsely, "you shall publicly apologise to a noble and virtuous woman whom you have outraged—now—at—once—on your knees—"

"You are mad, *Vicomte*," rejoined Déroulède coldly. "I am willing to ask your forgiveness for my blunder—"

"An apology—in public—on your knees—"

The boy had become more and more excited. He had suffered humiliation after humiliation. He was a mere lad, spoilt, adulated, pampered from his boyhood: the wine had got into his head, the intoxication of rage and hatred blinded his saner judgment.

"Coward!" he shouted again and again.

His seconds tried to interpose, but he waved them feverishly aside. He would listen to no one. He saw no one save the man who had insulted Adèle, and who was heaping further insults upon her, by refusing this public acknowledgment of her virtues.

De Marny hated Déroulède at this moment with the most deadly hatred the heart of man can conceive. The older man's calm, his chivalry, his consideration only enhanced the boy's anger and shame.

The hubbub had become general. Everyone seemed carried away with this strange fever of enmity, which was seething in the Vicomte's veins. Most of the young men crowded round De Marny, doing their best to pacify him. The Marquis de Villefranche declared that the matter was getting quite outside the rules.

No one took much notice of Déroulède. In the remote corners of the saloon a few elderly dandies were laying bets as to the ultimate issue of the quarrel.

Déroulède, however, was beginning to lose his temper. He had no friends in that room, and therefore there was no sympathetic observer there, to note the gradual darkening of his eyes, like the gathering of a cloud heavy with the coming storm.

"I pray you, *messieurs*, let us cease the argument," he said at last, in a loud, impatient voice. "M. le Vicomte de Marny desires a further lesson, and, by God! he shall have it. *En garde, M. le Vicomte!*"

The crowd quickly drew back. The seconds once more assumed the bearing and imperturbable expression which their important function demanded. The hubbub ceased as the swords began to clash.

Everyone felt that farce was turning to tragedy.

And yet it was obvious from the first that Déroulède merely meant once more to disarm his antagonist, to give him one more lesson, a little more severe perhaps than the last. He was such a brilliant swordsman, and De Marny was so excited, that the advantage was with him from the very first.

How it all happened, nobody afterwards could say. There is no doubt that the little *Vicomte's* sword-play had become more and more wild: that he uncovered himself in the most reckless way, whilst lunging wildly at his opponent's breast, until at last, in one of these mad, unguarded moments, he seemed literally to throw himself upon Déroulède's weapon.

The latter tried with lightning-swift motion of the wrist to avoid the fatal issue, but it was too late, and without a sigh or groan, scarce a tremor, the Vicomte de Marny fell.

The sword dropped out of his hand, and it was Déroulède himself who caught the boy in his arms.

It had all occurred so quickly and suddenly that no one had realised it all, until it was over, and the lad was lying prone on the ground, his elegant blue satin coat stained with red, and his antagonist bending over him.

There was nothing more to be done. Etiquette demanded that Déroulède should withdraw. He was not allowed to do anything for the boy whom he had so unwillingly sent to his death.

As before, no one took much notice of him. Silence, the awesome silence caused by the presence of the great Master, fell upon all those around. Only in the far corner a shrill voice was heard to say:

"I hold you at five hundred *louis*, Marquis. The *parvenu* is a good swordsman."

The groups parted as Déroulède walked out of the room, followed by the Colonel and M. de Quettare, who stood by him to the last. Both were old and proved soldiers, both had chivalry and courage in them, with which to do tribute to the brave man whom they had seconded.

At the door of the establishment, they met the leech who had been summoned some little time ago to hold himself in readiness for any eventuality.

The great eventuality had occurred: it was beyond the leech's learning. In the brilliantly lighted saloon above, the only son of the Duc de Marny was breathing his last, whilst Déroulède, wrapping his mantle closely round him, strode out into the dark street, all alone.

2

The head of the house of Marny was at this time barely seventy years of age. But he had lived every hour, every minute of his life, from the day when the *Grand Monarque* gave him his first appointment as gentleman page in waiting when he was a mere lad, barely twelve years of age, to the moment—some ten years ago now—when Nature's relentless hand struck him down in the midst of his pleasures, withered him in a flash as she does a sturdy old oak, and nailed him—a cripple, almost a dotard—to the invalid chair which he would only quit for his last resting place.

Juliette was then a mere slip of a girl, an old man's child, the spoilt darling of his last happy years. She had retained some of the melancholy which had characterised her mother, the gentle lady who had endured so much so patiently, and who had bequeathed this final tender burden—her baby girl—to the brilliant, handsome husband whom she had so deeply loved, and so often forgiven.

When the Duc de Marny entered the final awesome stage of his gilded career, that deathlike life which he dragged on for ten years wearily to the grave, Juliette became his only joy, his one gleam of happiness in the midst of torturing memories.

In her deep, tender eyes he would see mirrored the present, the future for her, and would forget his past, with all its gaieties, its mad, merry years, that meant nothing now but bitter regrets, and endless rosary of the might-have-beens.

And then there was the boy. The little *Vicomte*, the future Duc de Marny, who would in *his* life and with *his* youth recreate the glory of the family, and make France once more ring with the echo of brave deeds and gallant adventures, which had made the name of Marny so glorious in camp and court.

The *Vicomte* was not his father's love, but he was his father's pride, and from the depths of his huge, cushioned armchair, the old man would listen with delight to stories from Versailles and Paris, the young queen and the fascinating Lamballe, the latest play and the newest star in the theatrical firmament. His feeble, tottering mind would then take him back, along the paths of memory, to his own youth and his own triumphs, and in the joy and pride in his son, he would forget himself for the sake of the boy.

When they brought the *Vicomte* home that night, Juliette was the first to wake. She heard the noise outside the great gates, the coach slowly drawing up, the ring for the doorkeeper, and the sound of Matthieu's mutterings, who never liked to be called up in the middle of the night to let anyone through the gates.

Somehow a presentiment of evil at once struck the young girl: the footsteps sounded so heavy and muffled along the flagged courtyard, and up the great oak staircase. It seemed as if they were carrying something heavy, something inert or dead.

She jumped out of bed and hastily wrapped a cloak round her thin girlish shoulders and slipped her feet into a pair of heelless shoes, then she opened her bedroom door and looked out upon the landing.

Two men, whom she did not know, were walking upstairs abreast, two more were carrying a heavy burden, and Matthieu was behind moaning and crying bitterly.

Juliette did not move. She stood in the doorway rigid as a statue. The little *cortège* went past her. No one saw her, for the landings in the Hotel de Marny are very wide, and Matthieu's lantern only threw a dim, flickering light upon the floor.

The men stopped outside the *Vicomte's* room. Matthieu opened it, and then the five men disappeared within, with their heavy burden.

A moment later old Pétronelle, who had been Juliette's nurse, and was now her devoted slave, came to her, all bathed in tears.

She had just heard the news, and she could scarcely speak, but she folded the young girl, her dear pet lamb, in her arms, and rocking herself to and fro she sobbed and eased her aching, motherly heart.

But Juliette did not cry. It was all so sudden, so awful. She, at fourteen years of age, had never dreamed of death; and now there was her brother, her Philippe, in whom she had so much joy, so much pride—he was dead—and her father must be told—

The awfulness of this task seemed to Juliette like unto the last Judgment Day; a thing so terrible, so appalling, so impossible, that it would take a host of angels to proclaim its inevitableness.

The old cripple, with one foot in the grave, whose whole feeble mind, whose pride, whose final flicker of hope was concentrated in his boy, must be told that the lad had been brought home dead.

"Will you tell him, Pétronelle?" she asked repeatedly, during the brief intervals when the violence of the old nurse's grief subsided somewhat.

"No—no—darling, I cannot—I cannot—" moaned Pétronelle, amidst a renewed shower of sobs.

Juliette's entire soul—a child's soul it was—rose in revolt at thought of what was before her. She felt angered with God for having put such a thing upon her. What right had He to demand a girl of her years to endure so much mental agony?

To lose her brother, and to witness her father's grief! She couldn't! she couldn't! she couldn't! God was evil and unjust!

A distant tinkle of a bell made all her nerves suddenly quiver. Her father was awake then? He had heard the noise and was ringing his bell to ask for an explanation of the disturbance.

With one quick movement Juliette jerked herself free from the nurse's arms, and before Pétronelle could prevent her, she had run out of the room, straight across the dark landing to a large panelled door opposite.

The old Duc de Marny was sitting on the edge of his bed, with his long, thin legs dangling helplessly to the ground.

Crippled as he was, he had struggled to this upright position, he was making frantic, miserable efforts to raise himself still further. He, too, had heard the dull thud of feet, the shuffling gait of men when carrying a heavy burden.

His mind flew back half-a-century, to the days when he had witnessed scenes wherein he was then merely a half-interested spectator. He knew the *cortège* composed of valets and friends, with the leech walking beside that precious burden, which anon would be deposited on the bed and left to the tender care of a mourning family.

Who knows what pictures were conjured up before that enfeebled vision? But he guessed. And when Juliette dashed into his room and stood before him, pale, trembling, a world of misery in her great eyes, she knew that he guessed and that she need not tell him. God had already done that for her.

Pierre, the old *duc's* devoted valet, dressed him as quickly as he could. *M. le Duc* insisted on having his *habit de cérémonie*, the rich suit of black velvet with the priceless lace and diamond buttons, which he had worn when they laid *le Roi Soleil* to his eternal rest.

He put on his orders and buckled on his sword. The gorgeous clothes, which had suited him so well in the prime of his manhood, hung somewhat loosely on his attenuated frame, but he looked a grand and imposing figure, with his white hair tied behind with a great black bow, and the fine jabot of beautiful *point d'Angleterre* falling in a soft cascade below his chin.

Then holding himself as upright as he could, he sat in his invalid chair, and four flunkeys in full livery carried him to the deathbed of his son.

All the house was astir by now. Torches burned in great sockets in the vast hall and along the massive oak stairway, and hundreds of candles flickered ghostlike in the vast apartments of the princely mansion.

The numerous servants were arrayed on the landing, all dressed in the rich livery of the ducal house.

The death of an heir of the Marnys is an event that history makes a note of.

The old *Duc's* chair was placed close to the bed, where lay the dead body of the young *Vicomte*. He made no movement, nor did he utter a word or sigh. Some of those who were present at the time declared that his mind had completely given way, and that he neither felt nor understood the death of his son.

The Marquis de Villefranche, who had followed his friend to the last, took a final leave of the sorrowing house.

Juliette scarcely noticed him. Her eyes were fixed on her father. She would not look at her brother. A childlike fear had seized her, there, suddenly, between these two silent figures: the living and the dead.

But just as the Marquis was leaving the room, the old man spoke for the first time.

"Marquis," he said very quietly, "you forget—you have not yet told me who killed my son."

"It was in a fair fight, *M. de Duc*," replied the young Marquis, awed in spite of all his frivolity, his light-heartedness, by this strange, almost mysterious tragedy.

"Who killed my son, *M. le Marquis?*" repeated the old man mechanically. "I have the right to know," he added with sudden, weird energy.

"It was M. Paul Déroulède, *M. le Duc,*" replied the Marquis. "I repeat, it was in fair fight."

The old *Duc* sighed as if in satisfaction. Then with a courteous gesture of farewell reminiscent of the *grand siècle* he added:

"All thanks from me and mine to you, Marquis, would seem but a mockery. Your devotion to my son is beyond human thanks. I'll not detain you now. Farewell."

Escorted by two lacqueys, the Marquis passed out of the room.

"Dismiss all the servants, Juliette; I have something to say," said the old *Duc*, and the young girl, silent, obedient, did as her father bade her.

Father and sister were alone with their dead. As soon as the last hushed footsteps of the retreating servants died away in the distance.

The Duc de Marny seemed to throw away the lethargy which had enveloped him until now. With a quick, feverish gesture he seized his daughter's wrist, and murmured excitedly:

"His name. You heard his name, Juliette?"

"Yes, father," replied the child.

"Paul Déroulède! Paul Déroulède! You'll not forget it?"

"Never, father!"

"He killed your brother! You understand that? Killed my only son, the hope of my house, the last descendant of the most glorious race that has ever added lustre to the history of France."

"In fair fight, father!" protested the child.

"'Tis not fair for a man to kill a boy," retorted the old man, with furious energy.

"Déroulède is thirty: my boy was scarce out of his teens: may the vengeance of God fall upon the murderer!"

Juliette, awed, terrified, was gazing at her father with great, wondering eyes. He seemed unlike himself. His face wore a curious expression of ecstasy and of hatred, also of hope and exultation, whenever he looked steadily at her.

That the final glimmer of a tottering reason was fast leaving the poor, aching head she was too young to realise. Madness was a word that had only a vague meaning for her. Though she did not understand her father at the present moment, though she was half afraid of him, she would have rejected with scorn and horror any suggestion that he was mad.

Therefore, when he took her hand and, drawing her nearer to the bed and to himself, placed it upon her dead brother's breast, she recoiled at the touch of the inanimate body, so unlike anything she had ever touched before, but she obeyed her father without any question, and listened to his words as to those of a sage.

"Juliette, you are now fourteen, and able to understand what I am going to ask of you. If I were not chained to this miserable chair, if I were not a hopeless, abject cripple, I would not depute anyone, not even you, my only child, to do that, which God demands that one of us should do."

He paused a moment, then continued earnestly:

"Remember, Juliette, that you are of the house of Marny, that you are a Catholic, and that God hears you now. For you shall swear an oath before Him and me, an oath from which only death can relieve you. Will you swear, my child?"

"If you wish it, father."

"You have been to confession lately, Juliette?"

"Yes, father; also, to holy communion, yesterday," replied the child. "It was the *Fête-Dieu*, you know."

"Then you are in a state of grace, my child?"

"I was yesterday morning, father," replied the young girl naïvely, "but I have committed some little sins since then."

"Then make your confession to God in your heart now. You must be in a state of grace when you speak the oath."

The child closed her eyes, and as the old man watched her, he could see the lips framing the words of her spiritual confession.

Juliette made the sign of the cross, then opened her eyes and looked at her father.

"I am ready, father," she said; "I hope God has forgiven me the little sins of yesterday."

"Will you swear, my child?"

"What, father?"

"That you will avenge your brother's death on his murderer?"

"But, father—"

"Swear it, my child!"

"How can I fulfil that oath, father?—I don't understand—"

"God will guide you, my child. When you are older you will understand."

For a moment Juliette still hesitated. She was just on that borderland between childhood and womanhood when all the sensibilities, the nervous system, the emotions, are strung to their highest pitch.

Throughout her short life she had worshipped her father with a whole-hearted, passionate devotion, which had completely blinded her to his weakening faculties and the feebleness of his mind.

She was also in that initial stage of enthusiastic piety which overwhelms every girl of temperament, if she be brought up in the Roman Catholic religion, when she is first initiated into the mysteries of the Sacraments.

Juliette had been to confession and communion. She had been confirmed by *Monseigneur*, the Archbishop. Her ardent nature had responded to the full to the sensuous and ecstatic expressions of the ancient faith.

And somehow her father's wish, her brother's death, all seemed mingled in her brain with that religion, for which in her juvenile enthusiasm she would willingly have laid down her life.

She thought of all the saints, whose lives she had been reading. Her young heart quivered at the thought of *their* sacrifices, their martyrdoms, their sense of duty.

An exaltation, morbid perhaps, superstitious and overwhelming, took possession of her mind; also, perhaps, far back in the innermost recesses of her heart, a pride in her own importance, her mission in life, her individuality: for she was a girl after all, a mere child, about to become a woman.

But the old *Duc* was waxing impatient.

"Surely you do not hesitate, Juliette, with your dead brother's body clamouring mutely for revenge? You, the only Marny left now!—for from this day I too shall be as dead."

"No, father," said the young girl in an awed whisper, "I do not hesitate. I will swear, just as you bid me."

"Repeat the words after me, my child."

"Yes, father."

"Before the face of Almighty God, who sees and hears me—"

"Before the face of Almighty God, who sees and hears me," repeated Juliette firmly.

"I swear that I will seek out Paul Déroulède."

"I swear that I will seek out Paul Déroulède."

"And in any manner which God may dictate to me encompass his death, his ruin or dishonour, in revenge for my brother's death."

"And in any manner which God may dictate to me encompass his death, his ruin or dishonour, in revenge for my brother's death," said Juliette solemnly.

"May my brother's soul remain in torment until the final Judgment Day if I should break my oath, but may it rest in eternal peace the day on which his death is fitly avenged."

"May my brother's soul remain in torment until the final Judgment Day if I should break my oath, but may it rest in eternal peace the day on which his death is fitly avenged."

The child fell upon her knees. The oath was spoken, the old man was satisfied.

He called for his valet and allowed himself quietly to be put to bed.

One brief hour had transformed a child into a woman. A dangerous transformation when the brain is overburdened with emotions, when the nerves are overstrung and the heart full to breaking.

For the moment, however, the childlike nature reasserted itself for the last time, for Juliette, sobbing, had fled out of the room, to the privacy of her own apartment, and thrown herself passionately into the arms of kind old Pétronelle.

CHAPTER 1

Paris, 1793: The Outrage

It would have been very difficult to say why Citizen Déroulède was quite so popular as he was. Still more difficult would it have been to state the reason why he remained immune from the prosecutions, which were being conducted at the rate of several scores a day, now against the moderate Gironde, *anon* against the fanatic Mountain, until the whole of France was transformed into one gigantic prison, that daily fed the guillotine.

But Déroulède remained unscathed. Even Merlin's law of the suspect had so far failed to touch him. And when, last July, the murder of Marat brought an entire holocaust of victims to the guillotine—from Adam Lux, who would have put up a statue in honour of Charlotte Corday, with the inscription: "Greater than Brutus," to Chalier, who would have had her publicly tortured and burned at the stake for her crime—Déroulède alone said nothing and was allowed to remain silent.

The most seething time of that seething revolution. No one knew in the morning if his head would still be on his own shoulders in the evening, or if it would be held up by Citizen Samson the headsman, for the *sansculottes* of Paris to see.

Yet Déroulède was allowed to go his own way.

Marat once said of him: "*Il n'est pas dangereux*." The phrase had been taken up. Within the precincts of the National Convention, Marat was still looked upon as the great protagonist of Liberty, a martyr to his own convictions carried to the extreme, to squalor and dirt, to the downward levelling of man to what is the lowest type in humanity. And his sayings were still treasured up: even the Girondins did not dare to attack his memory. Dead Marat was more powerful than his living presentment had been.

And he had said that Déroulède was not dangerous. Not dangerous to Republicanism, to liberty, to that downward, levelling process, the tearing down of old traditions, and the annihilation of past pretensions.

Déroulède had once been very rich. He had had sufficient prudence to give away in good time that which, undoubtedly, would have been taken away from him later on.

But when he gave willingly, at a time when France needed it most, and before she had learned how to help herself to what she wanted.

And somehow, in this instance, France had not forgotten: an invisible fortress seemed to surround Citizen Déroulède and keep his enemies at bay. They were few, but they existed. The National Convention trusted him. "He was not dangerous" to them. The people looked upon him as one of themselves, who gave whilst he had something to give. Who can gauge that most elusive of all things: *Popularity?*

He lived a quiet life and had never yielded to the omni-prevalent temptation of writing pamphlets, but lived alone with his mother and Anne Mie, the little orphaned cousin whom old Madame Déroulède had taken care of, ever since the child could toddle.

Everyone knew his house in the Rue Ecole de Médecine, not far from the one wherein Marat lived and died, the only solid, stone house in the midst of a row of hovels, evil-smelling and squalid.

The street was narrow then, as it is now, and whilst Paris was cutting off the heads of her children for the sake of Liberty and Fraternity, she had no time to bother about cleanliness and sanitation.

Rue Ecole de Médecine did little credit to the school after which it was named, and it was a most unattractive crowd that usually thronged its uneven, muddy pavements.

A neat gown, a clean kerchief, were quite an unusual sight down this way, for Anne Mie seldom went out, and old Madame Déroulède hardly ever left her room. A good deal of brandy was being drunk at the two drinking bars, one at each end of the long, narrow street, and by five o'clock in the afternoon it was undoubtedly best for women to remain indoors.

The crowd of dishevelled elderly Amazons who stood gossiping at the street corner could hardly be called women now. A ragged petticoat, a greasy red kerchief round the head, a tattered, stained shift—to this pass of squalor and shame had Liberty brought the daughters of France.

And they jeered at any passer-by less filthy, less degraded than themselves.

"*Ah! voyons l'aristo!*" they shouted every time a man in decent clothes, a woman with tidy cap and apron, passed swiftly down the street.

And the afternoons were very lively. There was always plenty to see: first and foremost, the long procession of tumbrils, winding its way from the prisons to the *Place de la Révolution*. The forty-four thousand sections of the Committee of Public Safety sent their quota, each in their turn, to the guillotine.

At one time these tumbrils contained royal ladies and gentlemen, *ci-devant* dukes and princesses, aristocrats from every county in France, but now this stock was becoming exhausted. The wretched Queen Marie Antoinette still lingered in the Temple with her son and daughter. Madame Elisabeth was still allowed to say her prayers in peace, but *ci-devant* dukes and counts were getting scarce: those who had not perished at the hand of Citizen Samson were plying some trade in Germany or England.

There were aristocratic joiners, innkeepers, and hairdressers. The proudest names in France were hidden beneath trade signs in London and Hamburg. A good number owed their lives to that mysterious Scarlet Pimpernel, that unknown Englishman who had snatched scores of victims from the clutches of Tinville the Prosecutor, and sent M. Chauvelin, baffled, back to France.

Aristocrats were getting scarce, so it was now the turn of deputies of the National Convention, of men of letters, men of science or of art, men who had sent others to the guillotine a twelvemonth ago, and men who had been loudest in defence of anarchy and its Reign of Terror.

They had revolutionised the Calendar: The Citizen-Deputies, and every good citizen of France, called this 19th day of August 1793 the 2nd *Fructidor* of the year 2 of the New Era.

At six o'clock on that afternoon a young girl suddenly turned the angle of the Rue Ecole de Médecine, and after looking quickly to the right and left she began deliberately walking along the narrow street.

It was crowded just then. Groups of excited women stood jabbering before every doorway. It was the home-coming hour after the usual spectacle on the *Place de la Révolution*. The men had paused at the various drinking booths, crowding the women out. It would be the turn of these Amazons next, at the brandy bars; for the moment they were left to gossip, and to jeer at the passer-by.

At first the young girl did not seem to heed them. She walked quickly along, looking defiantly before her, carrying her head erect, and stepping carefully from cobblestone to cobblestone, avoiding the mud, which could have dirtied her dainty shoes.

The harridans passed the time of day to her, and the time of day meant some obscene remark unfit for women's ears. The young girl wore a simple grey dress, with fine lawn kerchief neatly folded across her bosom, a large hat with flowing ribbons sat above the fairest face that ever gladdened men's eyes to see.

Fairer still it would have been, but for the look of determination which made it seem hard and old for the girl's years.

She wore the tricolour scarf round her waist, else she had been more seriously molested ere now. But the Republican colours were her safeguard: whilst she walked quietly along, no one could harm her.

Then suddenly a curious impulse seemed to seize her. It was just outside the large stone house belonging to Citizen-Deputy Déroulède. She had so far taken no notice of the groups of women which she had come across. When they obstructed the footway, she had calmly stepped out into the middle of the road.

It was wise and prudent, for she could close her ears to obscene language and need pay no heed to insult.

Suddenly she threw up her head defiantly.

"Will you please let me pass?" she said loudly, as a dishevelled Amazon stood before her with arms akimbo, glancing sarcastically at the lace petticoat, which just peeped beneath the young girl's simple grey frock.

"Let her pass? Let her pass? Ho! ho! ho!" laughed the old woman, turning to the nearest group of idlers, and apostrophising them with a loud oath. "Did *you* know, citizeness, that this street had been specially made for *aristos* to pass along?"

"I am in a hurry, will you let me pass at once?" commanded the young girl, tapping her foot impatiently on the ground.

There was the whole width of the street on her right, plenty of room for her to walk along. It seemed positive madness to provoke a quarrel singlehanded against this noisy group of excited females, just home from the ghastly spectacle around the guillotine.

And yet she seemed to do it wilfully, as if coming to the end of her patience, all her proud, aristocratic blood in revolt against this evil-smelling crowd which surrounded her.

Half-tipsy men and noisome, naked urchins seemed to have sprung from everywhere.

"*Oho, quelle aristo!*" they shouted with ironical astonishment, gazing at the young girl's face, fingering her gown, thrusting begrimed, hate-distorted faces close to her own.

Instinctively she recoiled and backed towards the house immediately on her left. It was adorned with a porch made of stout oak beams, with a tiled roof; an iron lantern descended from this, and there was a stone parapet below, and a few steps, at right angles from the pavement, led up to the massive door.

On these steps the young girl had taken refuge. Proud, defiant, she confronted the howling mob, which she had so wilfully provoked.

"Of a truth, Citizeness Margot, that grey dress would become you well!" suggested a young man, whose red cap hung in tatters over an evil and dissolute-looking face.

"And all that fine lace would make a splendid jabot round the *aristo's* neck when Citizen Samson holds up her head for us to see," added another, as with mock elegance he stooped and with two very grimy fingers slightly raised the young girl's grey frock, displaying the lace-edged petticoat beneath.

A volley of oaths and loud, ironical laughter greeted this sally.

"'Tis mighty fine lace to be thus hidden away," commented an elderly harridan. "Now, would you believe it, my fine madam, but my legs are bare underneath my kirtle?"

"And dirty, too, I'll lay a wager," laughed another. "Soap is dear in Paris just now."

"The lace on the *aristo's* kerchief would pay the baker's bill of a whole family for a month!" shouted an excited voice.

Heat and brandy further addled the brains of this group of French citizens; hatred gleamed out of every eye. Outrage was imminent. The young girl seemed to know it, but she remained defiant and self-possessed, gradually stepping back and back up the steps, closely followed by her assailants.

"To the Jew with the gewgaw, then!" shouted a thin, haggard female viciously, as she suddenly clutched at the young girl's kerchief, and with a mocking, triumphant laugh tore it from her bosom.

This outrage seemed to be the signal for the breaking down of the final barriers which ordinary decency should have raised. The language and vituperation became such as no chronicler could record.

The girl's dainty white neck, her clear skin, the refined contour of shoulders and bust, seemed to have aroused the deadliest lust of hate in these wretched creatures, rendered bestial by famine and squalor.

It seemed almost as if one would vie with the other in seeking for words which would most offend these small aristocratic ears.

The young girl was now crouching against the doorway, her hands held up to her ears to shut out the awful sounds. She did not seem frightened, only appalled at the terrible volcano which she had provoked.

Suddenly a miserable harridan struck her straight in the face, with hard, grimy fist, and a long shout of exultation greeted this monstrous deed.

Then only did the girl seem to lose her self-control.

"À *moi*," she shouted loudly, whilst hammering with both hands against the massive doorway. "À *moi!* Murder! Murder! Citoyen Déroulède, à *moi!*"

But her terror was greeted with renewed glee by her assailants. They were now roused to the highest point of frenzy: the crowd of brutes would in the next moment have torn the helpless girl from her place of refuge and dragged her into the mire, an outraged prey, for the satisfaction of an ungovernable hate.

But just as half-a-dozen pairs of talon-like hands clutched frantically at her skirts, the door behind her was quickly opened. She felt her arm seized firmly, and herself dragged swiftly within the shelter of the threshold.

Her senses, overwrought by the terrible adventure which she had just gone through, were threatening to reel; she heard the massive door close, shutting out the yells of baffled rage, the ironical laughter, the obscene words, which sounded in her ears like the shrieks of Dante's damned.

She could not see her rescuer, for the hall into which he had hastily dragged her was only dimly lighted. But a peremptory voice said quickly:

"Up the stairs, the room straight in front of you, my mother is there. Go quickly."

She had fallen on her knees, cowering against the heavy oak beam which supported the ceiling, and was straining her eyes to catch sight of the man, to whom at this moment she perhaps owed more than her life: but he was standing against the doorway, with his hand on the latch.

"What are you going to do?" she murmured.

"Prevent their breaking into my house in order to drag you out of it," he replied quietly; "so, I pray you, do as I bid you."

Mechanically she obeyed him, drew herself to her feet, and, turning towards the stairs, began slowly to mount the shallow steps. Her knees were shaking under her, her whole body was trembling with horror at the awesome crisis she had just traversed.

She dared not look back at her rescuer. Her head was bent, and her lips were murmuring half-audible words as she went.

Outside the hooting and yelling was becoming louder and louder. Enraged fists were hammering violently against the stout oak door.

At the top of the stairs, moved by an irresistible impulse, she turned and looked into the hall.

She saw his figure dimly outlined in the gloom, one hand on the latch, his head thrown back to watch her movements.

A door stood ajar immediately in front of her. She pushed it open and went within.

At that moment he too opened the door below. The shrieks of the howling mob once more resounded close to her ears. It seemed as if they had surrounded him. She wondered what was happening and marvelled how he dared to face that awful crowd alone.

The room into which she had entered was gay and cheerful-looking with its dainty chintz hangings and graceful, elegant pieces of furniture. The young girl looked up, as a kindly voice said to her, from out the depths of a capacious armchair:

"Come in, come in, my dear, and close the door behind you! Did those wretches attack you? Never mind. Paul will speak to them. Come here, my dear, and sit down; there's no cause now for fear."

Without a word the young girl came forward. She seemed now to be walking in a dream, the chintz hangings to be swaying ghostlike around her, the yells and shrieks below to come from the very bowels of the earth.

The old lady continued to prattle on. She had taken the girl's hand in hers and was gently forcing her down on to a low stool beside her armchair. She was talking about Paul, and said something about Anne Mie, and then about the National Convention, and those beasts and savages, but mostly about Paul.

The noise outside had subsided. The girl felt strangely sick and tired. Her head seemed to be whirling round, the furniture to be dancing round her; the old lady's face looked at her through a swaying veil, and then—and then—

Tired Nature was having her way at last; she folded the quivering young body in her motherly arms and wrapped the aching senses beneath her merciful mantle of unconsciousness.

Chapter 2

Citizen-Deputy

When, presently, the young girl awoke, with a delicious feeling of rest and well-being, she had plenty of leisure to think.

So, then, this was his house! She was actually a guest, a rescued *protégé*, beneath the roof of Citoyen Déroulède.

He had dragged her from the clutches of the howling mob which she had provoked; his mother had made her welcome, a sweet-faced, young girl scarce out of her teens, sad-eyed and slightly deformed, had waited upon her and made her happy and comfortable.

Juliette de Marny was in the house of the man, whom she had sworn before her God and before her father to pursue with hatred and revenge.

Ten years had gone by since then.

Lying upon the sweet-scented bed which the hospitality of the Déroulèdes had provided for her, she seemed to see passing before her the spectres of these past ten years—the first four, after her brother's death, until the old Duc de Marny's body slowly followed his soul to its grave.

After that last glimmer of life beside the deathbed of his son, the old *Duc* had practically ceased to be. A mute, shrunken figure, he merely existed; his mind vanished, his memory gone, a wreck whom Nature fortunately remembered at last, and finally took away from the invalid chair which had been his world.

Then came those few years at the Convent of the Ursulines. Juliette had hoped that she had a vocation; her whole soul yearned for a secluded, a religious, life, for great barriers of solemn vows and days spent in prayer and contemplation, to interpose between herself and the memory of that awful night when, obedient to her father's will, she had made the solemn oath to avenge her brother's death.

She was only eighteen when she first entered the convent, directly after her father's death, when she felt very lonely—both morally and mentally lonely—and followed by the obsession of that oath.

She never spoke of it to anyone except to her confessor, and he, a simple-minded man of great learning and a total lack of knowledge of the world, was completely at a loss how to advise.

The Archbishop was consulted. He could grant a dispensation and release her of that most solemn vow.

When first this idea was suggested to her, Juliette was exultant. Her entire nature, which in itself was wholesome, light-hearted, the very reverse of morbid, rebelled against this unnatural task placed upon her young shoulders. It was only religion—the strange, warped religion of that extraordinary age—which kept her to it, which forbade her breaking lightly that most unnatural oath.

The Archbishop was a man of many duties, many engagements. He agreed to give this strange "*cas de conscience*" his most earnest attention. He would make no promises. But Mademoiselle de Marny was rich: a munificent donation to the poor of Paris, or to some cause dear to the Holy Father himself, might perhaps be more acceptable to God than the fulfilment of a compulsory vow.

Juliette, within the convent walls, was waiting patiently for the Archbishop's decision at the very moment, when the greatest upheaval the world has ever known was beginning to shake the very foundations of France.

The Archbishop had other things now to think about than isolated cases of conscience. He forgot all about Juliette, probably. He was busy consoling a monarch for the loss of his throne and preparing himself and his royal patron for the scaffold.

The Convent of the Ursulines was scattered during the Terror. Everyone remembers the Thermidor massacres, and the thirty-four nuns, all daughters of ancient families of France, who went so cheerfully to the scaffold.

Juliette was one of those who escaped condemnation. How or why, she herself could not have told. She was very young, and still a postulant; she was allowed to live in retirement with Pétronelle, her old nurse, who had remained faithful through all these years.

Then the Archbishop was prosecuted and imprisoned. Juliette made frantic efforts to see him, but all in vain. When he died, she looked upon her spiritual guide's death as a direct warning from God, that nothing could relieve her of her oath.

She had watched the turmoils of the Revolution through the attic window of her tiny apartment in Paris. Waited upon by faithful Pétronelle, she had been forced to live on the savings of that worthy old soul, as all her property, all the Marny estates, the *dot* she took with her to the convent—everything, in fact—had been seized by the Revolutionary Government, self-appointed to level fortunes, as well as individuals.

From that attic window she had seen beautiful Paris writhing under the pitiless lash of the demon of terror which it had provoked; she had heard the rumble of the tumbrils, dragging day after day their load of victims to the insatiable maker of this Revolution of Fraternity—the Guillotine.

She had seen the gay, light-hearted people of this Star-City turned to howling beasts of prey, its women changed to sexless vultures, with murderous talons implanted in everything that is noble, high or beautiful.

She was not twenty when the feeble, vacillating monarch and his imperious consort were dragged back—a pair of humiliated prisoners—to the capital from which they had tried to flee.

Two years later, she had heard the cries of an entire people exulting over a regicide. Then the murder of Marat, by a young girl like herself, the pale-faced, large-eyed Charlotte, who had committed a crime for the sake of a conviction. "Greater than Brutus!" some had called her. Greater than Joan of Arc, for it was to a mission of evil and of sin that she was called from the depths of her Breton village, and not to one of glory and triumph.

"Greater than Brutus!"

Juliette followed the trial of Charlotte Corday with all the passionate ardour of her exalted temperament.

Just think what an effect it must have had upon the mind of this young girl, who for nine years—the best of her life—had also lived with the idea of a sublime mission pervading her very soul.

She watched Charlotte Corday at her trial. Conquering her natural repulsion for such scenes, and the crowds which usually watched them, she had forced her way into the foremost rank of the narrow gallery which overlooked the Hall of the Revolutionary Tribunal.

She heard the indictment, heard Tinville's speech and the calling of the witnesses.

"All this is unnecessary. I killed Marat!"

Juliette heard the fresh young voice ringing out clearly above the murmur of voices, the howls of execration; she saw the beautiful young face, clear, calm, impassive.

"I killed Marat!"

And there in the special space allotted to the Citizen-Deputies, sitting among those who represented the party of the Moderate Gironde, was Paul Déroulède, the man whom she had sworn to pursue with a vengeance as great, as complete, as that which guided Charlotte Corday's hand.

She watched him during the trial and wondered if he had any presentiment of the hatred which dogged him, like unto the one which had dogged Marat.

He was very dark, almost swarthy a son of the South, with brown hair, free from powder, thrown back and revealing the brow of a student rather than that of a legislator. He watched Charlotte Corday earnestly, and Juliette who watched him saw the look of measureless pity, which softened the otherwise hard look of his close-set eyes.

He made an impassioned speech for the defence: a speech which has become historic. It would have cost any other man his head.

Juliette marvelled at his courage; to defend Charlotte Corday was equivalent to acquiescing in the death of Marat: Marat, the friend of the people; Marat, whom his funeral orators had compared to the Great, the Sacred Leveller of Mankind!

But Déroulède's speech was not a defence, it was an appeal. The most eloquent man of that eloquent age, his words seemed to find that hidden bit of sentiment which still lurked in the hearts of these strange protagonists of Hate.

Everyone round Juliette listened as he spoke: "It is Citoyen Déroulède!" whispered the bloodthirsty Amazons, who sat knitting in the gallery.

But there was no further comment. A huge, magnificently-equipped hospital for sick children had been thrown open in Paris that very morning, a gift to the nation from Citoyen Déroulède. Surely, he was privileged to talk a little, if it pleased him. His hospital would cover quite a good many defalcations.

Even the rabid Mountain, Danton, Merlin, Santerre, shrugged their shoulders. "It is Déroulède, let him talk an he list. Murdered Marat said of him that he was not dangerous."

Juliette heard it all. The knitters round her were talking loudly. Even Charlotte was almost forgotten whilst Déroulède talked. He had a fine voice, of strong calibre, which echoed powerfully through the hall.

He was rather short, but broad-shouldered and well knit, with an expressive hand, which looked slender and delicate below the fine lace ruffle.

Charlotte Corday was condemned. All Déroulède's eloquence could not save her.

Juliette left the court in a state of mad exultation. She was very young: the scenes she had witnessed in the past two years could not help but excite the imagination of a young girl, left entirely to her own intellectual and moral resources.

What scenes! Great God!

And now to wait for an opportunity! Charlotte Corday, the half-educated little provincial should not put to shame Mademoiselle de Marny, the daughter of a hundred dukes, of those who had made

France before she took to unmaking herself.

But she could not formulate any definite plans. Pétronelle, poor old soul, her only confidante, was not of the stuff that heroines are made of. Juliette felt impelled by duty, and duty at best is not so prompt a counsellor as love or hate.

Her adventure outside Déroulède's house had not been premeditated. Impulse and coincidence had worked their will with her.

She had been in the habit, daily, for the past month, of wandering down the Rue Ecole de Médecine, ostensibly to gaze at Marat's dwelling, as crowds of idlers were wont to do, but really in order to look at Déroulède's house. Once or twice she saw him coming or going from home. Once she caught sight of the inner hall, and of a young girl in a dark kirtle and snow-white kerchief bidding him goodbye at his door. Another time she caught sight of him at the corner of the street, helping that same young girl over the muddy pavement. He had just met her, and she was carrying a basket of provisions: he took it from her and carried it to the house.

Chivalrous—eh?—and innately so, evidently, for the girl was slightly deformed: hardly a hunchback, but weak and unattractive-looking, with melancholy eyes, and a pale, pinched face.

It was the thought of that little act of simple chivalry, witnessed the day before, which caused Juliette to provoke the scene which, but for Déroulède's timely interference, might have ended so fatally. But she reckoned on that interference: the whole thing had occurred to her suddenly, and she had carried it through.

Had not her father said to her that when the time came, God would show her a means to the end?

And now she was inside the house of the man who had murdered her brother and sent her sorrowing father, a poor, senseless maniac, tottering to the grave.

Would God's finger point again, and show her what to do next, how best to accomplish what she had sworn to do?

Chapter 3

Hospitality

"Is there anything more I can do for you now, *mademoiselle?*"

The gentle, timid voice roused Juliette from the contemplation of the past.

She smiled at Anne Mie and held her hand out towards her.

"You have all been so kind," she said, "I want to get up now and thank you all."

"Don't move unless you feel quite well."

"I am quite well now. Those horrid people frightened me so, that is why I fainted."

"They would have half-killed you, if—"

"Will you tell me where I am?" asked Juliette.

"In the house of M. Paul Déroulède—I should have said of Citizen-Deputy Déroulède. He rescued you from the mob and pacified them. He has such a beautiful voice that he can make anyone listen to him, and—"

"And you are fond of him, *mademoiselle?*" added Juliette, suddenly feeling a mist of tears rising to her eyes.

"Of course, I am fond of him," rejoined the other girl simply, whilst a look of the most tender-hearted devotion seemed to beautify her pale face. "He and Madame Déroulède have brought me up; I never knew my parents. They have cared for me, and he has taught me all I know."

"What do they call you, *mademoiselle?*"

"My name is Anne Mie."

"And mine, Juliette—Juliette Marny," she added after a slight hesitation. "I have no parents either. My old nurse, Pétronelle, has brought me up, and—But tell me more about M. Déroulède—I owe him so much, I'd like to know him better."

"Will you not let me arrange your hair?" said Anne Mie as if purposely evading a direct reply. "M. Déroulède is in the *salon* with *Madame.* You can see him then."

Juliette asked no more questions, but allowed Anne Mie to tidy her hair for her, to lend her a fresh kerchief and generally to efface all traces of her terrible adventure. She felt puzzled and tearful. Anne Mie's gentleness seemed somehow to jar on her spirits. She could not understand the girl's position in the Déroulède household. Was she a relative, or a superior servant? In these troublous times she might easily have been both.

In any case she was a childhood's companion of the Citizen-Deputy—whether on an equal or a humbler footing, Juliette would have given much to ascertain.

With the marvellous instinct peculiar to women of temperament, she had already divined Anne Mie's love for Déroulède. The poor young cripple's very soul seemed to quiver magnetically at the bare mention of his name, her whole face became transfigured: Juliette even thought her beautiful then.

She looked at herself critically in the glass, and adjusted a curl, which looked its best when it was rebellious. She scrutinised her own face carefully; why? she could not tell: another of those subtle feminine instincts perhaps.

The becoming simplicity of the prevailing mode suited her to perfection. The waist line, rather high but clearly defined—a precursor of the later more accentuated fashion—gave grace to her long slender limbs and emphasised the lissomness of her figure. The kerchief, edged with fine lace, and neatly folded across her bosom, softened the contour of her girlish bust and shoulders.

And her hair was a veritable glory round her dainty, piquant face. Soft, fair, and curly, it emerged in a golden halo from beneath the prettiest little lace cap imaginable.

She turned and faced Anne Mie, ready to follow her out of the room, and the young crippled girl sighed as she smoothed down the folds of her own apron and gave a final touch to the completion of Juliette's attire.

The time before the evening meal slipped by like a dream-hour for Juliette.

She had lived so much alone, had led such an introspective life, that she had hardly realised and understood all that was going on around her. At the time when the inner vitality of France first asserted itself and then swept away all that hindered its mad progress, she was tied to the invalid chair of her half-demented father; then, after that, the sheltering walls of the Ursuline Convent had hidden from her mental vision the true meaning of the great conflict, between the Old Era and the New.

Déroulède was neither a pedant nor yet a revolutionary: his theories were Utopian and he had an extraordinary overpowering sympathy for his fellow-men.

After the first casual greetings with Juliette, he had continued a discussion with his mother, which the young girl's entrance had interrupted.

He seemed to take but little notice of her, although at times his dark, keen eyes would seek hers, as if challenging her for a reply.

He was talking of the mob of Paris, whom he evidently understood so well. Incidents such as the one which Juliette had provoked, had led to rape and theft, often to murder, before now: but outside Citizen-Deputy Déroulède's house everything was quiet, half-an-hour after

Juliette's escape from that howling, brutish crowd.

He had merely spoken to them, for about twenty minutes, and they had gone away quite quietly, without even touching one hair of his head. He seemed to love them: to know how to separate the little good that was in them, from that hard crust of evil, which misery had put around their hearts.

Once he addressed Juliette somewhat abruptly: "Pardon me, *mademoiselle*, but for your own sake we must guard you a prisoner here awhile. No one would harm you under this roof, but it would not be safe for you to cross the neighbouring streets tonight."

"But I must go, *monsieur*. Indeed, indeed I must!" she said earnestly. "I am deeply grateful to you, but I could not leave Pétronelle."

"Who is Pétronelle?"

"My dear old nurse, *monsieur*. She has never left me. Think how anxious and miserable she must be, at my prolonged absence."

"Where does she live?"

"At No. 15 Rue Taitbout, but—"

"Will you allow me to take her a message?—telling her that you are safe and under my roof, where it is obviously more prudent that you should remain at present."

"If you think it best, *monsieur*," she replied.

Inwardly she was trembling with excitement. God had not only brought her to this house but willed that she should stay in it.

"In whose name shall I take the message, *mademoiselle?*" he asked.

"My name is Juliette Marny."

She watched him keenly as she said it, but there was not the slightest sign in his expressive face, to show that he had recognised the name.

Ten years is a long time, and everyone had lived through so much during those years! A wave of intense wrath swept through Juliette's soul, as she realised that he had forgotten. The name meant nothing to him! It did not recall to him the fact that his hand was stained with blood. During ten years she had suffered, she had fought with herself, fought for him as it were, against the Fate which she was destined to mete out to him, whilst he had forgotten, or at least had ceased to think.

He bowed to her and went out of the room.

The wave of wrath subsided, and she was left alone with Madame Déroulède: presently Anne Mie came in.

The three women chatted together, waiting for the return of the master of the house. Juliette felt well and, in spite of herself, almost happy. She had lived so long in the miserable, little attic alone with Pétronelle that she enjoyed the well-being of this refined home. It was not so grand or gorgeous of course as her father's princely palace opposite the Louvre, a wreck now, since it was annexed by the Committee of National Defence, for the housing of soldiery. But the Déroulèdes' home was essentially a refined one. The delicate china on the tall chimney-piece, the few bits of Buhl and Vernis Martin about the room, the vision through the open doorway of the supper-table spread with a fine white cloth, and sparkling with silver, all spoke of fastidious tastes, of habits of luxury and elegance, which the spirit of Equality and Anarchy had not succeeded in eradicating.

When Déroulède came back, he brought an atmosphere of breezy cheerfulness with him.

The street was quiet now, and when walking past the hospital—his own gift to the Nation—he had been loudly cheered. One or two ironical voices had asked him what he had done with the *aristo* and her lace furbelows, but it remained at that and Mademoiselle Marny need have no fear.

He had brought Pétronelle along with him: his careless, lavish hospitality would have suggested the housing of Juliette's entire domestic establishment, had she possessed one.

As it was, the worthy old soul's deluge of happy tears had melted his kindly heart. He offered her and her young mistress shelter, until the small cloud should have rolled by.

After that he suggested a journey to England. Emigration now was the only real safety, and Mademoiselle Marny had unpleasantly draw on herself the attention of the Paris rabble. No doubt, within the next few days her name would figure among the "suspect." She would be safest out of the country and could not do better than place herself under the guidance of that English enthusiast, who had helped so many persecuted Frenchmen to escape from the terrors of the Revolution: the man who was such a thorn in the flesh of the Committee of Public Safety, and who went by the nickname of the Scarlet Pimpernel.

Chapter 4

The Faithful House-Dog

After supper they talked of Charlotte Corday.

Juliette clung to the vision of that heroine and liked to talk of her.

She appeared as a justification of her own actions, which somehow seemed to require justification.

She loved to hear Paul Déroulède talk; liked to provoke his enthusiasm and to see his stern, dark face light up with the inward fire of the enthusiast.

She had openly avowed herself as the daughter of the Duc de Marny. When she actually named her father, and her brother killed in duel, she saw Déroulède looking long and searchingly at her. Evidently, he wondered if she knew everything: but she returned his gaze fearlessly and frankly, and he apparently was satisfied.

Madame Déroulède seemed to know nothing of the circumstances of that duel. Déroulède tried to draw Juliette out, to make her speak of her brother. She replied to his questions quite openly, but there was nothing in what she said, suggestive of the fact that she knew who killed her brother.

She wanted him to know who she was. If he feared an enemy in her, there was yet time enough for him to close his doors against her.

But less than a minute later, he had renewed his warmest offers of hospitality.

"Until we can arrange for your journey to England," he added with a short sigh, as if reluctant to part from her.

To Juliette his attitude seemed one of complete indifference for the wrong he had done to her and to her father: feeling that she was an avenging spirit, with flaming sword in hand, pursuing her brother's murderer like a relentless Nemesis, she would have preferred to see him cowed before her, even afraid of her, though she was only a young and delicate girl.

She did not understand that in the simplicity of his heart, he only wished to make amends. The quarrel with the young Vicomte de Marny had been forced upon him, the fight had been honourable and fair, and on his side fought with every desire to spare the young man. He had merely been the instrument of Fate, but he felt happy that Fate once more used him as her tool, this time to save the sister.

Whilst Déroulède and Juliette talked together Anne Mie cleared the supper-table, then came and sat on a low stool at *Madame's* feet. She took no part in the conversation, but every now and then Juliette felt the girl's melancholy eyes fixed almost reproachfully upon her.

When Juliette had retired with Pétronelle, Déroulède took Anne Mie's hand in his.

"You will be kind to my guest, Anne Mie, won't you? She seems very lonely and has gone through a great deal."

"Not more than I have," murmured the young girl involuntarily.

"You are not happy, Anne Mie? I thought—"

"Is a wretched, deformed creature ever happy?" she said with sudden vehemence, as tears of mortification rushed to her eyes, in spite of herself.

"I did not think that you were wretched," he replied with some sadness, "and neither in my eyes, nor in my mother's, are you in any way deformed."

Her mood changed at once. She clung to him, pressing his hand between her own.

"Forgive me! I—I don't know what's the matter with me tonight," she said with a nervous little laugh. "Let me see, you asked me to be kind to *Mademoiselle* Marny, did you not?"

He nodded with a smile.

"Of course, I'll be kind to her. Isn't everyone kind to one who is young and beautiful, and has great, appealing eyes, and soft, curly hair? Ah me! how easy is the path in life for some people! What do you want me to do, Paul? Wait on her? Be her little maid? Soothe her nerves or what? I'll do it all, though in her eyes I shall remain both wretched and deformed, a creature to pity, the harmless, necessary house-dog—"

She paused a moment: said "Goodnight" to him, and turned to go, candle in hand, looking pathetic and fragile, with that ugly contour of shoulder, which Déroulède assured her he could not see.

The candle flickered in the draught, illumining the thin, pinched face, the large melancholy eyes of the faithful house-dog.

"Who can watch and bite!" she said half-audibly as she slipped out of the room. "For I do not trust you, my fine madam, and there was something about that comedy this afternoon, which somehow, I don't quite understand."

Chapter 5

A Day in the Woods

But whilst men and women set to work to make the towns of France hideous with their shrieks and their hootings, their mock-trials and bloody guillotines, they could not quite prevent Nature from working her sweet will with the country.

June, July, and August had received new names—they were now called *Messidor, Thermidor,* and *Fructidor,* but under these new names they continued to pour forth upon the earth the same old fruits, the same flowers, the same grass in the meadows and leaves upon the trees.

Messidor brought its quota of wild roses in the hedgerows, just as archaic June had done. *Thermidor* covered the barren cornfields with its flaming mantle of scarlet poppies, and *Fructidor*, though now called August, still tipped the wild sorrel with dots of crimson, and laid the first wash of tender colour on the pale cheeks of the ripening peaches.

And Juliette—young, girlish, feminine and inconsequent—had sighed for country and sunshine, had longed for a ramble in the woods, the music of the birds, the sight of the meadows sugared with marguerites.

She had left the house early: accompanied by Pétronelle, she had been rowed along the river as far as Suresnes. They had brought some bread and fresh butter, a little wine and fruit in a basket, and from here she meant to wander homewards through the woods.

It was all so peaceful, so remote: even the noise of shrieking, howling Paris did not reach the leafy thickets of Suresnes.

It almost seemed as if this little old-world village had been forgotten by the destroyers of France. It had never been a royal residence, the woods had never been preserved for royal sport: there was no vengeance to be wreaked upon its peaceful glades and sleepy, fragrant meadows.

Juliette spent a happy day; she loved the flowers, the trees, the birds, and Pétronelle was silent and sympathetic. As the afternoon wore on, and it was time to go home, Juliette turned townwards with a sigh.

You all know that road through the woods, which lies to the northwest of Paris: so leafy, so secluded. No large, hundred-year-old trees, no fine oaks or antique elms, but numberless delicate stems of hazelnut and young ash, covered with honeysuckle at this time of year, sweet-smelling and so peaceful after that awful turmoil of the town.

Obedient to Madame Déroulède's suggestion, Juliette had tied a tricolour scarf round her waist, and a Phrygian cap of crimson cloth, with the inevitable rosette on one side, adorned her curly head.

She had gathered a huge bouquet of poppies, marguerites and blue lupin —Nature's tribute to the national colours—and as she wandered through the sylvan glades she looked like some quaint dweller of the woods—a sprite, mayhap—with old mother Pétronelle trotting behind her, like an attendant witch.

Suddenly she paused, for in the near distance she had perceived the sound of footsteps upon the leafy turf, and the next moment Paul Déroulède emerged from out the thicket and came rapidly towards her.

"We were so anxious about you at home!" he said, almost by way of an apology. "My mother became so restless—"

"That to quiet her fears you came in search of me!" she retorted with a gay little laugh, the laugh of a young girl, scarce a woman as yet, who feels that she is good to look at, good to talk to, who feels her wings for the first time, the wings with which to soar into that mad, merry, elusive and called Romance. Ay, her wings! but her power also! that sweet, subtle power of the woman: the yoke which men love, rail at, and love again, the yoke that enslaves them and gives them the joy of kings.

How happy the day had been! Yet it had been incomplete!

Pétronelle was somewhat dull, and Juliette was too young to enjoy long companionship with her own thoughts. Now suddenly the day seemed to have become perfect. There was someone there to appreciate the charm of the woods, the beauty of that blue sky peeping though the tangled foliage of the honeysuckle-covered trees. There was someone to talk to, someone to admire the fresh white frock Juliette had put on that morning.

"But how did you know where to find me?" she asked with a quaint touch of immature *coquetry*.

"I didn't know," he replied quietly. "They told me you had gone to Suresness and meant to wander homewards through the woods. It frightened me, for you will have to go through the north-west barrier, and—"

"Well?"

He smiled and looked earnestly for a moment at the dainty apparition before him.

"Well, you know!" he said gaily, "that tricolour scarf and the red cap are not quite sufficient as a disguise: you look anything but a staunch friend of the people. I guessed that your muslin frock would be clean, and that there would still be some tell-tale lace upon it."

She laughed again, and with delicate fingers lifted her pretty muslin frock, displaying a white *frou-frou* of flounces beneath the hem.

"How careless and childish!" he said, almost roughly.

"Would you have me coarse and grimy to be a fitting match for your partisans?" she retorted.

His tone of mentor nettled her, his attitude seemed to her priggish and dictatorial, and as the sun disappearing behind a sudden cloud, so her childish merriment quickly gave place to a feeling of unexplainable disappointment.

"I humbly beg your pardon," he said quietly, "And must crave your kind indulgence for my mood: but I have been so anxious—"

"Why should you be anxious about me?"

She had meant to say this indifferently, as if caring little what the reply might be: but in her effort to seem indifferent her voice became haughty, a reminiscence of the days when she still was the daughter of the Duc de Marny, the richest and most high-born heiress in France.

"Was that presumptuous?" he asked, with a slight touch of irony, in response to her own *hauteur.*

"It was merely unnecessary," she replied. "I have already laid too many burdens on your shoulders, without wishing to add that of anxiety."

"You have laid no burden on me," he said quietly, "save one of gratitude."

"Gratitude? What have I done?"

"You committed a foolish, thoughtless act outside my door, and gave me the chance of easing my conscience of a heavy load."

"In what way?"

"I had never hoped that the Fates would be so kind as to allow me to render a member of your family a slight service."

"I understand that you saved my life the other day, Monsieur Déroulède. I know that I am still in peril and that I owe my safety to you—"

"Do you also know that your brother owed his death to me?"

She closed her lips firmly, unable to reply, wrathful with him, for having suddenly and without any warning, placed a clumsy hand upon that hidden sore.

"I always meant to tell you," he continued somewhat hurriedly; "for it almost seemed to me that I have been cheating you, these last few days. I don't suppose that you can quite realise what it means to me to tell you this just now; but I owe it to you, I think. In later years you might find out, and then regret the days you spent under my roof. I called you childish a moment ago, you must forgive me; I know that you are a woman and hope therefore that you will understand me. I killed your brother in fair fight. He provoked me as no man was ever provoked before—"

"Is it necessary, M. Déroulède, that you should tell me all this?" she interrupted him with some impatience.

"I thought you ought to know."

"You must know, on the other hand, that I have no means of hearing the history of the quarrel from my brother's point of view now."

The moment the words were out of her lips she had realised how cruelly she had spoken. He did not reply; he was too chivalrous, too gentle, to reproach her. Perhaps he understood for the first time how bitterly she had felt her brother's death, and how deeply she must be suffering, now that she knew herself to be face to face with his murderer.

She stole a quick glance at him, through her tears. She was deeply penitent for what she had said. It almost seemed to her as if a dual nature was at war within her.

The mention of her brother's name, the recollection of that awful night beside his dead body, of those four years whilst she watched her father's moribund reason slowly wandering towards the grave, seemed to rouse in her a spirit of rebellion, and of evil, which she felt was not entirely of herself.

The woods had become quite silent. It was late afternoon, and they had gradually wandered farther and farther away from pretty sylvan Suresness, towards great, anarchic, death-dealing Paris. In this part of the woods the birds had left their homes; the trees, shorn of their lower branches looked like gaunt spectres, raising melancholy heads towards the relentless, silent sky.

In the distance, from behind the barriers, a couple of miles away, the boom of a gun was heard.

"They are closing the barriers," he said quietly after a long pause. "I am glad I was fortunate enough to meet you."

"It was kind of you to seek for me," she said meekly. "I didn't mean what I said just now—"

"I pray you, say no more about it. I can so well understand. I only wish—"

"It would be best I should leave your house," she said gently; "I have so ill repaid your hospitality. Pétronelle and I can easily go back to our lodgings."

"You would break my mother's heart if you left her now," he said, almost roughly. "She has become very fond of you, and knows, just as well as I do, the dangers that would beset you outside my house. My coarse and grimy partisans," he added, with a bitter touch of sarcasm, "have that advantage, that they are loyal to me, and would not harm you while under my roof."

"But you—" she murmured.

She felt somehow that she had wounded him very deeply and was half angry with herself for her seeming ingratitude, and yet childishly glad to have suppressed in him that attitude of mentorship, which he was beginning to assume over her.

"You need not fear that my presence will offend you much longer, *mademoiselle*," he said coldly. "I can quite understand how hateful it must be to you, though I would have wished that you could believe at least in my sincerity."

"Are you going away then?"

"Not out of Paris altogether. I have accepted the post of Governor of the *Conciergerie*."

"Ah!—where the poor queen—"

She checked herself suddenly. Those words would have been called treasonable to the people of France.

Instinctively and furtively, as everyone did in these days, she cast a rapid glance behind her.

"You need not be afraid," he said; "there is no one here but Pétronelle."

"And you."

"Oh! I echo your words. Poor Marie Antoinette!"

"You pity her?"

"How can I help it?"

"But you are that horrible National Convention, who will try her, condemn her, execute her as they did the king."

"I am of the National Convention. But I will not condemn her, nor be a party to another crime. I go as Governor of the *Conciergerie*, to help her, if I can."

"But your popularity—your life—if you befriend her?"

"As you say, *mademoiselle*, my life, if I befriend her," he said simply.

She looked at him with renewed curiosity in her gaze.

How strange were men in these days! Paul Déroulède, the republican, the recognised idol of the lawless people of France, was about to risk his life for the woman he had helped to dethrone.

Pity with him did not end with the rabble of Paris; it had reached Charlotte Corday, though it failed to save her, and now it extended to the poor dispossessed queen. Somehow, in his face this time, she saw either success or death.

"When do you leave?" she asked.

"Tomorrow night."

She said nothing more. Strangely enough, a tinge of melancholy had settled over her spirits. No doubt the proximity of the town was the cause of this. She could already hear the familiar noise of muffled drums, the loud, excited shrieking of the mob, who stood round the gates of Paris, at this time of the evening, waiting to witness some important capture, perhaps that of a hated aristocrat striving to escape from the people's revenge.

The had reached the edge of the wood, and gradually, as she walked, the flowers she had gathered fell unheeded out of her listless hands one by one.

First the blue lupins: their bud-laden heads were heavy and they dropped to the ground, followed by the white marguerites, that lay thick behind her now on the grass like a shroud. The red poppies were the lightest, their thin gummy stalks clung to her hands longer than the rest. At last she let them fall too, singly, like great drops of blood, that glistened as her long white gown swept them aside.

Déroulède was absorbed in his thoughts and seemed not to heed her. At the barrier, however, he roused himself and took out the passes which alone enabled Juliette and Pétronelle to re-enter the town unchallenged. He himself as Citizen-Deputy could come and go as he wished.

Juliette shuddered as the great gates closed behind her with a heavy clank. It seemed to shut out even the memory of this happy day, which for a brief space had been quite perfect.

She did not know Paris very well, and wondered where lay that gloomy *Conciergerie*, where a dethroned queen was living her last days, in an agonised memory of the past. But as they crossed the bridge she recognised all round her the massive towers of the great city: Notre Dame, the grateful spire of La Sainte Chapelle, the sombre outline of St. Gervais, and behind her the Louvre with its great history and irreclaimable grandeur. How small her own tragedy seemed in the midst of this great sanguinary drama, the last act of which had not yet even begun. Her own revenge, her oath, her tribulations, what were they in comparison with that great flaming Nemesis which had swept away a throne, that vow of retaliation carried out by thousands against other thousands, that long story of degradation, of regicide, of fratricide, the awesome chapters of which were still being unfolded one by one?

She felt small and petty: ashamed of the pleasure she had felt in the woods, ashamed of her high spirits and light-heartedness, ashamed of that feeling of sudden pity and admiration for the man who had done her and her family so deep an injury, which she was too feeble, too vacillating to avenge.

The majestic outline of the Louvre seemed to frown sarcastically on her weakness, the silent river to mock her and her wavering purpose. The man beside her had wronged her and hers far more deeply than the Bourbons had wronged their people. The people of France were taking their revenge, and God had at the close of this last happy day of her life pointed once more to the means for her great end.

CHAPTER 6

The Scarlet Pimpernel

It was some few hours later. The ladies sat in the drawing-room, silent and anxious.

Soon after supper a visitor had called and had been closeted with Paul Déroulède in the latter's study for the past two hours.

A tall, somewhat lazy-looking figure, he was sitting at a table face to face with the Citizen-Deputy. On a chair beside him lay a heavy caped coat, covered with the dust and the splashings of a long journey, but he himself was attired in clothes that suggested the most fastidious taste, and the most perfect of tailors; he wore with apparent ease the eccentric fashion of the time, the short-waisted coat of many lapels, the double waistcoat and billows of delicate lace. Unlike Déroulède he was of great height, with fair hair and a somewhat lazy expression in his good-natured blue eyes, and as he spoke, there was just a soupçon of foreign accent in the pronunciation of the French vowels, a certain drawl of o's and a's, that would have betrayed the Britisher to an observant ear.

The two men had been talking earnestly for some time, the tall Englishman was watching his friend keenly, whilst an amused, pleasant smile lingered round the corners of his firm mouth and jaw. Déroulède, restless and enthusiastic, was pacing to and fro.

"But I don't understand now, how you managed to reach Paris, my dear Blakeney!" said Déroulède at last, placing an anxious hand on his friend's shoulder. "The government has not forgotten the Scarlet Pimpernel."

"*La!* I took care of that!" responded Blakeney with his short, pleasant laugh. "I sent Tinville my autograph this morning."

"You are mad, Blakeney!"

"Not altogether, my friend. My faith! 'twas on only foolhardiness caused me to grant that devilish prosecutor another sight of my scarlet device. I knew what you maniacs would be after, so I came across in the *Daydream*, just to see if I couldn't get my share of the fun."

"Fun, you call it?" queried the other bitterly.

"Nay! what would you have me call it? A mad, insane, senseless tragedy, with but one issue?—the guillotine for you all."

"The why did you come?"

"To—What shall I say, my friend?" rejoined Sir Percy Blakeny, with that inimitable drawl of his. "To give your demmed government something else to think about, whilst you are all busy running your heads into a noose."

"What makes you think we are doing that?"

"Three things, my friend—may I offer you a pinch of snuff—No?—Ah well!—" And with the graceful gesture of an accomplished dandy, Sir Percy flicked off a grain of dust from his immaculate Mechlin ruffles.

"Three things," he continued quietly; "an imprisoned queen, about to be tried for her life, the temperament of a Frenchman—some of them—and the idiocy of mankind generally. These three things make me think that a certain section of hot-headed Republicans with yourself, my dear Déroulède, *en* tête, are about to attempt the most stupid, senseless, purposeless thing that was ever concocted by the excitable brain of a demmed Frenchman."

Déroulède smiled.

"Does it not seem amusing to you, Blakeney, that you should sit there and condemn anyone for planning mad, insane, senseless things."

"*La!* I'll not sit, I'll stand!" rejoined Blakeney with a laugh, as he drew himself up to his full height, and stretched his long, lazy limbs. "And now let me tell you, friend, that my league of the Scarlet Pimpernel never attempted the impossible, and to try and drag the queen out of the clutches of these murderous rascals now, is attempting the unattainable."

"And yet we mean to try."

"I know it. I guessed it, that is why I came: that is also why I sent a pleasant little note to the Committee of Public Safety, signed with the device they know so well: The Scarlet Pimpernel."

"Well?"

"Well! the result is obvious. Robespierre, Danton, Tinville, Merlin, and the whole of the demmed murderous crowd, will be busy looking after me—a needle in a haystack. They'll put the abortive attempt down to me, and you may—*ma foi!* I only suggest that you *may* escape safely out of France—in the *Daydream*, and with the help of your humble servant."

"But in the meanwhile, they'll discover you, and they'll not let you escape a second time."

"My friend! if a terrier were to lose his temper, he never would run a rat to earth. Now your Revolutionary Government has lost its temper with me, ever since I slipped through Chauvelin's fingers; they are blind with their own fury, whilst I am perfectly happy and cool as a cucumber. My life has become valuable to me, my friend. There is someone over the water now who weeps when I don't return—No! no! never fear—they'll not get the Scarlet Pimpernel this journey—"

He laughed, a gay, pleasant laugh, and his strong, firm face seemed to soften at thought of the beautiful wife, over in England, who was waiting anxiously for his safe return.

"And yet you'll not help us to rescue the queen?" rejoined Déroulède, with some bitterness.

"By every means in my power," replied Blakeney, "save the insane. But I will help to get you all out of the demmed hole, when you have failed."

"We'll not fail," asserted the other hotly.

Sir Percy Blakeney went close up to his friend and placed his long, slender hand, with a touch of almost womanly tenderness upon the latter's shoulder.

"Will you tell me your plans?"

In a moment Déroulède was all fire and enthusiasm.

"There are not many of us in it," he began, "although half France will be in sympathy with us. We have plenty of money, of course, and also the necessary disguise for the royal lady."

"Yes?"

"I, in the meanwhile, have asked for and obtained the post of Governor of the *Conciergerie*; I go into my new quarters tomorrow. In the meanwhile, I am making arrangements for my mother and—and those dependent upon me to quit France immediately."

Blakeney had perceived the slight hesitation when Déroulède mentioned those dependent upon him. He looked scrutinisingly at his friend, who continued quickly:

"I am still very popular among the people. My family can go about unmolested. I must get them out of France, however, in case—in case—"

"Of course," rejoined the other simply.

"As soon as I am assured that they are safe, my friends and I can prosecute our plans. You see the trial of the queen has not yet been decided on, but I know that it is in the air. We hope to get her away, disguised in one of the uniforms of the National Guard. As you know, it will be my duty to make the final round every evening in the prison, and to see that everything is safe for the night. Two fellows watch all night, in the room next to that occupied by the queen. Usually they drink and play cards all night long. I want an opportunity to drug their brandy, and thus to render them more loutish and idiotic than usual; then for a blow on the head that will make them senseless. It should be easy, for I have a strong fist, and after that—"

"Well? After that, friend?" rejoined Sir Percy earnestly, "after that? Shall I fill in the details of the picture?—the guard twenty-five strong outside the *Conciergerie*, how will you pass them?"

"I as the Governor, followed by one of my guards—"

"To go whither?"

"I have the right to come and go as I please."

"I' faith! so you have, but 'one of your guards'—eh? Wrapped to the eyes in a long mantle to hide the female figure beneath. I have been in Paris but a few hours, and yet already I have realised that there is not one demmed citizen within its walls, who does not at this moment suspect some other demmed citizen of conniving at the queen's escape. Even the sparrows on the house-tops are objects of suspicion. No figure wrapped in a mantle will from this day forth leave Paris unchallenged."

"But you yourself, friend?" suggested Déroulède. "You think you can quit Paris unrecognised—then why not the queen?"

"Because she is a woman and has been a queen. She has nerves, poor soul, and weaknesses of body and of mind now. Alas for her! Alas for France! who wreaks such idle vengeance on so poor an enemy? Can you take hold of Marie Antoinette by the shoulders, shove her into the bottom of a cart and pile sacks of potatoes on the top of her? I did that to the Comtesse de Tournai and her daughter, as stiff-necked a pair of French aristocrats as ever deserved the guillotine for their insane prejudices. But can you do it to Marie Antoinette? She'd rebuke you publicly, and betray herself and you in a flash, sooner than submit to a loss of dignity."

"But would you leave her to her fate?"

"Ah! there's the trouble, friend. Do you think you need appeal to the sense of chivalry of my league? We are still twenty strong, and heart and soul in sympathy with your mad schemes. The poor, poor

Queen! But you are bound to fail, and then who will help you all, if we too are put out of the way?"

"We should succeed if you helped us. At one time you used proudly to say: 'The League of the Scarlet Pimpernel has never failed.'"

"Because it attempted nothing which it could not accomplish. But, *la!* since you put me on my mettle—Demm it all! I'll have to think about it!"

And he laughed that funny, somewhat inane laugh of his, which had deceived the clever men of two countries as to his real personality.

Déroulède went up to the heavy oak desk which occupied a conspicuous place in the centre of one of the walls. He unlocked it and drew forth a bundle of papers.

"Will you look through these?" he asked, handing them to Sir Percy Blakeney.

"What are they?"

"Different schemes I have drawn up, in case my original plan should not succeed."

"Burn them, my friend," said Blakeney laconically. "Have you not yet learned the lesson of never putting your hand to paper?"

"I can't burn these. You see, I shall not be able to have long conversations with Marie Antoinette. I must give her my suggestions in writing, that she may study them and not fail me, through lack of knowledge of her part."

"Better that than papers in these times, my friend: these papers, if found, would send you, untried, to the guillotine."

"I am careful, and, at present, quite beyond suspicion. Moreover, among the papers is a complete collection of passports, suitable for any character the Queen and her attendant may be forced to assume. It has taken me some months to collect them, so as not to arouse suspicion; I gradually got them together, on one pretence or another: now I am ready for any eventuality—"

He suddenly paused. A look in his friend's face had given him a swift warning.

He turned, and there in the doorway, holding back the heavy *portière*, stood Juliette, graceful, smiling, a little pale, this no doubt owing to the flickering light of the unsnuffed candles.

So young and girlish did she look in her soft, white muslin frock that at sight of her the tension in Déroulède's face seemed to relax. Instinctively he had thrown the papers back into the desk, but his look had softened, from the fire of obstinate energy to that of inexpressible tenderness.

Blakeney was quietly watching the young girl as she stood in the doorway, a little bashful and undecided.

"Madame Déroulède sent me," she said hesitatingly, "she says the hour is getting late and she is very anxious. M. Déroulède, would you come and reassure her?"

"In a moment, *mademoiselle*," he replied lightly, "my friend and I have just finished our talk. May I have the honour to present him?—Sir Percy Blakeney, a traveller from England. Blakeney, this is Mademoiselle Juliette de Marny, my mother's guest."

Chapter 7

A Warning

Sir Percy bowed very low, with all the graceful flourish and elaborate gesture the eccentric customs of the time demanded.

He had not said a word, since the first exclamation of warning, with which he had drawn his friend's attention to the young girl in the doorway.

Noiselessly, as she had come, Juliette glided out of the room again, leaving behind her an atmosphere of wild flowers, of the bouquet she had gathered, then scattered in the woods.

There was silence in the room for a while. Déroulède was locking up his desk and slipping the keys into his pocket.

"Shall we join my mother for a moment, Blakeney?" he said, moving towards the door.

"I shall be proud to pay my respects," replied Sir Percy; "but before we close the subject, I think I'll change my mind about those papers. If I am to be of service to you I think I had best look through them and give you my opinion of your schemes."

Déroulède looked at him keenly for a moment.

"Certainly," he said at last, going up to his desk. "I'll stay with you whilst you read them through."

"*La!* not tonight, my friend," said Sir Percy lightly; "the hour is late, and *Madame* is waiting for us. They'll be quite safe with me, and you'll entrust them to my care."

Déroulède seemed to hesitate. Blakeney had spoken in his usual airy manner and was even now busy readjusting the set of his perfectly-tailored coat.

"Perhaps you cannot quite trust me?" laughed Sir Percy gaily. "I seemed too lukewarm just now."

"No; it's not that, Blakeney!" said Déroulède quietly at last. "There is no mistrust in me, all the mistrust is on your side."

"Faith!—" began Sir Percy.

"Nay! do not explain. I understand and appreciate your friendship, but I should like to convince you how unjust is your mistrust of one of God's purest angels, that ever walked the earth."

"Oho! that's it, is it, friend Déroulède? Methought you had foresworn the sex altogether, and now you are in love."

"Madly, blindly, stupidly in love, my friend," said Déroulède with a sigh. "Hopelessly, I fear me!"

"Why hopelessly?"

"She is the daughter of the late Duc de Marny, one of the oldest names in France; a Royalist to the backbone—"

"Hence your overwhelming sympathy for the Queen!"

"Nay! you wrong me there, friend. I'd have tried to save the Queen, even if I had never learned to love Juliette. But you see now how unjust were your suspicions."

"Had I any?"

"Don't deny it. You were loud in urging me to burn those papers a moment ago. You called them useless and dangerous and now—"

"I still think them useless and dangerous, and by reading them would wish to confirm my opinion and give weight to my arguments."

"If I were to part from them now I would seem to be mistrusting her."

"You are a mad idealist, my dear Déroulède!"

"How can I help it? I have lived under the same roof with her for three weeks now. I have begun to understand what a saint is like."

"And 'twill be when you understand that your idol has feet of clay that you'll learn the real lesson of love," said Blakeney earnestly.

"Is it love to worship a saint in heaven, whom you dare not touch, who hovers above you like a cloud, which floats away from you even as you gaze? To love is to feel one being in the world at one with us, our equal in sin as well as in virtue. To love, for us men, is to clasp one woman with our arms, feeling that she lives and breathes just as we do, suffers as we do, thinks with us, loves with us, and, above all, sins with us. Your mock saint who stands in a niche is not a woman if she have not suffered, still less a woman if she have not sinned. Fall at the feet of your idol an' you wish, but drag her down to your level after that—the only level she should ever reach, that of your heart."

Who shall render faithfully a true account of the magnetism which poured forth from this remarkable man as he spoke: this well-dressed, foppish apostle of the greatest love that man has ever known. And as he spoke the whole story of his own great, true love for the woman who once had so deeply wronged him seemed to stand clearly written in the strong, lazy, good-humoured, kindly face glowing with tenderness for her.

Déroulède felt this magnetism, and therefore did not resent the implied suggestion, anent the saint whom he was still content to worship.

A dreamer and an idealist, his mind held spellbound by the great social problems which were causing the upheaval of a whole country, he had not yet had the time to learn the sweet lesson which Nature teaches to her elect—the lesson of a great, a true, human and passionate love. To him, at present, Juliette represented the perfect embodiment of his most idealistic dreams. She stood in his mind so far above him that if she proved unattainable, he would scarce have suffered. It was such a foregone conclusion.

Blakeney's words were the first to stir in his heart a desire for something beyond that quasi-mediaeval worship, something weaker and yet infinitely stronger, something more earthy and yet almost divine.

"And now, shall we join the ladies?" said Blakeney after a long pause, during which the mental workings of his alert brain were almost visible, in the earnest look which he cast at his friend. "You shall keep the papers in your desk, give them into the keeping of your saint, trust her all in all rather than not at all, and if the time should come that your heaven-enthroned ideal fall somewhat heavily to earth, then give me the privilege of being a witness to your happiness."

"You are still mistrustful, Blakeney," said Déroulède lightly. "If you say much more I'll give these papers into Mademoiselle Marny's keeping until tomorrow."

Chapter 8

Anne Mie

That night, when Blakeney, wrapped in his cloak, was walking down the Rue Ecole de Médecine towards his own lodgings, he suddenly felt a timid hand upon his sleeve.

Anne Mie stood beside him, her pale, melancholy face peeping up at the tall Englishman, through the folds of a dark hood closely tied under her chin.

"*Monsieur*," she said timidly, "do not think me very presumptuous. I—I would wish to have five minutes' talk with you—may I?"

He looked down with great kindness at the quaint, wizened little figure, and the strong face softened at the sight of the poor, deformed shoulder, the hard, pinched look of the young mouth, the general look of pathetic helplessness which appeals so strongly to the chivalrous.

"Indeed, *mademoiselle*," he said gently, "you make me very proud; and I can serve you in any way, I pray you command me. But," he added, seeing Anne Mie's somewhat scared look, "this street is scarce fit for private conversation. Shall we try and find a better spot?"

Paris had not yet gone to bed. In these times it was really safest to be out in the open streets. There, everybody was more busy, more on the move, on the lookout for suspected houses, leaving the wanderer alone.

Blakeney led Anne Mie towards the Luxembourg Gardens, the great devastated pleasure-ground of the *ci-devant* tyrants of the people. The beautiful Anne of Austria, and the Medici before her, Louis XIII, and his gallant musketeers—all have given place to the great cannon-forging industry of this besieged Republic. France, attacked on every side, is forcing her sons to defend her: persecuted, martyrised, done to death by her, she is still their Mother: *La Patrie*, who needs their arms against the foreign foe. England is threatening the north, Prussia and Austria the east. Admiral Hood's flag is flying on Toulon Arsenal.

The siege of the Republic!

And the Republic is fighting for dear life. The Tuileries and Luxembourg Gardens are transformed into a township of gigantic smithies; and Anne Mie, with scared eyes, and clinging to Blakeney's arm, cast furtive, terrified glances at the huge furnaces and the begrimed, darkly scowling faces of the workers within.

"The people of France in arms against tyranny!" Great placards, bearing these inspiriting words, are affixed to gallows-shaped posts, and flutter in the evening breeze, rendered scorching by the heat of the furnaces all around.

Farther on, a group of older men, squatting on the ground, are busy making tents, and some women—the same *Megaeras* who daily shriek round the guillotine—are plying their needles and scissors for the purpose of making clothes for the soldiers.

The soldiers are the entire able-bodied male population of France.

"The people of France in arms against tyranny!"

That is their sign, their trademark; one of these placards, fitfully illumined by a torch of resin, towers above a group of children busy tearing up scraps of old linen—their mothers', their sisters' linen —in order to make lint for the wounded.

Loud curses and suppressed mutterings fill the smoke-laden air.

The people of France, in arms against tyranny, is bending its broad back before the most cruel, the most absolute and brutish slave-driving ever exercised over mankind.

Not even mediaeval Christianity has ever dared such wholesale enforcements of its doctrines, as this constitution of Liberty and Fraternity.

Merlin's "Law of the Suspect" has just been formulated. From now onward each and every citizen of France must watch his words, his looks, his gestures, lest they be suspect. Of what—of treason to the Republic, to the people? Nay, worse! lest they be suspect of being suspect to the great era of Liberty.

Therefore, in the smithies and among the groups of tent-makers a moment's negligence, a careless attention to the work, might lead to a brief trial on the morrow and the inevitable guillotine. Negligence is treason to the higher interests of the Republic.

Blakeney dragged Anne Mie away from the sight. These roaring furnaces frightened her; he took her down the Place St Michel, towards the river. It was quieter here.

"What dreadful people they have become," she said, shuddering; "even I can remember how different they used to be."

The houses on the banks of the river were mostly converted into hospitals, preparatory for the great siege. Some hundred *mètres* lower down, the new children's hospital, endowed by Citizen-Deputy Déroulède, loomed, white, clean, and comfortable-looking, amidst its more squalid fellows.

"I think it would be best not to sit down," suggested Blakeney, "and wiser for you to throw your hood away from your face."

He seemed to have no fears for himself; many had said that he bore a charmed life; and yet ever since Admiral Hood had planted his flag on Toulon Arsenal, the English were more feared than ever, and the Scarlet Pimpernel more hated than most.

"You wished to speak to me about Paul Déroulède," he said kindly, seeing that the young girl was making desperate efforts to say what lay on her mind. "He is my friend, you know."

"Yes; that is why I wished to ask you a question," she replied.

"What is it?"

"Who is Juliette de Marny, and why did she seek an entrance into Paul's house?"

"Did she seek it, then?"

"Yes; I saw the scene from the balcony. At the time it did not strike me as a farce. I merely thought that she had been stupid and foolhardy. But since then I have reflected. She provoked the mob of the street, wilfully, just at the very moment when she reached M. Déroulède's door. She meant to appeal to his chivalry, and called for help, well knowing that he would respond."

She spoke rapidly and excitedly now, throwing off all shyness and reserve. Blakeney was forced to check her vehemence, which might have been thought "suspicious" by some idle citizen unpleasantly inclined.

"Well? And now?" he asked, for the young girl had paused, as if ashamed of her excitement.

"And now she stays in the house, on and on, day after day," continued Anne Mie, speaking more quietly, though with no less intensity. "Why does she not go? She is not safe in France. She belongs to the most hated of all the classes—the idle, rich aristocrats of the old *régime*. Paul has several times suggested plans for her emigration to England. Madame Déroulède, who is an angel, loves her, and would not like to part from her, but it would be obviously wiser for her to go, and yet she stays. Why?"

"Presumably because—"

"Because she is in love with Paul?" interrupted Anne Mie vehemently. "No, no; she does not love him—at least—Oh! sometimes I don't know. Her eyes light up when he comes, and she is listless when he goes. She always spends a longer time over her toilet, when we expect him home to dinner," she added, with a touch of *naïve* femininity. "But—if it be love, then that love is strange and unwomanly; it is a love that will not be for his good—"

"Why should you think that?"

"I don't know," said the girl simply. "Isn't it an instinct?"

"Not a very unerring one in this case, I fear."

"Why?"

"Because your own love for Paul Déroulède has blinded you—Ah! you must pardon me, *mademoiselle*; you sought this conversation and not I, and I fear me I have wounded you. Yet I would wish you to know how deep is my sympathy with you, and how great my desire to render you a service if I could."

"I was about to ask a service of you, *monsieur*."

"Then command me, I beg of you."

"You are Paul's friend—persuade him that that woman in his house is a standing danger to his life and liberty."

"He would not listen to me."

"Oh! a man always listens to another."

"Except on one subject—the woman he loves."

He had said the last words very gently but very firmly. He was deeply, tenderly sorry for the poor, deformed, fragile girl, doomed to be a witness of that most heartrending of human tragedies, the passing away of her own scarce-hoped-for happiness. But he felt that at this moment the kindest act would be one of complete truth. He knew that Paul Déroulède's heart was completely given to Juliette de Marny; he too, like Anne Mie, instinctively mistrusted the beautiful girl and her strange, silent ways, but, unlike the poor hunchback, he knew that no sin which Juliette might commit would henceforth tear her from out the heart of his friend; that if, indeed, she turned out to be false, or even treacherous, she would, nevertheless, still hold a place in Déroulède's very soul, which no one else would ever fill.

"You think he loves her?" asked Anne Mie at last.

"I am sure of it."

"And she?"

"Ah! I do not know. I would trust your instinct—a woman's—sooner than my own."

"She is false, I tell you, and is hatching treason against Paul."

"Then all we can do is to wait."

"Wait?"

"And watch carefully, earnestly, all the time. There! shall I pledge you my word that Déroulède shall come to no harm?"

"Pledge me your word that you'll part him from that woman."

"Nay; that is beyond my power. A man like Paul Déroulède only loves once in life, but when he does, it is for always."

Once more she was silent, pressing her lips closely together, as if afraid of what she might say.

He saw that she was bitterly disappointed and sought for a means of tempering the cruelty of the blow.

"It will be your task to watch over Paul," he said; "with your friendship to guard and protect him, we need have no fear for his safety, I think."

"I will watch," she replied quietly.

Gradually he had led her steps back towards the Rue Ecole de Médecine.

A great melancholy had fallen over his bold, adventurous spirit. How full of tragedies was this great city, in the last throes of its insane and cruel struggle for an unattainable goal. And yet, despite its guillotine and mock trials, its tyrannical laws and overfilled prisons, its very sorrows paled before the dead, dull misery of this deformed girl's heart.

A wild exaltation, a fever of enthusiasm lent glamour to the scenes which were daily enacted on the *Place de la Revolution*, turning the final acts of the tragedies into glaring, lurid melodrama, almost unreal in its poignant appeal to the sensibilities.

But here there was only this dead, dull misery, an aching heart, a poor, fragile creature in the throes of an agonised struggle for a fast-disappearing happiness.

Anne Mie hardly knew now what she had hoped, when she sought this interview with Sir Percy Blakeney. Drowning in a sea of hopelessness, she had clutched at what might prove a chance of safety. Her reason told her that Paul's friend was right. Déroulède was a man who would love but once in his life. He had never loved—for he had too much pitied—poor, pathetic little Anne Mie.

Nay; why should we say that love and pity are akin?

Love, the great, the strong, the conquering god—Love that subdues a world, and rides roughshod over principle, virtue, tradition, over home, kindred, and religion—what cares he for the easy conquest of the pathetic being, who appeals to his sympathy?

Love means equality—the same height of heroism or of sin. When Love stoops to pity, he has ceased to soar in the boundless space, that rarefied atmosphere wherein man feels himself made at last truly in the image of God.

Chapter 9

Jealousy

At the door of her home Blakeney parted from Anne Mie, with all the courtesy with which he would have bade *adieu* to the greatest lady in his own land.

Anne Mie let herself into the house with her own latch-key. She closed the heavy door noiselessly, then glided upstairs like a quaint little ghost.

But on the landing above she met Paul Déroulède.

He had just come out of his room and was still fully dressed.

"Anne Mie!" he said, with such an obvious cry of pleasure, that the young girl, with beating heart, paused a moment on the top of the stairs, as if hoping to hear that cry again, feeling that indeed he was glad to see her, had been uneasy because of her long absence.

"Have I made you anxious?" she asked at last.

"Anxious!" he exclaimed. "Little one, I have hardly lived this last hour, since I realised that you had gone out so late as this, and all alone."

"How did you know?"

"Mademoiselle de Marny knocked at my door an hour ago. She had gone to your room to see you, and, not finding you there, she searched the house for you, and finally, in her anxiety, come to me. We did not dare to tell my mother. I won't ask you where you have been, Anne Mie, but another time, remember, little one, that the streets of Paris are not safe, and that those who love you suffer deeply, when they know you to be in peril."

"Those who love me!" murmured the girl under her breath.

"Could you not have asked me to come with you?"

"No; I wanted to be alone. The streets were quite safe, and—I wanted to speak with Sir Percy Blakeney."

"With Blakeney?" he exclaimed in boundless astonishment. "Why, what in the world did you want to say him?"

The girl, so unaccustomed to lying, had blurted out the truth, almost against her will.

"I thought he could help me, as I was much perturbed and restless."

"You went to him sooner than to me?" said Déroulède in a tone of gentle reproach, and still puzzled at this extraordinary action on the part of the girl, usually so shy and reserved.

"My anxiety was about you, and you would have mocked me for it."

"Indeed, I should never mock you, Anne Mie. But why should you be anxious about me?"

"Because I see you wandering blindly on the brink of a great danger, and because I see you confiding in those, whom you had best mistrust."

He frowned a little and bit his lip to check the rough word that was on the tip of his tongue.

"Is Sir Percy Blakeney one of those whom I had best mistrust?" he said lightly.

"No," she answered curtly.

"Then, dear, there is no cause for unrest. He is the only one of my friends whom you have not known intimately. All those who are round me now, you know that you can trust and that you can love," he added earnestly and significantly.

He took her hand; it was trembling with obvious suppressed agitation. She knew that he had guessed what was passing in her mind, and now was deeply ashamed of what she had done. She had been tortured with jealousy for the past three weeks, but at least she had suffered quite alone: on one had been allowed to touch that wound, which more often than not, excites derision rather than pity. Now, by her own actions, two men knew her secret. Both were kind and sympathetic; but Déroulède resented her imputations, and Blakeney had been unable to help her.

A wave of morbid introspection swept over her soul. She realised in a moment how petty and base had been her thoughts and how purposeless her actions. She would have given her life at this moment to eradicate from Déroulède's mind the knowledge of her own jealousy; she hoped that at least he had not guessed her love.

She tried to read his thoughts, but in the dark passage, only dimly lighted by the candles in Déroulède's room beyond, she could not see the expression of his face, but the hand which held hers was warm and tender. She felt herself pitied and blushed at the thought. With a hasty goodnight she fled down the passage, and locked herself in her room, alone with her own thoughts at last.

Chapter 10
Denunciation

But what of Juliette?

What of this wild, passionate, romantic creature tortured by a Titanic conflict? She, but a girl, scarcely yet a woman, torn by the greatest antagonistic powers that ever fought for a human soul. On the one side duty, tradition, her dead brother, her father—above all, her religion and the oath she had sworn before God; on the other justice and honour, a case of right and wrong, honesty and pity.

How she fought with these powers now!

She fought with them, struggled with them on her knees. She tried to crush memory, tried to forget that awful midnight scene ten years ago, her brother's dead body, her father's avenging hand holding her own, as he begged her to do that, which he was too feeble, too old to accomplish.

His words rang in her ears from across that long vista of the past.

"Before the face of Almighty God, who sees and hears me, I swear—"

And she had repeated those words loudly and of her own free will, with her hand resting on her brother's breast, and God Himself looking down upon her, for she had called upon Him to listen.

"I swear that I will seek out Paul Déroulède, and in any manner which God may dictate to me encompass his death, his ruin, or dishonour in revenge for my brother's death. May my brother's soul remain in torment until the final Judgment Day if I should break my oath, but may it rest in eternal peace, the day on which his death is fitly avenged."

Almost it seemed to her as if father and brother were standing by her side, as she knelt and prayed.—Oh! how she prayed!

In many ways she was only a child. All her years had been passed in confinement, either beside her dying father or, later, between the four walls of the Ursuline Convent. And during those years her soul had been fed on a contemplative, ecstatic religion, a kind of sanctified superstition, which she would have deemed sacrilege to combat.

Her first step into womanhood was taken with that oath upon her lips; since then, with a stoical sense of duty, she had lashed herself into a daily, hourly remembrance of the great mission imposed upon her.

To have neglected it would have been, to her, equal to denying God.

She had but vague ideas of the doctrinal side of religion. Purgatory was to her merely a word, but a word representing a real spiritual state—one of expectancy, of restlessness, of sorrow. And vaguely, yet determinedly, she believed that her brother's soul suffered, because she had been too weak to fulfil her oath.

The Church had not come to her rescue. The ministers of her religion were scattered to the four corners of besieged, agonising France. She had no one to help her, no one to comfort her. That very peaceful, contemplative life she had led in the convent, only served to enhance her feeling of the solemnity of her mission.

It was true, it was inevitable, because it was so hard.

To the few who, throughout those troublous times, had kept a feeling of veneration for their religion, this religion had become one of abnegation and martyrdom.

A spirit of uncompromising Jansenism seemed to call forth sacrifices and renunciation, whereas the happy-go-lucky Catholicism of the past century had only suggested an easy, flowered path, to a comfortable, well-upholstered heaven.

The harder the task seemed with was set before her, the more real it became to Juliette. God, she firmly believed, had at last, after ten years, shown her the way to wreak vengeance upon her brother's murderer. He had brought her to this house, caused her to see and hear part of the conversation between Blakeney and Déroulède, and this at the moment of all others, when even the semblance of a conspiracy against the Republic would bring the one inevitable result in its train: disgrace first, the hasty mock trial, the hall of justice, and the guillotine.

She tried not to hate Déroulède. She wished to judge him coldly and impartially, or rather to indict him before the throne of God, and to punish him for the crime he had committed ten years ago. Her personal feelings must remain out of the question.

Had Charlotte Corday considered her own sensibilities, when with her own hand she put an end to Marat?

Juliette remained on her knees for hours. She heard Anne Mie come home, and Déroulède's voice of welcome on the landing. That was perhaps the most bitter moment of this awful soul conflict, for it brought to her mind the remembrance of those others who would suffer too, and who were innocent—Madame Déroulède and poor, crippled Anne Mie. They had done no wrong, and yet how heavily would they be punished!

And then the saner judgment, the human, material code of ethics gained for a while the upper hand. Juliette would rise from her knees, dry her eyes, prepare quietly to go to bed, and to forget all about the awful, relentless Fate which dragged her to the fulfilment of its will, and then sink back, broken-hearted, murmuring impassioned prayers for forgiveness to her father, her brother, her God.

The soul was young and ardent, and it fought for abnegation, martyrdom, and stern duty; the body was childlike, and it fought for peace, contentment, and quiet reason.

The rational body was conquered by the passionate, powerful soul.

Blame not the child, for in herself she was innocent. She was but another of the many victims of this cruel, mad, hysterical time, that spirit of relentless tyranny, forcing its doctrines upon the weak.

With the first break of dawn Juliette at last finally rose from her knees, bathed her burning eyes and head, tidied her hair and dress, then she sat down at the table, and began to write.

She was a transformed being now, no longer a child, essentially a woman—a Joan of Arc with a mission, a Charlotte Corday going to martyrdom, a human, suffering, erring soul, committing a great crime for the sake of an idea.

She wrote out carefully and with a steady hand the denunciation of Citizen-Deputy Déroulède which has become an historical document and is preserved in the chronicles of France.

You have all seen it at the Musée Carnavalet in its glass case, its yellow paper and faded ink revealing nothing of the soul conflict of which it was the culminating victory. The cramped, somewhat schoolgirlish writing is the mute, pathetic witness of one of the saddest tragedies, that era of sorrow and crime has ever known:

> To the Representatives of the People now sitting in Assembly at the National Convention
> You trust and believe in the Representative of the people: Citizen-Deputy Paul Déroulède. He is false, and a traitor to the Republic. He is planning, and hopes to effect, the release of *ci-devant* Marie Antoinette, widow of the traitor Louis Capet. Haste! ye representatives of the people! proofs of his assertion, papers and plans, are still in the house of the Citizen-Deputy Déroulède. This statement is made by one who knows.
> 1. The 23rd *Fructidor.*

When her letter was written she read it through carefully, made the one or two little corrections, which are still visible in the document, then folded her missive, hid it within the folds of her kerchief, and, wrapping a dark cloak and hood round her, she slipped noiselessly out of her room.

The house was all quiet and still. She shuddered a little as the cool morning air fanned her hot cheeks: it seemed like the breath of ghosts.

She ran quickly down the stairs, and as rapidly as she could, pushed back the heavy bolts of the front door, and slipped out into the street.

Already the city was beginning to stir. There was no time for sleep, when so much had to be done for the safety of the threatened Republic. As Juliette turned her steps towards the river, she met the crowd of workmen, whom France was employing for her defence.

Behind her, in the Luxembourg Gardens, and all along the opposite bank of the river, the furnaces were already ablaze, and the smiths at work forging the guns.

At every step now, Juliette came across the great placards, pinned to the tall gallows-shaped posts, which proclaim to every passing citizen, that the people of France are up and in arms.

Right across the *Place de l'Institut* a procession of market carts, laden with vegetables and a little fruit, wends its way slowly towards the centre of the town. They each carry tiny tricolour flags, with a Pike and Cap of Liberty surmounting the flagstaff.

They are good patriots the market-gardeners, who come in daily to feed the starving mob of Paris, with the few handfuls of watery potatoes, and miserable, vermin-eaten cabbages, which that fraternal Revolution still allows them to grow without hindrance.

Everyone seems busy with their work thus early in the morning: the business of killing does not begin until later in the day.

For the moment Juliette can get along quite unmolested: the women and children mostly hurrying on towards the vast encampments in the Tuileries, where lint, and bandages, and coats for the soldiers are manufactured all the day.

The walls of all the houses bear the great patriotic device: "*Liberté, Egalité, Fraternité, sinon La Mort*"; others are more political in their proclamation: "*La République une et indivisible.*"

But on the walls of the Louvre, of the great palace of whilom kings, where the *Roi Soleil* held his Court, and flirted with the prettiest women in France, there the new and great Republic has affixed its final mandate.

A great poster glued to the wall bears the words: "*La Loi concernan les Suspects.*" Below the poster is a huge wooden box with a slit at the top.

This is the latest invention for securing the safety of this one and indivisible Republic.

Henceforth everyone becomes a traitor at one word of denunciation from an idler or an enemy, and, as in the most tyrannical days of the Spanish Inquisition one-half of the nation was set to spy upon the other, that wooden box, with its slit, is put there ready to receive denunciations from one hand against another.

Had Juliette paused but for the fraction of a second, had she stopped to read the placard setting forth this odious law, had she only reflected, then she would even now have turned back, and fled from that gruesome box of infamies, as she would from a dangerous and noisome reptile or from the pestilence.

But her long vigil, her prayers, her ecstatic visions of heroic martyrs had now completely numbed her faculties. Her vitality, her sensibilities were gone: she had become an automaton gliding to her doom, without a thought or a tremor.

She drew the letter from her bosom, and with a steady hand dropped it into the box. The irreclaimable had now occurred. Nothing she could henceforth say or do, no prayers or agonised vigils, no miracles even, could undo her action or save Paul Déroulède from trial and guillotine.

One or two groups of people hurrying to their work had seen her drop the letter into the box. A couple of small children paused, finger in mouth, gazing at her with inane curiosity; one woman uttered a coarse jest, all of them shrugged their shoulders, and passed on, on their way. Those who habitually crossed this spot were used to such sights.

That wooden box, with its mouthlike slit was like an insatiable monster that was constantly fed yet was still gaping for more.

Having done the deed Juliette turned, and as rapidly as she had come, so she went back to her temporary home.

A home no more now; she must leave it at once, today if possible. This much she knew, that she no longer could touch the bread of the man she had betrayed. She would not appear at breakfast, she could plead a headache, and in the afternoon Pétronelle should pack her things.

She turned into a little shop close by and asked for a glass of milk and a bit of bread. The woman who served her eyed her with some curiosity, for Juliette just now looked almost out of her mind.

She had not yet begun to think, and she had ceased to suffer.

Both would come presently, and with them the memory of this last irretrievable hour and a just estimate of what she had done.

CHAPTER 11

"Vengeance is mine"

The pretence of a headache enabled Juliette to keep in her room the greater part of the day. She would have liked to shut herself out from the entire world during those hours which she spent face to face with her own thoughts and her own sufferings.

The sight of Anne Mie's pathetic little face as she brought her food and delicacies and various little comforts, was positive torture to the poor, harrowed soul.

At very sound in the great, silent house she started up, quivering with apprehension and horror. Had the sword of Damocles, which she herself had suspended, already fallen over the heads of those who had shown her nothing but kindness?

She could not think of Madame Déroulède or of Anne Mie without the most agonising, the most torturing shame.

And what of him—the man she had so remorselessly, so ruthlessly betrayed to a tribunal which would know no mercy?

Juliette dared not think of him.

She had never tried to analyse her feelings with regard to him. At the time of Charlotte Corday's trial, when his sonorous voice rang out in its pathetic appeal for the misguided woman, Juliette had given him ungrudging admiration. She remembered now how strongly his magnetic personality had roused in her a feeling of enthusiasm for the poor girl, who had come from the depths of her quiet provincial home, in order to accomplish the horrible deed which would immortalise her name through all the ages to come and cause her countrymen to proclaim her "greater than Brutus."

Déroulède was pleading for the life of that woman, and it was his very appeal which had aroused Juliette's dormant energy, for the cause which her dead father had enjoined her not to forget. It was Déroulède again whom she had seen but a few weeks ago, standing alone before the mob who would have torn her to pieces, haranguing them on her behalf, speaking to them with that quiet, strong voice of his, ruling them with the rule of love and pity, and turning their wrath to gentleness.

Did she hate him, then?

Surely, surely, she hated him for having thrust himself into her life, for having caused her brother's death and covered her father's declining years with sorrow. And, above all, she hated him—indeed, indeed it was hate!—for being the cause of this most hideous action of her life: an action to which she had been driven against her will, one of basest ingratitude and treachery, foreign to every sentiment within her heart, cowardly, abject, the unconscious outcome of this strange magnetism which emanated from him and had cast a spell over her, transforming her individuality and will power, and making of her an unconscious and automatic instrument of Fate.

She would not speak of God's finger again: it was Fate—pagan, devilish Fate!—the weird, shrivelled women who sit and spin their interminable thread. They had decreed; and Juliette, unable to fight, blind and broken by the conflict, had succumbed to the *Megaeras* and their relentless wheel.

At length silence and loneliness became unendurable. She called Pétronelle and ordered her to pack her boxes.

"We leave for England today," she said curtly.

"For England?" gasped the worthy old soul, who was feeling very happy and comfortable in this hospitable house and was loath to leave it. "So soon?"

"Why, yes; we had talked of it for some time. We cannot remain here always. My cousins De Crécy are there, and my aunt De Coudremont. We shall be among friends, Pétronelle, if we ever get there."

"If we ever get there!" sighed poor Pétronelle; "we have but very little money, *ma chérie*, and no passports. Have you thought of asking M. Déroulède for them."

"No, no," rejoined Juliette hastily; "I'll see to the passports somehow, Pétronelle. Sir Percy Blakeney is English; he'll tell me what to do."

"Do you know where he lives, my jewel?"

"Yes; I heard him tell Madame Déroulède last night that he was lodging with a provincial named Brogard at the Sign of the Cruche Cassée. I'll go seek him, Pétronelle; I am sure he will help me. The English are so resourceful and practical. He'll get us our passports, I know, and advise us as to the best way to proceed. Do stay here and get all our things ready. I'll not be long."

She took up a cloak and hood, and, throwing them over her arm, she slipped out of the room.

Déroulède had left the house earlier in the day. She hoped that he had not yet returned, and ran down the stairs quickly, so that she might go out unperceived.

The house was quite peaceful and still. It seemed strange to Juliette that there did not hang over it some sort of pall-like presentiment of coming evil.

From the kitchen, at some little distance from the hall, Anne Mie's voice was heard singing an old ditty:

De ta tige détachée
Pauvre feuille désséchée
Où vas-tu?

Juliette paused a moment. An awful ache had seized her heart; her eyes unconsciously filled with tears, as they roamed round the walls of this house which had sheltered her so hospitably, these three weeks past.

And now whither was she going? Like the poor, dead leaf of the song, she was wastrel, torn from the parent bough, homeless, friendless, having turned against the one hand which, in this great time of peril, had been extended to her in kindness and in love.

Conscience was beginning to rise up against her, and that hydra-headed tyrant Remorse. She closed her eyes to shut out the hideous vision of her crime; she tried to forget this home which her treachery had desecrated.

Je vais où va toute chose
Où va la feuille de rose
Et la feuille de laurier,

. . . .sang Anne Mie plaintively.

A great sob broke from Juliette's aching heart. The misery of it all was more than she could bear. Ah, pity her if you can! She had fought and striven and been conquered. A girl's soul is so young, so impressionable; and she had grown up with that one, awful, all-pervading idea of duty to accomplish, a most solemn oath to fulfil, one sworn to her dying father, and on the dead body of her brother. She had begged for guidance, prayed for release, and the voice from above had remained silent. Weak, miserable, cringing, the human soul, when torn with earthly passion, must look at its own strength for the fight.

And now the end had come. That swift, scarce tangible dream of peace, which had flitted through her mind during the past few weeks, had vanished with the dawn, and she was left desolate, alone with her great sin and its lifelong expiation.

Scarce knowing what she did, she fell on her knees, there on that threshold, which she was about to leave for ever. Fate had placed on her young shoulders a burden too heavy for her to bear.

"Juliette!"

At first, she did not move. It was his voice coming from the study behind her. Its magic thrilled her, as it had done that day in the Hall of Justice. Strong, passionate, tender, it seemed now to raise every echo of response in her heart. She thought it was a dream and remained there on her knees lest it should be dispelled.

Then she heard his footsteps on the flagstones of the hall. Anne Mie's plaintive singing had died away in the distance. She started, and jumped to her feet, hastily drying her eyes. The momentary dream was dispelled, and she was ashamed of her weakness.

He, the cause of all her sorrows, of her sin, and of her degradation, had no right to see her suffer.

She would have fled out of the house now, but it was too late. He had come out of his study, and, seeing her there on her knees weeping, he came quickly forward, trying, with all the innate chivalry of his upright nature, not to let her see that he had been a witness to her tears.

"You are going out, *mademoiselle?*" he said courteously, as, wrapping her cloak around her, she was turning towards the door.

"Yes, yes," she replied hastily; "a small errand, I—"

"Is it anything I can do for you?"

"No."

"If—" he added, with visible embarrassment, "if your errand would brook a delay, might I crave the honour of your presence in my study for a few moments?"

"My errand brooks of no delay, Citizen Déroulède," she said as composedly as she could, "and perhaps on my return I might—"

"I am leaving almost directly, *mademoiselle*, and I would wish to bid you goodbye."

He stood aside to allow her to pass, either out, through the street door or across the hall to his study.

There had been no reproach in his voice towards the guest, who was thus leaving him without a word of farewell. Perhaps if there had been any, Juliette would have rebelled. As it was, an unconquerable magnetism seemed to draw her towards him, and, making an almost imperceptible sign of acquiescence, she glided past him into his room.

The study was dark and cool; for the room faced the west, and the shutters had been closed, in order to keep out the hot August sun. At first Juliette could see nothing, but she felt his presence near her, as he followed her into the room, leaving the door slightly ajar.

"It is kind of you, *mademoiselle*," he said gently, "to accede to my request, which was perhaps presumptuous. But, you see, I am leaving this house today, and I had a selfish longing to hear your voice bidding me farewell."

Juliette's large, burning eyes were gradually piercing the semi-gloom around her. She could see him distinctly now, standing close beside her, in an attitude of the deepest, almost reverential respect.

The study was as usual neat and tidy, denoting the orderly habits of a man of action and energy. On the ground there was a valise, ready strapped as if or a journey, and on the top of it a bulky letter-case of stout pigskin, secured with a small steel lock. Juliette's eyes fastened upon this case with a look of fascination and of horror. Obviously, it contained Déroulède's papers, the plans for Marie Antoinette's escape, the passports of which he had spoken the day before to his friend, Sir Percy Blakeney—the proofs, in fact, which she had offered to the representatives of the people, in support of her denunciation of the Citizen-Deputy.

After his request he had said nothing more. He was waiting for her to speak; but her voice felt parched; it seemed to her as if hands of steel were gripping her throat, smothering the words she would have longed to speak.

"Will you not wish me Godspeed, *mademoiselle?*" he repeated gently.

"Godspeed?" Oh! the awful irony of it all! Should God speed him to a mock trial and to the guillotine? He was going thither, though he did not know it, and was even now trying to take the hand which had deliberately sent him there.

At last she made an effort to speak, and in a toneless, even voice she contrived to murmur:

"You are not going for long, Citizen-Deputy?"

"In these times, *mademoiselle*," he replied, "any farewell might be for ever. But I am actually going for a month to the *Conciergerie*, to take charge of the unfortunate prisoner there."

"For a month!" she repeated mechanically.

"Oh yes!" he said, with a smile. "You see, our present government is afraid that poor Marie Antoinette will exercise her fascinations over any lieutenant-governor of her prison, if he remain near her long enough, so a new one is appointed every month. I shall be in charge during this coming *Vendémiaire*. I shall hope to return before the equinox, but—who can tell?"

"In any case then, Citoyen Déroulède, the farewell I bid you tonight will be a very long one."

"A month will seem a century to me," he said earnestly, "since I must spend it without seeing you, but—"

He looked long and searchingly at her. He did not understand her in her present mood, so scared and wild did she seem, so unlike that girlish, light-hearted self, which had made the dull old house so bright these past few weeks.

"But I should not dare to hope," he murmured, "that a similar reason would cause you to call that month a long one."

She turned perhaps a trifle paler than she had been hitherto, and her eyes roamed round the room like those of a trapped hare seeking to escape.

"You misunderstand me, Citoyen Déroulède," she said at last hurriedly. "You have all been kind—very kind—but Pétronelle and I can no longer trespass on your hospitality. We have friends in England, and many enemies here—"

"I know," he interrupted quietly; "it would be the most arrant selfishness on my part to suggest, that you should stay here an hour longer than necessary. I fear that after today my roof may no longer prove a sheltering one for you. But will you allow me to arrange for your safety, as I am arranging for that of my mother and Anne Mie? My English friend Sir Percy Blakeney, has a yacht in readiness off the Normandy coast. I have already seen to your passports and to all the arrangements of your journey as far as there, and Sir Percy, or one of his friends, will see you safely on board the English yacht. He has given me his promise that he will do this, and I trust him as I would myself. For the journey through France, my name is a sufficient guarantee that you will be unmolested; and if you will allow it, my mother and Anne Mie will travel in your company. Then—"

"I pray you stop, Citizen Déroulède," she suddenly interrupted excitedly. "You must forgive me, but I cannot allow thus to make any arrangements for me. Pétronelle and I must do as best we can. All your time and trouble should be spent for the benefit of those who have a claim upon you, whilst I—"

"You speak unkindly, *mademoiselle*; there is no question of claim."

"And you have no right to think—" she continued, with a growing, nervous excitement, drawing her hand hurriedly away, for he had tried to seize it.

"Ah! pardon me," he interrupted earnestly, "there you are wrong. I have the right to think of you and for you—the inalienable right conferred upon me by my great love for you."

"Citizen-Deputy!"

"Nay, Juliette; I know my folly, and I know my presumption. I know the pride of your caste and of your party, and how much you despise the partisan of the squalid mob of France. Have I said that I aspired to gain your love? I wonder if I have ever dreamed it? I only know, Juliette, that you are to me something akin to the angels, something white and ethereal, intangible, and perhaps ununderstandable.

Yet, knowing my folly, I glory in it, my dear, and I would not let you go out of my life without telling you of that, which has made every hour of the past few weeks a paradise for me—my love for you, Juliette."

He spoke in that low, impressive voice of his, and with those soft, appealing tones with which she had once heard him pleading for poor Charlotte Corday. Yet now he was not pleading for himself, not for his selfish wish or for his own happiness, only pleading for his love, that she should know of it, and, knowing it, have pity in her heart for him, and let him serve her to the end.

He did not say anything more for a while; he had taken her hand, which she no longer withdrew from him, for there was sweet pleasure in feeling his strong fingers close tremblingly over hers. He pressed his lips upon her hand, upon the soft palm and delicate wrist, his burning kisses bearing witness to the tumultuous passion, which his reverence for her was holding in check.

She tried to tear herself away from him, but he would not let her go:

"Do not go away just yet, Juliette," he pleaded. "Think! I may never see you again; but when you are far from me—in England, perhaps—amongst your own kith and kin, will you try sometimes to think kindly of one who so wildly, so madly worships you?"

She would have stilled, an she could, the beating of her heart, which went out to him at last with all the passionate intensity of her great, pent-up love. Every word he spoke had its echo within her very soul, and she tried not to hear his tender appeal, not to see his dark head bending in worship before her. She tried to forget his presence, not to know that he was there—he, the man whom she had betrayed to serve her own miserable vengeance, whom in her mad, exalted rage she had thought that she hated, but whom she now knew that she loved better than her life, better than her soul, her traditions, or her oath.

Now, at this moment, she made every effort to conjure up the vision of her brother brought home dead upon a stretcher, of her father's declining years, rendered hideous by the mind unhinged through the great sorrow.

She tried to think of the avenging finger of God pointing the way to the fulfilment of her oath and called to Him to stand by her in this terrible agony of her soul.

And God spoke to her at last; through the eternal *vistas* of boundless universe, from that heaven which had known no pity, His voice came to her now, clear, awesome, and implacable:

Vengeance is mine! I will repay!

Chapter 12

The Sword of Damocles

"In the name of the Republic!"

Absorbed in his thoughts, his dreams, his present happiness, Déroulède had heard nothing of what was going on in the house, during the past few seconds.

At first, to Anne Mie, who was still singing her melancholy ditty over her work in the kitchen, there had seem nothing unusual in the peremptory ring at the front-door bell. She pulled down her sleeves over her thin arms, smoothed down her cooking apron, then only did she run to see who the visitor might be.

As soon as she had opened the door, however, she understood.

Five men were standing before her, four of whom wore the uniform of the National Guard, and the fifth, the tricolour scarf fringed with gold, which denoted service under the Convention.

This man seemed to be in command of the others, and he immediately stepped into the hall, followed by his four companions, who at a sign from him, effectively cut off Anne Mie from what had been her imminent purpose—namely, to run to the study and warn Déroulède of his danger.

That it was danger of the most certain, the most deadly kind she never doubted for one moment. Even had her instinct not warned her, she would have guessed. One glance at the five men had sufficed to tell her: their attitude, their curt word of command, their air of authority as they crossed the hall—everything revealed the purpose of their visit: a domiciliary search in the house of Citizen-Deputy Déroulède.

Merlin's Law of the Suspect was in full operation. Someone had denounced the Citizen-Deputy to the Committee of Public Safety; and in this year of grace, 1793, and I of the Revolution, men and women were daily sent to the guillotine on suspicion.

Anne Mie would have screamed, had she dared, but instinct such as hers was far too keen, to betray her into so injudicious an act. She felt that, were Paul Déroulède's eyes upon her at this moment, he would wish her to remain calm and outwardly serene.

The foremost man—he with the tricolour scarf—had already

crossed the hall and was standing outside the study door. It was his word of command which first roused Déroulède from his dream:

"In the name of the Republic!"

Déroulède did not immediately drop the small hand, which a moment ago he had been covering with kisses. He held it to his lips once more, very gently, lingering over this last fond caress, as if over an eternal farewell, then he straightened out his broad, well-knit figure, and turned to the door.

He was very pale, but there was neither fear nor even surprise expressed in his earnest, deep-set eyes. They still seemed to be looking afar, gazing upon a heaven-born vision, which the touch of her hand and the avowal of his love had conjured up before him.

"In the name of the Republic'"

Once more, for the third time—according to custom—the words rang out, clear, distinct, peremptory.

In that one fraction of a second, whilst those six words were spoken, Déroulède's eyes wandered swiftly towards the heavy letter-case, which now held his condemnation, and a wild, mad thought—the mere animal desire to escape from danger—surged up in his brain.

The plans for the escape of Marie Antoinette, the various passports, worded in accordance with the possible disguises the unfortunate Queen might assume—all these papers were more than sufficient proof of what would be termed his treason against the Republic.

He could already hear the indictment against him, could see the filthy mob of Paris dancing a wild saraband round the tumbril, which bore him towards the guillotine; he could hear their yells of execration, could feel the insults hurled against him, by those who had most admired, most envied him. And from all this he would have escaped if he could, if it had not been too late.

It was but a second, or less, whilst the words were spoken outside his door, and whilst all other thoughts in him were absorbed in this one mad desire for escape. He even made a movement, as if to snatch up the letter-case and to hide it about his person. But it was heavy and bulky; it would be sure to attract attention and might bring upon him the additional indignity of being forced to submit to a personal search.

He caught Juliette's eyes fixed upon him with an intensity of gaze which, in that same one mad moment, revealed to him the depths of her love. Then the second's weakness was gone; he was once more quiet, firm, the man of action, accustomed to meet danger boldly, to rule and to subdue the most turgid mob.

With a quiet shrug of the shoulders, he dismissed all thought of the compromising letter-case, and went to the door.

Already, as no reply had come to the third word of command, it had been thrown open from outside, and Déroulède found himself face to face with the five men.

"Citizen Merlin!" he said quietly, as he recognised the foremost among them.

"Himself, Citizen-Deputy," rejoined the latter, with a sneer, "at your service."

Anne Mie, in a remote corner of the hall, had heard the name, and felt her very soul sicken at its sound.

Merlin! Author of that infamous Law of the Suspect which had set man against man, a father against his son, brother against brother, and friend against friend, had made of every human creature a bloodhound on the track of his fellowmen, dogging in order not to be dogged, denouncing, spying, hounding, in order not to be denounced.

And he, Merlin, gloried in this, the most fiendishly evil law ever perpetrated for the degradation of the human race.

There is that sketch of him in the Musée Carnavalet, drawn just before he, in his turn, went to expiate his crimes on that very guillotine, which he had sharpened and wielded so powerfully against his fellows. The artist has well caught the slouchy, slovenly look of his loosely knit figure, his long limbs and narrow head, with the snakelike eyes and slightly receding chin. Like Marat, his model and prototype, Merlin affected dirty, ragged clothes. The real *Sansculottism*, the downward levelling of his fellowmen to the lowest rung of the social ladder, pervaded every action of this noted product of the great Revolution.

Even Déroulède, whose entire soul was filled with a great, all-understanding pity for the weaknesses of mankind, recoiled at sight of this incarnation of the spirit of squalor and degradation, of all that was left of the noble Utopian theories of the makers of the Revolution.

Merlin grinned when he saw Déroulède standing there, calm, impassive, well dressed, as if prepared to receive an honoured guest, rather than a summons to submit to the greatest indignity a proud man has ever been called upon to suffer.

Merlin had always hated the popular Citizen-Deputy. Friend and boon-companion of Marat and his gang, he had for over two years now exerted all the influence he possessed in order to bring Déroulède under a cloud of suspicion.

But Déroulède had the ear of the populace. No one understood as he did the tone of a Paris mob; and the National Convention, ever terrified of the volcano it had kindled, felt that a popular member of its assembly was more useful alive than dead.

But now at last Merlin was having his way. An anonymous denunciation against Déroulède had reached the Public Prosecutor that day. Tinville and Merlin were the fastest of friends, so the latter easily obtained the privilege of being the first to proclaim to his hated enemy, the news of his downfall.

He stood facing Déroulède for a moment, enjoying the present situation to its full. The light from the vast hall struck full upon the powerful figure of the Citizen-Deputy and upon his firm, dark face and magnetic, restless eyes. Behind him the study, with its closely-drawn shutters, appeared wrapped in gloom.

Merlin turned to his men, and, still delighted with his position of a cat playing with a mouse, he pointed to Déroulède, with a smile and a shrug of the shoulders.

"*Voyez-moi donc* çà," he said, with a coarse jest, and expectorating contemptuously upon the floor, "the aristocrat seems not to understand that we are here in the name of the Republic. There is a very good proverb, Citizen-Deputy," he added, once more addressing Déroulède, "which you seem to have forgotten, and that is that the pitcher which goes too often to the well breaks at last. You have conspired against the liberties of the people for the past ten years. Retribution has come to you at last; the people of France have come to their senses. The National Convention wants to know what treason you are hatching between these four walls, and it has deputed me to find out all there is to know."

"At your service, Citizen-Deputy!" said Déroulède, quietly stepping aside, in order to make way for Merlin and his men.

Resistance was useless, and, like all strong, determined natures, he knew when it was best to give in.

During this while, Juliette had neither moved nor uttered a sound. Little more than a minute had elapsed since the moment when the first peremptory order, to open in the name of the Republic, had sounded like the tocsin through the stillness of the house. Déroulède's kisses were still hot upon her hand, his words of love were still ringing in her ears.

And now this awful, deadly peril, which she with her own hand had brought on the man she loved!

If in one moment's anguish the soul be allowed to expiate a lifelong sin, then indeed did Juliette atone during this one terrible second.

Her conscience, her heart, her entire being rose in revolt against her crime. Her oath, her life, her final denunciation appeared before her in all their hideousness.

And now it was too late.

Déroulède stood facing Merlin, his most implacable enemy. The latter was giving orders to his men, preparatory to searching the house, and there, just on the top of the valise, lay the letter-case, obviously containing those papers, to which the day before she had overheard Déroulède making allusion, whilst he spoke to his friend, Sir Percy Blakeney.

An unexplainable instinct seemed to tell her that the papers were in that case. Her eyes were riveted on it, as if fascinated. An awful terror held her enthralled for one second more, whilst her thoughts, her longings, her desires were all centred on the safety of that one thing.

The next instant she had seized it and thrown it upon the sofa. Then seating herself beside it, with the gesture of a queen and the grace of a Parisienne, she had spread the ample folds of her skirts over the compromising case, hiding it entirely from view.

Merlin in the hall was ordering two men to stand one on each side of Déroulède, and two more to follow him into the room. Now he entered it himself, his narrow eyes trying to pierce the semi-obscurity, which was rendered more palpable by the brilliant light in the hall.

He had not seen Juliette's gesture, but he had heard the *frou-frou* of her skirts, as she seated herself upon the sofa.

"You are not alone Citizen-Deputy, I see," he said, with a sneer, as his snakelike eyes lighted upon the young girl.

"My guest, Citizen Merlin," replied Déroulède as calmly as he could—"Citizen Juliette Marny. I know that it is useless, under these circumstances, to ask for consideration for a woman, but I pray you to remember, as far as is possible, that although we are all Republicans, we are also Frenchmen, and all still equal in our sentiment of chivalry towards our mothers, our sisters, or our guests."

Merlin chuckled and gazed for a moment ironically at Juliette. He had held, between his talon-like fingers, that very morning, a thin scrap of paper, on which a schoolgirlish hand had scrawled the denunciation against Citizen-Deputy Déroulède.

Coarse in nature, and still coarser in thoughts, this representative of the people had very quickly arrived at a conclusion in his mind, with regard to this so-called guest in the Déroulède household.

"A discarded mistress," he muttered to himself. "Just had another scene, I suppose. He's got tired of her, and she's given him away out of spite."

Satisfied with this explanation of the situation, he was quite inclined to be amiable to Juliette. Moreover, he had caught sight of the valise, and almost thought that the young girl's eyes had directed his attention towards it.

"Open those shutters!" he commanded, "this place is like a vault."

One of the men obeyed immediately, and as the brilliant August sun came streaming into the room, Merlin once more turned to Déroulède.

"Information has been laid against you, Citizen-Deputy," he said, "by an anonymous writer, who states that you have just now in your possession correspondence or other papers intended for the Widow Capet: and the Committee of Public Safety has entrusted me and these citizens to seize such correspondence and make you answerable for its presence in your house."

Déroulède hesitated for one brief fraction of a second. As soon as the shutters had been opened, and the room flooded in daylight, he had at once perceived that his letter-case had disappeared, and guessed, from Juliette's attitude upon the sofa, that she had concealed it about her person. It was this which caused him to hesitate.

His heart was filled with boundless gratitude to her for her noble effort to save him, but he would have given his life at this moment, to undo what she had done.

The Terrorists were no respecters of persons or of sex. A domiciliary search order, in those days, conferred full powers on those in authority, and Juliette might at any moment now be peremptorily ordered to rise. Through her action she had made herself one with the Citizen-Deputy; if the case were found under the folds of her skirts, she would be accused of connivance, or at any rate of the equally grave charge of shielding a traitor.

The manly pride in him rebelled at the thought of owing his immediate safety to a woman, yet he could not now discard her help, without compromising her irretrievably.

He dared not even to look again towards her, for he felt that at this moment her life as well as his own lay in the quiver of an eyelid; and Merlin's keen, narrow eyes were fixed upon him in eager search for a tremor, a flash, which might betray fear or prove an admission of guilt.

Juliette sat there, calm, impassive, disdainful, and she seemed to Déroulède more angelic, more unattainable even than before. He could have worshipped her for her heroism, her resourcefulness, her quiet aloofness from all these coarse creatures who filled the room with the odour of their dirty clothes, with their rough jests, and their noisome suggestions.

"Well, Citizen-Deputy," sneered Merlin after a while, "you do not reply, I notice."

"The insinuation is unworthy of a reply, citizen," replied Déroulède quietly; "my services to the Republic are well known. I should have thought that the Committee of Public Safety would disdain an anonymous denunciation against a faithful servant of the people of France."

"The Committee of Public Safety knows its own business best, Citizen-Deputy," rejoined Merlin roughly. "If the accusation prove a calumny, so much the better for you. I presume," he added with a sneer, "that you do not propose to offer any resistance whilst these citizens and I search your house."

Without another word Déroulède handed a bunch of keys to the man by his side. Every kind of opposition, argument even, would be worse than useless.

Merlin had ordered the valise and desk to be searched, and two men were busy turning out the contents of both on to the floor. But the desk now only contained a few private household accounts, and notes for the various speeches which Déroulède had at various times delivered in the assemblies of the National Convention. Among these, a few pencil jottings for his great defence of Charlotte Corday were eagerly seized upon by Merlin, and his grimy, clawlike hands fastened upon this scrap of paper, as upon a welcome prey.

But there was nothing else of any importance. Déroulède was a man of thought and of action, with all the enthusiasm of real conviction, but none of the carelessness of a fanatic. The papers which were contained in the letter-case, and which he was taking with him to the *Conciergerie*, he considered were necessary to the success of his plans, otherwise he never would have kept them, and they were the only proofs that could be brought up against him.

The valise itself was only packed with the few necessaries for a month's sojourn at the *Conciergerie*; and the men, under Merlin's guidance, were vainly trying to find something, anything that might be construed into treasonable correspondence with the unfortunate prisoner there.

Merlin, whilst his men were busy with the search, was sprawling in one of the big leather-covered chairs, on the arms of which his dirty finger-nails were beating an impatient devil's tattoo. He was at no pains to conceal the intense disappointment which he would experience, were his errand to prove fruitless.

His narrow eyes every now and then wandered towards Juliette, as if asking for her help and guidance. She, understanding his frame of mind, responded to the look. Shutting her mentality off from the coarse suggestion of his attitude towards her, she played her part with cunning, and without flinching. With a glance here and there, she directed the men in their search. Déroulède himself could scarcely refrain from looking at her; he was puzzled, and vaguely marvelled at the perfection, with which she carried through her *rôle* to the end.

Merlin found himself baffled.

He knew quite well that Citizen-Deputy Déroulède was not a man to be lightly dealt with. No mere suspicion or anonymous denunciation would be sufficient in his case, to bring him before the tribunal of the Revolution. Unless there were proofs—positive, irrefutable, damnable proofs—of Paul Déroulède's treachery, the Public Prosecutor would never dare to frame an indictment against him. The mob of Paris would rise to defend its idol; the hideous hags, who plied their knitting at the foot of the scaffold, would tear the guillotine down, before they would allow Déroulède to mount it.

That was Déroulède's stronghold: the people of Paris, whom he had loved through all their infamies, and whom he had succoured and helped in their private need; and above all the women of Paris, whose children he had caused to be tended in the hospitals which he had built for them—this they had not yet forgotten, and Merlin knew it. One day they would forget—soon, perhaps—then they would turn on their former idol, and, howling, send him to his death, amidst cries of rancour and execration. When that day came there would be no need to worry about treason or about proofs. When the populace had forgotten all that he had done, then Déroulède would fall.

But that time was not yet.

The men had finished ransacking the room; every scrap of paper, every portable article had been eagerly seized upon.

Merlin, half blind with fury, had jumped to his feet.

"Search him!" he ordered peremptorily.

Déroulède set his teeth, and made no protest, calling up every fibre of moral strength within him, to aid him in submitting to this indignity. At a coarse jest from Merlin, he buried his nails into the palms of his hand, not to strike the foulmouthed creature in the face. But he submitted, and stood impassive by, whilst the pockets of his coat were turned inside out by the rough hands of the soldiers.

All the while Juliette had remained silent, watching Merlin as any hawk would its prey. But the Terrorist, through the very coarseness of his nature, was in this case completely fooled.

He knew that it was Juliette who had denounced Déroulède and had satisfied himself as to her motive. Because he was low and brutish and degraded, he never once suspected the truth, never saw in that beautiful young woman, anything of the double nature within her, of that curious, self-torturing, at times morbid sense of religion and of duty, at war with her own upright, innately heathy disposition.

The low-born, self-degraded Terrorist had put his own construction on Juliette's action, and with this he was satisfied, since it answered to his own estimate of the human race, the race which he was doing his best to bring down to the level of the beast.

Therefore, Merlin did not interfere with Juliette, but contented himself with insinuating, by jest and action, what her share in this day's work had been. To these hints Déroulède, of course, paid no heed. For him Juliette was as far above political intrigue as the angels. He would as soon have suspected one of the saints enshrined in Notre Dame as this beautiful, almost ethereal creature, who had been send by Heaven to gladden his heart and to elevate his very thought.

But Juliette understood Merlin's attitude and guessed that her written denunciation had come into his hands. Her every thought, every living sensation within her, was centred in this one thing: to save the man she loved from the consequences of her own crime against him. And for this, even the shadow of suspicion must be removed from him. Merlin's iniquitous law should not touch him again.

When Déroulède at last had been released, after the outrage to which he had been personally subjected, Merlin was literally, and figuratively too, looking about him for an issue to his present dubious position.

Judging others by his own standard of conduct, he feared now that the popular Citizen-Deputy would incite the mob against him, in revenge for the indignities which he had had to suffer. And with it all the Terrorist was convinced that Déroulède was guilty, that proofs of his treason did exist, if only he knew where to lay hands on them.

He turned to Juliette with an unexpressed query in his adder-like eyes. She shrugged her shoulders and made a gesture as if pointing towards the door.

"There are other rooms in the house besides this," her gesture seemed to say; "try them. The proofs are there, 'tis for you to find them."

Merlin had been standing between her and Déroulède, so that the latter saw neither query nor reply.

"You are cunning, Citizen-Deputy," said Merlin now, turning towards him, "and no doubt you have been at pains to put your treasonable correspondence out of the way. You must understand that the Committee of Public Safety will not be satisfied with a mere examination of your study," he added, assuming an air of ironical benevolence, "and I presume you will have no objection, if I and these citizen soldiers pay a visit to other portions of your house."

"As you please," responded Déroulède drily.

"You will accompany us, Citizen-Deputy," commanded the other curtly.

The four men of the National Guard formed themselves into line outside the study door; with a peremptory nod, Merlin ordered Déroulède to pass between them, then he too prepared to follow. At the door he turned, and once more faced Juliette.

"As for you, citizeness," he said, with a sudden access of viciousness against her, "if you have brought us here on a fool's errand, it will go ill with you, remember. Do not leave the house until our return. I may have some questions to put to you."

Chapter 13

Tangled Meshes

Juliette waited a moment or two, until the footsteps of the six men died away up the massive oak stairs.

For the first time, since the sword of Damocles had fallen, she was alone with her thoughts.

She had but a few moments at her command in which to devise an issue out of these tangled meshes, which she had woven round the man she loved.

Merlin and his men would return anon. The comedy could not be kept up through another visit from them, and while the compromising letter-case remained in Déroulède's private study he was in imminent danger at the hands of his enemy.

She thought for a moment of concealing the case about her person, but a second's reflection showed her the futility of such a move.

She had not seen the papers themselves; any one of them might be an absolute proof of Déroulède's guilt; the correspondence might be in his handwriting.

If Merlin, furious, baffled, vicious, were to order her to be searched! The horror of the indignity made her shudder, but she would have submitted to that, if thereby she could have saved Déroulède. But of this she could not be sure until after she had looked through the papers, and this she had not the time to do.

Her first and greatest idea was to get out of this room, his private study, with the compromising papers. Not a trace of them must be found here, if he were to remain beyond suspicion.

She rose from the sofa and peeped through the door. The hall was now deserted; from the left wing of the house, on the floor above, the heavy footsteps of the soldiers and Merlin's occasional brutish laugh could be distinctly heard.

Juliette listened for a moment, trying to understand what was happening. Yes; they had all gone to Déroulède's bedroom, which was on the extreme left, at the end of the first-floor landing. There might be just time to accomplish what she had now resolved to do.

As best she could, she hid the bulky leather case in the folds of her skirt. It was literally neck or nothing now. If she were caught on the stairs by one of the men nothing could save her or—possibly—Déroulède.

At any rate, by remaining where she was, by leaving the events to shape themselves, discovery was absolutely certain. She chose to take the risk.

She slipped noiselessly out of the room and up the great oak stairs. Merlin and his men, busy with their search in Déroulède's bedroom, took no heed of what was going on behind them; Juliette arrived on the landing, and turned sharply to her right, running noiselessly along the thick Aubusson carpet, and thence quickly to her own room.

All this had taken less than a minute to accomplish. The very next moment she heard Merlin's voice ordering one of his men to stand at attention on the landing, but by that time she was safe inside her room. She closed the door noiselessly.

Pétronelle, who had been busy all the afternoon packing up her young mistress' things, had fallen asleep in an armchair. Unconscious of the terrible events which were rapidly succeeding each other in the house, the worthy old soul was snoring peaceably, with her hands complacently folded on her ample bosom.

Juliette, for the moment, took no notice of her. As quickly and as dexterously as she could, she was tearing open the heavy leather case with a sharp pair of scissors, and very soon its contents were scattered before her on the table.

One glance at them was sufficient to convince her that most of the papers would undoubtedly, if found, send Déroulède to the guillotine. Most of the correspondence was in the Citizen-Deputy's handwriting. She had, of course, no time to examine it more closely, but instinct naturally told her that it was of a highly compromising character.

She gathered the papers up into a heap, tearing some of them up into strips; then she spread them out upon the ash-pan in front of the large earthenware stove, which stood in a corner of the room.

Unfortunately, this was a hot day in August. Her task would have been far easier if she had wished to destroy a bundle of papers in the depth of winter, when there was a good fire burning in the stove.

But her purpose was firm and her incentive, the greatest that has ever spurred mankind to heroism.

Regardless of any consequences to herself, she had but the one object in view, to save Déroulède at all costs.

On the wall facing her bed, and immediately above a velvet-covered *prie-dieu*, there was a small figure of the Virgin and Child—one of those quaintly pretty devices for holding holy water, which the reverent superstition of the past century rendered a necessary adjunct of every girl's room.

In front of the figure a small lamp was kept perpetually burning. This Juliette now took between her fingers, carefully, lest the tiny flame should die out. First, she poured the oil over the fragments of paper in the ash-pan, then with the wick she set fire to the whole compromising correspondence.

The oil helped the paper to burn quickly; the smell, or perhaps the presence of Juliette in the room caused worthy old Pétronelle to wake.

"It's nothing, Pétronelle," said Juliette quietly; "only a few old letters I am burning. But I want to be alone for a few moments—will you go down to the kitchen until I call you?"

Accustomed to do as her young mistress commanded, Pétronelle rose without a word.

"I have finished putting away your few things, my jewel. There, there! why didn't you tell me to burn your papers for you? You have soiled your dear hands, and—"

"Sh! Sh! Pétronelle!" said Juliette impatiently, and gently pushing the garrulous old woman towards the door. "Run to the kitchen now quickly, and don't come out of it until I call you. And, Pétronelle," she added, "you will see soldiers about the house perhaps."

"Soldiers! The good God have mercy!"

"Don't be frightened, Pétronelle. But they may ask you questions."

"Questions?"

"Yes; about me."

"My treasure, my jewel," exclaimed Pétronelle in alarm, "have those devils—?"

"No, no; nothing has happened as yet, but, you know, in these times there is always danger."

"Good God! Holy Mary! Mother of God!"

"Nothing'll happen if you try to keep quite calm and do exactly as I tell you. Go to the kitchen and wait there until I call you. If the soldiers come in and question you, if they try to frighten you, remember that we have nothing to fear from men, and that our lives are in God's keeping."

All the while that Juliette spoke, she was watching the heap of paper being gradually reduced to ashes. She tried to fan the flames as best she could, but some of the correspondence was on tough paper, and was slow in being consumed. Pétronelle, tearful but obedient, prepared to leave the room. She was overawed by her mistress' air of aloofness, the pale face rendered ethereally beautiful by the sufferings she had gone through. The eyes glowed large and magnetic, as if in presence of spiritual visions beyond mortal ken; the golden hair looked like a saintly halo above the white, immaculate young brow.

Pétronelle made the sign of the cross, as if she were in the presence of a saint.

As she opened the door there was a sudden draught, and the last flickering flame died out in the ash-pan. Juliette, seeing that Pétronelle had gone, hastily turned over the few half-burnt fragments of paper that were left. In none of them had the writing remained legible. All that was compromising to Déroulède was effectually reduced to dust. The small wick in the lamp at the foot of the Virgin and Child had burned itself out for want of oil; there was no means for Juliette to strike another light and to destroy what remained. The leather case was, of course, still there, with its sides ripped open, an indestructible thing.

There was nothing to be done about that. Juliette after a second's hesitation threw it among her dresses in the valise.

Then she too went out of the room.

Chapter 14

A Happy Moment

The search in the Citizen-Deputy's bedroom had proved as fruitless as that in his study. Merlin was beginning to have vague doubts as to whether he had been effectively fooled.

His manner towards Déroulède had undergone a change. He had become suave and unctuous, a kind of elephantine irony pervading his laborious attempts at conciliation. He and the Public Prosecutor would be severely blamed for this day's work, if the popular Deputy, relying upon the support of the people of Paris, chose to take his revenge.

In France, in this glorious year of the Revolution, there was but one step between censure and indictment. And Merlin knew it. Therefore, although he had not given up all hope of finding proofs of Déroulède's treason, although by the latter's attitude he remained quite convinced that such proof did exist, he was already reckoning upon the cat's paw, the sop he would offer to that Cerberus, the Committee of Public Safety, in exchange for his own exculpation in the matter.

This sop would be Juliette, the denunciator instead of Déroulède the denounced.

But he was still seeking for the proofs.

Somewhat changing his tactics, he had allowed Déroulède to join his mother in the living-room and had betaken himself to the kitchen in search of Anne Mie, whom he had previously caught sight of in the hall. There he also found old Pétronelle, whom he could scare out of her wits to his heart's content, but from whom he was quite unable to extract any useful information. Pétronelle was too stupid to be dangerous, and Anne Mie was too much on the alert.

But, with a vague idea that a cunning man might choose the most unlikely places for the concealment of compromising property, he was ransacking the kitchen from floor to ceiling.

In the living-room Déroulède was doing his best to reassure his mother, who, in her turn, was forcing herself to be brave, and not to show by her tears how deeply she feared for the safety of her son. As soon as Déroulède had been freed from the presence of the soldiers, he had hastened back to his study, only to find that Juliette had gone, and that the letter-case had also disappeared. Not knowing what to think, trembling for the safety of the woman he adored, he was just debating whether he would seek for her in her own room, when she came towards him across the landing.

There seemed a halo around her now. Déroulède felt that she had never been so beautiful and to him so unattainable. Something told him then, that at this moment she was as far away from him, as if she were an inhabitant of another, more ethereal planet.

When she saw him coming towards her, she put a finger to her lips, and whispered:

"Sh! sh! the papers are destroyed, burned."

"And I owe my safety to you!"

He had said it with his whole soul, an infinity of gratitude filled his heart, a joy and pride in that she had cared for his safety.

But at his words she had grown paler than she was before. Her eyes, large, dilated, and dark, were fixed upon him with an intensity of gaze which almost startled him. He thought that she was about to faint, that the emotions of the past half hour had been too much for her overstrung nerves. He took her hand, and gently dragged her into the living-room.

She sank into a chair, as if utterly weary and exhausted, and he, forgetting his danger, forgetting the world and all else besides, knelt at her feet, and held her hands in his.

She sat bolt upright, her great eyes still fixed upon him. At first it seemed as if she could not be satiated with looking at her; he felt as if he had never, never really seen her. She had been a dream of beauty to him ever since that awful afternoon when he had held her, half fainting, in his arms, and had dragged her under the shelter of his roof.

From that hour he had worshipped her: she had cast over him the magic spell of her refinement, her beauty, that aroma of youth and innocence which makes such a strong appeal to the man of sentiment.

He had worshipped her and not tried to understand. He would have deemed it almost sacrilege to pry into the mysteries of her inner self, of that second nature in her which at times mad her silent, and almost morose, and cast a lurid gloom over her young beauty.

And though his love for her had grown in intensity, it had remained as heaven born as he deemed her to be—the love of a mortal for a saint, the ecstatic adoration of a St Francis for his Madonna.

Sir Percy Blakeney had called Déroulède an idealist. He was that, in the strictest sense, and Juliette had embodied all that was best in his idealism.

It was for the first time today, that he had held her hand just for a moment longer than mere conventionality allowed. The first kiss on her finger-tips had sent the blood rushing wildly to his heart; but he still worshipped her and gazed upon her as upon a divinity.

She sat bolt upright in the chair, abandoning her small, cold hands to his burning grasp.

His very senses ached with the longing to clasp her in his arms, to draw her to him, and to feel her pulses beat closer against his. It was almost torture now to gaze upon her beauty—that small, oval face, almost like a child's, the large eyes which at times had seemed to be blue but which now appeared to be a deep, unfathomable colour, like the tempestuous sea.

"Juliette!" he murmured at last, as his soul went out to her in a passionate appeal for the first kiss.

A shudder seemed to go through her entire frame, her very lips turned white and cold, and he, not understanding, timorous, chivalrous and humble, thought that she was repelled by his ardour and frightened by a passion to which she was too pure to respond.

Nothing but that one word had been spoken—just her name, an appeal from a strong man, overmastered at last by his boundless love—and she, poor, stricken soul, who had so much loved, so deeply wronged him, shuddered at the thought of what she might have done, had Fate not helped her to save him.

Half ashamed of his passion, he bowed his dark head over her hands, and, once more forcing himself to be calm now, he kissed her finger-tips reverently.

When he looked up again the hard lines in her face had softened, and two tears were slowly trickling down her pale cheeks.

"Will you forgive me, Madonna?" he said gently. "I am only a man and you are very beautiful. No—don't take your little hands away. I am quite calm now and know how one should speak to angels."

Reason, justice, rectitude—everything was urging Juliette to close her ears to the words of love, spoken by the man whom she had betrayed. But who shall blame her for listening to the sweetest sound the ears of a woman can ever hear—the sound of the voice of the loved one in his first declaration of love?

She sat and listened, whilst he whispered to her those soft, endearing words, of which a strong man alone possesses the enchanting secret.

She sat and listened, whilst all around her was still. Madame Déroulède, at the farther end of the room, was softly muttering a few prayers.

They were all alone these two in the mad and beautiful world, which man has created for himself—the world of romance—that world more wonderful than any heaven, where only those may enter who have learned the sweet lesson of love. Déroulède roamed in it at will. He had created his own romance, wherein he was as a humble worshipper, spending his life in the service of his Madonna.

And she too forgot the earth, forgot the reality, her oath, her crime and its punishment, and began to think that it was good to live, good to love, and good to have at her feet the one man in all the world whom she could fondly worship.

Who shall tell what he whispered? Enough that she listened and that she smiled; and he, seeing her smile, felt happy.

Chapter 15

Detected

The opening and shutting of the door roused them both from their dreams.

Anne Mie, pale, trembling, with eyes looking wild and terrified, had glided into the room.

Déroulède had sprung to his feet. In a moment he had thrust his own happiness into the background at sight of the poor child's obvious suffering. He went quickly towards her, and would have spoken to her, but she run past him up to Madame Déroulède, as if she were beside herself with some unexplainable terror.

"Anne Mie," he said firmly, "what is it? Have those devils dared—"

In a moment reality had come rushing back upon him with full force, and bitter reproaches surged up in his heart against himself, for having in this moment of selfish joy forgotten those who looked up to him for help and protection.

He knew the temper of the brutes who had been set upon his track, knew that low-minded Merlin and his noisome ways, and blamed himself severely for having left Anne Mie and Pétronelle alone with him even for a few moments.

But Anne Mie quickly reassured him.

"They have not molested us much," she said, speaking with a visible effort and enforced calmness. "Pétronelle and I were together, and they made us open all the cupboards and uncover all the dishes. They then asked us many questions."

"Questions? Of what kind?" asked Déroulède.

"About you, Paul," replied Anne Mie, "and about *maman*, and also about—about the citizeness, your guest."

Déroulède looked at her closely, vaguely wondering at the strange attitude of the child. She was evidently labouring under some strong excitement, and in her thin, brown little hand she was clutching a piece of paper.

"Anne Mie! Child," he said very gently, "you seem quite upset—as if something terrible had happened. What is that paper you are holding, my dear?"

Anne Mie gazed down upon it. She was obviously making frantic efforts to maintain her self-possession.

Juliette at first sight of Anne Mie seemed literally to have been turned to stone. She sat upright, rigid as a statue, her eyes fixed upon the poor, crippled girl as if upon an inexorable judge, about to pronounce sentence upon her of life or death.

Instinct, that keen sense of coming danger which Nature sometimes gives to her elect, had told her that, within the next few seconds, her doom would be sealed; that Fate would descend upon her, holding the sword of Nemesis; and it was Anne Mie's tiny, half-shrivelled hand which had placed that sword into the grasp of Fate.

"What is that paper? Will you let me see it, Anne Mie?" repeated Déroulède.

"Citizen Merlin gave it to me just now," began Anne Mie more quietly; "he seems very wroth at finding nothing compromising against you, Paul. They were a long time in the kitchen, and now they have gone to search my room and Pétronelle's; but Merlin—oh! that awful man!—he seemed like a beast infuriated with his disappointment."

"Yes, yes."

"I don't know what he hoped to get out of me, for I told him that you never spoke to your mother or to me about your political business, and that I was not in the habit of listening at the keyholes."

"Yes. And—"

"Then he began to speak of—of our guest—but, of course, there again I could tell him nothing. He seemed to be puzzled as to who had denounced you. He spoke about an anonymous denunciation, which reached the Public Prosecutor early this morning. It was written on a scrap of paper, and thrown into the public box, it seems, and—"

"It is indeed very strange," said Déroulède, musing over this extraordinary occurrence, and still more over Anne Mie's strange excitement in the telling of it. "I never knew I had a hidden enemy. I wonder if I shall ever find out—"

"That is just what I said to Citizen Merlin," rejoined Anne Mie.

"What?"

"That I wondered if you, or—or any of us who love you, will ever find out who your hidden enemy might be."

"It was a mistake to talk so fully with such a brute, little one."

"I didn't say much, and I thought it wisest to humour him, as he seemed to wish to talk on that subject."

"Well? And what did he say?"

"He laughed and asked me if I would very much like to know."

"I hope you said No, Anne Mie?"

"Indeed, indeed, I said Yes," she retorted with sudden energy, her eyes fixed now upon Juliette, who still sat rigid and silent, watching every movement of Anne Mie from the moment in which she began to tell her story.

"Would I not wish to know who is your enemy, Paul—the creature who was base and treacherous enough to attempt to deliver you into the hands of those merciless villains? What wrong had you done to anyone?"

"Sh! Hush, Anne Mie! you are too excited," he said, smiling now, in spite of himself, at the young girl's vehemence over what he thought was but a trifle—the discovery of his own enemy.

"I am sorry, Paul. How can I help being excited," rejoined Anne Mie with quaint, pathetic gentleness, "when I speak of such base treachery, as that which Merlin has suggested?"

"Well? And what did he suggest?"

"He did more than suggest," whispered Anne Mie almost inaudibly; "he gave me this paper—the anonymous denunciation which reached the Public Prosecutor this morning—he thought one of us might recognise the handwriting."

Then she paused, some five steps away from Déroulède, holding out towards him the crumpled paper, which up to now she had clutched determinedly in her hand. Déroulède was about to take it from her, and just before he had turned to do so, his eyes lighted on Juliette.

She said nothing, she had merely risen instinctively, and had reached Anne Mie's side in less than the fraction of a second.

It was all a flash, and there was dead silence in the room, but in that one-hundredth part of a second, Déroulède had read guilt in the face of Juliette.

It was nothing but instinct, a sudden, awful, unexplainable revelation. Her soul seemed suddenly to stand before him in all its misery and in all its sin.

It was if the fire from heaven had descended in one terrific crash, burying beneath its devastating flames his ideals, his happiness, and his divinity. She was no longer there. His Madonna had ceased to be.

There stood before him a beautiful woman, on whom he had lavished all the pent-up treasures of his love, whom he had succoured, sheltered, and protected, and who had repaid him thus.

She had forced an entry into his house; she had spied upon him, dogged him, lied to him. The moment was too sudden, too awful for him to make even a wild guess at her motives. His entire life, his whole past, the present, and the future, were all blotted out in this awful dispersal of his most cherished dream. He had forgotten everything else save her appalling treachery; how could he even remember that once, long ago, in fair fight, he had killed her brother?

She did not even try now to hide her guilt.

A look of appeal, touching in its trustfulness, went out to him, begging him to spare her further shame. Perhaps she felt that love, such as his, could not be killed in a flash.

His entire nature was full of pity, and to that pity she made a final appeal, lest she should be humiliated before Madame Déroulède and Anne Mie.

And he, still under the spell of those magic moments when he had knelt at her feet, understood her prayer, and closing his eyes just for one brief moment in order to shut out for ever that radiant vision of a pure angel whom he had worshipped, turned quietly to Anne Mie.

"Give me that paper, Anne Mie," he said coldly. "I may perhaps recognise the handwriting of my most bitter enemy."

"'Tis unnecessary now," replied Anne Mie slowly, still gazing at the face of Juliette, in which she too had read what she wished to read.

The paper dropped out of her hand.

Déroulède stooped to pick it up. He unfolded it, smoothed it out, and then saw that it was blank.

"There is nothing written on this paper," he said mechanically.

"No," rejoined Anne Mie; "no other words save the story of her treachery."

"What you have done is evil and wicked, Anne Mie."

"Perhaps so; but I had guessed the truth, and I wished to know.

God showed me this way, how to do it, and how to let you know as well."

"The less you speak of God just now, Anne Mie, the better, I think. Will you attend to *maman?* she seems faint and ill."

Madame Déroulède, silent and placid in her armchair, had watched the tragic scene before her, almost like a disinterested spectator. All her ideas and all her thoughts had been paralysed, since the moment when the first summons at the front door had warned her of the imminence of the peril to her son.

The final discovery of Juliette's treachery had left her impassive. Since her son was in danger, she cared little as to whence that danger had come.

Obedient to Déroulède's wish, Anne Mie was attending to the old lady's comforts. The poor, crippled girl was already feeling the terrible reaction of her deed.

In her childish mind she had planned this way, in which to bring the traitor to shame. Anne Mie knew nothing, cared nothing, about the motives which had actuated Juliette; all she knew was that a terrible Judas-like deed had been perpetrated against the man, on whom she herself had lavished her pathetic, hopeless love.

All the pent-up jealousy which had tortured her for the past three weeks rose up and goaded her into unmasking her rival.

Never for a moment did she doubt Juliette's guilt. The god of love may be blind, tradition has so decreed it, but the demon of jealousy has a hundred eyes, more keen than those of the lynx.

Anne Mie, pushed aside by Merlin's men when they forced their way into Déroulède's study, had, nevertheless, followed them to the door. When the curtains were drawn aside and the room filled with light, she had seen Juliette enthroned, apparently calm and placid, upon the sofa.

It was instinct, the instinct born of her own rejected passion, which caused her to read in the beautiful girl's face all that lay hidden behind the pale, impassive mask. That same second sight made her understand Merlin's hints and allusions. She caught every inflection of his voice, heard everything, saw everything.

And in the midst of her anxiety and her terrors for the man she loved, there was the wild, primitive, intensely human joy at the thought of bringing that enthroned idol, who had stolen his love, down to earth at last.

Anne Mie was not clever; she was simple and childish, with no complexity of passions or devious ways of intellect. It was her elemental jealousy which suggested the cunning plan for the unmasking of Juliette. She would make the girl cringe and fear, threaten her with discovery, and through her very terror shame her before Paul Déroulède.

And now it was all done; it had all occurred as she had planned it. Paul knew that his love had been wasted upon a liar and a traitor, and Juliette stood pale, humiliated, a veritable wreck of shamed humanity.

Anne Mie had triumphed, and was profoundly, abjectly wretched in her triumph. Great sobs seemed to tear at her very heart-strings. She had pulled down Paul's idol from her pedestal, but the one look she had cast at his face had shown her that she had also wrecked his life.

He seemed almost old now. The earnest, restless gaze had gone from his eyes; he was staring mutely before him, twisting between nerveless fingers that blank scrap of paper, which had been the means of annihilating his dream.

All energy of attitude, all strength of bearing, which were his chief characteristics, seemed to have gone. There was a look of complete blankness, of hopelessness in his listless gesture.

"How he loved her!" sighed Anne Mie, as she tenderly wrapped the shawl round Madame Déroulède's shoulders.

Juliette had said nothing; it seemed as if her very life had gone out of her. She was a mere statue now, her mind numb, her heart dead, her very existence a fragile piece of mechanism. But she was looking at Déroulède. That one sense in her had remained alive: her sight.

She looked and looked: and saw every passing sign of mental agony on his face: the look of recognition of her guilt, the bewilderment at the appalling crash, and now that hideous deathlike emptiness of his soul and mind.

Never once did she detect horror or loathing. He had tried to save her from being further humiliated before his mother, but there was no hatred or contempt in his eyes, when he realised that she had been unmasked by a trick.

She looked and looked, for there was no hope in her, not even despair. There was nothing in her mind, nothing in her soul, but a great pall-like blank.

Then gradually, as the minutes sped on, she saw the strong soul within him make a sudden fight against the darkness of his despair: the movement of the fingers became less listless; the powerful, energetic figure straightened itself out; remembrance of other matters, other interests than his own began to lift the overwhelming burden of his grief.

He remembered the letter-case containing the compromising papers. A vague wonder arose in him as to Juliette's motives in warding off, through her concealment of it, the inevitable moment of its discovery by Merlin.

The thought that her entire being had undergone a change, and that she now wished to save him, never once entered his mind; if it had, he would have dismissed it as the outcome of maudlin sentimentality, the conceit of the fop, who believes his personality to be irresistible.

His own self-torturing humility pointed but to the one conclusion: that she had fooled him all along; fooled him when she sought his protection; fooled him when she taught him to love her; fooled him, above all, at the moment when, subjugated by the intensity of his passion, he had for one brief second ceased to worship in order to love.

When the bitter remembrance of that moment of sweetest folly rushed back to his aching brain, then at last did he look up at her with one final, agonised look of reproach, so great, so tender, and yet so final, that Anne Mie, who saw it, felt as if her own heart would break with the pity of it all.

But Juliette had caught the look too. The tension of her nerves seemed suddenly to relax. Memory rushed back upon her with tumultuous intensity. Very gradually her knees gave beneath her, and at last she knelt down on the floor before him, her golden head bent under the burden of her guilt and her shame.

Chapter 16

Under Arrest

Déroulède did not attempt to go to her.

Only presently, when the heavy footsteps of Merlin and his men were once more heard upon the landing, she quietly rose to her feet.

She had accomplished her act of humiliation and repentance, there before them all. She looked for the last time upon those whom she had so deeply wronged, and in her heart spoke an eternal farewell to that great, and mighty, and holy love which she had called forth and then had so hopelessly crushed.

Now she was ready for the atonement.

Merlin had already swaggered into the room. The long and arduous search throughout the house had not improved either his temper or his personal appearance. He was more covered with grime than he had been before, and his narrow forehead had almost disappeared beneath the tangled mass of his ill-kempt hair, which he had perpetually tugged forward and roughed up in his angry impatience.

One look at his face had already told Juliette what she wished to know. He had searched her room, and found the fragments of burnt paper, which she had purposely left in the ash-pan.

How he would act now was the one thing of importance left for Juliette to ponder over. That she would not escape arrest and condemnation was at once made clear to her. Merlin's look of sneering contempt, when he glanced towards her, had told her that.

Déroulède himself had been conscious of a feeling of intense relief when the men re-entered the room. The tension had become unendurable. When he saw his dethroned Madonna kneel in humiliation at his feet, an overwhelming pain had wrenched his very heart-strings.

And yet he could not go to her. The passionate, human nature within him felt a certain proud exultation at seeing her there.

She was not above him now, she was no longer akin to the angels.

He had given no further thought to his own immediate danger. Vaguely he guessed that Merlin would find the leather case. Where it was he could not tell; perhaps Juliette herself had handed it to the soldiers. She had only hidden it for a few moments, out of impulse perhaps, fearing lest, at the first instant of its discovery, Merlin might betray her.

He remembered now those hints and insinuations which had gone out from the Terrorist to Juliette whilst the search was being conducted in the study. At the time he had merely looked upon these as a base attempt at insult, and had tortured himself almost beyond bearing, in the endeavour to refrain from punishing that evil-mouthed creature, who dared to bandy words with his Madonna.

But now he understood and felt his very soul writhing with shame at the remembrance of it all.

Oh yes; the return of Merlin and his men, the presence of these grimy, degraded brutes, was welcome now. He would have wished to crowd in the entire world, the universe and its population, between him and his fallen idol.

Merlin's manner towards him had lost nothing of its ironical benevolence. There was even a touch of obsequiousness apparent in the ugly face, as the representative of the people approached the popular Citizen-Deputy.

"Citizen-Deputy," began Merlin, "I have to bring you the welcome news, that we have found nothing in your house that in any way can cast suspicion upon your loyalty to the Republic. My orders, however, were to bring you before the Committee of Public Safety, whether I had found proofs of your guilt or not. I have found none."

He was watching Déroulède keenly, hoping even at this eleventh hour to detect a look or a sign, which would furnish him with the proofs for which he was seeking. The slightest suggestion of relief on Déroulède's part, a sigh of satisfaction, would have been sufficient at this moment, to convince him and the Committee of Public Safety that the Citizen-Deputy was guilty after all.

But Déroulède never moved. He was sufficiently master of himself not to express either surprise or satisfaction. Yet he felt both—satisfaction not for his own safety, but because of his mother and Anne Mie, whom he would immediately send out of the country, out of all danger; and also because of her, of Juliette Marny, his guest, who, whatever she may have done against him, had still a claim on his protection. His feeling of surprise was less keen, and quite transient. Merlin had not found the letter-case. Juliette, stricken with tardy remorse perhaps, had succeeded in concealing it. The matter had practically ceased to interest him. It was equally galling to owe his betrayal or his ultimate safety to her.

He kissed his mother tenderly, bidding her goodbye, and pressed Anne Mie's timid little hand warmly between his own. He did what he could to reassure them, but, for their own sakes, he dared say nothing before Merlin, as to his plans for their safety.

After that he was ready to follow the soldiers.

As he passed close to Juliette he bowed, and almost inaudibly whispered:

"*Adieu!*"

She heard the whisper but did not respond. Her look alone gave him the reply to his eternal farewell.

His footsteps and those of his escort were heard echoing down the staircase, then the hall door to open and shut. Through the open window came the sound of hoarse cheering as the popular Citizen-Deputy appeared in the street.

Merlin, with two men beside him, remained under the portico; he told off the other two to escort Déroulède as far as the Hall of Justice, where sat the members of the Committee of Public Safety. The Terrorist had a vague fear that the Citizen-Deputy would speak to the mob.

An unruly crowd of women had evidently been awaiting his appearance. The news had quickly spread along the streets that Merlin, Merlin himself, the ardent, bloodthirsty Jacobin, had made a descent upon Paul Déroulède's house, escorted by four soldiers. Such an indignity, put upon the man they most trusted in the entire assembly of the Convention, had greatly incensed the crowd. The women jeered at the soldiers as soon as they appeared, and Merlin dared not actually forbid Déroulède to speak.

"À *la lanterne, vieux crétin!*" shouted one of the women, thrusting her fist under Merlin's nose.

"Give the word, Citizen-Deputy," rejoined another, "and we'll break his ugly face. *Nous lui casserons la gueule!*"

"À *la lanterne!* À *la lanterne!*"

One word from Déroulède now would have caused an open riot, and in those days self defence against the mob was construed into enmity against the people.

Merlin's work, too, was not yet accomplished. He had had no intention of escorting Déroulède himself; he had still important business to transact inside the house which he had just quitted and had merely wished to get the Citizen-Deputy well out of the way, before he went upstairs again.

Moreover, he had expected something of a riot in the streets. The temper of the people of Paris was at fever heat just now. The hatred of the populace against a certain class, and against certain individuals, was only equalled by their enthusiasm in favour of others.

They had worshipped Marat for his squalor and his vices; they worshipped Danton for his energy and Robespierre for his calm; they worshipped Déroulède for his voice, his gentleness and his pity, for his care of their children and the eloquence of his speech.

It was that eloquence which Merlin feared now; but he little knew the type of man he had to deal with.

Déroulède's influence over the most unruly, the most vicious populace the history of the world has ever known, was not obtained through fanning its passions. That popularity, though brilliant, is always ephemeral. The passions of a mob will invariably turn against those who have helped to rouse them. Marat did not live to see the waning of his star; Danton was dragged to the guillotine by those whom he had taught to look upon that instrument of death as the only possible and unanswerable political argument; Robespierre succumbed to the orgies of bloodshed he himself had brought about. But Déroulède remained master of the people of Paris for as long as he chose to exert that mastery. When they listened to him they felt better, nobler, less hopelessly degraded.

He kept up in their poor, misguided hearts that last flickering sense of manhood which their bloodthirsty tyrants, under the guise of Fraternity and Equality, were doing their best to smother.

Even now, when he might have turned the temper of the small crowd outside his door to his own advantage, he preferred to say nothing; he even pacified them with a gesture.

He well knew that those whom he incited against Merlin now would, once their blood was up, probably turn against him in less than half-an-hour.

Merlin, who all along had meant to return to the house, took his opportunity now. He allowed Déroulède and the two men to go on ahead, and beat a hasty retreat back into the house, followed by the jeers of the women.

"À *la lanterne, vieux crétin!*" they shouted as soon as the hall door was once more closed in their faces. A few of them began hammering against the door with their fists; then they realised that their special favourite, Citizen-Deputy Déroulède, was marching along between two soldiers, as if he were a prisoner. The word went round that he was under arrest, and was being taken to the Hall of Justice—a prisoner.

This was not to be. The mob of Paris had been taught that it was the master in the city, and it had learned its lesson well. For the moment it had chosen to take Paul Déroulède under its special protection, and as a guard of honour to him—the women in ragged kirtles, the men with bare legs and stripped to the waist, the children all yelling, hooting, and shrieking—followed him, to see that none dared harm him.

CHAPTER 17

Atonement

Merlin waited a while in the hall, until he heard the noise of the shrieking crowd gradually die away in the distance, then with a grunt of satisfaction he one more mounted the stairs.

All these events outside had occurred during a very few minutes, and Madame Déroulède and Anne Mie had been too anxious as to what was happening in the streets, to take any notice of Juliette.

They had not dared to step out on to the balcony to see what was going on, and, therefore, did not understand what the reopening and shutting of the front door had meant.

The next instant, however, Merlin's heavy, slouching footsteps on the stairs had caused Anne Mie to look round in alarm.

"It is only the soldiers come back for me," said Juliette quietly.

"For you?"

"Yes; they are coming to take me away. I suppose they did not wish to do it in the presence of Mr. Déroulède, for fear—"

She had no time to say more. Anne Mie was still looking at her in awed and mute surprise, when Merlin entered the room.

In his hand he held a leather case, all torn, and split at one end, and a few tiny scraps of half-charred paper. He walked straight up to Juliette, and roughly thrust the case and papers into her face.

"These are yours?" he said roughly.

"Yes."

"I suppose you know where they were found?"

She nodded quietly in reply.

"What were these papers which you burnt?"

"Love letters."

"You lie!"

She shrugged her shoulders.

"As you please," she said curtly.

"What were these papers?" he repeated, with a loud obscene oath which, however, had not the power to disturb the young girl's serenity.

"I have told you," she said: "love letters, which I wished to burn."

"Who was your lover?" he asked.

Then as she did not reply he indicated the street, where cries of "Déroulède! *Vive* Déroulède!" still echoed from afar.

"Were the letters from him?"

"No."

"You had more than one lover, then?"

He laughed, and a hideous leer seemed further to distort his ugly countenance.

He thrust his face quite close to hers, and she closed her eyes, sick with the horror of this contact with the degraded wretch. Even Anne Mie had uttered a cry of sympathy at sight of this evil-smelling, squalid creature torturing, with his close proximity, the beautiful, refined girl before him.

With a rough gesture he put his clawlike hand under her delicate chin, forcing her to turn round and to look at him. She shuddered at the loathsome touch, but her quietude never forsook her for a moment.

It was into the power of wretches such as this man, that she had wilfully delivered the man she loved. This brutish creature's familiarity put the finishing touch to her own degradation, but it gave her the courage to carry through her purpose to the end.

"You had more than one lover, then?" said Merlin, with a laugh which would have pleased the devil himself. "And you wished to send one of them to the guillotine in order to make way for the other? Was that it?"

"Was that it?" he repeated, suddenly seizing one of her wrists, and giving it as savage twist, so that she almost screamed with the pain.

"Yes," she replied firmly.

"Do you know that you brought me here on a fool's errand?" he asked viciously; "that the Citizen-Deputy Déroulède cannot be sent to the guillotine on mere suspicion, eh? Did you know that, when you wrote out that denunciation?"

"No; I did not know."

"You thought we could arrest him on mere suspicion?"

"Yes."

"You knew he was innocent?"

"I knew it."

"Why did you burn your love letters?"

"I was afraid that they would be found and would be brought under the notice of the Citizen-Deputy."

"A splendid combination, *ma foi!*" said Merlin, with an oath, as he turned to the two other women, who sat pale and shrinking in a corner of the room, not understanding what was going on, not knowing what to think or what to believe. They had known nothing of Déroulède's plans for the escape of Marie Antoinette, they didn't know what the letter-case had contained, and yet they both vaguely felt that the beautiful girl, who stood up so calmly before the loathsome Terrorist, was not a wanton, as she tried to make out, but only misguided, mad perhaps—perhaps a martyr.

"Did you know anything of this?" queried Merlin roughly from trembling Anne Mie.

"Nothing," she replied.

"No one knew anything of my private affairs or of my private correspondence," said Juliette coldly; "as you say, it was a splendid combination. I had hoped that it would succeed. But I understand now that Citizen-Deputy Déroulède is a personage of too much importance to be brought to trial on mere suspicion, and my denunciation of him was not based on facts."

"And do you know, my fine aristocrat," sneered Merlin viciously, "that it is not wise either to fool the Committee of Public Safety, or to denounce without cause one of the representatives of the people?"

"I know," she rejoined quietly, "that you, Citizen Merlin, are determined that someone shall pay for this day's blunder. You dare not now attack the Citizen-Deputy, and so you must be content with me."

"Enough of this talk now; I have no time to bandy words with *aristos*," he said roughly.

"Come now, follow the men quietly. Resistance would only aggravate your case."

"I am quite prepared to follow you. May I speak two words to my friends before I go?"

"No."

"I may never be able to speak to them again."

"I have said No, and I mean No. Now then, forward. March! I have wasted too much time already."

Juliette was too proud to insist any further. She had hoped, by one word, to soften Madame Déroulède's and Anne Mie's heart towards her. She did not know whether they believed that miserable lie which she had been telling to Merlin; she only guessed that for the moment they still thought her the betrayer of Paul Déroulède.

But that one word was not to be spoken. She would have to go forth to her certain trial, to her probable death, under the awful cloud, which she herself had brought over her own life.

She turned quietly, and walked towards the door, where the two men already stood at attention.

Then it was that some heaven-born instinct seemed suddenly to guide Anne Mie. The crippled girl was face to face with a psychological problem, which in itself was far beyond her comprehension, but vaguely she felt that it was a problem. Something in Juliette's face had already caused her to bitterly repent her action towards her, and now, as this beautiful, refined woman was about to pass from under the shelter of this roof, to the cruel publicity and terrible torture of that awful revolutionary tribunal, Anne Mie's whole heart went out to her in boundless sympathy.

Before Merlin or the men could prevent her, she had run up to Juliette, taken her hand, which hung listless and cold, and kissed it tenderly.

Juliette seemed to wake as if from a dream. She looked down at Anne Mie with a glance of hope, almost of joy, and whispered:

"It was an oath—I swore it to my father and my dead brother. Tell him."

Anne Mie could only nod; she could not speak, for her tears were choking her.

"But I'll atone—with my life. Tell him," whispered Juliette.

"Now then," shouted Merlin, "out of the way, hunchback, unless you want to come along too."

"Forgive me," said Anne Mie through her tears.

Then the men pushed her roughly aside. But at the door Juliette turned to her once more, and said:

"Pétronelle—take care of her—"

And with a firm step she followed the soldiers out of the room.

Presently the front door was heard to open, then to shut with a loud bang, and the house in the Rue Ecole de Médecine was left in silence.

Chapter 18

In the Luxembourg Prison

Juliette was alone at last—that is to say, comparatively alone, for there were too many aristocrats, too many criminals and traitors, in the prisons of Paris now, to allow of any seclusion of those who were about to be tried, condemned, and guillotined.

The young girl had been marched through the crowded streets of Paris, followed by a jeering mob, who readily recognised in the gentle, high-bred girl the obvious prey, which the Committee of Public Safety was wont, from time to time to throw to the hungry hydra-headed dog of the Revolution.

Lately the squalid spectators of the noisome spectacle on the Place de la Guillotine had had few of these very welcome sights: an aristocrat—a real, elegant, refined woman, with white hands and proud, pale face—mounting the steps of the same scaffold on which perished the vilest criminals and most degraded brutes.

Madame Guillotine was, above all, catholic in her tastes, her gaunt arms, painted blood red, were open alike to the murderer and the thief, the aristocrats of ancient lineage, and the proletariat from the gutter.

But lately the executions had been almost exclusively of a political character. The Girondins were fighting their last upon the bloody arena of the Revolution. One by one they fell still fighting, still preaching moderation, still foretelling disaster and appealing to that people, whom they had roused from one slavery, in order to throw it headlong under a tyrannical yoke more brutish, more absolute than before.

There were twelve prisons in Paris then, and forty thousand in France, and they were all full. An entire army went round the country recruiting prisoners. There was no room for separate cells, no room for privacy, no cause or desire for the most elementary sense of delicacy.

Women, men, children—all were herded together, for one day, perhaps two, and a night or so, and then death would obliterate the petty annoyances, the womanly blushes caused by this sordid propinquity.

Death levelled all, erased everything.

When Marie Antoinette mounted the guillotine, she had forgotten that for six weeks she practically lived day and night in the immediate companionship of a set of degraded soldiery.

Juliette, as she marched through the streets between two men of the National Guard, and followed by Merlin, was hooted and jeered at, insulted, pelted with mud. One woman tried to push past the soldiers, and to strike her in the face—a woman! not thirty!—and who was dragging a pale, squalid little boy by the hand.

"*Crache donc sur l'aristo, voyons!*" the woman said to this poor, miserable little scrap of humanity as the soldiers pushed her roughly aside. "Spit on the aristocrat!" And the child tortured its own small, parched mouth so that, in obedience to its mother, it might defile and bespatter a beautiful, innocent girl.

The soldiers laughed and improved the occasion with another insulting jest. Even Merlin forgot his vexation, delighted at the incident.

But Juliette had seen nothing of it all.

She was walking as in a dream. The mob did not exist for her; she heard neither insult nor vituperation. She did not see the evil, dirty faces pushed now and then quite close to her; she did not feel the rough hands of the soldiers jostling her through the crowd: she had gone back to her own world of romance, where she dwelt alone now with the man she loved. Instead of the squalid houses of Paris, with their eternal device of Fraternity and Equality, there were beautiful trees and shrubs of laurel and of roses around her, making the air fragrant with their soft, intoxicating perfumes; sweet voices from the land of dreams filled the atmosphere with their tender murmur, whilst overhead a cloudless sky illumined this earthly paradise.

She was happy—supremely, completely happy. She had saved him from the consequences of her own iniquitous crime, and she was about to give her life for him, so that his safety might be more completely assured.

Her love for him he would never know; now he knew only her crime, but presently, when she would be convicted and condemned, confronted with a few scraps of burned paper and a torn letter-case, then he would know that she had stood her trial, self-accused, and meant to die for him.

Therefore, the past few moments were now wholly hers. She had the rights to dwell on those few happy seconds when she listened to the avowal of his love. It was ethereal, and perhaps not altogether human, but it was hers. She had been his divinity, his Madonna; he had loved in her that, which was her truer, her better self.

What was base in her was not truly her. That awful oath, sworn so solemnly, had been her relentless tyrant; and her religion—a religion of superstition and of false ideals—had blinded her, and dragged her into crime.

She had arrogated to herself that which was God's alone—"Vengeance!" which is not for man.

That through it all she should have known love, and learned its tender secrets, was more than she deserved. That she should have felt his burning kisses on her hand was heavenly compensation for all she would have to suffer.

And so, she allowed them to drag her through the *sansculotte* mob of Paris, who would have torn her to pieces then and there, so as not to delay the pleasure of seeing her die.

They took her to the Luxembourg, once the palace of the Medici, the home of proud "*Monsieur*" in the days of the Great Monarch, now a loathsome, overfilled prison.

It was then six o'clock in the afternoon, drawing towards the close of this memorable day. She was handed over to the governor of the prison, a short, thick-set man in black trousers and black-shag woollen shirt, and wearing a dirty red cap, with tricolour rosette on the side of his unkempt head.

He eyed her up and down as she passed under the narrow doorway, then murmured one swift query to Merlin:

"Dangerous?"

"Yes," replied Merlin laconically.

"You understand," added the governor; "we are so crowded. We ought to know if individual attention is required."

"Certainly," said Merlin, "you will be personally responsible for this prisoner to the Committee of Public Safety."

"Any visitors allowed?"

"Certainly not, without the special permission of the Public Prosecutor."

Juliette heard this brief exchange of words over her future fate.

No visitor would be allowed to see her. Well, perhaps that would be best. She would have been afraid to meet Déroulède again, afraid to read in his eyes that story of his dead love, which alone might have destroyed her present happiness.

And she wished to see no one. She had a memory to dwell on—a short, heavenly memory. It consisted of a few words, a kiss—the last one—on her hand, and that passionate murmur which had escaped from his lips when he knelt at her feet:

"Juliette!"

Chapter 19

Complexities

Citizen-Deputy Déroulède had been privately interviewed by the Committee of Public Safety, and temporarily allowed to go free.

The brief proceedings had been quite private, the people of Paris were not to know as yet that their favourite was under a cloud. When he had answered all the question put to him, and Merlin—just returned from his errand at the Luxembourg Prison—had given his version of the domiciliary visitation in the Citizen-Deputy's house, the latter was briefly told that for the moment the Republic had no grievance against him.

But he knew quite well what that meant. He would be henceforth under suspicion, watched incessantly, as a mouse is by the cat, and pounced upon, the moment time would be considered propitious for his final downfall.

The inevitable waning of his popularity would be noted by keen, jealous eyes; and Déroulède, with his sure knowledge of mankind and of character, knew well enough that his popularity was bound to wane sooner or later, as all such ephemeral things do.

In the meanwhile, during the short respite which his enemies would leave him, his one thought and duty would be to get his mother and Anne Mie safely out of the country.

And also—

He thought of *her*, and wondered what had happened. As he walked swiftly across the narrow footbridge, and reached the other side of the river, the events of the past few hours rushed upon his memory with terrible, overwhelming force.

A bitter ache filled his heart at the remembrance of her treachery. The baseness of it all was so appalling. He tried to think if he had ever wronged her; wondered if perhaps she loved someone else and wished *him* out of her way.

But, then, he had been so humble, so unassuming in his love. He had arrogated nothing unto himself, asked for nothing, demanded nothing in virtue of his protecting powers over her.

He was torturing himself with this awful wonderment of why she had treated him thus.

Out of revenge for her brother's death—that was the only explanation he could find, the only palliation for her crime.

He knew nothing of her oath to her father, and, of course, had never heard of the sad history of this young, sensitive girl placed in one terrible moment between her dead brother and her demented father. He only thought of common, sordid revenge for a sin he had been practically forced to commit.

And how he had loved her! Yes, *loved*—for that was in the past now.

She had ceased to be a saint or a Madonna; she had fallen from her pedestal so low that he could not find the way to descend and grope after the fragments of his ideal.

At his own door he was met by Anne Mie in tears.

"She has gone," murmured the young girl. "I feel as if I had murdered her."

"Gone? Who? Where?" queried Déroulède rapidly, an icy feeling of terror gripping him by the heart-strings.

"Juliette has gone," replied Anne Mie; "those awful brutes took her away."

"When?"

"Directly after you left. That man Merlin found some ashes and scraps of paper in her room—"

"Ashes?"

"Yes; and a torn letter-case."

"Great God!"

"She said that they were love letters, which she had been burning for fear you should see them."

"She said so? Anne Mie, Anne Mie, are you quite sure?"

It was all so horrible, and he did not quite understand it all; his brain, which was usually so keen and so active, refused him service at this terrible juncture.

"Yes; I am quite sure," continued Anne Mie, in the midst of her tears. "And oh! that awful Merlin said some dastardly things. But she persisted in her story, that she had—another lover. Oh, Paul, I am sure it is not true. I hated her because—because—you loved her so, and I mistrusted her, but I cannot believe that she was quite as base as that."

"No, no, child," he said in a toneless, miserable voice; "she was not so base as that. Tell me more of what she said."

"She said very little else. But Merlin asked her whether she had denounced you so as to get you out of the way. He hinted that—that—"

"That I was her lover too?"

"Yes," murmured Anne Mie.

She hardly liked to look at him; the strong face had become hard and set in its misery.

"And she allowed them to say all this?" he asked at last.

"Yes. And she followed them without a murmur, as Merlin said she would have to answer before the Committee of Public Safety, for having fooled the representatives of the people."

"She'll answer for it with her life," murmured Déroulède. "And with mine!" he added half audibly.

Anne Mie did not hear him; her pathetic little soul was filled with a great, an overwhelming pity of Juliette and for Paul.

"Before they took her away," she said, placing her thin, delicate-looking hands on his arm. "I ran to her and bade her farewell. The soldiers pushed me roughly aside; but I contrived to kiss her—and then she whispered a few words to me."

"Yes? What were they?"

"'It was an oath,' she said. 'I swore it to my father and to my dead brother. Tell him,'" repeated Anne Mie slowly.

An oath!

Now he understood, and oh! how he pitied her. How terribly she must have suffered in her poor, harassed soul when her noble, upright nature fought against this hideous treachery.

That she was true and brave in herself, of that Déroulède had no doubt. And now this awful sin upon her conscience, which must be causing her endless misery.

And, alas! the atonement would never free her from the load of self-condemnation. She had elected to pay with her life for her treason against him and his family. She would be arraigned before a tribunal which would inevitably condemn her. Oh! the pity of it all!

One moment's passionate emotion, a lifelong superstition and mistaken sense of duty, and now this endless misery, this terrible atonement of a wrong that could never be undone.

And she had never loved him!

That was the true, the only sting which he knew now; it rankled more than her sin, more than her falsehood, more than the shattering of his ideal.

With a passionate desire for his safety, she had sacrificed herself in order to atone for the material evil which she had done.

But there was the wreck of his hopes and of his dreams!

Never until now, when he had irretrievably lost her, did Déroulède realise how great had been his hopes; how he had watched day after day for a look in her eyes, a word from her lips, to show him that she too —his unattainable saint—would one day come to earth, and respond to his love.

And now and then, when her beautiful face lighted up at sight of him, when she smiled a greeting to him on his return from his work, when she looked with pride and admiration on him from the public bench in the assemblies of the Convention—then he had begun to hope, to think, to dream.

And it was all a sham! A mask to hide the terrible conflict that was raging within her soul, nothing more.

She did not love him, of that he felt convinced. Man like, he did not understand to the full that great and wonderful enigma, which has puzzled the world since primeval times: a woman's heart.

The eternal contradictions which go to make up the complex nature of an emotional woman were quite incomprehensible to him. Juliette had betrayed him to serve her own sense of what was just and right, her revenge and her oath. Therefore, she did not love him.

It was logic, sound common-sense, and, aided by his own diffidence where women were concerned, it seemed to him irrefutable.

To a man like Paul Déroulède, a man of thought, of purpose, and of action, the idea of being false to the thing loved, of hate and love being interchangeable, was absolutely foreign and unbelievable. He had never hated the thing he loved or loved the thing he hated. A man's feelings in these respects are so much less complex, so much less contradictory.

Would a man betray his friend? No—never. He might betray his enemy, the creature he abhorred, whose downfall would cause him joy. But his friend? The very idea was repugnant, impossible to an upright nature.

Juliette's ultimate access of generosity in trying to save him, when she was at last brought face to face with the terrible wrong she had committed, *that* he put down to one of those noble impulses of which he knew her soul to be fully capable, and even then, his own diffidence suggested that she did it more for the sake of his mother or for Anne Mie rather than for him.

Therefore, what mattered life to him now? She was lost to him forever, whether he succeeded in snatching her from the guillotine or not. He had but little hope to save her, but he would not owe his life to her.

Anne Mie, seeing him wrapped in his own thoughts, had quietly withdrawn. Her own good sense told her already that Paul Déroulède's first step would be to try and get his mother out of danger, and out of the country, while there was yet time.

So, without waiting for instructions, she began that same evening to pack up her belongings and those of Madame Déroulède.

There was no longer any hatred in her heart against Juliette. Where Paul Déroulède had failed to understand, there Anne Mie had already made a guess. She firmly believed that nothing now could save Juliette from death, and a great feeling of tenderness had crept into her heart, for the woman whom she had looked upon as an enemy and a rival.

She too had learnt in those brief days the great lesson that revenge belongs to God alone.

Chapter 20

The Cheval Borgne

It was close upon midnight.

The place had become suffocatingly hot; the fumes of rank tobacco, of rancid butter, and or raw spirits hung like a vapour in mid-air.

The principal room in the "*Auberge du Cheval Borgne*" had been used for the past five years now as the chief meeting-place of the ultra-*sansculotte* party of the Republic.

The house itself was squalid and dirty, up one of those mean streets which, by their narrow way and shelving buildings, shut out sun, air, and light from their miserable inhabitants.

The Cheval Borgne was one of the most wretched-looking dwellings in this street of evil repute. The plaster was cracked, the walls themselves seemed bulging outward, preparatory to a final collapse. The ceilings were low and supported by beams black with age and dirt.

At one time it had been celebrated for its vast cellarage, which had contained some rare old wines. And in the days of the Grand Monarch young bucks were wont to quit the gay *salons* of the ladies, in order to repair to the Cheval Borgne for a night's carouse.

In those days the vast cellarage was witness of many a dark encounter, of many a mysterious death; could the slimy walls have told their own tale, it would have been one which would have put to shame the wildest chronicles of M. Vidoq.

Now it was no longer so.

Things were done in broad daylight on the *Place de la Révolution*: there was no need for dark, mysterious cellars, in which to accomplish deeds of murder and of revenge.

Rats and vermin of all sorts worked their way now in the underground portion of the building. They ate up each other, and held their orgies in the cellars, whilst men did the same sort of thing in the rooms above.

It was a club of Equality and Fraternity. Any passer-by was at liberty to enter and take part in the debates, his only qualification for this temporary membership being an inordinate love for Madame la Guillotine.

It was from the sordid rooms of the Cheval Borgne that most of the denunciations had gone forth which led but to the one inevitable ending—death.

They sat in conclave here, some two-score or so at first, the rabid patriots of this poor, downtrodden France. They talked of Liberty mostly, with many oaths and curses against the tyrants, and then started a tyranny, an autocracy, ten thousand times more awful than any wielded by the dissolute Bourbons.

And this was the temple of Liberty, this dark, damp, evil-smelling brothel, with is narrow, cracked window-panes, which let in but an infinitesimal fraction of air, and that of the foulest, most unwholesome kind.

The floor was of planks roughly put together; now they were worm-eaten, bare, save for a thick carpet of greasy dust, which deadened the sound of booted feet. The place only boasted of a couple of chairs, both of which had to be propped against the wall lest they should break and bring the sitter down upon the floor; otherwise a number of empty wine barrels did duty for seats, and rough deal boards on broken trestles for tables.

There had once been a paper on the walls, now it hung down in strips, showing the cracked plaster beneath. The whole place had a tone of yellowish-grey grime all over it, save where, in the centre of the room, on a rough double post, shaped like the guillotine, a scarlet cap of Liberty gave a note of lurid colour to the dismal surroundings.

On the walls here and there the eternal device, so sublime in conception, so sordid in execution, recalled the aims of the so-called club: "*Liberté, Fraternité, Egalité, sinon la Mort.*"

Below the device, in one or two corners of the room, the wall was further adorned with rough charcoal sketches, mostly of an obscene character, the work of one of the members of the club, who had chosen this means of degrading his art.

Tonight, the assembly had been reduced to less than a score.

Even according to the dictates of these apostles of Fraternity: "*la guillotine va toujours*"—the guillotine goes on always. She had become the most potent factor in the machinery of government, of this great Revolution, and she had been daily, almost hourly fed through the activity of this nameless club, which held its weird and awesome sittings in the dank coffee-room of the Cheval Borgne.

The number of the active members had been reduced. Like the rats in the cellars below, they had done away with one another, swallowed one another up, torn each other to pieces in this wild rage for a Utopian fraternity.

Marat, founder of the organisation, had been murdered by a girl's hand; but Charon, Manuel, Osselin had gone the usual way, denounced by their colleagues, Rabaut, Custine, Bison, who in their turn were sent to the guillotine by those more powerful, perhaps more eloquent, than themselves.

It was merely a case of who could shout the loudest at an assembly of the National Convention.

"*La guillotine va toujours!*"

After the death of Marat, Merlin became the most prominent member of the club—he and Foucquier-Tinville, his bosom friend, Public Prosecutor, and the most bloodthirsty homicide of this homicidal age.

Bosom friend both, yet they worked against one another, undermining each other's popularity, whispering persistently, one against the other: "He is a traitor!" It had become just a neck-to-neck race between them towards the inevitable goal—the guillotine.

Foucquier-Tinville is in the ascendant for the moment. Merlin had been given a task which he had failed to accomplish. For days now, weeks even, the debates of this noble assembly had been chiefly concerned with the downfall of Citizen-Deputy Déroulède. His popularity, his calm security in the midst of this reign of terror and anarchy, had been a terrible thorn in the flesh of these rabid Jacobins.

And now the climax had been reached. An anonymous denunciation had roused the hopes of these sanguinary patriots. It all sounded perfectly plausible. To try and save that traitor, Marie Antoinette, the widow of Louis Capet, was just the sort of scheme that would originate in the brain of Paul Déroulède.

He had always been at heart an aristocrat, and the feeling of chivalry for a persecuted woman was only the outward signs of his secret adherence to the hated class.

Merlin had been sent to search the Deputy's house for proofs of the latter's guilt.

And Merlin had come back empty-handed.

The arrest of a female *aristo*—the probable mistress of Déroulède, who obviously had denounced him—was but small compensation for the failure of the more important capture.

As soon as Merlin joined his friends in the low, ill-lit, evil-smelling room he realised at once that there was a feeling of hostility against him.

Tinville, enthroned on one of the few chairs of which the Cheval Borgne could boast, was surrounded by a group of surly adherents.

On the rough trestles a number of glasses, half filled with raw potato-spirit, gave the keynote to the temper of the assembly.

All those present were dressed in the black-shag spencer, the seedy black breeches, and down-at-heel boots, which had become recognised as the distinctive uniform of the *sansculotte* party. The inevitable Phrygian cap, with its tricolour cockade, appeared on the heads of all those present, in various stages of dirt and decay.

Tinville had chosen to assume a sarcastic tone with regard to his whilom bosom friend, Merlin. Leaning both elbows on the table, he was picking his teeth with a steel fork, and in the intervals of his interesting operation, gave forth his views on the broad principles of patriotism.

Those who sat round him felt that his star was in the ascendant and assumed the position of satellites. Merlin as he entered had grunted a sullen "Good-eve," and sat himself down in a remote corner of the room.

His greeting had been responded to with a few jeers and a good many dark, threatening looks. Tinville himself had bowed to him with mock sarcasm and an unpleasant leer.

One of the patriots, a huge fellow, almost a giant, with heavy, coarse fists and broad shoulders that obviously suggested coal-heaving, had, after a few satirical observations, dragged one of the empty wine barrels to Merlin's table, and sat down opposite him.

"Take care, Citizen Lenoir," said Tinville, with an evil laugh, "Citizen-Deputy Merlin will arrest you instead of Deputy Déroulède, whom he has allowed to slip through his fingers."

"Nay; I've no fear," replied Lenoir, with an oath. "Citizen Merlin is too much of an *aristo* to hurt anyone; his hands are too clean; he does not care to do the dirty work of the Republic. Isn't that so, Monsieur Merlin?" added the giant, with a mock bow, and emphasising the appellation which had fallen into complete disuse in these days of equality.

"My patriotism is too well known," said Merlin roughly, "to fear any attacks from jealous enemies; and as for my search in the Citizen-Deputy's house this afternoon, I was told to find proofs against him, and I found none."

Lenoir expectorated on the floor, crossed his dark hairy arms over the table, and said quietly:

"Real patriotism, as the true Jacobin understands it, makes the proofs it wants and leaves nothing to chance."

A chorus of hoarse murmurs of "*Vive la Liberté*!" greeted this harangue of the burly coal-heaver.

Feeling that he had gained the ear and approval of the gallery, Lenoir seemed, as it were, to spread himself out, to arrogate to himself the leadership of this band of malcontents, who, disappointed in their lust of Déroulède's downfall, were ready to exult over that of Merlin.

"You were a fool, Citizen Merlin," said Lenoir with slow significance, "not to see that the woman was playing her own game."

Merlin had become livid under the grime on his face. With this ill-kempt *sansculotte* giant in front of him, he almost felt as if he were already arraigned before that awful, merciless tribunal, to which he had dragged so many innocent victims.

Already he felt, as he sat ensconced behind a table in the far corner of the room, that he was a prisoner at the bar, answering for his failure with his life.

His own laws, his own theories now stood in bloody array against him. Was it not he who had framed the indictments against General Custine for having failed to subdue the cities of the south? against General Westerman and Brunet and Beauharnais for having failed and failed and failed?

And now it was his turn.

These bloodthirsty jackals had been cheated of their prey; they would tear him to pieces in compensation of their loss.

"How could I tell?" he murmured roughly, "the woman had denounced him."

A chorus of angry derision greeted this feeble attempt at defence.

"By your own law, Citizen-Deputy Merlin," commented Tinville sarcastically, "it is a crime against the Republic to be suspected of treason. It is evident, however, that it is quite one thing to frame a law and quite another to obey it."

"What could I have done?"

"Hark at the innocent!" rejoined Lenoir, with a sneer. "What could he have done? Patriots, friends, brothers, I ask you, what could he have done?"

The giant had pushed the wine cask aside, it rolled away from under him, and in the fulness of his contempt for Merlin and his impotence, he stood up before them all, strong in his indictment against treasonable incapacity.

"I ask you," he repeated, with a loud oath, "what any patriot would do, what you or I would have done, in the house of a man whom we all *know* is a traitor to the Republic? Brothers, friends, Citizen-Deputy Merlin found a heap of burn paper in a grate, he found a letter-case which had obviously contained important documents, and he asks us what he could do!"

"Déroulède is too important a man to be tried without proofs. The whole mob of Paris would have turned on us for having arraigned him, for having dared lay hands upon his sacred person."

"Without proofs? Who said there were no proofs?" queried Lenoir.

"I found the burnt papers and torn letter-case in the woman's room. She owned that they were love letters, and that she had denounced Déroulède in order to be rid of him."

"Then let me tell you, Citizen-Deputy Merlin, that a true patriot would have found those papers in Déroulède's, and not the woman's room; that in the hands of a faithful servant of the Republic those documents would not all have been destroyed, for he would have 'found' one letter addressed to the Widow Capet, which would have proved conclusively that Citizen-Deputy Déroulède was a traitor. That is what a true patriot would have done—what I would have done. *Pardi!* since Déroulède is so important a personage, since we must all put on kid gloves when we lay hands upon him, then let us fight him with other weapons. Are we aristocrats that we should hesitate to play the part of jackal to this cunning fox? Citizen-Deputy Merlin, are you the son of some *ci-devant* duke or prince that you dared not *forge* a document which would bring a traitor to his doom? Nay; let me tell you, friends, that the Republic has no use for curs, and calls him a traitor who allows one of her enemies to remain inviolate through his cowardice, his terror of that intangible and fleeting shadow—the wrath of a Paris mob."

Thunderous applause greeted this peroration, which had been delivered with an accompaniment of violent gesture and a wealth of obscene epithets, quite beyond the power of the mere chronicler to render. Lenoir had a harsh, strident voice, very high pitched, and he spoke with a broad, provincial accent, somewhat difficult to locate, but quite unlike the hoarse, guttural tones of the low-class Parisian. His enthusiasm made him seem impressive. He looked, in his ragged, dust-stained clothes, the very personification of the squalid herd which had driven culture, art, refinement to the scaffold in order to make way for sordid vice, and satisfied lusts of hate.

Chapter 21

A Jacobin Orator

Tinville alone had remained silent during Lenoir's impassioned speech. It seemed to be his turn now to become surly. He sat picking his teeth, and staring moodily at the enthusiastic orator, who had so obviously diverted popular feeling in his own direction. And Tinville brooked popularity only for himself.

"It is easy to talk now, Citizen—er—Lenoir. Is that your name? Well, you are a comparative stranger here, Citizen Lenoir, and have not yet proved to the Republic that you can do ought else but talk."

"If somebody did not talk, Citizen Tinville—is that your name?" rejoined Lenoir, with a sneer—"if somebody didn't talk, nothing would get done. You all sit here, and condemn the Citizen-Deputy Merlin for being a fool, and I must say I am with you there, but—"

"*Pardi!* tell us your 'but' citizen," said Tinville, for the coal-heaver had paused, as if trying to collect his thoughts. He had dragged a wine barrel to collect his thoughts. He had dragged a wine barrel close to the trestle table, and now sat astride upon it, facing Tinville and the group of Jacobins. The flickering tallow candle behind him threw into bold silhouette his square, massive head, crowned with its Phrygian cap, and the great breadth of his shoulders, with the shabby knitted spencer and low, turned-down collar.

He had long, thin hands, which were covered with successive coats of coal dust, and with these he constantly made weird gestures, as if in the act of gripping some live thing by the throat.

"We all know that the Deputy Déroulède is a traitor, eh?" he said, addressing the company in general.

"We do," came with uniform assent from all those present.

"Then let us put it to the vote. The Ayes mean death, the Noes freedom."

"Ay, ay!" came from every hoarse, parched throat; and twelve gaunt hand were lifted up demanding death for Citizen-Deputy Déroulède.

"The Ayes have it," said Lenoir quietly, "Now all we need do is to decide how best to carry out our purpose."

Merlin, very agreeable surprised to see public attention thus diverted from his own misdeeds, had gradually lost his surly attitude. He too dragged one of the wine barrels, which did duty for chairs, close to the trestle table, and thus the members of the nameless Jacobin club made a compact group, picturesque in its weird horror, its uncompromising, flaunting ugliness.

"I suppose," said Tinville, who was loth to give up his position as leader of these extremists—"I suppose, Citizen Lenoir, that you are in position to furnish me with proofs of the Citizen-Deputy's guilt?"

"If I furnish you with such proofs, Citizen Tinville," retorted the other, "will you, as Public Prosecutor, carry the indictment through?"

"It is my duty to publicly accuse those who are traitors to the Republic."

"And you, Citizen Merlin," queried Lenoir, "will you help the Republic to the best of your ability to be rid of a traitor?"

"My services to the cause of our great Revolution are too well known—" began Merlin.

But Lenoir interrupted him with impatience.

"*Pardi!* but we'll have no rhetoric now, Citizen Merlin. We all know that you have blundered, and that the Republic cares little for those of her sons who have failed, but whilst you are still Minister of Justice the people of France have need of you—for bringing *other* traitors to the guillotine."

He spoke this last phrase slowly and significantly, lingering on the word "other," as if he wished its whole awesome meaning to penetrate well into Merlin's brain.

"What is your advice then, Citizen Lenoir?"

Apparently, by unanimous consent, the coalheaver, from some obscure province of France, had been tacitly acknowledged the leader of the band. Merlin, still in terror for himself, looked to him for advice; even Tinville was ready to be guided by him. All were at one in their desire to rid themselves of Déroulède, who by his clean living, his aloofness from their own hideous orgies and deadly hates, seemed a living reproach to them all; and they all felt that in Lenoir there must exist some secret dislike of the popular Citizen-Deputy, which would give him a clear insight of how best to bring about his downfall.

"What is your advice?" had been Merlin's query, and everyone there listened eagerly for what was to come.

"We are all agreed," commenced Lenoir quietly, "that just at this moment it would be unwise to arraign the Citizen-Deputy without material proof. The mob of Paris worship him and would turn against those who had tried to dethrone their idol. Now, Citizen Merlin failed to furnish us with proofs of Déroulède's guilt. For the moment he is a free man, and I imagine a wise one; within two days he will have quitted this country, well knowing that, if he stayed long enough to see his popularity wane, he would also outstay his welcome on earth altogether."

"Ay! Ay! said some of the men approvingly, whilst others laughed hoarsely at the weird jest.

"I propose, therefore," continued Lenoir after a slight pause, "that it shall be Citizen-Deputy Déroulède himself who shall furnish to the people of France proofs of his own treason against the Republic."

"But how? But how?" rapid, loud and excited queries greeted this extraordinary suggestion from the provincial giant.

"By the simplest means imaginable," retorted Lenoir with imperturbable calm. "Isn't there a good proverb which our grandmothers used to quote, that if you only give a man a sufficient length of rope, he is sure to hang himself? We'll give our aristocratic Citizen-Deputy plenty of rope, I'll warrant, if only our present Minister of Justice," he added, indicating Merlin, "will help us in the little comedy which I propose that we should play."

"Yes! Yes! Go on!" said Merlin excitedly.

"The woman who denounced Déroulède—that is our trump card," continued Lenoir, now waxing enthusiastic with his own scheme and his own eloquence. "She denounced him. Ergo, he had been her lover, whom she wished to be rid of—why? Not, as Citizen Merlin supposed, because he had discarded her. No, no; she had another lover—she has admitted that. She wished to be rid of Déroulède to make way for the other, because he was too persistent—ergo, because he loved her."

"Well, and what does that prove?" queried Tinville with dry sarcasm.

"It proves that Déroulède, being in love with the woman, would do much to save her from the guillotine."

"Of course."

"*Pardi!* let him try, say I," rejoined Lenoir placidly. "Give him the rope with which to hang himself."

"What does he mean?" asked one or two of the men, whose dull brains had not quite as yet grasped the full meaning of this monstrous scheme.

"You don't understand what I mean, citizens; you think I am mad, or drunk, or a traitor like Déroulède? *Eh bien!* give me your attention five minutes longer, and you shall see. Let me suppose that we have reached the moment when the woman—what is her name? Oh! ah! yes! Juliette Marny—stands in the Hall of Justice on her trial before the Committee of Public Safety. Citizen Foucquier-Tinville, one of our greatest patriots, reads the indictment against her: the papers surreptitiously burnt, the torn, mysterious letter-case found in her room. If these are presumed, in the indictment, to be treasonable correspondence with the enemies of the Republic, condemnation follows at once, then the guillotine. There is no defence, no respite.

"The Minister of Justice, according to Article IX of the Law framed by himself, allows no advocate to those directly accused of treason. But," continued the giant, with slow and calm impressiveness, "in the case of ordinary, civil indictments, offences against public morality or matters pertaining to the penal code, the Minister of Justice allows the accused to be publicly defended. Place Juliette Marny in the dock on a treasonable charge, she will be hustled out of the court in a few minutes, amongst a batch of other traitors, dragged back to her own prison, and executed in the early dawn, before Déroulède has had time to frame a plan for her safety or defence. If, then, he tries to move heaven and earth to rescue the woman he loves, the mob of Paris may,—who knows?—take his part warmly.

"They are mad where Déroulède is concerned; and we all know that two devoted lovers have ere now found favour with the people of France—a curious remnant of sentimentalism, I suppose—and the popular Citizen-Deputy knows better than anyone else on earth, how to play upon the sentimental feelings of the populace. Now, in the case of a penal offence, mark where the difference would be! The woman Juliette Marny, arraigned for wantonness, for an offence against public morals; the burnt correspondence, admitted to be the letters of a lover—her hatred for Déroulède suggesting the false denunciation. Then the Minister of Justice allows an advocate to defend her. She has none in court; but think you Déroulède would not step forward, and bring all the fervour of his eloquence to bear in favour of his mistress?

"Can you hear his impassioned speech on her behalf?—I can—the rope, I tell you, citizens, with which he'll hang himself. Will he admit in open court that the burnt correspondence was another lover's letters? No!—a thousand times no!—and, in the face of his emphatic denial of the existence of another lover for Juliette, it will be for our clever Public Prosecutor to bring him down to an admission that the correspondence was his, that it was treasonable, that she burnt them to save him."

He paused, exhausted at last, mopping his forehead, then drinking large gulps of brandy to ease his parched throat.

A veritable chorus of enthusiasm greeted the end of his long peroration. The Machiavellian scheme, almost devilish in its cunning, in its subtle knowledge of human nature and of the heart-strings of a noble organisation like Déroulède's, commended itself to these patriots, who were thirsting for the downfall of a superior enemy.

Even Tinville lost his attitude of dry sarcasm; his thin cheeks were glowing with the lust of the fight.

Already for the past few months, the trials before the Committee of Public Safety had been dull, monotonous, uninteresting. Charlotte Corday had been a happy diversion, but otherwise it had been the case of various deputies, who had held views that had become too moderate, or of the generals who had failed to subdue the towns or provinces of the south.

But now this trial on the morrow—the excitement of it all, the trap laid for Déroulède, the pleasure of seeing him take the first step towards his own downfall. Everyone there was eager and enthusiastic for the fray. Lenoir, having spoken at such length, had now become silent, but everyone else talked, and drank brandy, and hugged his own hate and likely triumph.

For several hours, far into the night, the sitting was continued. Each one of the score of members had some comment to make on Lenoir's speech, some suggestion to offer.

Lenoir himself was the first to break up this weird gathering of human jackals, already exulting over their prey. He bad his companions a quiet goodnight, then passed out into the dark street.

After he had gone there were a few seconds of complete silence in the dark and sordid room, where men's ugliest passions were holding absolute sway. The giant's heavy footsteps echoed along the ill-paved street, and gradually died away in the distance.

Then at last Foucquier-Tinville, the Public Prosecutor, spoke:

"And who is that man?" he asked, addressing the assembly of patriots.

Most of them did not know.

"A provincial from the north," said one of the men at last; "he has been here several times before now, and last year he was a fairly constant attendant. I believe he is a butcher by trade, and I fancy he comes from Calais. He was originally brought here by Citizen Brogard, who is good patriot enough."

One by one the members of this bond of Fraternity began to file out of the Cheval Borgne. They nodded curt goodnights to each other, and then went to their respective abodes, which surely could not be dignified with the name of home.

Tinville remained one of the last; he and Merlin seemed suddenly to have buried the hatchet, which a few hours ago had threatened to destroy one of the other of these whilom bosom friends.

Two or three of the most ardent of these ardent extremists had gathered round the Public Prosecutor, and Merlin, the framer of the Law of the Suspect.

"What say you, citizens?" said Tinville at last quietly. "That man Lenoir, me seems, is too eloquent—eh?"

"Dangerous," pronounced Merlin, whilst the others nodded approval.

"But his scheme is good," suggested one of the men.

"And we'll avail ourselves of it," assented Tinville, "but afterwards—"

He paused, and once more everyone nodded approval.

"Yes; he is dangerous. We'll leave him in peace tomorrow, but afterwards—"

With a gentle hand Tinville caressed the tall double post, which stood in the centre of the room, and which was shaped like the guillotine. An evil look was on his face: the grin of a death-dealing monster, savage and envious. The others laughed in grim content. Merlin grunted a surly approval. He had no cause to love the provincial coal-heaver who had raised a raucous voice to threaten him.

Then, nodding to one another, the last of the patriots, satisfied with this night's work, passed out into the night.

The watchman was making his rounds, carrying his lantern, and shouting his customary cry:

"Inhabitants of Paris, sleep quietly. Everything is in order, everything is at peace."

Chapter 22

The Close of Day

Déroulède had spent the whole of this same night in a wild, impassioned search for Juliette.

Earlier in the day, soon after Anne Mie's revelations, he had sought out his English friend, Sir Percy Blakeney, and talked over with him the final arrangements for the removal of Madame Déroulède and Anne Mie from Paris.

Though he was a born idealist and a Utopian, Paul Déroulède had never for a moment had any illusions with regard to his own popularity. He knew that at any time, and for any trivial cause, the love which the mob bore him would readily turn to hate. He had seen Mirabeau's popularity wane, La Fayette's, Desmoulin's—was it likely that *he* alone would survive the inevitable death of so ephemeral a thing?

Therefore, whilst he was in power, whilst he was loved and trusted, he had, figuratively and actually, put his house in order. He had made full preparations for his own inevitable downfall, for that probable flight from Paris of those who were dependent upon him.

He had, as far back as a year ago, provided himself with the necessary passports, and bespoken with his English friend certain measures for the safety of his mother and his crippled little relative. Now it was merely a question of putting these measures into execution.

Within two hours of Juliette Marny's arrest, Madame Déroulède and Anne Mie had quitted the house in the Rue Ecole de Médecine. They had but little luggage with them and were ostensibly going into the country to visit a sick cousin.

The mother of the popular Citizen-Deputy was free to travel unmolested. The necessary passports which the safety of the Republic demanded were all in perfect order, and Madame Déroulède and Anne Mie passed through the north gate of Paris an hour before sunset, on that 24th day of *Fructidor*.

Their large travelling chaise took them some distance on the North Road, where they were to meet Lord Hastings and Lord Anthony Dewhurst, two of the Scarlet Pimpernel's most trusted lieutenants, who were to escort them as far as the coast, and thence see them safely aboard the English yacht.

On that score, therefore, Déroulède had no anxiety. His chief duty was to his mother and to Anne Mie, and that was now fully discharged.

Then there was old Pétronelle.

Ever since the arrest of her young mistress the poor old soul had been in a state of mind bordering on frenzy, and no amount of eloquence on Déroulède's part would persuade her to quit Paris without Juliette.

"If my pet lamb is to die," she said amidst heartbroken sobs, "then I have no cause to live. Let those devils take me along too, if they want a useless, old woman like me. But if my darling is allowed to go free, then what would become of her in this awful city without me? She and I have never been separated; she wouldn't know where to turn for a home. And who would cook for her and iron out her kerchiefs, I'd like to know?"

Reason and common sense were, of course, powerless in face of this sublime and heroic childishness. No one had the heart to tell the old woman that the murderous dog of the Revolution seldom loosened its fangs, once they had closed upon a victim.

All Déroulède could do was to convey Pétronelle to the old abode, which Juliette had quitted in order to come to him, and which had never been formally given up. The worthy soul, calmed and refreshed, deluded herself into the idea that she was waiting for the return of her young mistress, and became quite cheerful at sight of the familiar room.

Déroulède had provided her with money and necessaries. He had but few remaining hopes in his heart, but among them was the firmly implanted one that Pétronelle was too insignificant to draw upon herself the terrible attention of the Committee of Public Safety.

By the nightfall he had seen the good woman safely installed. Then only did he feel free.

At last he could devote himself to what seemed to him the one, the only, aim of his life—to find Juliette.

A dozen prisons in this vast Paris!

Over five thousand prisoners on that night, awaiting trial, condemnation and death.

Déroulède at first, strong in his own power, his personality, had thought that the task would be comparatively easy.

At the Palais de Justice they would tell him nothing: the list of new arrests had not yet been handled in by the commandant of Paris, Citizen Santerre, who classified and docketed the miserable herd of aspirants for the next day's guillotine.

The lists, moreover, would not be completed until the next day, when the trials of the new prisoners would already be imminent.

The work of the Committee of Public Safety was done without much delay.

Then began Déroulède's weary quest through those twelve prisons of Paris. From the Temple to the Conciergerie, from Palais Condé to the Luxembourg, he spent hours in the fruitless search.

Everywhere the same shrug of the shoulders, the same indifferent reply to his eager query:

"Juliette Marny? *Inconnue*."

Unknown! She had not yet been docketed, not yet classified; she was still one of that immense flock of cattle, sent in ever-increasing numbers to the slaughter-house.

Presently, tomorrow, after a trial which might last ten minutes, after a hasty condemnation and quick return to prison, she would be listed as one of the traitors, whom this great and beneficent Republic sent daily to the guillotine.

Vainly did Déroulède try to persuade, to entreat, to bribe. The sullen guardians of these twelve charnel-houses knew nothing of individual prisoners.

But the Citizen-Deputy was allowed to look for himself. He was conducted to the great vaulted rooms of the Temple, to the vast ballrooms of the Palais Condé, where herded the condemned and those still awaiting trial; he was allowed to witness there the grim farcical tragedies, with which the captives beguiled the few hours which separated them from death.

Mock trials were acted there; Tinville was mimicked; then the *Place de la Révolution*; Samson the headsman, with a couple of inverted chairs to represent the guillotine.

Daughters of dukes and princes, descendants of ancient lineage, acted in these weird and ghastly comedies. The ladies, with hair bound high over their heads, would kneel before the inverted chairs, and place the snow-white necks beneath this imaginary guillotine. Speeches were delivered to a mock populace, whilst a mock Santerre ordered a mock roll of drums to drown the last flow of eloquence of the supposed victim.

Oh! the horror of it all—the pity, pathos, and misery of this ghastly parody, in the very face of the sublimity of death!

Déroulède shuddered when first he beheld the scene, shuddered at the very thought of finding Juliette amongst these careless, laughing, thoughtless mimes.

His own, his beautiful Juliette, with her proud face and majestic, queen-like gestures; it was a relief not to see her there.

"Juliette Marny? *Inconnue*," was the final word he heard about her.

No one told him that by Deputy Merlin's strictest orders she had been labelled "dangerous", and placed in a remote wing of the Luxembourg Palace, together with a few, who, like herself, were allowed to see no one, communicate with no one.

Then when the *couvre-feu* had sounded, when all public places were closed, when the night watchman had begun his rounds, Déroulède knew that his quest for that night must remain fruitless.

But he could not rest. In and out the tortuous streets of Paris he roamed during the better part of that night. He was now only awaiting the dawn to publicly demand the right to stand beside Juliette.

A hopeless misery was in his heart, a longing for a cessation of life; only one thing kept his brain active, his mind clear: the hope of saving Juliette.

The dawn was breaking in the far east when, wandering along the banks of the river, he suddenly felt a touch on his arm.

"Come to my hovel," said a pleasant, lazy voice close to his ear, whilst a kindly hand seemed to drag him away from the contemplation of the dark, silent river. "And a demmed, beastly place it is too, but at least we can talk quietly there."

Déroulède, roused from his meditation, looked up, to see his friend, Sir Percy Blakeney, standing close beside him. Tall, *débonnair*, well-dressed, he seemed by his very presence to dissipate the morbid atmosphere which was beginning to weigh upon Déroulède's active mind.

Déroulède followed him readily enough through, the intricate mazes of old Paris, and down the Rue des Arts, until Sir Percy stopped outside a small hostelry, the door of which stood wide open.

"Mine host has nothing to lose from footpads and thieves," explained the Englishman as he guided his friend through the narrow doorway, then up a flight of rickety stairs, to a small room on the floor above. "He leaves all doors open for anyone to walk in, but, *la!* the interior of the house looks so uninviting that no one is tempted to enter."

"I wonder you care to stay here," remarked Déroulède, with a momentary smile, as he contrasted in his mind the fastidious appearance of his friend with the dinginess and dirt of these surroundings.

Sir Percy deposited his large person in the capacious depths of a creaky chair, stretched his long limbs out before him, and said quietly:

"I am only staying in this demmed hole until the moment when I can drag you out of this murderous city."

Déroulède shook his head.

"You'd best go back to England, then," he said, "for I'll never leave Paris now."

"Not without Juliette Marny, shall we say?" rejoined Sir Percy placidly.

"And I fear me that she has placed herself beyond our reach," said Déroulède sombrely.

"You know that she is in the Luxembourg Prison?" queried the Englishman suddenly.

"I guessed it but could find no proof."

"And that she will be tried tomorrow?"

"They never keep a prisoner pining too long," replied Déroulède bitterly. "I guessed that too."

"What do you mean to do?"

"Defend her with the last breath in my body."

"You love her still, then?" asked Blakeney, with a smile.

"Still?" The look, the accent, the agony of a hopeless passion conveyed in that one word, told Sir Percy Blakeney all that he wished to know.

"Yet she betrayed you," he said tentatively.

"And to atone for that sin—an oath, mind you, friend, sworn to her father—she is already to give her life for me."

"And you are prepared to forgive?"

"To understand *is* to forgive," rejoined Déroulède simply, "and I love her."

"Your Madonna!" said Blakeney, with a gently ironical smile.

"No; the woman I love, with all her weaknesses, all her sins; the woman to gain whom I would give my soul, to save whom I will give my life."

"And she?"

"She does not love me—would she have betrayed me else?"

He sat beside the table and buried his head in his hands. Not even his dearest friend should see how much he had suffered, how deeply his love had been wounded.

Sir Percy said nothing, a curious, pleasant smile lurked round the corners of his mobile mouth. Through his mind there flitted the vision of beautiful Marguerite, who had so much loved yet so deeply wronged him, and, looking at his friend, he thought that Déroulède too would soon learn all the contradictions, which wage a constant war in the innermost recesses of a feminine heart.

He made a movement as if he would say something more, something of grave import, then seemed to think better of it, and shrugged his broad shoulders, as if to say:

"Let time and chance take their course now."

When Déroulède looked up again Sir Percy was sitting placidly in the arm-chair, with an absolutely blank expression on his face.

"Now that you know how much I love her, my friend," said Déroulède as soon as he had mastered his emotions, "will you look after her when they have condemned me, and save her for my sake?"

A curious, enigmatic smile suddenly illumined Sir Percy's earnest countenance.

"Save her? Do you attribute supernatural powers to me, then, or to The League of the Scarlet Pimpernel?"

"To you, I think," rejoined Déroulède seriously.

Once more it seemed as if Sir Percy were about to reveal something of great importance to his friend, then once more he checked himself. The Scarlet Pimpernel was, above all, far-seeing and practical, a man of action and not of impulse. The glowing eyes of his friend, his nervous, febrile movements, did not suggest that he was in a fit state to be entrusted with plans, the success of which hung on a mere thread.

Therefore, Sir Percy only smiled, and said quietly:

"Well, I'll do my best."

Chapter 23

Justice

The day had been an unusually busy one.

Five and thirty prisoners, arraigned before the bar of the Committee of Public Safety, had been tried in the last eight hours—an average of rather more than four to the hour; twelve minutes and a half in which to send a human creature, full of life and health, to solve the great enigma which lies hidden beyond the waters of the Styx.

And Citizen-Deputy Foucquier-Tinville, the Public Prosecutor, had surpassed himself. He seemed indefatigable.

Each of these five and thirty prisoners had been arraigned for treason against the Republic, for conspiracy with her enemies, and all had to have irrefutable proofs of their guilt brought before the Committee of Public Safety. Sometimes a few letters, written to friends abroad, and seized at the frontier; a word of condemnation of the measures of the extremists; and expression of horror at the massacres on the *Place de la Révolution*, where the guillotine creaked incessantly—these were irrefutable proofs; or else perhaps a couple of pistols, or an old family sword seized in the house of a peaceful citizen, would be brought against a prisoner, as an irrefutable proof of his warlike dispositions against the Republic.

Oh! it was not difficult!

Out of five and thirty indictments, Foucquier-Tinville had obtained thirty convictions.

No wonder his friends declared that he had surpassed himself. It had indeed been a glorious day, and the glow of satisfaction as much as the heat, caused the Public Prosecutors to mop his high, bony cranium before he had adjourned for the much-needed respite for refreshment.

The day's work was not yet done.

The "politicals" had been disposed of, and there had been such an accumulation of them recently that it was difficult to keep pace with the arrests.

And in the meanwhile, the criminal record of the great city had not diminished. Because men butchered one another in the name of Equality, there were none the fewer among the Fraternity of thieves and petty pilferers, of ordinary cut-throats and public wantons.

And these too had to be dealt with by law. The guillotine was impartial, and fell with equal velocity on the neck of the proud duke and the gutter-born *fille de joie*, on a descendant of the Bourbons and the wastrel born in a brothel.

The ministerial decrees favoured the proletariat. A crime against the Republic was indefensible, but one against the individual was dealt with, with all the paraphernalia of an elaborate administration of justice. There were citizen judges and citizen advocates, and the rabble, who crowded in to listen to the trials, acted as honorary jury.

It was all thoroughly well done. The citizen criminals were given every chance.

The afternoon of this hot August day, one of the last of glorious *Fructidor*, had begun to wane, and the shades of evening to slowly creep into the long, bare room where this travesty of justice was being administered.

The Citizen-President sat at the extreme end of the room, on a rough wooden bench, with a desk in front of him littered with papers.

Just above him, on the bare, whitewashed wall, the words: "*La République: une et indivisible*," and below them the device: "*Liberté, Egalité, Fraternité!*"

To the right and left of the Citizen-President, four clerks were busy making entries in that ponderous ledger, that amazing record of the foulest crimes the world has ever known, the *Bulletin du Tribunal Révolutionnaire.*

At present no one is speaking, and the grating of the clerks' quill pens against the paper is the only sound which disturbs the silence of the hall.

In front of the President, on a bench lower than his, sits Citizen Foucquier-Tinville, rested and refreshed, ready to take up his occupation, for as many hours as his country demands it of him.

On every desk a tallow candle, smoking and spluttering, throws a weird light, and more weird shadows, on the faces of clerks and President, on blank walls and ominous devices.

In the centre of the room a platform surrounded by an iron railing is ready for the accused. Just in front of it, from the tall, raftered ceiling above, there hangs a small brass lamp, with a green *abat-jour.*

Each side of the long, whitewashed walls there are three rows of benches, beautiful old carved oak pews, snatched from Nôtre Dame and from the Churches of St Eustache and St Germain l'Auxerrois. Instead of the pious worshippers of mediaeval times, they now accommodate the lookers-on of the grim spectacle of unfortunates, in their brief halt before the scaffold.

The front row of these benches is reserved for those citizen-deputies who desire to be present at the debates of the Tribunal Révolutonnaire. It is their privilege, almost their duty, as representatives of the people, to see that the sittings are properly conducted.

These benches are already well filled. At one end, on the left, Citizen Merlin, Minister of Justice, sits; next to him Citizen-Minister Lebrun; also, Citizen Robespierre, still in the height of his ascendancy, and watching the proceedings with those pale, watery eyes of his and that curious, disdainful smile, which have earned for him the nickname of "the sea-green incorruptible."

Other well-known faces are there also, dimly outlined in the fast-gathering gloom. But everyone notes Citizen-Deputy Déroulède, the idol of the people, as he sits on the extreme end of a bench on the right, with arms tightly folded across his chest, the light from the hanging lamp falling straight on his dark head and proud, straight brows, with the large, restless, eager eyes.

Anon the Citizen-President rings a hand-bell, and there is a discordant noise of hoarse laughter and loud curses, some pushing, jolting, and swearing, as the general public is admitted into the hall.

Heaven save us! What a rabble! Has humanity really such a scum?

Women with a single ragged kirtle and shift, through the interstices of which the naked, grime-covered flesh shows shamelessly: with bare legs, and feet thrust into heavy sabots, hair dishevelled, and evil, spirit-sodden faces: women without a semblance of womanhood, with shrivelled, barren breasts, and dry, parched lips, that have never known how to kiss. Women without emotion save that of hate, without desire, save for the satisfaction of hunger and thirst, and lust for revenge against their sisters less wretched, less unsexed than themselves. They crowd in, jostling one another, swarming into the front rows of the benches, where they can get a better view of the miserable victims about to be pilloried before them.

And the men without a semblance of manhood. Bent under the heavy care of their own degradation, dead to pity, to love, to chivalry; dead to all save an inordinate longing for the sight of blood.

And God help them all! for there were the children too. Children—save the mark!—with pallid, precocious little faces, pinched with the ravages of starvation, gazing with dim, filmy eyes on this world of rapacity and hideousness. Children who have seen death!

Oh, the horror of it! Not beautiful, peaceful death, a slumber or a dream, a loved parent or fond sister or brother lying all in white amidst a wealth of flowers, but death in its most awesome aspect, violent, lurid, horrible.

And now they stare around them with eager, greedy eyes, awaiting the amusement of the spectacle; gazing at the President, with his tall Phrygian cap; at the clerks wielding their indefatigable quill pens, writing, writing, writing; at the flickering lights, throwing clouds of sooty smoke, up to the dark ceiling above.

Then suddenly the eyes of one little mite—a poor, tiny midget not yet in her teens—alight on Paul Déroulède's face, on the opposite side of the rooms.

"*Tiens!* Papa Déroulède!" she says, pointing an attenuated little finger across at him, and turning eagerly to those around her, her eyes dilating in wishful recollection of a happy afternoon spent in Papa Déroulède's house, with fine white bread to eat in plenty, and great jars of foaming milk.

He rouses himself from his apathy, and his great earnest eyes lose their look of agonised misery, as he responds to the greeting of the little one.

For one moment—oh! a mere fraction of a second—the squalid faces, the miserable, starved expressions of the crowd, soften at sight of him. There is a faint murmur among the women, which perhaps God's recording angel registered as a blessing. Who knows?

Foucquier-Tinville suppresses a sneer, and the Citizen-President impatiently rings his hand-bell again.

"Bring forth the accused!" he commands in stentorian tones.

There is a movement of satisfaction among the crowd, and the angel of God is forced to hide his face again.

Chapter 24

The Trial of Juliette

It is all indelibly placed on record in the *Bulletin du Tribunal Révolutionnaire*, under date 25th *Fructidor*, year 1 of the Revolution.

Anyone who cares may read, for the *Bulletin* is in the Archives of the *Bibliothèque Nationale* of Paris.

One by one the accused had been brought forth, escorted by two men of the National Guard in ragged, stained uniforms of red, white, and blue; they were then conducted to the small raised platform in the centre of the hall, and made to listen to the charge brought against them by Citizen Foucquier-Tinville, the Public Prosecutor.

They were petty charges mostly: pilfering, fraud, theft, occasionally arson or manslaughter. One man, however, was arraigned for murder with highway robbery, and a woman for the most ignoble traffic, which evil feminine ingenuity could invent.

These two were condemned to the guillotine, the others sent to the galleys at Brest or Toulon—the forger along with the petty thief, the housebreaker with the absconding clerk.

There was no room in the prison for ordinary offences against the criminal code; they were overfilled already with so-called traitors against the Republic.

Three women were sent to the penitentiary at the Salpêtriere and were dragged out of the court shrilly protesting their innocence, and followed by obscene jeers from the spectators on the benches.

Then there was a momentary hush.

Juliette Marny had been brought in.

She was quite calm, and exquisitely beautiful, dressed in a plain grey bodice and kirtle, with a black band round her slim waist and a soft white kerchief folded across her bosom. Beneath the tiny, white cap her golden hair appeared in dainty, curly profusion; her child-like, oval face was very white, but otherwise quite serene.

She seemed absolutely unconscious of her surroundings and walked with a firm step up to the platform, looking neither to the right nor to the left of her.

Therefore, she did not see Déroulède. A great, a wonderful radiance seemed to shine in her large eyes—the radiance of self-sacrifice.

She was offering not only her life, but everything a woman of refinement holds most dear, for the safety of the man she loved.

A feeling that was almost physical pain, so intense was it, overcame Déroulède, when at last he heard her name loudly called by the Public Prosecutor.

All day he had waited for this awful moment, forgetting his own misery, his own agonised feeling of an irretrievable loss, in the horrible thought of what *she* would endure, what *she* would think, when first she realised the terrible indignity, which was to be put upon her.

Yet for the sake of her, of her chances of safety and of ultimate freedom, it was undoubtedly best that it should be so.

Arraigned for conspiracy against the Republic, she was liable to secret trial, to be brought up, condemned, and executed before he could even hear of her whereabouts, before he could throw himself before her judges and take all guilt upon himself.

Those suspected of treason against the Republic forfeited, according to Merlin's most iniquitous Law, their rights of citizenship, in publicity of trial and in defence.

It all might have been finished before Déroulède knew anything of it.

The other way was, of course, more terrible. Brought forth amongst the scum of criminal Paris, on a charge, the horror of which, he could but dimly hope that she was too innocent to fully understand, he dared not even think of what she would suffer.

But undoubtedly it was better so.

The mud thrown at her robes of purity could never cling to her, and at least her trial would be public; he would be there to take all infamy, all disgrace, all opprobrium on himself.

The strength of his appeal would turn her judges' wrath from her to him; and after these few moments of misery, she would be free to leave Paris, France, to be happy, and to forget him and the memory of him.

An overwhelming, all-compelling love filled his entire soul for the beautiful girl, who had so wronged, yet so nobly tried to save him. A longing for her made his very sinews ache; she was no longer Madonna, and her beauty thrilled him, with the passionate, almost sensuous desire to give his life for her.

The indictment against Juliette Marny has become history now.

On that day, the 25th *Fructidor*, at seven o'clock in the evening, it was read out by the Public Prosecutor, and listened to by the accused —so the *Bulletin* tells us—with complete calm and apparent indifference. She stood up in that same pillory where once stood poor, guilty Charlotte Corday, where presently would stand proud, guiltless Marie Antoinette.

And Déroulède listened to the scurrilous document, with all the outward calm his strength of will could command. He would have liked to rise from his seat then and there, at once, and in mad, purely animal fury have, with a blow of his fist, quashed the words in Foucquier-Tinville's lying throat.

But for her sake he was bound to listen, and, above all, to act quietly, deliberately, according to form and procedure, so as in no way to imperil her cause.

Therefore, he listened whilst the Public Prosecutor spoke.

"Juliette Marny, you are hereby accused of having, by a false and malicious denunciation, slandered the person of a representative of the people; you caused the Revolutionary Tribunal, through this same mischievous act, to bring a charge against this representative of the people, to institute a domiciliary search in his house, and to waste valuable time, which otherwise belonged to the service of the Republic. And this you did, not from a misguided sense of duty towards your country, but in wanton and impure spirit, to be rid of the surveillance of one who had your welfare at heart, and who tried to prevent your leading the immoral life which had become a public scandal, and which has now brought you before this court of justice, to answer to a charge of wantonness, impurity, defamation of character, and corruption of public morals.

"In proof of which I now place before the court your own admission, that more than one citizen of the Republic has been led by you into immoral relationship with yourself; and further, your own admission, that your accusation against Citizen-Deputy Déroulède was false and mischievous; and further, and finally, your immoral and obscene correspondence with some persons unknown, which you vainly tried to destroy. In consideration of which, and in the name of the people of France, whose spokesman I am, I demand that you be taken hence from this Hall of Justice to the *Place de la Révolution*, in full view of the citizens of Paris and its environs, and clad in a soiled white garment, emblem of the smirch upon your soul, that there you be publicly whipped by the hands of Citizen Samson, the public executioner; after which, that you be taken to the prison of the Salpêtriere, there to be further detained at the discretion of the Committee of Public Safety. And now, Juliette Marny, you have heard the indictment preferred against you, have you anything to say, why the sentence which I have demanded shall not be passed upon you?"

Jeers, shouts, laughter, and curses greeted this speech of the Public Prosecutor.

All that was most vile and most bestial in this miserable, misguided people struggling for Utopia and Liberty, seemed to come to the surface, whilst listening to the reading of this most infamous document.

The delight of seeing this beautiful, ethereal woman, almost unearthly in her proud aloofness, smirched with the vilest mud to which the vituperation of man can contrive to sink, was a veritable treat to the degraded wretches.

The women yelled hoarse approval; the children, not understanding, laughed in mirthless glee; the men, with loud curses, showed their appreciation of Foucquier-Tinville's speech.

As for Déroulède, the mental agony he endured surpassed any torture which the devils, they say, reserve for the damned. His sinews cracked in his frantic efforts to control himself; he dug his finger-nails into his flesh, trying by physical pain to drown the sufferings of his mind.

He thought that his reason was tottering, that he would go mad if he heard another word of this infamy. The hooting and yelling of that filthy mob sounded like the cries of lost souls, shrieking from hell. All his pity for them was gone, his love for humanity, his devotion to the suffering poor.

A great, an immense hatred for this ghastly Revolution and the people it professed to free filled his whole being, together with a mad, hideous desire to see them suffer, starve, die a miserable, loathsome death. The passion of hate, that now overwhelmed his soul, was at least as ugly as theirs. He was, for one brief moment, now at one with them in their inordinate lust for revenge.

Only Juliette throughout all this remained calm, silent, impassive.

She had heard the indictment, heard the loathsome sentence, for her white cheeks had gradually become ashy pale, but never for a moment did she depart from her attitude of proud aloofness.

She never once turned her head towards the mob who insulted her. She waited in complete passiveness until the yelling and shouting had subsided, motionless save for her finger-tips, which beat an impatient tattoo upon the railing in front of her.

The Bulletin says that she took out her handkerchief and wiped her face with it. *Elle s'essuya le front qui fut perlé de sueur.* The heat had become oppressive.

The atmosphere was overcharged with the dank, penetrating odour of steaming, dirty clothes. The room, though vast, was close and suffocating, the tallow candles flickering in the humid, hot air threw the faces of the President and clerks into bold relief, with curious caricature effects of light and shade.

The petrol lamp above the head of the accused had flared up, and begun to smoke, causing the chimney to crack with a sharp report. This diversion effected a momentary silence among the crowd, and the Public Prosecutor was able to repeat his query:

"Juliette Marny, have you anything to say in reply to the charge brought against you, and why the sentence which I have demanded should not be passed against you?"

The sooty smoke from the lamp came down in small, black, greasy particles; Juliette with her slender finger-tips flicked one of these quietly off her sleeve, the she replied:

"No; I have nothing to say."

"Have you instructed an advocate to defend you, according to your rights of citizenship, which the Law allows?" added the Public Prosecutor solemnly.

Juliette would have replied at once; her mouth had already framed the No with which she meant to answer.

But now at last had come Déroulède's hour. For this he had been silent, had suffered and had held his peace, whilst twice twenty-four hours had dragged their weary lengths along, since the arrest of the woman he loved.

In a moment he was on his feet before them all, accustomed to speak, to dominate, to command.

"Citiziness Juliette Marny has entrusted me with her defence," he said, even before the No had escaped Juliette's white lips, "and I am here to refute the charges brought against her, and to demand in the name of the people of France full acquittal and justice for her."

Chapter 25

The Defence

Intense excitement, which found vent in loud applause, greeted Déroulède's statement.

"Ça *ira!* ça *ira! vas-y Déroulède!*" came from the crowded benches round; and men, women, and children, wearied with the monotony of the past proceedings, settled themselves down for a quarter of an hour's keen enjoyment.

If Déroulède had anything to do with it, the trial was sure to end in excitement. And the people were always ready to listen to their special favourite.

The citizen-deputies, drowsy after the long, oppressive day, seemed to rouse themselves to renewed interest. Lebrun, like a big, shaggy dog, shook himself free from creeping somnolence. Robespierre smiled between his thin lips and looked across at Merlin to see how the situation affected him. The enmity between the Minister of Justice and Citizen Déroulède was well known, and everyone noted, with added zest, that the former wore a keen look of anticipated triumph.

High up, on one of the topmost benches, sat Citizen Lenoir, the stage-manager of this palpitating drama. He looked down, with obvious satisfaction, at the scene which he himself had suggested last night to the members of the Jacobin Club. Merlin's sharp eyes had tried to pierce the gloom, which wrapped the crowd of spectators, searching vainly to distinguish the broad figure and massive head of the provincial giant.

The light from the petrol lamp shone full on Déroulède's earnest, dark countenance as he looked Juliette's infamous accuser full in the face, but the tallow candles, flickering weirdly on the President's desk, threw Tinville's short, spare figure and large, unkempt head into curious grotesque silhouette.

Juliette apparently had lost none of her calm, and there was no one there sufficiently interested in her personality to note the tinge of delicate colour which, at the first word of Déroulède, had slowly mounted to her pale cheeks.

Tinville waited until the wave of excitement had broken upon the shoals of expectancy.

Then he resumed:

"Then, Citizen Déroulède, what have *you* to say, why sentence should not be passed upon the accused?"

"I have to say that the accused is innocent of every charge brought against her in your indictment," replied Déroulède firmly.

"And how do you substantiate this statement, Citizen-Deputy?" queried Tinville, speaking with mock unctuousness.

"Very simply, Citizen Tinville. The correspondence to which you refer did not belong to the accused, but to me. It consisted of certain communications, which I desired to hold with Marie Antoinette, now a prisoner in the *Conciergerie*, during my state there as lieutenant-governor. The Citizeness Juliette Marny, by denouncing me, was serving the Republic, for my communications with Marie Antoinette had reference to my own hopes of seeing her quit this country and take refuge in her own native land."

Gradually, as Déroulède spoke, a murmur, like the distant roar of a monstrous breaker, rose among the crowd on the upper benches. As he continued quietly and firmly, so it grew in volume and in intensity, until his last words were drowned in one mighty, thunderous shout of horror and execration.

Déroulède, the friend and idol of the people, the privileged darling of this unruly population, the father of the children, the friend of the women, the sympathiser in all troubles, Papa Déroulède as the little ones called him—he a traitor, self-accused, plotting and planning for an ex-tyrant, a harlot who had called herself a queen, for Marie Antoinette the Austrian, who had desired and worked for the overthrow of France! He, Déroulède, a traitor!

In one moment, as he spoke, the love which in their crude hearts they bore him, that animal primitive love, was turned to sudden, equally irresponsible hate. He had deceived them, laughed at them, tried to bribe them by feeding their little ones!

Bah! the bread of the traitor! It might have choked the children.

Surprise at first had taken their breath away. Already they had marvelled why he should stand up to defend a wanton. And now, probably feeling that he was on the point of being found out, he thought it better to make a clean breast of his own treason, trusting in his popularity, in his power over the people.

Bah!!!

Not one extenuating circumstance did they find in their hardened hearts for him.

He had been their idol, enshrined in their squalid, degraded minds, and now he had fallen, shattered beyond recall, and they hated and loathed him as much as they had loved him before.

And this his enemies noted and smiled with complete satisfaction.

Merlin heaved a sigh of relief. Tinville nodded his shaggy head, in token of intense delight.

What that provincial coal-heaver had foretold had indeed come to pass.

The populace, that most fickle of all fickle things in this world, had turned all at once against its favourite. This Lenoir had predicted, and the transition had been even more rapid than he had anticipated.

Déroulède had been given a length of rope, and, figuratively speaking, had already hanged himself.

The reality was a mere matter of a few hours now. At dawn tomorrow the guillotine; and the mob of Paris, who yesterday would have torn his detractors, limb from limb, would on the morrow be dragging him, with hoots and yells and howls of execration, to the scaffold.

The most shadowy of all footholds, that of the whim of a populace, had already given way under him. His enemies knew it and were exulting in their triumph. He knew it himself, and stood up, calmly defiant, ready for any event, if only he succeeded in snatching her beautiful head from the ready embrace of the guillotine.

Juliette herself had remained as if entranced. The colour had again fled from her cheeks, leaving them paler, more ashen than before. It seemed as if in this moment she suffered more than human creature could bear, more than any torture she had undergone hitherto.

He would not owe his life to her.

That was the one overwhelming thought in her, which annihilated all others. His love for her was dead, and he would not accept the great sacrifice at her hands.

Thus, these two in the supreme moment of their life saw each other, yet did not understand. A word, a touch would have given them both the key to one another's heart, and it now seemed as if death would part them for ever, whilst that great enigma remained unsolved.

The Public Prosecutor had been waiting until the noise had somewhat subsided, and his voice could be heard above the din, then he said, with a smile of ill-concealed satisfaction:

"And is the court, then, to understand, Citizen-Deputy Déroulède, that it was you who tried to burn the treasonable correspondence and to destroy the case which contained it?"

"The treasonable correspondence was mine, and it was I who destroyed it."

"But the accused admitted before Citizen Merlin that she herself was trying to burn certain love letters, that would have brought to light her illicit relationship with another man than yourself," argued Tinville suavely. The rope was perhaps not quite long enough; Déroulède must have all that could be given him, ere this memorable sitting was adjourned.

Déroulède, however, instead of directing his reply straight to his enemy, now turned towards the dense crowd of spectators, on the benches opposite to him.

"Citizens, friends, brothers," he said warmly, "the accused is only a girl, young, innocent knowing nothing of peril or of sin. You all have mothers, sisters, daughters—have you not watched those dear to you in the many moods of which a feminine heart is capable; have you not seen them affectionate, tender, and impulsive? Would you love them so dearly but for the fickleness of their moods? Have you not worshipped them in your hearts, for those sublime impulses which put all man's plans and calculations to shame? Look on the accused, citizens. She loves the Republic, the people of France, and feared that I, an unworthy representative of her sons, was hatching treason against our great mother.

"That was her first wayward impulse—to stop me before I committed the awful crime, to punish me, or perhaps only to warn me. Does a young girl calculate, citizens? She acts as her heart dictates; her reason but awakes from slumber later on, when the act is done. Then comes repentance sometimes: another impulse of tenderness which we all revere. Would you extract vinegar from rose leaves? Just as readily could you find reason in a young girl's head. Is that a crime? She wished to thwart me in my treason; then, seeing me in peril, the sincere friendship she had for me gained the upper hand once more. She loved my mother, who might be losing a son; she loved my crippled foster-sister; for *their* sakes, not for mine—a traitor's—did she yield to another, a heavenly impulse, that of saving me from the consequences of my own folly.

"Was *that* a crime, citizens? When you are ailing, do not your mothers, sisters, wives tend you? when you are seriously ill, would they not give their heart's blood to save you? and when, in the dark hours of your lives, some deed which you would not openly avow before the world over-weights your soul with its burden of remorse, is it not again your womenkind who come to you, with tender words and soothing voices, trying to ease your aching conscience, bringing solace, comfort, and peace? And so, it was with the accused, citizens. She had seen my crime and longed to punish it; she saw those who had befriended her in sorrow, and she tried to ease their pain by taking *my* guilt upon her shoulders.

"She has suffered for the noble lie, which she had told on my behalf, as no woman has ever been made to suffer before. She has stood, white and innocent as your new-born children, in the pillory of infamy. She was ready to endure death, and what was ten thousand times worse than death, because of her own warm-hearted affection. But you, citizens of France, who, above all, are noble, true, and chivalrous, you will not allow the sweet impulses of young and tender womanhood to be punished with the ban of felony. To you, women of France, I appeal in the name of your childhood, your girlhood, your motherhood; take her to your hearts, she is worthy of it, worthier now for having blushed before you, worthier than any heroine in the great roll of honour of France."

His magnetic voice went echoing along the rafters of the great, sordid Hall of Justice, filling it with a glory it had never known before. His enthusiasm thrilled his hearers, his appeal to their honour and chivalry roused all the finer feelings within them. Still hating him for his treason, his magical appeal had turned their hearts towards her.

They had listened to him without interruption, and now at last, when he paused, it was very evident, by muttered exclamations and glances cast at Juliette, that popular feeling, which up to the present had practically ignored her, now went out towards her personality with overwhelming sympathy.

Obviously at the present moment, if Juliette's fate had been put to the plebiscite, she would have been unanimously acquitted.

Merlin, as Déroulède spoke, had once or twice tried to read his friend Foucquier-Tinville's enigmatical expression, but the Public Prosecutor, with his face in deep shadow, had not moved a muscle during the Citizen-Deputy's noble peroration. He sat at his desk, chin resting on hand, staring before him with an expression of indifference, almost of boredom.

Now, when Déroulède finished speaking, and the outburst of human enthusiasm had somewhat subsided, he rose slowly to his feet, and said quietly:

"So, you maintain, Citizen-Deputy, that the accused is a chaste and innocent girl, unjustly charged with immorality?"

"I do," protested Déroulède loudly.

"And will you tell the court why you are so ready to publicly accuse yourself of treason against the Republic, knowing full well all the consequences of your action?"

"Would any Frenchman care to save his own life at the expense of a woman's honour?" retorted Déroulède proudly.

A murmur of approval greeted these words, and Tinville remarked unctuously:

"Quite so, quite so. We esteem your chivalry, Citizen-Deputy. The same spirit, no doubt, actuates you to maintain that the accused knew nothing of the papers which you say you destroyed?"

"She knew nothing of them. I destroyed them; I did not know that they had been found; on my return to my house I discovered that the Citizeness Juliette Marny had falsely accused herself of having destroyed some papers surreptitiously."

"She said they were love letters."

"It is false."

"You declare her to be pure and chaste?"

"Before the whole world."

"Yet you were in the habit of frequenting the bedroom of this pure and chaste girl, who dwelt under your roof," said Tinville with slow and deliberate sarcasm.

"It is false."

"If it be false, Citizen Déroulède," continued the other with the same unctuous suavity, "then how comes it that the correspondence which you admit was treasonable, and therefore presumably secret—how comes it that it was found, still smouldering, in the chaste young woman's bedroom, and the torn letter-case concealed among her dresses in a valise?"

"It is false."

"The Minister of Justice, Citizen-Deputy Merlin, will answer for the truth of that."

"It is the truth," said Juliette quietly.

Her voice rang out clear, almost triumphant, in the midst of the breathless pause, caused by the previous swift questions and loud answers.

Déroulède now was silent.

This one simple fact he did not know. Anne Mie, in telling him the events in connection with the arrest of Juliette, had omitted to give him the one little detail, that the burnt letters were found in the young girl's bedroom.

Up to the moment when the Public Prosecutor confronted him with it, he had been under the impression that she had destroyed the papers and the letter-case in the study, where she had remained alone after Merlin and his men had left the room. She could easily have burnt them there, as a tiny spirit lamp was always kept alight on a side table for the use of smokers.

This little fact now altered the entire course of events. Tinville had but to frame an indignant ejaculation:

"Citizens of France, see how you are being befooled and hoodwinked!"

Then he turned once more to Déroulède.

"Citizen Déroulède—" he began.

But in the tumult that ensued he could no longer hear his own voice. The pent-up rage of the entire mob of Paris seemed to find vent for itself in the howls with which the crowd now tried to drown the rest of the proceedings.

As their brutish hearts had been suddenly melted on behalf of Juliette, in response to Déroulède's passionate appeal, so now they swiftly changed their sympathetic attitude to one of horror and execration.

Two people had fooled and deceived them. One of these they had reverenced and trusted, as much as their degraded minds were capable of reverencing anything, therefore *his* sin seemed doubly damnable.

He and that pale-face aristocrat had for weeks now, months, or year perhaps, conspired against the Republic, against the Revolution, which had been made by a people thirsting for liberty. During these months and years, *he* had talked to them, and they had listened; he had poured forth treasures of eloquence, cajoled them, as he had done just now.

The noise and hubbub were growing apace. If Tinville and Merlin had desired to infuriate the mob, they had more than succeeded. All that was most bestial, most savage in this awful Parisian populace rose to the surface now in one wild, mad desire for revenge.

The crowd rushed down from the benches, over one another's heads, over children's fallen bodies; they rushed down because they wanted to get at him, their whilom favourite, and at his pale-faced mistress, and tear them to pieces, hit them, scratch out their eyes. They snarled like so many wild beasts, the women shrieked, the children cried, and the men of the National Guard, hurrying forward, had much ado to keep back this food-tide of hate.

Had any of them broken loose, from behind the barrier of bayonets hastily raised against them, it would have fared ill with Déroulède and Juliette.

The President wildly rang his bell, and his voice, quivering with excitement, was heard once or twice above the din.

"Clear the court! Clear the court!"

But the people refused to be cleared out of court.

"À *la lanterne les traîtres! Mort à Déroulède.* À *la lanterne! l'aristo!*"

And in the thickest of the crowd, the broad shoulders and massive head of Citizen Lenoir towered above the others.

At first it seemed as if he had been urging on the mob in its fury. His strident voice, with its broad provincial accent, was heard distinctly shouting loud vituperations against the accused.

Then at a given moment, when the tumult was at its height, when the National Guard felt their bayonets giving way before this onrushing tide of human jackals, Lenoir changed his tactics.

"*Tiens! c'est* bête!" he shouted loudly, "we shall do far better with the traitors when we get them outside. What say you, citizens? Shall we leave the judges here to conclude the farce, and arrange for its sequel ourselves outside the '*Tigre Jaune*'?"

At first but little heed was paid to his suggestion, and he repeated it once or twice, adding some interesting details:

"One is freer in the streets, where these apes of the National Guard can't get between the people of France and their just revenge. *Ma foi!*" he added, squaring his broad shoulders, and pushing his way through the crowd towards the door, "I for one am going to see where hangs the most suitable *lanterne*."

Like a flock of sheep the crowd now followed him.

"The nearest *lanterne!*" they shouted. "In the streets—in the streets! À *la lanterne!* The traitors!"

And with many a jeer, many a loathsome curse, and still more loathsome jests, some of the crowd began to file out. A few only remained to see the conclusion of the farce.

Chapter 26

Sentence of Death

The *Bulletin du Tribunal Révolutionnaire* tells us that both the accused had remained perfectly calm during the turmoil which raged within the bare walls of the Hall of Justice.

Citizen-Deputy Déroulède, however, so the chroniclers aver, though outwardly impassive, was evidently deeply moved. He had very expressive eyes, clear mirrors of the fine, upright soul within, and in them there was a look of intense emotion as he watched the crowd, which he had so often dominated and controlled, now turning in hatred against him.

He seemed actually to be seeing with a spiritual vision, his own popularity wane and die.

But when the thick of the crowd had pushed and jostled itself out of the hall, that transient emotion seemed to disappear, and he allowed himself quietly to be led from the front bench, where he had sat as a privileged member of the National Convention, to a place immediately behind the dock, and between two men of the National Guard.

From that moment he was a prisoner, accused of treason against the Republic, and obviously his mock trial would be hurried through by his triumphant enemies, whilst the temper of the people was at boiling point against him.

Complete silence had succeeded to the raging tumult of the past few moments. Nothing now could be heard in the vast room, save Foucquier-Tinville's hastily whispered instructions to the clerk nearest to him, and the scratch of the latter's quill pen against the paper.

The President was, with equal rapidity, affixing his signature to various papers handed up to him by the other clerks. The few remaining spectators, the deputies, and those among the crowd who had elected to see the close of the debate, were silent and expectant.

Merlin was mopping his forehead as if in intense fatigue after a hard struggle; Robespierre was coolly taking snuff.

From where Déroulède stood, he could see Juliette's graceful figure silhouetted against the light of the petrol lamp. His heart was torn between intense misery at having failed to save her and a curious, exultant joy at thought of dying beside her.

He knew the procedure of this revolutionary tribunal well—knew that within the next few moments he too would be condemned, that they would both be hustled out of the crowd and dragged through the streets of Paris, and finally thrown into the same prison, to herd with those who, like themselves, had but a few hours to live.

And then tomorrow at dawn, death for them both under the guillotine. Death in public, with all its attendant horrors: the packed tumbril; the priest, in civil clothes, appointed by this godless government, muttering conventional prayers and valueless exhortations.

And in his heart, there was nothing but love for her—love and an intense pity—for the punishment she was suffering was far greater than her crime. He hoped that in her heart remorse would not be too bitter; and he looked forward with joy to the next few hours, which he would pass near her, during which he could perhaps still console and soothe her.

She was but the victim of an ideal, of Fate stronger than her own will. She stood, an innocent martyr to the great mistake of her life.

But the minutes sped on. Foucquier-Tinville had evidently completed his new indictments.

The one against Juliette Marny was read out first. She was now accused of conspiring with Paul Déroulède against the safety of the Republic, by having cognisance of a treasonable correspondence carried on with the prisoner, Marie Antoinette; by virtue of which accusation the Public Prosecutor asked her if she had anything to say.

"No," she replied loudly and firmly. "I pray to God for the safety and deliverance of our Queen, Marie Antoinette, and for the overthrow of this Reign of Terror and Anarchy."

These words, registered in the *Bulletin du Tribunal Révolutionnaire* were taken as final and irrefutable proofs of her guilt, and she was then summarily condemned to death.

She was then made to step down from the dock and Déroulède to stand in her place.

He listened quietly to the long indictment which Foucquier-Tinville had already framed against him the evening before, in readiness for this contingency. The words "treason against the Republic" occurred conspicuously and repeatedly. The document itself is at one with the thousands of written charges, framed by that odious Foucquier-Tinville during these periods of bloodshed, and which in themselves are the most scathing indictments against the odious travesty of Justice, perpetrated with his help.

Self-accused, and avowedly a traitor, Déroulède was not even asked if he had anything to say; sentence of death was passed on him, with the rapidity and callousness peculiar to these proceedings.

After which Paul Déroulède and Juliette Marny were led forth, under strong escort, into the street.

Chapter 27

The Fructidor Riots

Many accounts, more or less authentic, have been published of the events known to history as the "*Fructidor* Riots."

But this is how it all happened: at any rate it is the version related some few days later in England to the Prince of Wales by no less a personage than Sir Percy Blakeney; and who indeed should know better than the Scarlet Pimpernel himself?

Déroulède and Juliette Marny were the last of the batch of prisoners who were tried on that memorable day of *Fructidor*.

There had been such a number of these, that all the covered carts in use for the conveyance of prisoners to and from the Hall of Justice had already been despatched with their weighty human load; thus, it was that only a rough wooden cart, hoodless and rickety, was available, and into this Déroulède and Juliette were ordered to mount.

It was now close on nine o'clock in the evening. The streets of Paris, sparsely illuminated here and there with solitary oil lamps swung across from house to house on wires, presented a miserable and squalid appearance. A thin, misty rain had begun to fall, transforming the ill-paved roads into morasses of sticky mud.

The Hall of Justice was surrounded by a howling and shrieking mob, who, having imbibed all the stores of brandy in the neighbouring drinking bars, was now waiting outside in the dripping rain for the express purpose of venting its pent-up, spirit-sodden lust of rage against the man whom it had once worshipped, but whom now it hated. Men, women, and even children swarmed round the principal entrances of the Palais de Justice, along the bank of the river as far as the Pont au Change, and up towards the Luxembourg Palace, now transformed into the prison, to which the condemned would no doubt be conveyed.

Along the river-bank, and immediately facing the Palais de Justice, a row of gallows-shaped posts, at intervals of a hundred yards or more, held each a smoky petrol lamp, at a height of some eight feet from the ground.

One of these lamps had been knocked down, and from the post itself there now hung ominously a length of rope, with a noose at the end.

Around this improvised gallows a group of women sat, or rather squatted, in the mud; their ragged shifts and kirtles, soaked through with the drizzling rain, hung dankly on their emaciated forms; their hair, in some cases grey, and in others dark or straw-coloured, clung matted round their wet faces, on which the dirt and the damp had drawn weird and grotesque lines.

The men were restless and noisy, rushing aimlessly hither and thither, from the corner of the bridge, up the Rue du Palais, fearful lest their prey be conjured away ere their vengeance was satisfied.

Oh, how they hated their former idol now! Citizen Lenoir, with his broad shoulders and powerful, grime-covered head, towered above the throng; his strident voice, with its raucous, provincial accent, could be distinctly heard above the din, egging on the men, shouting to the women, stirring up hatred against the prisoners, wherever it showed signs of abating in intensity.

The coal-heaver, hailing from some distant province, seemed to have set himself the grim task of provoking the infuriated populace to some terrible deed of revenge against Déroulède and Juliette.

The darkness of the street, the fast-falling mist which obscured the light from the meagre oil lamps, seemed to add a certain weirdness to this moving, seething multitude. No one could see his neighbour. In the blackness of the night the muttering or yelling figures moved about like some spectral creatures from hellish regions—the Akous of Brittany who call to those about to die; whilst the women squatting in the oozing mud, beneath that swinging piece of rope, looked like a group of ghostly witches, waiting for the hour of their Sabbath.

As Déroulède emerged into the open, the light from a swinging lantern in the doorway fell upon his face. The foremost of the crowd recognised him; a howl of execration went up to the cloud-covered sky, and a hundred hands were thrust out in deadly menace against him.

It seemed as if they wished to tear him to pieces.

"*À la lanterne! À la lanterne! le traître!*"

He shivered slightly, as if with the sudden blast of cold, humid air, but he stepped quietly into the cart, closely followed by Juliette.

The strong escort of the National Guard, with Commandant Santerre and his two drummers, had much ado to keep back the mob. It was not the policy of the revolutionary government to allow excesses of summary justice in the streets: the public execution of traitors on the *Place de la Révolution,* the processions in the tumbrils, were thought to be wholesome examples for other would-be traitors to mark and digest.

Citizen Santerre, military commandant of Paris, had ordered his men to use their bayonets ruthlessly, and, to further overawe the populace, he ordered a prolonged roll of drums, lest Déroulède took it into his head to speak to the crowd.

But Déroulède had no such intention: he seemed chiefly concerned in shielding Juliette from the cold; she had been made to sit in the cart beside him, and he had taken off his coat, and was wrapping it round her against the penetrating rain.

The eye-witnesses of these memorable events have declared that, at a given moment, he looked up suddenly with a curious, eager expression in his eyes, and then raised himself in the cart and seemed to be trying to penetrate the gloom round him, as if in search of a face, or perhaps a voice.

"*À la lanterne! À la lanterne!*" was the continual hoarse cry of the mob.

Up to now, flanked in their rear by the outer walls of the Palais de Justice, the soldiers had found it a fairly easy task to keep the crowd at bay. But there came a time when the cart was bound to move out into the open, in order to convey the prisoners along, by the Rue du Palais, up to the Luxembourg Prison.

This task, however, had become more and more difficult every moment. The people of Paris, who for two years had been told by its tyrants that it was supreme lord of the universe, was mad with rage at seeing its desires frustrated by a few soldiers.

The drums had been greeted by terrific yells, which effectually drowned their roll; the first movement of the cart was hailed by a veritable tumult.

Only the women who squatted round the gallows had not moved from their position of vantage; one of these *Mægæras* was quietly readjusting the rope, which had got out of place.

But all the men and some of the women were literally besieging the cart, and threatening the soldiers, who stood between them and the object of their fury.

It seemed as if nothing now could save Déroulède and Juliette from an immediate and horrible death.

"À *mort!* À *mort!* À *la lanterne les traîtres!*"

Santerne himself, who had shouted himself hoarse, was at a loss what to do. He had sent one man to the nearest cavalry barracks, but reinforcements would still be some little time coming; whilst in the meanwhile his men were getting exhausted, and the mob, more and more excited, threatened to break through their line at every moment.

There was not another second to be lost.

Santerre was for letting the mob have its way, and he would willingly have thrown it the prey for which it clamoured; but orders were orders, and in the year I. of the Revolution it was not good to disobey.

At this supreme moment of perplexity, he suddenly felt a respectful touch on his arm.

Close behind him a soldier of the National Guard—not one of his own men—was standing at attention, and holding a small, folded paper in his hand.

"Sent to you by the Minister of Justice," whispered the soldier hurriedly. "The citizen-deputies have watched the tumult from the Hall; they say, you must not lose an instant."

Santerre withdrew from the front rank, up against the side of the cart, where a rough stable lantern had been fixed. He took the paper from the soldier's hand, and, hastily tearing it open, he read it by the dim light of the lantern.

As he read, his thick, coarse features expressed the keenest satisfaction.

"You have two more men with you?" he asked quickly.

"Yes, citizen," replied the man, pointing towards his right; "and the Citizen-Minister said you would give me two more."

"You'll take the prisoners quietly across to the Prison of the Temple —you understand that?"

"Yes, citizen; Citizen Merlin has given me full instructions. You can have the cart drawn back a little more under the shadow of the portico, where the prisoners can be made to alight; they can then given into my charge. You in the meantime are to stay here with your men, round the empty cart, as long as you can. Reinforcements have been sent for and must soon be here. When they arrive, you are to move along with the cart, as if you were making for the Luxembourg Prison. This manoeuvre will give us time to deliver the prisoners safely at the Temple."

The man spoke hurriedly and peremptorily, and Santerne was only too ready to obey. He felt relieved at thought of reinforcements, and glad to be rid of the responsibility of conducting such troublesome prisoners.

The thick mist, which grew more and more dense, favoured the new manoeuvre, and the constant roll of drums drowned the hastily given orders.

The cart was drawn back into the deepest shadow of the great portico, and whilst the mob were howling their loudest, and yelling out frantic demands for the traitors, Déroulède and Juliette were summarily ordered to step out of the cart. No one saw them, for the darkness here was intense.

"Follow quietly!" whispered a raucous voice in their ears as they did so, "or my orders are to shoot you where you stand."

But neither of them had any wish for resistance. Juliette, cold and numb, was clinging to Déroulède, who had placed a protecting arm round her.

Santerne had told off two of his men to join the new escort of the prisoners, and presently the small party, skirting the walls of the Palais de Justice, began to walk rapidly away from the scene of the riot.

Déroulède noted that some half-dozen men seemed to be surrounding him and Juliette, but the drizzling rain blurred every outline. The blackness of the night too had become absolutely dense, and in the distance the cries of the populace grew more and more faint.

Chapter 28

The Unexpected

The small party walked on in silence. It seemed to consist of a very few men of the National Guard, whom Santerne had placed under the command of the soldier who had transmitted to him the orders of the Citizen-Deputies.

Juliette and Déroulède both vaguely wondered whither they were being led; to some other prison mayhap, away from the fury of the populace. They were conscious of a sense of satisfaction at thought of being freed from that pack of raging wild beasts.

Beyond that they cared nothing. Both felt already the shadow of death hovering over them. The supreme moment of their lives had come and had found them side by side.

What neither fear nor remorse, sorrow nor joy, could do, that the great and mighty Shadow accomplished in a trice.

Juliette, looking death bravely in the face, held out her hand, and sought that of the man she loved.

There was not one word spoken between them, not even a murmur.

Déroulède, with the unerring instinct of his own unselfish passion, understood all that the tiny hand wished to convey to him.

In a moment everything was forgotten save the joy of this touch. Death, or the fear of death, had ceased to exist. Life was beautiful, and in the soul of these two human creatures there was perfect peace, almost perfect happiness.

With one grasp of the hand they had sought and found one another's soul. What mattered the yelling crowd, the noise and tumult of this sordid world? They had found one another, and, hand-in-hand, shoulder-to-shoulder, they had gone off wandering into the land of dreams, where dwelt neither doubt nor treachery, where there was nothing to forgive.

He no longer said: "She does not love me—would she have betrayed me else?" He felt the clinging, trustful touch of her hand, and knew that, with all her faults, her great sin and her lasting sorrow, her woman's heart, Heaven's most priceless treasure, was indeed truly his.

And she knew that he had forgiven—nay, that he had naught to forgive —for Love is sweet and tender, and judges not. Love is Love—whole, trustful, passionate. Love is perfect understanding and perfect peace.

And so, they followed their escort whithersoever it chose to lead them.

Their eyes wandered aimlessly over the mist-laden landscape of this portion of deserted Paris. They had turned away from the river now and were following the Rue des Arts. Close by on the right was the dismal little hostelry, "*La Cruche Cassée*," where Sir Percy Blakeney lived. Déroulède, as they neared the place, caught himself vaguely wondering what had become of his English friend.

But it would take more than the ingenuity of the Scarlet Pimpernel to get two noted prisoners out of Paris today. Even if—

"Halt!"

The word of command rang out clearly and distinctly through the rain-soaked atmosphere.

Déroulède threw up his head and listened. Something strange and unaccountable in that same word of command had struck his sensitive ear.

Yet the party had halted, and there was a click as of bayonets or muskets levelled ready to fire.

All had happened in less than a few seconds. The next moment there was a loud cry:

"À *moi,* Déroulède! 'tis the Scarlet Pimpernel!"

A vigorous blow from an unseen hand had knocked down and extinguished the nearest street lantern.

Déroulède felt that he and Juliette were being hastily dragged under an adjoining doorway even as the cheery voice echoed along the narrow street.

Half-a-dozen men were struggling below in the mud, and there was a plentiful supply of honest English oaths. It looked as if the men of the National Guard had fallen upon one another, and had it not been for those same English oaths perhaps Déroulède and Juliette would have been slower to understand.

"Well done, Tony! Gadzooks, Ffoulkes, that was a smart bit of work!"

The lazy, pleasant voice was unmistakable, but, God in heaven! where did it come from?

Of one thing there could be no doubt. The two men despatched by Santerne were lying disabled on the ground, whilst three other soldiers were busy pinioning them with ropes.

What did it all mean?

"*La,* friend Déroulède! you had not thought, I trust, that I would leave Mademoiselle Juliette in such a demmed, uncomfortable hole?"

And there, close beside Déroulède and Juliette, stood the tall figure of the Jacobin orator, the bloodthirsty Citizen Lenoir. The two young people gazed and gazed, then looked again, dumfounded, hardly daring to trust their vision, for through the grime-covered mask of the gigantic coal-heaver a pair of merry blue eyes was regarding them with lazy-amusement.

"*La!* I do look a miserable object, I know," said the pseudo coal-heaver at last, "but 'twas the only way to get those murderous devils to do what I wanted. A thousand pardons, *mademoiselle*; 'twas I brought you to such a terrible pass, but *la!* you are amongst friends now. Will you deign to forgive me?"

Juliette looked up. Her great, earnest eyes, now swimming in tears, sought those of the brave man who had so nobly stood by her and the man she loved.

"Blakeney—" began Déroulède.

But Sir Percy quickly interrupted him:

"Hush, man! we have but a few moments. Remember you are in Paris still, and the Lord only knows how we shall all get out of this murderous city tonight. I have said that you and *mademoiselle* are among friends. That is all for the moment. I had to get you together, or I should have failed. I could only succeed by subjecting you and mademoiselle to terrible indignities. Our League could plan but one rescue, and I had to adopt the best means at my command to have you condemned and led away together. Faith!" he added, with a pleasant laugh, "my friend Tinville will not be pleased when he realises that Citizen Lenoir has dragged the Citizen-Deputies by the nose."

Whilst he spoke he had led Déroulède and Juliette into a dark and narrow room on the ground floor of the hostelry, and presently he called loudly for Brogard, the host of this uninviting abode.

"Brogard!" shouted Sir Percy. "Where is that ass Brogard? *La!* man," he added as Citizen Brogard, obsequious and fussy, and with pockets stuffed with English gold, came shuffling along, "where do you hide your engaging countenance? Here! another length of rope for the gallant soldiers. Bring them in here, then give them that potion down their throats, as I have prescribed. Demm it! I wish we need not have brought them along, but that devil Santerre might have been suspicious else. They'll come to no harm, though, and can do us no mischief."

He prattled along merrily. Innately kind and chivalrous, he wished to give Déroulède and Juliette time to recover from their dazed surprise.

The transition from dull despair to buoyant hope had been so sudden: it had all happened in less than three minutes.

The scuffle had been short and sudden outside. The two soldiers of Santerne had been taken completely unawares, and the three young lieutenants of the Scarlet Pimpernel had fallen on them with such vigour that they had hardly had time to utter a cry of "Help!"

Moreover, that cry would have been useless. The night was dark and wet, and those citizens who felt ready for excitement were busy mobbing the Hall of Justice, a mile and a half away. One or two heads had appeared at the small windows of the squalid houses opposite, out it was too dark to see anything, and the scuffle had very quickly subsided.

All was silent now in the Rue des Arts, and in the grimy coffee-room of the Cruche Cassée two soldiers of the National Guard were lying bound and gagged, whilst three others were gaily laughing, and wiping their rain-soaked hand and faces.

In the midst of them all stood the tall, athletic figure of the bold adventurer who had planned this impudent coup.

"*La!* we've got so far, friends, haven't we?" he said cheerily, "and now for the immediate future. We must all be out of Paris tonight, or the guillotine for the lot of us tomorrow."

He spoke gaily, and with that pleasant drawl of his which was so well known in the fashionable assemblies of London; but there was a ring of earnestness in his voice, and his lieutenants looked up at him, ready to obey him in all things, but aware that danger was looming threateningly ahead.

Lord Anthony Dewhurst, Sir Andrew Ffoulkes, and Lord Hastings, dressed as soldiers of the National Guard, had played their part to perfection. Lord Hastings had presented the order to Santerre, and the three young bucks, at the word of command from their chief, had fallen upon and overpowered the two men whom the commandant of Paris had despatched to look after the prisoners.

So far all was well. But how to get out of Paris? Everyone looked to the Scarlet Pimpernel for guidance.

Sir Percy now turned to Juliette, and with the consummate grace which the elaborate etiquette of the times demanded, he made her a courtly bow.

"Mademoiselle de Marny," he said, "allow me to conduct you to a room, which though unworthy of your presence will, nevertheless, enable you to rest quietly for a few minutes, whilst I give my friend Déroulède further advice and instructions. In the room you will find a disguise, which I pray you to don with all haste. La! they are filthy rags, I own, but your life and—and ours depend upon your help."

Gallantly he kissed the tips of her fingers and opened the door of an adjoining room to enable her to pass through; then he stood aside, so that her final look, as she went, might be for Déroulède.

As soon as the door had closed upon her he once more turned to the men.

"Those uniforms will not do now," he said peremptorily; "there are bundles of abominable clothes here, Tony. Will you all don them as quickly as you can? We must all look as filthy a band of *sansculottes* tonight as ever walked the streets of Paris."

His lazy drawl had deserted him now. He was the man of action and of thought, the bold adventurer who held the lives of his friends in the hollow of his hand.

The four men hastily obeyed. Lord Anthony Dewhurst—one of the most elegant dandies of London society—had brought forth from a dank cupboard a bundle of clothes, mere rags, filthy but useful.

Within ten minutes the change was accomplished, and four dirty, slouchy figures stood confronting their chief.

"That's capital!" said Sir Percy merrily.

"Now for Mademoiselle de Marny."

Hardly had he spoken when the door of the adjoining room was pushed open, and a horrible apparition stood before the men. A woman in filthy bodice and skirt, with face covered in grime, her yellow hair, matted and greasy, thrust under a dirty and crumpled cap.

A shout of rapturous delight greeted this uncanny apparition.

Juliette, like the true woman she was, had found all her energy and spirits now that she felt that she had an important part to play. She woke from her dream to realise that noble friends had risked their lives for the man she loved and for her.

Of herself she did not think; she only remembered that her presence of mind, her physical and mental strength, would be needed to carry the rescue to a successful end.

Therefore, with the rags of a Paris *tricotteuse* she had also donned her personality. She played her part valiantly, and one look at the perfection of her disguise was sufficient to assure the leader of this band of heroes that his instructions would be carried through to the letter.

Déroulède too now looked the ragged *sansculotte* to the life, with bare and muddy feet, frayed breeches, and shabby, black-shag spencer. The four men stood waiting together with Juliette, whilst Sir Percy gave them his final instructions.

"We'll mix with the crowd," he said, "and do all that the crowd does. It is for us to see that that unruly crowd does what we want. Mademoiselle de Marny, a thousand congratulations. I entreat you to take hold of my friend Déroulède's hand, and not to let go of it, on any pretext whatever. *La!* not a difficult task, I ween," he added, with his genial smile; "and yours, Déroulède, is equally easy. I enjoin you to take charge of Mademoiselle Juliette, and on no account to leave her side until we are out of Paris."

"Out of Paris!" echoed Déroulède, with a troubled sigh.

"Aye!" rejoined Sir Percy boldly; "out of Paris! with a howling mob at our heels causing the authorities to take double precautions. And above all remember, friends, that our rallying cry is the shrill call of the sea-mew thrice repeated. Follow it until you are outside the gates of Paris. Once there, listen for it again; it will lead you to freedom and safety at last. Aye! Outside Paris, by the grace of God."

The hearts of his hearers thrilled as they heard him. Who could help but follow this brave and gallant adventurer, with the magic voice and the noble bearing?

"And now *en route!*" said Blakeney finally, "that ass Santerre will have dispersed the pack of yelling hyenas with his cavalry by now. They'll to the Temple prison to find their prey; we'll in their wake. À *moi*, friends! and remember the sea-gull's cry."

Déroulède drew Juliette's hand in his.

"We are ready," he said; "and God bless the Scarlet Pimpernel."

Then the five men, with Juliette in their midst, went out into the street once more.

Chapter 29

Père Lachaise

It was not difficult to guess which way the crowd had gone; yells, hoots, and hoarse cries could be heard from the farther side of the river.

Citizen Santerne had been unable to keep the mob back until the arrival of the cavalry reinforcements. Within five minutes of the abduction of Déroulède and Juliette the crowd had broken through the line of soldiers, and had stormed the cart, only to find it empty, and the prey disappeared.

"They are safe in the Temple by now!" shouted Santerne hoarsely, in savage triumph at seeing them all baffled.

At first it seemed as if the wrath of the infuriated populace, fooled in its lust for vengeance, would vent itself against the commandant of Paris and his soldiers; for a moment even Santerre's ruddy cheeks had paled at the sudden vision of this unlooked for danger.

Then just as suddenly the cry was raised.

"To the Temple!"

"To the Temple! To the Temple!" came in ready response.

The cry was soon taken up by the entire crowd, and in less than two minutes the purlieus of the Hall of Justice were deserted, and the Pont St Michel, then the Cité and the Pont au Change, swarmed with the rioters. Thence along the north bank of the river, and up the Rue du Temple, the people still yelling, muttering, singing the "Ça *ira*," and shouting: "*À la lanterne! À la lanterne!*"

Sir Percy Blakeney and his little band of followers had found the Pont Neuf and the adjoining streets practically deserted. A few stragglers from the crowd, soaked through with the rain, their enthusiasm damped, and their throats choked with the mist, were sulkily returning to their homes.

The desultory group of six *sansculottes* attracted little or no attention, and Sir Percy boldly challenged every passer-by.

"The way to the Rue du Temple, citizen?" he asked once or twice, or:

"Have they hung the traitor yet? Can you tell me, citizeness?"

A grunt or an oath were the usual replies, but no one took any further notice of the gigantic coal-heaver and his ragged friends.

At the corner of one of the cross streets, between the Rue du Temple and the Rue des Archives, Sir Percy Blakeney suddenly turned to his followers:

"We are close to the rabble now," he said in a whisper, and speaking in English; "do you all follow the nearest stragglers and get as soon as possible into the thickest of the crowd. We'll meet again outside the prison—and remember the sea-gull's cry."

He did not wait for an answer, and presently disappeared in the mist.

Already a few stragglers, hangers-on of the multitude, were gradually coming into view, and the yells could be distinctly heard. The mob had evidently assembled in the great square outside the prison and was loudly demanding the object of its wrath.

The moment for cool-headed action was at hand. The Scarlet Pimpernel had planned the whole thing, but it was for his followers and for those, whom he was endeavouring to rescue from certain death, to help him heart and soul.

Déroulède's grasp tightened on Juliette's little hand.

"Are you frightened, my beloved?" he whispered.

"Not whilst you are near me," she murmured in reply.

A few more minutes' walk up the Rue des Archives and they were in the thick of the crowd. Sir Andrew Ffoulkes, Lord Anthony Dewhurst, and Lord Hastings, the three Englishmen, were in front; Déroulède and Juliette immediately behind them.

The mob itself now carried them along. A motley throng they

were, soaked through with the rain, drunk with their own baffled rage, and with the brandy which they had imbibed.

Everyone was shouting; the women louder than the rest; one of them was dragging the length of rope, which might still be useful.

"Ça *ira!* ça *ira! À la lanterne! À la lanterne! les traîtres!*"

And Déroulède, holding Juliette by the hand, shouted lustily with them:

"Ça *ira!*"

Sir Andrew Ffoulkes turned, and laughed. It was rare sport for these young bucks, and they all entered into the spirit of the situation. They all shouted "À *la lanterne!*" egging and encouraging those around them.

Déroulède and Juliette felt the intoxication of the adventure. They were drunk with the joy of their reunion, and seized with the wild, mad, passionate desire for freedom and for life... Life and love!

So, they pushed and jostled on in the mud, followed the crowd, sang and yelled louder than any of them. Was not that very crowd the great bulwark of their safety?

As well have sought for the proverbial needle in the haystack, as for two escaped prisoners in this mad, heaving throng.

The large open space in front of the Temple Prison looked like one great, seething, black mass.

The darkness was almost thick here, the ground like a morass, with inches of clayey mud, which stuck to everything, whilst the sparse lanterns, hung to the prison walls and beneath the portico, threw practically no light into the square.

As the little band, composed of the three Englishmen, and of Déroulède, holding Juliette by the hand, emerged into the open space, they heard a strident cry, like that of a sea-mew thrice repeated, and a hoarse voice shouting from out the darkness:

"*Ma foi!* I'll not believe that the prisoners are in the Temple now! It is my belief, friends, citizens, that we have been fooled once more!"

The voice, with its strange, unaccountable accent, which seemed to belong to no province of France, dominated the almost deafening noise; it penetrated through, even into the brandy-soddened minds of the multitude, for the suggestion was received with renewed shouts of the wildest wrath.

Like one great, living, seething mass the crowd literally bore down upon the huge and frowning prison. Pushing, jostling, yelling, the women screaming, the men cursing, it seemed as if that awesome day—the 14th of July—was to have its sanguinary counterpart tonight, as if the Temple were destined to share the fate of the Bastille.

Obedient to their leader's orders the three young Englishmen remained in the thick of the crowd: together with Déroulède they contrived to form a sturdy rampart round Juliette, effectually protecting her against rough buffetings.

On their right, towards the direction of Ménilmontant, the seamew's cry at intervals gave the strength and courage.

The foremost rank of the crowd had reached the portico of the building, and, with howls and snatches of their gutter song, were loudly clamouring for the guardian of the grim prison.

No one appeared; the great gates with their massive bars and hinges remained silent and defiant.

The crowd was becoming dangerous: whispers of the victory of the Bastille, five years ago, engendered thoughts of pillage and of arson.

Then the strident voice was heard again:

"*Pardi!* the prisoners are not in the Temple! The dolts have allowed them to escape, and now are afraid of the wrath of the people!"

It was strange how easily the mob assimilated this new idea. Perhaps the dark, frowning block of massive buildings had overawed them with its peaceful strength, perhaps the dripping rain and oozing clay had damped their desire for an immediate storming of the grim citadel; perhaps it was merely the human characteristic of a wish for something new, something unexpected.

Be that as it may, the cry was certainly taken up with marvellous, quick-change rapidity.

"The prisoners have escaped! The prisoners have escaped!"

Some were for proceeding with the storming of the Temple, but they were in the minority. All along, the crowd had been more inclined for private revenge than for martial deeds of valour; the Bastille had been taken by daylight; the effort might not have been so successful on a pitch-black night such as this, when one could not see one's hand before one's eyes, and the drizzling rain went through to the marrow.

"They've got through one of the barriers by now!" suggested the same voice from out the darkness.

"The barriers—the barriers!" came in sheeplike echo from the crowd.

The little group of fugitives and their friends tightened their hold on one another.

They had understood at last.

"It is for us to see that the crowd does what we want," the Scarlet Pimpernel had said.

He wanted it to take him and his friends out of Paris, and, by God! he was like to succeed.

Juliette's heart within her beat almost to choking; her strong little hand gripped Déroulède's fingers with the wild strength of a mad exultation.

Next to the man to whom she had given her love and her very soul she admired and looked up to the remarkable and noble adventurer, the high-born and exquisite dandy, who with grime-covered face, and strong limbs encased in filthy clothes, was playing the most glorious part ever enacted upon the stage.

"To the barriers—to the barriers!"

Like a herd of wild horses, driven by the whip of the herdsmen, the mob began to scatter in all directions. Not knowing what it wanted, not knowing what it would find, half forgetting the very cause and object of its wrath, it made one gigantic rush for the gates of the great city through which the prisoners were supposed to have escaped.

The three Englishmen and Déroulède, with Juliette well protected in their midst, had not joined the general onrush as yet. The crowd in the open place was still very thick, the outward-branching streets were very narrow: through these the multitude, scampering, hurrying, scurrying, like a human torrent let out of a whirlpool, rushed down headlong towards the barriers.

Up the Rue Turbigo to the Belleville gate, the Rue des Filles, and the Rue du Chemin Vert, towards Popincourt, they ran, knocking each other down, jostling the weaker ones on one side, trampling others underfoot. They were all rough, coarse creatures, accustomed to these wild *bousculades*, ready to pick themselves up, again after any number of falls; whilst the mud was slimy and soft to tumble on, and those who did the trampling had no shoes on their feet.

They rushed out from the dark, open place, these creatures of the night, into streets darker still.

On they ran—on! on!—now in thick, heaving masses, *anon* in loose, straggling groups—some north, some south, some east, some west.

But it was from the east that came the seagull's cry.

The little band rand boldly towards the east. Down the Rue de la République they followed their leader's call. The crowd was very thick here; the Barrière Ménilmontant was close by, and beyond it there was the cemetery of Père Lachaise. It was the nearest gate to the Temple Prison, and the mob wanted to be up and doing, not to spend too much time running along the muddy streets and getting wet and cold, but to repeat the glorious exploits of the 14th of July, and capture the barriers of Paris by force of will rather than force of arms.

In this rushing mob the four men, with Juliette in their midst, remained quite unchallenged, mere units in an unruly crowd.

In a quarter of an hour Ménilmontant was reached.

The great gates of the city were well guarded by detachments of the National Guard, each under command of an officer. Twenty strong at most—what was that against such a throng?

Who had ever dreamed of Paris being stormed from within?

At every gate to the north and east of the city there was now a rabble some four or five thousand strong, wanting it knew not what. Everyone had forgotten what it was that caused him or her to rush on so blindly, so madly, towards the nearest barrier.

But everyone knew that he or she wanted to get through that barrier, to attack the soldiery, to knock down the captain of the Guard.

And with a wild cry every city gate was stormed.

Like one huge wind-tossed wave, the populace on that memorable night of *Fructidor*, broke against the cordon of soldiery, that vainly tried to keep it back. Men and women, drunk with brandy and exultation, shouted "*Quatorze Juillet!*" and amidst curses and threats demanded the opening of the gates.

The people of France *would* have its will.

Was it not the supreme lord and ruler of the land, the arbiter of the Fate of this great, beautiful, and maddened country?

The National Guard was powerless; the officers in command could offer but feeble resistance.

The desultory fire, which in the darkness and the pouring rain did very little harm, had the effect of further infuriating the mob.

The drizzle had turned to a deluge, a veritable heavy summer downpour, with occasional distant claps of thunder and incessant sheet-lightning, which ever and *anon* illumined with its weird, fantastic flash this heaving throng, these begrimed faces, crowned with red caps of Liberty, these witchlike female creatures with wet, straggly hair and gaunt, menacing arms.

Within half-an-hour the people of Paris was outside its own gates.

Victory was complete. The Guard did not resist; the officers had surrendered; the great and mighty rabble had had its way.

Exultant, it swarmed around the fortifications and along the *terrains vauges,* which it had conquered by its will.

But the downpour was continuous, and with victory came satiety—satiety coupled with wet skins, muddy feet, tired, wearied bodies, and throats parched with continual shouting.

At Ménilmontant, where the crowd had been thickest, the tempers highest, and the yells most strident, there now stretched before this tired, excited throng, the peaceful vastness of the cemetery of Père Lachaise.

The great alleys of sombre monuments, the weird cedars with their fantastic branches, like arms of a hundred ghosts, quelled and awed these hooting masses of degraded humanity.

The silent majesty of this city of the dead seemed to frown with withering scorn on the passions of the sister city.

Instinctively the rabble was cowed. The cemetery looked dark, dismal, and deserted. The flashed of lightning seemed to reveal ghost-like processions of the departed heroes of France, wandering silently amidst the tombs.

And the populace turned with a shudder away from this vast place of eternal peace.

From within the cemetery gates, there was suddenly heard the sound of a sea-mew calling thrice to its mate. And five dark figures, wrapped in cloaks, gradually detached themselves from the throng, and one by one slipped into the grounds of Père Lachaise through that break in the wall, which is quite close to the main entrance.

Once more the sea-gull's cry.

Those in the crowd who heard it, shivered beneath their dripping clothes. They thought it was a soul in pain risen from one of the graves, and some of the women, forgetting the last few years of godlessness, hastily crossed themselves, and muttered an invocation to the Virgin Mary.

Within the gates all was silent and at peace. The sodden earth gave forth no echo of the muffled footsteps, which slowly crept towards the massive block of stone, which covers the graves of the immortal lovers —Abélard and Heloïse.

Chapter 30

Conclusion

There is but little else to record.

History has told us how, shamefaced, tired, dripping, the great, all-powerful people of Paris quietly slunk back to their homes, even before the first cock-crow in the villages beyond the gates, acclaimed the pale streak of dawn.

But long before that, even before the church bells of the great city had tolled the midnight hour, Sir Percy Blakeney and his little band of followers had reached the little tavern which stand close to the farthest gate of Père Lachaise.

Without a word, like six silent ghosts, they had traversed the vast cemetery, and reached the quiet hostelry, where the sounds of the seething revolution only came, attenuated by their passage through the peaceful city of the dead.

English gold had easily purchased silence and good will from the half-starved keeper of this wayside inn. A huge travelling chaise already stood in readiness, and four good Flanders horses had been pawing the ground impatiently for the past half hour. From the window of the chaise old Pétronelle's face, wet with anxious tears, was peering anxiously.

A cry of joy and surprise escaped Déroulède and Juliette, and both turned, with a feeling akin to awe, towards the wonderful man who had planned and carried through this bold adventure.

"Nay, my friend," said Sir Percy, speaking more especially to Déroulède; "if you only knew how simple it all was! Gold can do so many things, and my only merit seems to be the possession of plenty of that commodity. You told me yourself how you had provided for old Pétronelle. Under the most solemn assurance that she would meet her young mistress here, I got her to leave Paris. She came out most bravely this morning in one of the market carts. She is so obviously a woman of the people, that no one suspected her.

"As for the worthy couple who keep this wayside hostel, they have been well paid, and money soon procures a chaise and horses. My English friends and I, we have our own passports, and one for Mademoiselle Juliette, who must travel as an English lady, with her old nurse, Pétronelle. There are some decent clothes in readiness for us all in the inn. A quarter of an hour in which to don them and we must on our way. You can use your own passport, of course; your arrest has been so very sudden that it has not yet been cancelled, and we have an eight hours' start of our enemies. They'll wake up tomorrow morning, begad! and find that you have slipped through their fingers."

He spoke with easy carelessness, and that slow drawl of his, as if he were talking airy nothings in a London drawing-room, instead of recounting the most daring, most colossal piece of effrontery the adventurous brain of man could conceive.

Déroulède could say nothing. His own noble heart was too full of gratitude towards his friend to express it all in a few words.

And time, of course, was precious.

Within the prescribed quarter of an hour the little band of heroes had doffed their grimy, ragged clothes, and now appeared dressed as respectable *bourgeois* of Paris *en route* for the country. Sir Percy Blakeney had donned the livery of a coachman of a well-to-do house, whilst Lord Anthony Dewhurst wore that of an English lacquey.

Five minutes later Déroulède had lifted Juliette into the travelling chaise, and in spite of fatigue, of anxiety, and emotion, it was immeasurable happiness to feel her arm encircling his shoulders in perfect joy and trust.

Sir Andrew Ffoulkes and Lord Hastings joined them inside the chaise; Lord Anthony sat next to Sir Percy on the box.

And whilst the crowd of Paris was still wondering why it had stormed the gates of the city, the escaped prisoners were borne along the muddy roads of France at breakneck speed northward to the coast.

Sir Percy Blakeney held the reins himself. With his noble heart full of joy, the gallant adventurer himself drove his friends to safety.

They had an eight hours' start, and the league of the Scarlet Pimpernel had done its work thoroughly: well provided with passports, and with relays awaiting them at every station of fifty miles or so, the journey, though wearisome was free from further adventure.

At Le Havre the little party embarked on board Sir Percy Blakeney's yacht the *Daydream*, where they met Madame Déroulède and Anne Mie.

The two ladies, acting under the instructions of Sir Percy, had as originally arranged, pursued their journey northwards, to the populous seaport town.

Anne Mie's first meeting with Juliette was intensely pathetic. The poor little cripple had spent the last few days in an agony of remorse, whilst the heavy travelling chaise bore her farther and farther away from Paris.

She thought Juliette dead, and Paul a prey to despair, and her tender soul ached when she remembered that it was she who had given the final deadly stab to the heart of the man she loved.

Hers was the nature born to abnegation: aye! and one destined to find bliss therein. And when one glance in Paul Déroulède's face told her that she was forgiven, her cup of joy at seeing him happy beside his beloved, was unalloyed with any bitterness.

******

It was in the beautiful, rosy dawn of one of the last days of that memorable *Fructidor*, when Juliette and Paul Déroulède, standing on the deck of the *Daydream*, saw the shores of France gradually receding from their view.

Déroulède's arm was round his beloved, her golden hair, fanned by the breeze, brushed lightly against his cheek.

"Madonna!" he murmured.

She turned her head to him. It was the first time that they were quite alone, the first time that all thought of danger had become a mere dream.

What had the future in store for them, in that beautiful, strange land to which the graceful yacht was swiftly bearing them?

England, the land of freedom, would shelter their happiness and their joy; and they looked out towards the North, where lay, still hidden in the arms of the distant horizon, the white cliffs of Albion, whilst the mist even now was wrapping it its obliterating embrace the shores of the land where they had both suffered, where they had both learned to love.

He took her in his arms.

"My wife!" he whispered.

The rosy light touched her golden hair; he raised her face to his, and soul met soul in one long, passionate kiss.